PRAISE FOR *WITH LOVE,*

"An electric, utterly unique workplace romance that burrowed deep into my heart, starring polar opposites with off-the-charts sexual tension and a truly unforgettable setting that feels like a character in itself. *With Love, from Cold World* is a steamy delight sure to keep you warm all through the winter. I need everything Alicia Thompson writes beamed directly into my brain."

—Rachel Lynn Solomon, *New York Times* bestselling author of *Business or Pleasure*

"Alicia Thompson writes stories that are so uniquely real to me, with characters who are flawed and lovable and achingly relatable, alongside writing that balances trauma and humor with incredible skill and heart. I was invested in Lauren, Asa, and the quirky world of Cold World from the jump, and I loved their story every step of the way. A new forever favorite."

—Anita Kelly, author of *Something Wild & Wonderful*

"I fell hard for the characters in this world—Asa and Lauren are complicated and flawed and so easy to root for, and I loved watching them become tentative friends, passionate lovers, and, finally, committed, confident partners to each other. Imaginative and sexy and thoughtful, *With Love, from Cold World* will warm you from the inside out."

—Kate Clayborn, author of *Georgie, All Along*

"With this swoony enemies-to-lovers rom-com, Thompson gets in well ahead of the annual slew of Christmas romances, taking readers to Florida's Cold World amusement park, where the winter holidays are celebrated year-round. . . . This will have readers dreaming of sugarplums at any time of year." —*Publishers Weekly*

"*With Love, from Cold World*, appealing and funny, is a lovely romance, featuring bisexual representation, a cast of quirky characters, and the best kind of happily-ever-after. Somehow cozy and comforting in spite of its chilly setting and sexy scenes, this novel is bound to leave readers with a smile." —Shelf Awareness

PRAISE FOR *LOVE IN THE TIME OF SERIAL KILLERS*

"Unique, sexy, hilarious, charming, *Love in the Time of Serial Killers* is to die for: the perfect beach read for anyone who loves witty banter, intelligent plotting, and compelling characters. . . . The true crime is NOT reading this novel!"

—Ali Hazelwood, *New York Times* bestselling author of *Not in Love*

"A criminally addictive romance. With excellent wry humor, lovably messy characters, and so many heart-squeezing moments, this book is sheer perfection from beginning to end."

—Rachel Lynn Solomon, *New York Times* bestselling author of *Business or Pleasure*

"Phoebe is an immensely relatable and likable character, one whose prickly exterior hides a deep fear of vulnerability. It's a joy to watch her realize that the only thing scarier than a grisly murder is falling in love." —Kerry Winfrey, author of *Faking Christmas*

"Smart, clever, and slow-burn steamy, *Love in the Time of Serial Killers* is a fresh, lovable rom-com that tackles facing our fear of not only the worst life can bring but the very best, and being brave enough to take a chance on love."

—Chloe Liese, author of *Better Hate than Never*

"*Love in the Time of Serial Killers* is funny, sharp, and thoughtful."

—Sarah Hogle, author of *Old Flames and New Fortunes*

"It's criminal how much we enjoyed *Love in the Time of Serial Killers*, the perfect pairing of intrigue with utterly charming romance and a deeply relatable story of how sometimes life's most complicated mystery is how to open your heart."

—Emily Wibberley and Austin Siegemund-Broka,
authors of *The Breakup Tour*

"With toe-curling swoons, witty banter, and enough true crime references to make Truman Capote proud, this is not one to be missed."

—Sonia Hartl, author of *Rent to Be*

"Fans of Christina Lauren and Rachel Lynn Solomon will adore this ode to true crime and its poignant message of opening your heart to love, even when that's the scariest thing of all."

—Amy Lea, author of *The Catch*

"The perfect blend of romantic comedy and true crime you didn't know you needed. A charming and darkly funny read, this book is a love letter to murderinos, romancerinos, and those of us still trying to figure out who the heck we are."

—Nicole Tersigni, author of *Men to Avoid in Art and Life*

"Thompson's clever premise is a trendy hook for a romance that explores family, grief, and the relationships that define us."

—*Washington Independent Review of Books*

"The fast-paced plot is alternately hilarious and touching, and readers won't be able to put it down. True crime is an incredibly popular genre, and this book is a must-read for crossover romance fans."

—*Library Journal* (starred review)

"Highly recommended for romance readers who enjoy flirty dialogue, pop-culture references, strong female characters, and, of course, true crime."

—*Booklist* (starred review)

THE ART OF

Catching Feelings

ALICIA THOMPSON

BERKLEY ROMANCE

NEW YORK

BERKLEY ROMANCE
Published by Berkley
An imprint of Penguin Random House LLC
penguinrandomhouse.com

Library of Congress Cataloging-in-Publication Data

Names: Thompson, Alicia, author.
Title: The art of catching feelings / Alicia Thompson.
Description: First edition. | New York: Berkley Romance, 2024.
Identifiers: LCCN 2023048266 | ISBN 9780593640937 (trade paperback) |
ISBN 9780593640944 (ebook)
Subjects: LCGFT: Romance fiction. | Novels.
Classification: LCC PS3620.H64775 A88 2024 | DDC 813/.6—dc23/eng/20231013
LC record available at https://lccn.loc.gov/2023048266

First Edition: June 2024

Printed in the United States of America
1st Printing

Book design by George Towne
Illustrations on pages vi, vii, and xv by Jenifer Prince

for Ryan

you are Clayton Krewshal to my life

Love is the most important thing in the world,
but baseball is pretty good, too.

—*Yogi Berra*

AUTHOR'S NOTE

This book contains backstories involving divorce and the loss of a loved one to suicide. There are on-the-page depictions of panic attacks. There is also some pregnancy/baby content, mostly involving a side character.

THE ART OF

Catching
Feelings

ONE

THE CROWD ERUPTED IN A SHOUT—OBVIOUSLY, SOMETHING WAS happening—but Daphne didn't bother to look up as she turned a page in her book. She hadn't *meant* to read at the baseball game, but she had a book in her purse and her best friend Kim was running late, so . . . here she was.

Not that the words were sinking in. She'd read the same paragraph three times, and still her brain pounded with the same two words over and over.

I'm divorced I'm divorced I'm divorced

She was about to put the book away—there was no point—when the people next to her stood up, allowing Kim to make her way down the aisle. "Sorry," Kim said cheerfully to each one of them. "Excuse me, sorry." When she got to the empty seat next to Daphne, she plopped down and said, "Are you *reading* during America's Pastime?"

"More like America's Snoozefest," Daphne said, slipping the book back into her bag. "A guy throws a ball, another guy tries to hit it, and if they connect there's running involved. Beyond that, who knows."

"Well, *that's* sacrilege, especially since we have these sick seats. Layla hooked you up."

Daphne shrugged. Her sister-in-law Layla was the sideline reporter for the Carolina Battery, and her brother Donovan worked in Guest Services for the team. He acted like he was in the dugout from the way he carried on about all the perks their connection to the team got them. Daphne had never taken Layla up on an offer for tickets before, and she wouldn't have this time, either, if it hadn't been for extenuating circumstances involving her husband.

ex-husband ex-husband ex-husband

"Technically, *your* ticket was Justin's."

Kim pulled a face at the mention of Daphne's ex. "How was that even going to work?"

The goateed man on the other side of Daphne stood up so fast he jostled her elbow, muttering something about *couldn't fucking catch a cold out there.* She glanced toward the field, briefly curious about whatever had happened to upset this fan so much. The pitcher was getting set to throw again, the batter was still standing with his bat, and everyone else was standing where they'd been the whole game. She could feel the tension from the crowd hanging heavy in the humid Charleston air, but out there it looked placid as a lake.

A metaphor for her short-lived marriage, if ever there was one.

"You know Donovan," she said, trying to give a wry smile that she hoped didn't look as painful as it felt. "Justin's his best friend. He can't believe we're not going to work it out. So he gave us each a ticket to today's game, I guess hoping we'd somehow make up in time to go? Or just show up and find our way back to each other by the end, like we're in *Parent Trap* and he's Lindsay Lohan?"

"Your brother has the hair and freckles to be Lindsay, but not the gravitas."

This time, Daphne's smile was more natural. Unlike Donovan, her hair had turned more auburn as she'd gotten older, but Kim had a point about her family's coloring. Freckles had been her nemesis since she was in second grade.

"So when I saw Justin on Friday, he told me to forward my ticket to him." If he'd *asked*, she probably would've done it. She might've daydreamed about setting every single one of his Salt Life shirts on fire, but her spite didn't extend to subjecting herself to baseball just to cheat him out of the experience.

"But you didn't." Kim's eyes were glittering, like she knew things were about to get good.

Daphne was kind of proud of herself for this one, actually. "Nope. I said we could play rock paper scissors for them, best two out of three. He threw rock twice in a row. And I threw paper."

You're so predictable, he'd said after the first time. *I know you.* But he didn't. He never had.

Meanwhile, she knew him. He always threw rock on the first turn—she suspected because he was busy thinking what to throw, and didn't get his hand out of a fist in time. And he always repeated on the second turn, trying to outbluff your bluff.

"And then I had his lawyer write it into the divorce agreement—*Simultaneously herewith, Husband will transfer one (1) Carolina Battery ticket in his possession to Wife.* We had to initial the change and everything."

Kim pressed her hand over her heart. "Well, I'm honored you chose me to take that douchebag's place." Her eyes widened as she seemed to take in the full import of Daphne's story. "Wait—you saw him and his lawyer? So does that mean . . . ?"

"It's official."

It was rare to see her best friend speechless, but Daphne could tell that she didn't quite know how to react. Knowing Kim, her instinct would be to give Daphne a fierce hug, to start scream-singing "*freedom*" through the stadium like she was Aretha, to list all the ways Justin could go fuck himself. But her friend must've also seen something in Daphne's face, something fragile that said *I'm very close to losing it so please be careful with me.*

They were still locked in that stalemate when the guy next to Daphne shot to his feet, beer sloshing out of the bottle he still gripped in one hand while he used the other to gesture toward the field. "That throw was a mile high! Get him outta there!"

Daphne glanced at the action, such as it was, but she *still* couldn't tell what was happening. The guys in gray outfits were standing on the bases again? It looked like there might be more of them?

"What are you going to do now?" Kim asked.

She knew that Kim's question was mostly about logistics. Was Daphne going to be able to move out of the crappy studio unit she was living in? (No—he'd been the one to stay in the house they'd rented together. She couldn't afford it.) Was she going to start looking for a full-time job since her freelance copywriting work was so sporadic lately? (She was *trying*.) Was she ready to start dating again? (Oof. She couldn't even let herself think about that one.)

Strands of Daphne's curly hair were sticking to her cheeks, and she automatically reached for the hair-tie she usually kept looped around her wrist. But it wasn't there, and even though there could be any number of rational explanations why—she'd left it on the bathroom counter! it somehow snapped without her noticing!—it felt like just *one* more thing that wasn't right. She didn't want to think about her divorce, or the bleak ocean of her future disappearing into the horizon. She didn't want to think at all.

"I want to get really, really drunk," she said.

Kim quirked an eyebrow at her. "Well," she said. "That's one way to enjoy a baseball game."

SEVERAL BEERS LATER—THREE? FOUR? THEY WERE LOCAL CRAFT-brewed IPAs flavored with raspberry and vanilla and were surprisingly smooth—Daphne was in a much better mood. So what if her life was stalled out? The sun was shining and she was at a baseball game with her best friend, making more friends by the minute.

The older goateed guy next to her, for example. It turned out she didn't need to *understand* the game—just mimic his reactions. Soon they were high-fiving when the Battery scored a run, or he'd slap the netting in front of them and say, "You've got to be kidding me!" and she'd say, "I know, right?" and shake her head. Kim had limited herself to one beer—*someone* had to be sober to drive them home—and observed this new dynamic with amused indulgence.

"You're really getting into this, huh?" she said at one point. Daphne took another gulp of her beer before letting out a loud *boo* with the rest of the crowd.

"Come on, play the game!" she yelled. She was proud of herself for having figured this one out. Whenever the opposing pitcher threw over to first base instead of making another pitch, the entire crowd reacted, and the guy next to her would throw up his hands and say something similar to what she was now shouting herself. Only usually with more colorful language.

Another part that was really fun—you could heckle or cheer for players with little puns on their names. Daphne didn't have to be a baseball expert to figure that one out—she just glanced up at the scoreboard, where they put a picture and information about the batter currently on and the next one up. There was an opposing player named *Chapman*, which was a quick consonant change away from *Crapman*. She was pretty pleased with herself for that one.

It was especially easy when the players were *right there*. Kim had a point—Layla had given them great tickets, and they were just behind the on-deck circle, where the next batter up swung his practice swings while he waited his turn. If Daphne wanted to shout to the guy named *Bummer*—at her current inebriation level, she wasn't above picking some low-hanging fruit—she could. Meanwhile, Kim chose to focus her energies in a thirstier direction.

"Mmm, the *forearms*," Kim said as a bigger guy came to the on-deck circle. "You can have the infielders. I want those designated hitter muscles."

Daphne giggled. "He'll *hear* you."

"So?"

"Hey, Gutierrez!" Daphne yelled, until Kim pulled her in and clapped a hand over her mouth, laughing the whole time. Apparently she wasn't as sanguine about being perceived as she claimed to be. Daphne, on the other hand, had no such inhibitions at this point. Who cared? These guys made millions of dollars and were probably used to people shouting at them. It was a nice outlet. Like scream therapy.

The atmosphere had been buzzing with excitement when the Battery scored a few to take a narrow lead, but toward the end of the game, that lead was long gone and they had their backs against the wall. At least, that's what Goatee Guy reported, looking as red-faced and fired up as though he were on the team's coaching staff.

"And now it's Chris fucking Kepler on deck," he said, gesturing angrily toward the guy coming out of the dugout with his bat. "Bottom of the ninth and this joker's on the interstate. Hell, put me in to hit for him. Who's running this fucking team?"

"Dude," Kim said under her breath, "it's *April*. Chill out."

But Daphne liked Goatee's passion. He was just a man who cared about his team. Wasn't that a good thing? Shouldn't people *care* more? "Chris Kepler?" she said, more to feel the name in her mouth than anything else. Kepler. That was a hard name to do anything with. *Chris Kepler, watch your step-ler!* She'd sound like an after-school special rap battle. The very idea had her laughing so hard she almost choked on her beer.

"You are on another planet," Kim said, and Daphne couldn't tell, but she didn't look as amused anymore. More concerned, but truly, she had no reason to be. Daphne felt *great*. She'd gone to sporting events with Justin before and always felt like she was solely there to make sure *he* had a good time—hold his cup when he needed her to, make the snack run when he didn't want to miss any of the action, stay sober enough to drive them home. She'd *never* have been able to let loose like this on his watch. This was freedom, baby! She cupped her hand around her mouth.

"Chris!"

Kim wasn't wrong. Baseball players did have amazing forearms. There was netting between them and the players, but this guy was so close that she could practically *feel* the texture of the red clay streaked down one leg of his white pants. He twisted one foot every time he took a swing, flashing the bottom of his shoes, and she could see the clumps of grass and dirt stuck in his cleats. His back was to them, and there was a small nick on his left elbow, the dried blood of a scab. Daphne felt like she could reach out and open it up with the flick of a fingernail.

Which was an extremely weird thought to have.

She felt her mood starting to tilt precariously, like it was a boat on choppy waters she had to get back under control. Chris Kepler. What could she do with that?

"Yo, Chris!" she said, clinging to the netting in front of her. "Your name should be Christopher Robin, 'cause you're hitting like *Pooh*!"

Bam! She'd hit that one out of the park. A play on his name and a reference to a charming children's book—an all-star heckle if she'd ever heard one.

Then he turned and looked at her.

Her breath caught in her throat. For all the shouting she'd been doing for the last half hour, it had honestly never occurred to her that this could happen. It felt as strange as if she'd been watching the game on TV and one of the players had faced the camera to address her directly. Because she'd said something from her cushy seat in the stands, and suddenly here was this guy all dressed out in his uniform with the clay rubbed into it and the nick on his elbow, and he was *looking right at her.*

Weirder still was the *way* he was looking at her. She might've expected anger—it would've been uncomfortable and made her face flame even more than it probably already was, but he'd be justified in getting irritated with some random drunk woman telling him his playing was shit. She might even have expected a nonchalant, lighthearted clapback, the kind of thing she imagined famous people had to get really good at. Something that said, *Keep talking trash while I make fifty times your annual income,* but you know, in a fan-friendly way.

But this guy—*Chris Kepler,* a real name that belonged to a real person—didn't look like he was angry or like he was ready to take a little heckling in stride. He looked . . . stricken.

That was the only word she could think of.

His eyes were in shadow, his batting helmet low over his forehead, but somehow she still felt his reaction like a punch to her stomach. His lips were slightly parted, like he was about to say something, his knuckles white where they gripped his bat. He wore the navy blue jersey of Carolina's team, *Battery* in stitched-on letters across the chest, and for some reason it only *then* hit her. She'd been yelling at the home team. Why would she yell at the *home* team?

Music pumped through the PA system, a swinging drumbeat, but still he just looked at her. And suddenly she couldn't help but look at *him*—take in his broad shoulders and the way the fabric of his pants pulled tight over his thighs. Fuck, he was *hot.*

He was also noticeably affected by her words. The way he was looking at her made her feel ashamed for noticing his attractiveness now, made her regret that she'd shouted anything in the first place. It was like he saw right through her and didn't even register she was there, all at the same time. She felt his focus as a shiver up her spine, and she waited for him to break the tension, to *speak* and make the moment solidify into something concrete instead of just this unbearable crackle in the air. But instead he gave her one final glance before walking toward the game, ready to take his place at home plate. She was grateful he hadn't said anything.

She had a twisted, masochistic need to know what he might've said.

"You got his attention!" Goatee cackled from beside her. "Now hopefully he steps up. I'll believe it when I see it."

Daphne turned away, no longer as well disposed toward this hypercritical fan she'd been shouting with only minutes before. A thick wave of shame rolled through her, and she rested her elbows on her knees so she could lean forward and try to catch her breath.

"Oh my god," Kim said from her other side. "Did that just—"

"I think I'm going to be sick," Daphne said, and Kim must've seen how close she was, because she didn't say anything else. She just grasped Daphne by the elbow and helped her to her feet, guiding her through the crowd with more forceful words than she'd used to get in. No more *sorry* or *excuse me*, now it was all, *coming through, she's sick, we need to leave*. Behind her, Daphne was dimly aware that something must be happening, because the crowd stood up, a weird hush coming over everyone before the hum of conversation started again. She looked down before leaving the ballpark to see Chris Kepler striding away from home plate, head down, bat still in his hand. He'd struck out.

CHAPTER TWO

THE FIRST THING DAPHNE DID WHEN SHE GOT HOME WAS TO GET disgustingly, violently ill. Since she'd managed to keep it together in Kim's car, she suspected it had less to do with the heat and the amount of alcohol she'd drunk on an empty stomach—although neither helped—and more to do with finally being alone and able to let it all out.

And *let it all out* is exactly what she did. Afterward, she left her clothes right there on the bathroom floor and turned on the shower, sitting in the tub while the water pulsed over her shoulders until she felt strong enough to stand up and grab the soap.

She could've stayed in the shower forever, except that it was one of the worst places for her thoughts. She couldn't turn them off. They crowded her head, and the white noise of the running water did nothing to drown them out. She got out, fed her cat Milo, and wrapped herself in a thin satin bathrobe before turning on SZA as loud as she could without the neighbor complaining. The walls of her studio duplex unit were paper-thin. Sometimes she could hear when her neighbor had people over and they were chatting at the table she knew he had pushed against the shared wall behind her bed. The reciprocal problem was one Daphne never had to worry about, since she never had anyone over to her tiny matchbox of a place.

She lay on top of her covers, trying not to think about what an absolute ass she'd made of herself at the game. It didn't matter, right? Lots of people got drunk at sporting events and shouted at players. It was practically part of the experience. And sure, okay, normally those players may not be able to *hear* them . . . but they got paid millions of dollars to put up with that kind of shit, right?

Except in that moment when their eyes had met, Chris Kepler hadn't looked like an overpaid, untouchable celebrity. He'd looked like a guy. He'd looked *upset*. Because of what she said.

But he wasn't doing well in general. That's what the toxic grandpa sitting next to her had been ranting about—so maybe it wasn't about Daphne at all. Of course he was upset—his team was losing. She was an egomaniac if she thought anything *she* could say would have the ability to affect the way he felt.

Daphne rolled to her side, snuggling into her pillow. Chalk it up to a bad day. She'd had one; Chris Kepler had had one; but now it was almost over. And the good news was she didn't have to think about any of this ever again.

A PERSISTENT RINGING STARTLED DAPHNE OUT OF HER HEAVY, dreamy sleep. She had no idea how long she'd been out, but the glimpse of sky through her one broken blind was black and the steam from her shower had cleared out of her small space.

She almost just threw her pillow over her head and went back to sleep. But then the ringing came again. Only this time it was even more piercing, if possible, like the person on the other end had turned up some volume button.

"Okay, okay," she muttered, reaching to try to grab the phone off the nightstand without getting up. It was probably Kim. She'd texted after she'd gotten home, just to check in, but Daphne hadn't been in much of a state to say anything other than that she'd be fine as long as she never had to get off the bathroom floor. She could see how that wouldn't sound *that* encouraging.

It was Donovan. Panic rose in her chest even as she accepted the call, her mind already skipping ahead to whatever this could be about. Their parents were traveling the country by RV right now, living their early-retirement dream. Had something happened? Or was it Layla—was she okay?

But Daphne barely had time to say hello before Donovan launched into it. "Daph, what the *fuck?*"

"What?"

It came out fluttery and scared. She was only half-awake, and still not sure why her brother was calling. Why he was practically *yelling* at her.

"Turn on *SportsCenter*."

"I don't have—" She didn't even know where to start. Her "TV" was a large computer monitor, and she mostly used it to stream Spotify.

She could hear him muttering on the other end, and then her phone lit up with a text. "I just sent you a video. Call me back after you've watched it."

And then he hung up.

Right from the title, Daphne's heart sank. **Chris Kepler gets heckled and breaks down, a breakdown**. She clicked on the YouTube video, already dreading what she knew she'd see.

The Carolina Battery are playing the Toronto Blue Jays and the Jays are leading six to five in the bottom of the ninth. The Battery have two men on with one out, so they should be looking to tie the game at least, maybe a walk-off, right? Except they call on this guy.

Between the dry snark and the dramatic pause, she could tell this wasn't going to be good. It was weird, to see footage of the game that she was at earlier that day. Not that she'd had either the baseball knowledge or the sober wherewithal to know what was going on at any given point. But now the video was showing clips of Chris Kepler up at bat, clearly from various games earlier that month, swinging and missing, the ball sailing by him for a final strike, him popping up a foul ball easily caught by the catcher. The whole time, the video guy kept up a running commentary of each different way Chris Kepler had fucked up.

That's right, he said, *they called on* this *guy. The one who'd already cost them one run in the top of the third.*

Another clip from the game that day, this one of the ball cracking off a Blue Jay bat, Chris breaking to the right, his glove up, watching . . . waiting . . . and then the ball bounced off the edge of his glove, cutting sharply toward the outfield. He turned around, trying to locate it, but one of his teammates was already running to scoop it up, throwing it toward home plate. Not in time. The runner scored.

For a second, Daphne almost forgot the context in which she'd been sent this video, the part she must play in it later. She was impressed that someone had been able to edit this together so fast. It actually made her understand what was happening.

But then the camera turned to *her.* She was right there, behind the net, a purple can in her hand. If she never saw one of those raspberry beers again, she'd be fine. The older guy was to her right, and she could see Kim's leg to her left, the rest of her friend off camera.

This fan knows what's up, the video guy said. *She's not having it. She yells something at Kepler—his body is blocking our view here, so I can't read her lips for you. Probably something like, hey, hit the ball, buddy! And he's like, yeah, yeah, I'm trying. Maybe she's like, hey, remember hitting home runs? That was nice.*

The commentary was making the moment seem much bigger

than it had been. Right? She'd shouted one stupid Winnie the Pooh reference, which would make her more the target of ridicule in this video if he'd been able to figure that out, and then the player hadn't said anything. It was over in thirty seconds.

But the moment had felt pretty big, even as it was happening. Daphne's stomach twisted as she remembered that look on his face, like he was . . . haunted. By the words she'd said. Milo watched her from the floor, his tail twitching, like even he could sense that there was something going on.

No big deal, right? Fans heckle, it's what we do. I've shouted at a few jabronis in my time. It's all part of the game. But wait—this guy's not so great at the game right now.

Now it was the part she hadn't seen, while she'd been making her way through the crowd with Kim. He was crouched in his batter's stance, his hands gripping the bat, and then all of a sudden . . . his face crumpled.

That was the only way to describe it. He turned away, putting his hand up like he was calling for time, wiping at his eyes with the sleeve of his jersey.

Is he crying? He's crying. This guy is getting paid millions of dollars to suck and he's crying. There's no crying in baseball! I mean, maybe the fans can weep, since Carolina's twelve-and-sixteen to start the season . . .

Daphne paused the video, only just realizing she'd been biting her knuckle so hard she'd left an indentation in her skin. There were fifty-eight seconds left in the video, but she wasn't sure she could take any more.

In the end, she pressed play but turned the volume down, not wanting to hear this guy's no-doubt gleeful commentary. Chris finished his at-bat, his face stoic, and between the shadow from his batter's helmet and the eye black he wore on his cheekbones, it was almost like he'd never reacted at all. But there was that sheen in his eyes, which you could see when he moved his head. That look on his face, the way it had collapsed for that split second. The expression he'd had before, when he'd turned to make eye contact with her. Those couldn't be explained any other way.

She'd made him cry.

She was still staring down at her phone, frozen on a blurry still from the end of the video, when it buzzed in her hand with a call from Donovan. Now that she knew what he'd called about, she *really* didn't want to talk to him, but she picked up before the phone could ring again.

"Well?" Donovan demanded. "I know you had time to watch the video because I just finished rewatching it myself. Do you know how bad this makes me look? What did you *say* to him?"

"I—I just said he was Winnie the Pooh."

Silence.

"Or Christopher Robin? That he should be called Christopher Robin, because he played like Pooh."

Those raspberry vanilla beers had her feeling like Rodney Dangerfield at the time. Now she just felt stupid.

Donovan sighed. She couldn't tell if the sheer inanity of her insult made the situation better or worse.

"Justin said you made him give up his ticket?"

Her brother's censure had moved back to the personal, it seemed. She didn't feel like filling him in on everything that had happened with the divorce papers the other day, and it sounded like Justin had already filled him in anyway. He sure was quick to tell people what information cast him in the best light. Everything else, he shoved behind a closed door.

They'd had to live separately before they could be granted a divorce—hence the shoebox she was living in, since it was all she could find and afford at the time. In South Carolina, there were only a few grounds for divorce, and technically Justin hadn't cheated on her, hadn't hit her, hadn't abandoned her, and wasn't chronically drunk. There were no "reasons" for them not to be together, so the state insisted they live apart for a full year before it would let them go through with the dissolution.

And sometimes that was the hardest part. There wasn't any huge event Daphne could point to and say *that, that* was unacceptable. It had been a lot of little moments, times when she realized her marriage just didn't *feel* good. It had been a slow whittling away, an eventual realization that there was more negative space than anything substantial there.

Donovan sighed again, clearly taking her prolonged silence as a refusal to answer. Really, she'd just spaced out on his question. She found she was doing a lot of that lately.

"Look," he said. "It's late. We'll talk about this more tomorrow, yeah? They're probably going to call me into a meeting. They know Layla and I got you those tickets. Hope you enjoyed the game, because it's the last one we'll probably be able to get you into."

Her brother could be overdramatic, but she still tensed up when she heard him say that. "This won't cost you your job, right? Or Layla?"

God, she would absolutely die if this came back on her sister-in-law in any way. She was the first Turkish American woman to work the sideline in the MLB, and was great at her job. Daphne still figured her brother had been a nepotism hire, but she didn't want to see him down and out because of her shitty judgment, either.

"Layla, no," he said. "She's under contract. But me . . ."

He drew out the last word, and she wished she could tell if he was playing it up to make her feel bad, or if he really was worried.

"I'm so sorry," she said. "I'll make it better. I'll do anything to make it better."

He gave a snort that was far from encouraging. "Good night, Daph."

After hanging up, she tortured herself by watching the video again with no sound, and then scrolling down the comments before giving up. The gist was either that she was an obnoxious bitch who disrespected the game, or that he was a crybaby loser who disrespected the game. No matter what, commenters were positive that the game had been disrespected.

She wondered if he'd said anything about the incident. Her thumbs hovered over her phone, not even sure where to start, but eventually she just searched his name and filtered the results to the most recent.

At the top was a clip from an interview he'd apparently done with Layla after the game. One of the other side effects of Daphne leaving early—she hadn't even been able to see her sister-in-law other than a brief wave before the game started. She wasn't super close with Layla—not because she didn't want to be, but just because her sister-in-law was intimidating as hell.

Chris looked uncomfortable in the video, his body language closed off. Daphne heard Layla's familiar voice saying, not unkindly, that he'd seemed emotional, and what was going through his head in that last inning?

"They played us tough," he said. "I'm still making adjustments to my swing, and I know I wasn't at my best on the field. I've already talked to Marv and some of my teammates, and we know what we have to do in this upcoming road trip."

It was the most nonanswer Daphne had ever heard. But she was surprised by his voice—it was smooth and deep, the kind of voice you wished would narrate an eighteen-hour audiobook about a sweeping multigenerational saga. Something about him, in fact, gave her the impression of a 1940s soldier about to ship off to the German front. Maybe it was the short, utilitarian cut of his brown hair, or the hard line of his jaw.

"Chris," Layla said, her voice even gentler. Daphne had never heard her use that tone before. They'd been out to a restaurant and had people turn around and glare at their table before; that's how loud Layla usually was. "I have to ask—what happened before that last at-bat? Did a fan say something to upset you, or—"

If he looked uncomfortable before, it was nothing compared to the way he seemed now. His eyes cut to the side, almost like he was looking at someone off camera. Maybe he wanted someone to end the interview, if that was a thing you could even do. Daphne had no idea how that all worked.

"It's baseball," he said. "You want to win and it can get emotional. But I'm grateful to our fans for coming out and supporting us. I hope to earn that support as the season goes on. Thanks so much."

And with that, he was walking away, back toward the dugout, where only a few players remained. It was almost impressive, how little he'd managed to say. The way he'd left the interview felt casual, normal, like he was always supposed to talk to Layla for exactly twenty seconds and that's how much he'd done.

Somehow Daphne knew that wasn't true.

She sat up in her bed now, drawing her robe tighter around her. If she was going to creep on Chris Kepler's social media, she'd feel self-conscious flashing his Instagram feed. She found his account easily—the unimaginative combination of his name and his number, with a little verification check to prove it was the real him.

It was a nice-looking feed. Professional. Literally professional; she assumed the team had someone who took all these photos of him, crouched down by third base, on the run with his batting helmet flying off his head, leaning against the dugout with a teammate. There were no captions on any of the pictures except a short video posted last year, the crack of the bat as he hit a home run that apparently had won them the game.

This feeling, the caption said.

She scrolled back to the picture of Chris in the dugout. It was from last season, as most of the pictures seemed to be. In it, he was smiling, crinkle lines around his eyes. The guy she'd seen earlier that day, the one from the interview, didn't look like he'd ever smiled a day in his life, but here was proof that he had.

Daphne knew what it felt like to have a bad day, a bad month—hell, a bad year. She knew that the YouTuber and commenters had a point; this was his job and he was paid well to do it. But she hated the idea that she might've added one more brick to the pile, kicked him when he was down.

She'd feel better if she could at least apologize, or explain. It was probably pointless—she doubted he ran his own Instagram account, and even if he did, he wouldn't accept a random DM. But something made her click on the message button and start to type.

You don't know me, but I wanted to reach out to

"Reach out." God. She sounded like she was sending a business follow-up. She deleted the words and started again.

Hi. It's me—I'm the problem

Maybe quoting song lyrics was too flippant.

I was at the game earlier—I was actually the one who

Paranoia kicked in that she'd accidentally send the message before it was ready, so she opened up her Notes app instead, figuring she'd type it there first and then cut and paste it over.

And she should probably lead with his name, even though it was what had kicked off this entire nightmare scenario in the first place. **Chris**, she added to the beginning of her message, and then leaned back against her pillows, her thumbs hovering over her phone while she thought about what to say.

CHAPTER
THREE

CHRIS LEANED HIS HEAD BACK AGAINST HIS SEAT AND CLOSED HIS eyes. Beau had brought his Bluetooth speaker again, which meant that electronic music was pulsing through the plane like they were in a club flying thirty thousand feet. Earlier, one of the rookies had been sliding up and down the aisle on a flattened cardboard box like it was a sled. He'd come through on all the alcohol he was supposed to bring as one of his rookie duties, so everyone was in an indulgent mood. Or maybe just a mood to distract themselves from the fact that, thanks to today's game, they were officially in last place in their division.

Thanks to him. No one had said it directly to his face—it takes a team to win, it takes a team to lose, et cetera, et cetera—but everyone seemed fine giving him his space.

Or at least they had been. Randy Caminero, the Battery's twenty-five-year-old shortstop, slid next to Chris, nudging him with his elbow.

"They're crazy back there, man," he said.

"Yeah."

"You still down about the game? Don't be, man, it happens."

Chris felt like the only thing he could think to say was another lackluster *yeah*. So instead he stayed silent. But the thing about

Randy, for better or worse, was that he'd never met a silence he wasn't afraid to power right through.

"What did that chick say to you anyway?"

He squeezed his eyes shut, as if he had a headache. Hell, maybe he *did* have a headache. It was hard to tell. This might just be how he felt now.

Christopher Robin. He didn't want to think about it.

That moment was on *SportsCenter*, people were talking about it on social media, tomorrow there would be any number of sports analysis shows debating the natural passion that came with playing versus athletes needing to get over themselves versus overpaid crybabies versus toxic masculinity versus who knew what else. Already his phone had been blowing up with text messages, calls, notifications—mostly people in his life who were well-meaning, but who had no particular claim to any insider information. There were only two phone calls that mattered, and he'd ignored both of them.

His father had followed up by text with a terse Call me, while his agent had at least left a voicemail. *Chris—it might make sense to talk some strategy, given what's going on. Here for you.*

His agent wasn't a bad person, but she didn't even know what was "going on." And Chris wasn't naive. His agent was "there" to protect her asset as much as she was there to support her athlete.

Randy seemed to understand that he wasn't going to get an answer to his question, and moved on. "Hey, I got a buddy in LA who's got the hookup on some hot spots around town. You want in?"

Thirty-two wasn't *old*. But it felt old, especially in baseball. Chris tried to remember the last time he'd had the energy to make late-night plans during a road series in the middle of the week. His usual routine after a game, whether he was at home or away— maybe hit the weight room, stretch out with the trainer, get a shower, grab some food, head back to his condo or the hotel. Days could pass by in a monotonous blur of routines, the only difference being what color jersey he was wearing and which pitchers he faced and whether or not reporters cared to talk to him after the game.

Maybe going out with the guys was exactly what he needed.

"Sure," he said. "Thanks."

"Oh, shit!" Randy said, so loudly that Chris startled a little in his seat. "Sorry, I just didn't expect you to actually be down."

Great. So it had been a pity invite. "I don't have to—"

"No, no, no." Randy cut him off with a shake of his head. "This is sick. What kind of music you like? Techno, house, hip-hop, trip-hop . . . You know what, don't worry about it, I got it covered. We're gonna take this series and then we'll have some fun, am I right?"

Chris hoped he was right. But he had a sinking, superstitious feeling nonetheless, like maybe he shouldn't actually say it out loud. He settled for a short, noncommittal laugh before picking up his phone again, scrolling through it like he was looking for something in particular. Eventually, one of the guys in the back called for Randy, and the younger guy went off to join them, leaving Chris alone again.

Checking social media would be the absolute worst thing to do, like touching a stove you knew would be hot. So of course that was the first place Chris went. He had over three hundred notifications from the last time he'd checked, and a quick skim confirmed that most were people tagging him into their hot takes on what had happened at the game earlier.

if I was batting .173, I'd cry, too

watch them make some "mental health" thing out of this
#snowflakes

that bitch should've been thrown out of the game

Chris frowned. As much as he didn't love reading all the hate directed his way, he didn't want it directed toward that fan, either. As far as he could tell, no one had identified her to make her name part of the public conversation, and he hoped it stayed that way. Intellectually, he didn't blame her—he'd been heckled way worse before, and would probably get heckled more in the future, especially if he continued on the slide he'd been on lately.

Emotionally, though . . .

Christopher Robin. It had been what his brother used to call him, when they were kids. He hadn't yet started to shorten his name, because their mother hadn't liked it—*I named you Christopher for a reason,* she used to say. Back when she'd still been a part of his life anyway—she'd left when he was barely in elementary school, and he'd had very little contact with her since. But *Winnie the Pooh* had been one of his favorites as a toddler, so it had been an obvious nickname. He hadn't heard it in years, *decades,* but the minute he'd heard it shouted by that fan it had immediately brought him back. To a time when he was young, and hopeful.

To a time when his brother was alive.

He clicked over to Instagram. Normally, he didn't find it particularly restful to scroll through a bunch of people's random pictures, but right now he welcomed the distraction. A friend he kept up with had posted a few photos of him and his girlfriend hiking in Zion National Park, so he liked those, which would probably have him spinning out since Chris so often only lurked on social media. His agent had all his password information and occasionally posted a photo to his own feed, usually one provided by the team's Publicity Department or a repost of local media coverage. She always sent him a text, asking him any caption he wanted to include, but he rarely answered.

His DMs would be a cesspool just like his other notifications, but he opened them up anyway. No one he knew sent him messages via social media, because they were aware that he rarely checked it. There actually weren't as many message requests from today as he might've thought. It seemed most of the people who wanted to yell at him were over on other sites and hadn't yet thought to cross platforms. He started from the top and swiped to delete each of the unread messages, until one caught his eye.

His thumb hovered over the preview of the message. **I'm sorry about your pain. I don't pretend**

He almost swiped to delete it, but something made him click to open it instead.

I'm sorry about your pain, it began, just like in the preview, before continuing on.

I don't pretend to know what you might be going through. Maybe it's just about baseball, or maybe there's more to it than that. Maybe it's not "just" baseball when it's your job and your life. I don't know.

I do know what it's like to feel overwhelmed and sad. Lately it feels like I can't think too hard about what's already happened, and I can't think too hard about what might happen in the future. I have to stay aggressively in the present just to get through my day. Is that what all those yoga influencer accounts have been trying to say this whole time?

Chris surprised himself with his own snort of laughter. Then he schooled his features back into neutrality, not that anyone was even paying attention to him. It was second nature by this point.

Luckily, I work from home, so if I cry on the job nobody has to know. Well, except for my cat, Milo. He gives me the judgiest looks, like he can't believe I would be so unprofessional. But to be fair, that might just be how his face is. I'm not trying to resting-bitch-face-shame my cat. I also don't have jerks

coming to my workplace and shouting random shit at me! If you wanted to heckle me, I guess you could call me out for not including at least three affiliate links or forgetting the final word count on my invoice. Not very exciting stuff, but it's the reason they give for not paying me within thirty days so sometimes it can make me cry lol

Anyway, I'm rambling. Sorry. That's the only important part of this message, which I know you'll probably never even see. I'm so, so sorry.

It was a bizarre message. For one thing, there was a tone of familiarity in it, as though they already knew each other somehow. The username was *duckiesbooks*, the profile icon a rubber duckie, fittingly enough, on top of a stack of books. He clicked over to the profile, to see if anyone he knew followed the account, some real-life connection he might've missed. But there was nothing. The account had a couple hundred followers, and a quick scroll through the feed showed that it was only pictures of book covers or stacks of books, no selfies or other identifying pictures. Nothing to even indicate that this person was a big baseball fan, or why they would've reached out at all.

Maybe the most bizarre thing was how Chris *did* feel like he knew this person already, or that the person knew him. *I have to stay aggressively in the present just to get through my day.* In that one sentence, he felt like someone had made sense of the way he'd been feeling lately.

While he'd been reading, he'd stretched out on the seats, his back leaned against the window and his legs toward the aisle. At six foot three, he was hardly the tallest person on the team, but this was the part of the flight when he started to feel restless. Normally, he might get up, find a group of guys playing cards, or even just hit the bathroom as an excuse to stretch his legs. But today, he was happy to keep a lower profile.

His foot must've been sticking out in the aisle a bit, because Roberto Gutierrez, the veteran slugger the team had picked up from the Tigers right before spring training, stepped on it as he walked past. Chris winced slightly, pulling back in, and started to apologize.

"You gonna cry about it?" Gutierrez said, before continuing up the aisle.

Maybe it had been a joke. He'd already gotten some ribbing from his teammates, and genuine concern from guys he was friends with, like Randy. But this had felt more pointed.

It was late. They'd played a shitty game, and were now on a six-hour flight across the country to play a team who, despite Randy's optimism, was practically guaranteed to take at least two of three. He was sure all those factors were behind Gutierrez's irritable mood.

Maybe it's not "just" baseball when it's your job and your life.

He stared down at the message still pulled up on his phone. It didn't feel right to leave it completely unacknowledged. So, he typed a one-word response.

Thanks.

It had only been on the screen a few seconds when a little gray word appeared beneath it. Seen.

Fuck. He had no idea the app sold you out like that. Now he thought back to how long it had been since he'd first opened the message, how weird it must've seemed, the delay between him first seeing it and him responding to it. Or maybe the read receipt could've been the equivalent of a response, if he'd just left it alone. This was why he didn't mess with social media.

And yet the idea that there was a person on the other end, someone who was seeing these messages in real time, compelled him to keep going.

When I was a kid, I had a pug named Otis.

Three dots, like they were typing. Then the dots disappeared. Chris realized that his message was a bit of a non sequitur, so he started to add a bit more context. **Milo & Otis? It was about a dog and a cat . . .**

He actually didn't remember anything more than that. He clicked over to a search page, wanting to look up the movie real fast to jog his memory, before it occurred to him just how stupid this whole thing was. Who cared. He went back to Instagram to delete his unsent draft, but saw that there was new text from duckiesbooks already.

Milo & Otis! That's cute. Don't look it up but apparently there was some animal cruelty in the way they filmed that movie tho. 😔

Then, a second later: **Oh god, I'm sorry. What a downer thing to bring up! I haven't seen that movie since I was a kid. They used to show it in my after-school program on rainy days. I bet your pug was adorable.**

It occurred to him that he didn't really know anything about duckiesbooks, including their age. They'd mentioned working from home, which suggested they were an adult at least, but still it was a relief that they seemed to get his dated references and referred back to when they were a kid in a way that suggested it had been years ago. Still, it was a good reminder of yet another reason he didn't use social media—as someone who was at least quasi-famous, he had to be extra careful about boundaries. It would be best if he shut this down.

He was, he typed. **And don't worry, I won't look up the movie, but I appreciate the heads-up. Have a good night.**

But at the same time he sent his message, there was another from duckiesbooks.

Milo's actually named for the main character in The

Phantom Tollbooth by Norton Juster. It was one of my favorite childhood books. Basically, Milo is this super bored kid who thinks everything is pointless until he gets a mysterious package in the mail with a magical tollbooth and a map. He goes off on all these adventures through places like Dictionopolis and the Doldrums, and runs into these princesses Rhyme and Reason and this watchdog named Tock . . .

Chris was typing his response when another message popped up on the screen.

Have a good night!

He should be relieved that duckiesbooks had read the room correctly. It was the closure he'd wanted. And yet suddenly he realized he didn't want to drop the conversation just yet. He had no idea what time it was—his phone had probably updated to the local time zone for wherever they were flying over, but where that was, he had no clue. But for once, he wasn't thinking about baseball or about his brother, and that was hard to pass up.

C: For someone living aggressively in the present, that's the second time you've brought up your childhood.

D: I guess you can't escape the past after all.

D: anyway, you started it

Nope. He wasn't touching that.

He flicked back to Duckie's profile. There were her pronouns, right next to her username—she/her. And her bio was only a single quote—"A well-read woman is a dangerous creature," attributed to Lisa Kleypas. Although none of the thumbnails he scrolled through showed Duckie's face, there were several that showed part of her hands. In a recent one, she was holding up a green-and-black hardback book, an artistically blurred couple embracing behind the bold white brushstroke title. She had pretty hands from what he could see of them, graceful fingers. Her nail polish was chipped teal.

You could imagine so much of a stranger's life from these little moments. Already he was calling her *Duckie* in his head, like that was her actual name.

C: What time is it in South Carolina?

Full minutes went by without a response, longer than it should have been given that she was clearly active on the app—that little *Seen* notification had popped up again—and the time would be displayed on her phone or computer. He didn't know if he'd crossed a line by referencing their home state. But he'd figured she would be local—it wasn't like the Battery were a large-market team. And one of her recent posts had been of a book stack in front of the Charleston Library Society, the forced perspective making the books seem like the steps to the building.

The question had seemed safe when Chris volleyed it over. It was a simple request for factual information, an acknowledgment of the temporal moment they found themselves in. But the longer it went unanswered, the more the words seemed to pulse on the screen. The question peeled back so many layers he'd worked hard to reinforce. How distant he felt, how alone. Suddenly he could think of nothing more desperate than asking a stranger what time it was.

Then the dots appeared, blinking before her response came in.

FOUR

DAPHNE DIDN'T KNOW WHAT TO DO.

She'd barely expected Chris Kepler to check his messages, much less actually respond to her. Even in the alternate universe where he read her message, and decided to reply, she'd figured he might have some words of admonishment. Something about how he was a person, too, and maybe she should think about that next time she decided to mouth off at a game. Or he'd say something dismissive that made her feel ridiculous, like she was making a big deal out of nothing.

But instead he'd written about his childhood dog?

She scrolled back up to her first message, still trying to make sense of what was happening. And that's when she saw it. She'd typed and retyped her message a hundred times, trying to get the tone right—contrite but lighthearted, remorseful but friendly—and then when she'd cut and pasted it over from her Notes app she'd deleted the most important paragraph. The one where she actually said, *I was the heckler, and I'm sorry.*

SHE'D SENT AN APOLOGY MESSAGE AND DE-LETED THE APOLOGY.

There were still references to her being sorry, but without that introductory paragraph, it read more like she was *generally* sorry.

Instead of unmasking her as a piece of shit, if anything her message had made her seem like an even *better* person for caring enough to reach out.

And now he was writing about his childhood dog and asking her what time it was, and it was all so normal . . . so *nice*. It would be beyond awkward to say something now, like, *Oh, by the way, I'm the one who made fun of how bad you were at the game? But anyway, let me tell you more about my cat.*

Milo had that judgy face on again, and this time she knew she deserved it. She took a deep breath, trying to ignore the slippery feeling in her stomach as she typed her response to Chris' question.

D: 11:43.

She could've left it there, closed the door behind her. But damned if she didn't want to open the door a little bit more, even if it meant that she was crossing a line she couldn't venture back over.

D: Where are you?

"Stay in the present," she murmured to Milo, who'd flipped over onto his back, showing his belly even as he hid half his body underneath her bed. It was one of his favorite things to do, inviting tummy scratches while simultaneously making it impossible to administer them unless she crouched down and wedged her hand uncomfortably between the bed frame and his body. She leaned over to try her best, but Milo immediately rolled back over and slunk over to his favorite spot, curled up in the laundry on the floor of her closet.

C: Two hours behind. Not sure exactly where.

While they'd been talking, she'd pulled up the Battery's schedule. They were playing the Dodgers tomorrow, so she assumed that Chris was typing these messages from thousands of miles away and many more feet above the ground.

D: Now look who's in the past. What kind of plane traveler are you? Like do you put your seat back, earbuds in, do you prefer window or aisle, etc.? Once I got stuck sitting in the middle seat between an older couple and they talked about his golf game and her pecan pie recipe the entire flight right over me like I wasn't even there.

C: We have a private plane.

Well, she supposed she should've figured that.

D: So you do whatever you want?

C: Pretty much.

She couldn't get a read on him. His replies could be so short, and she kept waiting for him to wrap it up, or stop responding. He'd already kind of done it once. But then he just kept typing. Even now, she saw the three dots appear, and then a new message popped up at the bottom of the chat.

C: Seat back: occasionally. Earbuds in: usually. Window: preferably.

The fact that he answered each part of her question in order got to her a little. This wasn't a formal interview; he didn't owe her answers to anything at all. And yet he seemed to want her to know each of those details, because she'd asked about them, and she didn't know what to do with that.

Before she could second-guess herself, she decided to cut right to the chase.

D: Can I ask you a question?

C: . . .

D: Why are you talking to me?

D: Not that I mind.

D: I like talking to you.

D: I mean, I appreciate that you answered my DM. I'm just surprised.

Daphne groaned audibly into her empty apartment, causing

Milo to lift his head from the laundry. Everything she said was more cringeworthy than the last. Not to mention reminding her that the only reason this guy was talking to her in the first place was because she'd botched her apology so badly.

C: I can't sleep on planes.

Okay, so he was just bored. Weirdly, that made her feel better. She'd been in that kind of situation before—stuck in a doctor's waiting room, for example, with nothing to do but mess around on your phone and hope you got called soon. Those were the times when you stooped to interacting with branded social media accounts or answering all those mindless autofill prompts. *Type "I am [your Zodiac sign] and that's why" and then let predictive text fill in the rest.*

Bored made sense to her. Bored, she could handle.

D: Are you scared to fly? I'm not, but I hate it when anyone reminds you that you're 10x safer when you fly than when you drive. I know!!! That's why I'm more scared of cars!!!

C: I never used to be.

Huh. That implied that he was now, but he didn't follow up. Instead, his next message came in with another question for her.

C: Are you really scared of cars?

D: I got into a car accident in college—it wasn't even that bad, if my best friend were here she'd say, "It was a bump!" (She's the one who hit my car.) Anyway, ever since then I've been a nervous driver! Which I know doesn't help, only makes me more nervous, and on and on. It's a vicious cycle.

C: Have you been in a car accident since the bump?

Daphne smiled. She didn't know why it was so charming to her, that he'd used Kim's word for it.

D: No.

C: So in . . . how many years?

D: 7

She was probably reading too much into it, but suddenly Daphne wondered if that had been a clever way to ask how old she was. She decided to follow it up with more information, just in case.

D: (I was 20 at the time.)

C: It sounds like you're a pretty safe driver.

Justin had insisted on driving if they were going anywhere together. At the time, she'd been more than happy to give up control in that area, willing to accept his judgment that he was the better driver. If for any reason she did take the wheel—like if he'd had too much to drink and she'd had to drive them home—he would berate her the entire time, pointing out yellow lights she could've made it through or demanding why she hadn't turned down a particular street. Meanwhile, he was the one who'd navigated traffic like he was drafting in NASCAR.

It was maddening, what she'd put up with when she really thought about it. She wished she could go back in time and shout, *You're the one who backed into a parked semi! Not me!*

But she supposed her last chance to scream that kind of stuff had been a couple days ago. And she didn't actually want to replay any of it—she was just grateful she didn't have to live with that feeling anymore, always waiting to be put in her place. Now she was moving forward. Moving on.

D: I'm reading your Wikipedia now.

She'd thought it was somehow more honest to announce the fact, like she couldn't be accused of creeping if she owned it. But now, seeing the words so baldly in their chat, she wished she'd kept it to herself. She was going to have to get better at this if she was going to start online dating like Kim kept encouraging her to.

Not that this was the same. Not that she felt in any way ready to date. Still, it couldn't hurt to practice not being awkward as hell, if she could manage it for five seconds.

C: Is my driving history in there?

D: No, but happy birthday ☺ Did you do anything special?

The emoji was particularly embarrassing. She wished she could take it back, together with the inappropriate question—it wasn't any of her business what he did. She'd just never been able to stop herself if she found out someone's birthday had just passed or was coming up. She *had* to say happy birthday. It was a sickness.

C: Lost to the Diamondbacks. What else does it say?

She was impressed by how much information there was, actually. Minor league teams he'd played for in the A's organization, the teams he'd been traded to, various statistics about his batting average, how many home runs he'd hit, how many errors he'd made. Most of it was lost on her.

D: This says you're one of only 11 players in the MLB who eschews batting gloves. What do you have against batting gloves?

C: I like to feel the bat. "Eschews?" Interesting word choice.

D: Right? I love unusual words. In sixth grade I won a writing contest where we had to use all our vocabulary words in one essay. "Your homework should always be safely ensconced in your homework folder." I think that was the sentence that pushed mine over the top.

C: Well, no wonder. You wrote about responsible homework practices . . . for a school essay contest. You knew what you were doing.

Daphne bit her lip. She'd definitely been teacher's pet in school. Quiet, kept to herself, followed rules. It was only recently that she'd started asking herself if that was any way to go through life. She'd originally thought about going into elementary education, but she'd ended up majoring in communications and broadcasting in college, thinking one day maybe she'd combine her interests into something that could really reach people. It was a far cry from what she was doing now—writing dry corporate blog posts about setting up IT networks or writing quick clickbait listicles about movie stars and their most famous roles.

D: I was a nerdy kid. My favorite show was Reading Rainbow.

C: I remember that one. One of my favorite movies was Winnie the Pooh. I used to be inconsolable when he followed the bees into that hole and got stuck. My older brother roasted me so bad for that. If he even mentioned Winnie the Pooh getting stuck in the tree he could get me to cry.

It couldn't be a coincidence, him mentioning the same movie she'd referenced in her heckle. Maybe that was what all the crying had been about—some Pavlovian response to thinking of that movie again if that one small part had gotten to him so much as a kid. She wondered if it was possible that he *did* know she was his heckler after all, if she was the one who'd misread the earlier messages and her original intent had come through just fine. She started to scroll back up to the top of their conversation before another message came through.

C: Can I ask you a question?

She sat up a little straighter on her bed, trying to settle the sudden flutter in her stomach at the way he'd mirrored her earlier words. She racked her brain, trying to figure out what he could possibly want to know.

D: . . .

C: Why did you message me in the first place?

So he didn't know who she was. And now he'd given her the perfect opportunity to come clean—it would be like ripping off a Band-Aid. *I'm the one who heckled you at the game,* she'd type, and then he'd know. But then that led to so many more things she'd need to say—how sorry she was for doing that, how sorry she was now that she hadn't led with that information from the beginning.

"Sure," she said, more to herself than Milo, who took no more interest in whatever she was doing. "Here's a can of worms for you, go ahead and open it."

She started drafting her response, before eventually getting up, setting the phone temporarily on her bed while she went to fix herself a cup of tea. She was out of her Sleepytime tea and normally she wouldn't have caffeine this late, but tonight she would make an exception. She needed to think about how to explain, and for that, she needed to be awake.

CHAPTER
FIVE

CHRIS TAPPED HIS PHONE ON HIS THIGH WHILE HE WAITED FOR Duckie's answer. He knew she was composing something from the way the dots disappeared, then reappeared again, like maybe she'd thought twice about whatever she was going to write and had deleted it to start over. The thing was, she didn't seem like much of a baseball fan—or maybe it just didn't fit with her book-themed account; he didn't know. But something about the way she'd cut and pasted that fact from his Wikipedia, the way that they'd been chatting for almost half an hour at this point and she had yet to make any comment about the team's record, the season, what did he think about that decision from the commissioner or this year's chances that so-and-so would make the World Series . . .

He was glad not to talk baseball. It was refreshing. It was just unusual for him, especially on the internet, where his presence felt completely superfluous except in his limited capacity as Chris Kepler, third baseman for the Carolina Battery.

This was a terrible idea. What response did he expect, except some variation of *Because you seemed like a sad sack on TV and I felt sorry for you.*

Maybe it was better if he just got out in front of it. He wasn't ashamed of crying, per se, but he hated the fact that everyone was talking about it, weighing in on why he might've been upset and whether he had any right to be. He knew he had some control over the narrative—he could share more about what had been going through his head in that moment, stop the speculation, and give people the answers they clearly felt entitled to. But then everyone would be talking about *that*, which would be even worse.

He thought again of his father's text. *Call me.* He already knew without speaking to the man that he'd want Chris to stay quiet. *Keep your head down, keep playing ball, and for the love of god, swing* through. *You have a hitch that's holding you back, you have to swing* through.

We can use this, his agent would say, and she'd have a lot of strategic ideas about how. Ideas that would probably help his career, bolster his reputation, maybe even secure him some niche sponsorship deal. He didn't want to hear any of that, either.

C: My older brother died by suicide a few months ago.

He'd typed the sentence and clicked send before he could take it back. It was the first time he'd laid it out so plainly for someone who didn't already know, someone who wasn't a friend of the family or involved in his day-to-day life. He hadn't even told the Battery's manager, Marv, or his teammates—not because he didn't expect them to be supportive, but maybe even because he was afraid they would be. He didn't know if he could handle it, having people ask how he was doing or offer to let him take time off.

There was absolutely zero reason for him to share such a personal detail with this random stranger, but maybe that was part of the appeal. The anonymity of it.

Although, shit—nothing on the internet was anonymous, was it? He quickly typed a follow-up message.

C: That's not really public information. I'd appreciate if you didn't share it anywhere.

It was also a pretty heavy thing to just dump on someone. She'd felt bad about sharing the unethical working conditions for animals in a movie filmed decades ago, and he'd hit her with *this*? Via a social messaging app? At *midnight*? He wished there was a way to erase all of it, but the *Seen* stamp had already appeared below his texts.

D: I'm so sorry about your brother. "Sorry"—god, such an inadequate word. You must be devastated.

D: Of course I won't tell anyone.

D: Do you want to talk about it?

Did he want to talk about it? That was the big question. He kept thinking it was the last thing he wanted. And yet here he was, pouring his heart out to a stranger. Clearly his feelings were complicated.

C: It used to be that everything tunneled when I played baseball. It was just me and the ball, the field, my team . . . like in a photo where the crowd is all blurred, but I was crisp and clear in the center of the frame. That's how it felt. But now it's flipped. I'm the blur. And everything that used to be background is turned up so loud, I can't tune it out.

C: I don't know if any of that made sense.

He rubbed his hand over his face, surprised at the sting he felt at the outer corners of his eyes. This was another problem he'd been having lately. This urge to cry came over him at the oddest, most random moments. He'd sat in his condo alone only a few nights ago, *trying* to cry, willing himself to get it all out. It would be cathartic, he figured. But eventually he'd gone to bed, his eyes dry. Then, a couple days later, one throwaway Winnie the Pooh reference and it had hit him like a wave. He supposed he should just be thankful he'd managed to get himself back under control relatively quickly, that he'd finished his at-bat and the postgame interview without any further incident.

D: It makes perfect sense. Something like that would crater your entire world.

D: Is there anyone you can talk to—your coach or a team doctor . . . ? (I don't know anything about baseball, sorry.)

That made him smile a little. Yeah, he'd figured. The Battery's manager, Marvin Gordon, was a legend. Now in his seventies, he'd had a Hall of Fame–worthy career as a player before taking on leadership roles after he retired. He was one of only five Black managers to have ever managed a World Series team, back when he was in Atlanta. Marv was a great guy, but old-school—Chris could no more imagine talking to him about taking bereavement leave than he could imagine talking to him about pitching in the next game.

C: Maybe.

C: Sorry to lay all that on you. I'm just tired.

D: There's no need to apologize. You can talk more about it if you want to. If you were here I'd make you some tea.

D: (Metaphorically. Not like you'd actually be here, but you know what I mean.)

Around him, guys were starting to shift in their seats, pack up stuff they'd had out for the trip. There must've been an announcement that they were landing soon, but he'd missed it. This had been the fastest cross-country flight of his life.

C: I appreciate the offer (metaphorical or otherwise). Are you having a cup now?

D: Yeah, although I shouldn't. It's a black tea with apricot and currant. It'll keep me up all night. I just like the ritual of it—putting the kettle on the stove, steeping it for the exact right amount of time, adding honey, that kind of thing.

C: Rituals are good.

D: They are. What's one of yours?

Chris had to think about that one for a minute. He had so

many in baseball, some he'd done for years, since his days playing in high school. The order in which he did certain stretches before a game, for example, or if he had a good game the way he'd try to replicate certain conditions the next day, as though searching for the magical variable that had made the difference.

But he tried to think of something he did outside of the sport, something that brought him comfort, like making a hot cup of tea. The problem was that he was so rarely home, and the routines he had at his condo or whatever hotel he was at for the night felt less like rituals and more like part of the daily grind.

C: This isn't a ritual exactly, but I do have a superstition about the song "The Way" by Fastball. Have you heard it?

D: It sounds a little familiar? But I couldn't sing it for you or anything. (You wouldn't want me to sing regardless—I have a terrible voice.)

He almost caught himself responding to that, saying something along the lines of how he was sure her voice was just fine. But of course that was ridiculous, because he'd never heard her speak, let alone sing, and surely she would be in a better position to judge than he would. It was a knee-jerk reaction to her talking badly about herself.

C: Well, don't look it up. That's part of the superstition.

D: That you can't look up the song?

The plane was starting to descend, and he leaned forward, resting his elbows on his knees as he hurried to type his explanation.

C: There's something about when that song comes on. I've heard it in a grocery store, once at a Waffle House. It's serendipity. You can't seek it out or you'll ruin it. It has to find you, not the other way around.

D: You could say the same thing about most songs that come over the radio. What makes this one different?

C: I don't know, but it's special. Trust me.

D: Now I'm worried I won't know the song when I hear it. Since I can't look it up to study beforehand.

C: You'll know. Just keep your ears open.

His were starting to kill him. He couldn't remember it being this bad on other flights, but he'd also stayed in one position for a longer period of time than he usually did. He opened his jaw as if to yawn, stretching until he felt his ears pop.

D: Can I look up the lyrics?

Chris had never codified all the rules of this superstition. It lived in his gut, not his head. He didn't even know what the superstition was *about*—what the song was supposed to be an omen of, or what good luck it brought if you heard it. He just knew that it had to be protected.

C: I don't even know all the lyrics. I have no idea what the song is about and I don't want to know. It's more a vibe than anything else. Like seeing a double rainbow.

D: I feel like that may be more common than hearing this song.

He grinned.

C: Exactly.

D: Imagine one day you meet this band and you say, "I love your song so much I refuse to ever purposely listen to it."

Someone jostled the seat next to him, and he looked up. It was Randy, standing in the aisle with his bag already over his shoulder.

"Hey, man, you gonna bunk down on the plane?"

Half the team had already deboarded, and the other half were lined up in the aisle, still laughing and talking but with a bit of that bleary-eyed look that said everyone was looking forward to getting to the hotel and calling it a night.

Chris glanced back down at his phone. Three new messages had come in from Duckie after the last one, and he could tell his silence had made her second-guess herself.

D: Maybe that is the purest form of love tho

D: Am I allowed to Wikipedia the band?

D: Okay, I'll let the song come to me organically. Appreciate you giving me the heads-up so I didn't spoil the magic for myself.

"Who you chatting with?" Randy asked, craning his neck to see over Chris' shoulder. "You got yourself a girl?"

He could feel the tips of his ears go hot as he rushed to send one last message before putting his phone away. "Nah," he said. "It's no one."

SIX

JUST LANDED. HAVE A GOOD NIGHT.

Daphne flashed the phone screen to Kim, showing her the last words she'd received from Chris Kepler the night before. She'd filled her best friend in on the whole thing—well, most of it. She'd told her about how she'd reached out to apologize, how he'd actually responded, how they'd ended up talking. She hadn't gone into any specifics about what they'd talked *about*. Obviously, the stuff with his brother was private. And as for the rest of it . . . it felt private, too, like if she exposed it to air she risked it turning brown and wilting.

"Well, that certainly explains why we're *here*," Kim said, gesturing around the sports bar where they'd met to share a sampler platter and, yes, okay, to watch the Battery play the Dodgers on the road.

"It was just so abrupt," Daphne said.

"You held your own, though," Kim said, dipping a mozzarella stick into marinara sauce and taking a big, cheese-stretching bite. "Liking his message instead of replying to it. Brutal."

She hadn't necessarily intended it that way. It was more that he'd seemed to want to shut the conversation down, and she didn't want to be the one desperately trying to keep it going. A simple heart to acknowledge that she'd seen his last message seemed the only way to go.

And now she kept opening and closing the chat window, debating about sending a new message, trying to restart the conversation. It felt so unfinished, and she was surprised by how much she'd enjoyed talking to him. How much more she wanted to know about what he was thinking and feeling, how much more she wanted to say.

"He probably gets hundreds of thirsty DMs a day," Kim went on, before defensively holding up a mozzarella stick at Daphne's expression. "*Not* saying that's what yours was. Just saying I'm not surprised if he's flaky and weird, but it has nothing to do with you. I'm proud of you for taking some initiative. You could stand to do the same in other areas of your life—like I wish you'd slide into *more* DMs, if you feel me."

"The ink on the divorce papers is barely dry."

Kim rolled her eyes. "Okay, but you've been separated for a while. And even before that . . ."

She didn't need to go on. Daphne was well aware of what her marriage had been like.

Justin had been her brother's best friend since high school, and Daphne had had a crush on him for . . . well, practically since the first day they met. Donovan had invited a bunch of friends over, warning Daphne to stay out of the way and not embarrass him. There was only a two-year age gap between them, but once he'd started ninth grade that gap had been insurmountable, her seventh-grade self way beneath his notice. His friends had mostly ignored her, too, including Justin. But she couldn't help noticing him, his boyish good looks, the way he always managed to be the life of any party. He had a million stories and jokes, and would hold court in their den for hours while Daphne listened from her room. As someone who struggled to overcome her own natural shyness, she was in awe of anyone who could be that extroverted.

Maybe that had been part of the problem, in the end. Maybe she'd wanted to be *like* Justin more than she'd wanted to be *with* Justin. And then, once she was actually with him—once she'd gotten what she'd always told herself she wanted—she realized she didn't even want to be like him at all. They'd married in haste and were still repenting.

Daphne turned her head toward the TV screen over the bar, where the pregame announcers were talking about the game. The sound was off, but the closed-captioning briefly flashed with Chris' name before it cut to the now-ubiquitous clip of him starting to cry. She looked away, not wanting to see it again or even read what the commentators might be saying.

Her heart had ached for him when he revealed how he'd lost his brother. She couldn't even begin to imagine what he must be going through. He'd struck her as an intensely private person, and she hadn't wanted to pry any further. She just hoped he had *someone* he could talk to.

"Have you ever heard that song 'The Way'?" Daphne asked.

Kim had pulled her phone out and was scrolling through it, and Daphne could tell she only had half her friend's attention.

"No," Kim said distractedly. "Any good? Oh—this is the one I was looking for. You *have* to be on this app. It's not overrun with fuckboys, I promise. We can work on your profile together. It's going to be so fun to be single at the same time! Like college all over again."

Daphne studied the screen that Kim had pushed toward her. It looked like any other dating app, several of which she'd already started populating information in before giving up, either because they asked for too much upfront or she wasn't sure that she wanted to pay the money or she was ambivalent about the idea of dating at all. Kim seemed to have it in her head that this was what Daphne needed to get over Justin, but Daphne wasn't sure about that. She felt over her ex. She just didn't feel hopeful about anyone new.

So why did her mind turn immediately to the thought of how cozy it would be to sit down at her tiny countertop, drinking tea with another person and not just by herself? Why did her mind complete that image with not just a generic silhouette of a person, but a very specific person who'd fill her small space with his tall, rangy body?

I appreciate the offer (metaphorical or otherwise).

She wondered what kind of profile would get someone like Chris Kepler to swipe right. He would appreciate someone special, probably—someone unique. He liked a song he rarely heard because of how rarely he heard it. She was sure professional athletes dated pop stars, models, people like that. But when she'd talked to him, he'd seemed so . . . normal. He'd taken the time to assure her she sounded like a safe driver. Why would he do that?

She pulled out her own phone and downloaded the app Kim recommended. "Okay," she said. "I'm ready to fill out my profile."

Half an hour later, Daphne was *still* completing the monstrous survey at the beginning of the process, but starting to feel excited about the possibility of reinventing herself a little. So she'd never really been that outdoorsy. She could be! Long walks on the beach sounded nice. So she'd never been much of a partier—she could be! Just look at how she'd let loose at the baseball game . . . not that she wanted a repeat of *that* incident. And so she'd never been that great at first-date banter or small talk—she bet she could improve with practice.

For some reason, she thought of Chris again, the way he'd typed *You knew what you were doing.* That had felt a *little* flirty. Had they been flirting?

"Now it's asking what I'm looking for," Daphne said once she'd gotten to the part of the survey about her potential matches.

Kim made a gesture like, *And? What's the problem?*

The problem was that Daphne had no clue. Technically, Justin had ticked off every box she might've selected on this list. She'd thought he had a good sense of humor, but later she'd realized that what he really wanted was just to be the funniest person in the room. She'd thought he was supportive, but everything filtered through how it affected *him.*

She'd thought he was kind, but in the short fourteen months they'd been married, he'd shown he could be quite cruel.

"I just want someone to *know* me," Daphne said. "To love me for who I am but to also push me to be who I want to be."

Sometimes she thought finding the perfect partner had less to do with who they were and more about how they made you feel. But how could you screen for that?

Kim grabbed her phone from her. "Get outta here with that cheesy shit," she said. "We'll narrow down the age range to under forty and filter out anyone who selected 'unemployed' or 'self-employed' as their employment status."

"Technically *I'm* self-employed."

Kim blinked before tapping the phone a couple times. "Believe me, it's better to start this way. The last thing you want is some wannabe entrepreneur trying to hit you up for free graphic design work for his vending machine business. Ask me how I know."

In one corner of the bar, a group of guys erupted in a cheer, and Daphne looked up to the TV screen to see Chris rounding first base, stopping at second to point at someone in the dugout, an almost-smile tugging at the corner of his mouth. The instant replay showed the pitch coming toward him, the way he twisted his body to make contact with his bat, the moment he dropped the bat in the dirt and started running. After the replay the screen filled with footage from the last game *again*, this time going all the way back to the shot that YouTube video had shown of her yelling through the net. The closed-captioning was rolling across the bottom, too fast and garbled for her to make much sense of it, but she didn't need to know the specifics to know they were rehashing the same tired ground about how this had happened last game, looks like he has more reason to smile today, and on and on.

"Oh, shit," someone yelled in a deep baritone, and suddenly there was a commotion over in that corner. Daphne looked up and was surprised to see that they were staring directly at *her*. The guy who must've spoken pointed right at her, gesturing with his sloshing beer as though he were participating in pub trivia and determined to be first to answer. "That's her! That's the heckler!"

Even the bartender glanced over at the high-top, where moments before, Daphne and Kim had been quietly enjoying their meal. It only now occurred to Daphne that she was in a bar filled with Battery fans, and the fact that they'd all just seen her drunkenly roasting one of their players on TV was maybe . . . not the best.

"What do you have to say now?" one of the guys shouted. "Still want to talk trash?"

"Um, no," Daphne said, even as Kim was already tossing down a couple twenties onto the table.

"Come on," she said. "Let's get out of here."

The guys were still shouting after her as they left the bar, and several people had their phones out, obviously snapping pictures or shooting video of the whole encounter. Great. Just her luck, *that* would end up on *SportsCenter*, too, and then she'd never hear the end of it from her brother.

"Well," Kim said, digging through her purse for her pepper spray for the dark walk to their cars. "You did say you wanted someone to know you. So how does it feel?"

Daphne was saved from having to answer by her phone vibrating in her pocket. Unfortunately, it was her brother. She picked up the call, her stomach sinking. He couldn't have possibly already heard what had just gone down, right?

"Donovan —" she started, but he cut her off.

"It's Layla," he said. "We're at the hospital now. Can you come?"

DAPHNE SPOTTED HER BROTHER PACING IN THE HALLWAY OUTSIDE a hospital room, finishing up a phone call. By the way he signed off the conversation, she could tell he'd been talking to their parents. Any other time she would've asked how they were, how the trip was going, if their mom still boycotted using the tiny RV bathroom if their dad had used it in the hour beforehand. But now she was too focused on how her sister-in-law was doing.

"Is she in there?" she asked, gesturing toward the room. "What happened? How is she?"

Kim came up behind her, a little late from having to park. She touched Daphne's arm as if to say, *It's okay, calm down.*

But Daphne couldn't help it. Donovan had always been the typical older brother in that he didn't want to show any weakness in front of his little sister, so for him to call her that panicked had made *her* panic. Now that she was here, though, she noticed that he seemed okay. Tired, maybe, a little worried. But not devastated. Whatever the news was, it couldn't be *that* bad.

"They took her downstairs to run a couple tests," he said. "Right now they're saying something about an insufficient cervix, or incompetent cervix? I forget the term. She should be fine, and the baby should be fine, but they're recommending she go on bed rest to avoid going into labor too early. There's also some procedure they can do to possibly help, but they're still assessing that."

Daphne froze. "Donnie."

"Duckie." If she was going to use the childhood nickname she knew he hated, apparently he was going to fight back.

A slow smile spread over her face. "You're having a *baby*?"

It seemed to dawn on him, then, that he'd told the news in reverse order. He smiled, too, a full-out grin that told Daphne just how truly excited her brother was to be a dad. "Oh yeah," he said. "We were going to tell everyone when we were a little further in the second trimester. And then we were thinking of throwing some kind of party where we could tell everyone all at once and . . . yeah, whoops. You're going to be an aunt."

He barely got the last words out before Daphne was enveloping him in a huge hug, and then Kim was hugging her, and by the time they wheeled Layla back down the hallway toward her room, everyone was almost too busy laughing and hugging to even notice.

"Jeez, guys," she said dryly. "I can see you were really worried. Thanks so much for your concern."

"Layla, congratulations!" Daphne said, not bothering to wipe the tears out of her eyes as she gave her sister-in-law a hug. It was a little awkward, both because Daphne wasn't used to being taller than Layla and because she wasn't used to giving her polished sister-in-law hugs that weren't of the one-arm-patting-the-back variety. It was the hair. Layla's jet-black shiny hair was always so perfectly coiffed that Daphne was afraid to mess it up.

"We're just excited about the baby," she said. "But how is everything? Are you feeling okay?"

Layla sighed. "I feel fine now. I had some cramping and wasn't feeling well this morning when I was supposed to catch my flight to LA, so Donovan thought I should stay back. Then I had a little spotting, so we made a doctor's appointment just in case, and they sent me here . . . to keep a grisly story short, I guess they're worried about the baby just slipping right out of me if I'm on my feet too much."

"So what does bed rest mean?"

Layla rolled her eyes at Donovan's question, but she reached out to squeeze her husband's hand, a sign that she knew he'd been worried and appreciated his concern. "Technically it's called an *activity restriction*. It means pretty much what you think it does. No lifting anything or exerting myself too much. Looks like you're on your own to paint that nursery, sweetheart."

"I'm happy to help," Daphne cut in, even though she knew it was about more than just the logistics of getting a single room painted. Some people you could imagine sitting still for long periods of time—Layla wasn't one of them.

"What about work?" Donovan asked.

Layla shook her head. "I'll have to take a leave—even if they end up doing the stitch, they said too much activity can put the baby at risk. And here we were, congratulating ourselves on threading the needle with that October due date."

Daphne shot her brother a confused look, and he grimaced almost defensively. "What? The chances of the Battery making the playoffs are very, very low."

Ah. She understood now. They'd been trying to time their pregnancy around the baseball season. "Did they win tonight?"

Now it was her brother's turn to look confused. Which, fair. When was the last time she'd asked about the outcome of a game? But she'd been genuinely interested, before she'd been run out of the sports bar by the mob of fans who thought she'd been booing one of their own.

Okay, it had hardly been a *mob*. And she kinda *had* been booing one of their own. But still.

He checked his phone. "Shit," he said, and her heart dropped. Things had looked promising when they'd left. But then he bit his lower lip, pumping his fist once in victory. "They did, actually. Five to three. Not bad. The guy you hate scored a run in the second inning, and then put down a sac bunt in the ninth for the tying RBI."

"I don't *hate* him," Daphne said.

"Sorry," Donovan said, putting his phone back in his pocket. "The guy you reduced to tears. Better?"

Layla's eyes lit up. "That's right, that was *you*," she said. "Between us, that guy is one of my least favorite interviews."

"Really?" Daphne asked, trying not to look like the answer mattered that much to her. "Why?"

"He's probably a dick," Kim said. "Just think about the way he—"

Daphne gave her friend a sharp nudge to the rib cage, which was not at all subtle given that Kim immediately yelped, "Ow! What was *that* for?"

"Let her answer," Daphne said, trying to communicate with her eyes that she did *not* want to talk about the whole DMing-with-Chris-Kepler thing. It would needlessly complicate matters. Her brother would be angry that she was continuing to involve herself in his team and potentially his job, Layla would think she was a complete weirdo, and she'd be left trying to explain why she'd wanted to apologize but ended up somehow not apologizing at all.

Layla watched the interaction with a sharp look in her eyes. "Actually," she said slowly. "He's never been anything but polite. Almost *too* polite—that's the problem. You can't get anything out of him. He's a steel vault. What did you say to him, anyway, that made him get upset like that?"

"I told you this," Donovan interrupted. "She compared him to Winnie the Pooh."

"I said his *playing* was poo," Daphne clarified. "I was drunk.

I barely even knew what I was talking about. The guy next to me said . . . anyway, it doesn't matter. I feel terrible about it, and I'm really sorry if it caused you guys any problems."

Layla shrugged. "I don't see why anyone would care. It probably would've been better if you'd at least *paid* for the seat you were heckling him from, but it is what it is. If anything, I'm more worried about how all this time off is going to affect my job."

This was one reason her sister-in-law intimidated her so much. She could casually rip you to shreds with a single comment—*It probably would've been better if you'd at least* paid *for the seat—* but then pivot right to something else.

"They have to hold it for you, though, right?" Daphne asked. "Since it's medical leave?"

"Sure," Layla said. "Officially. But they'll have to get someone to take my place while I'm out, and who knows. If the fans like that person better, or that person brings something to the table I can't . . ."

"That won't happen," Donovan said, squeezing his wife's shoulder. "You're the best."

Layla made a face like, *I know I am*, and Daphne found herself wishing she could have that kind of confidence. As it was, she ended up apologizing in every email she ever sent, even when she knew she was in the right about something. *So sorry to bother you about this again, but* . . . and then she would reiterate her fourth request to be paid for work she'd already done and the client had already used. *Attached is a draft, but of course I'm open to suggestions if you had anything you wanted to add* . . . even though she knew she'd delivered exactly what the client had requested, and if they wanted anything more they should really have to pay her extra.

"That little dillweed Preston's been gunning for my job," Layla said. "And the frustrating part is I could still do *some* of it.

The prep work and the social media and all that—I just need someone to stand in front of the camera and point the microphone at Chris Kepler for his monosyllabic answers until I can return. Hell, *you* could do that."

"Me?" Daphne pointed at her own chest, even though Layla's eyes were clearly focused right on her.

"It'd be hilarious. Hand the heckler a microphone and let her actually talk to the players."

Daphne gave a nervous laugh. She was ninety-nine percent sure her sister-in-law was joking, but then again, Layla didn't joke much. "Yeah, hilarious."

"Most important," Donovan said, "is that you and the baby stay safe and healthy. We can figure out the job stuff as we go."

"Yes," Daphne agreed, relieved when Layla's attention turned back to her brother. "That is the most important part to remember."

SEVEN

AFTER WINNING THAT FIRST GAME, THE BATTERY HAD ENDED UP losing the series to the Dodgers. It didn't exactly put Chris in a "going out" kind of mood, but Randy insisted that it would be just what he needed.

"Tomorrow's a travel day," he pointed out, "and we can pour you onto the plane in the morning if we have to. Come on, man, live it up."

Advice that sounded easy enough coming from Randy, but it didn't come as naturally to Chris. Even once they were at the club, he felt awkward and out of place. The bass vibrated through his body so hard it made his bones hurt, and that was on top of his sore shoulder, which he'd injured last year and which still bothered him sometimes. Randy and a couple of the other guys immediately peeled off to hit the dance floor, but Chris leaned against the bar and ordered a whiskey. He'd have one, he decided, and then hang out long enough to say he'd done it.

While he waited for the bartender to pour his drink, he pulled out his phone, automatically opening it to Instagram. He'd been checking it more lately. His friend who'd been hiking in Zion had messaged him, reiterating his regrets about Chris' brother and saying he and his girlfriend might be in Colorado when the

Battery played there and would Chris want to try to get together? Chris typed a quick response, saying sure, even if he had a hard time thinking that far ahead.

Still no new message from Duckie. But what had he expected? He'd been the one to shut down the conversation so abruptly, and although she'd reacted to his message with a little heart that let him know she'd received it, she hadn't otherwise written anything new. He'd checked her own posts, just out of idle curiosity he told himself, and she'd posted once since the last time they'd communicated. It was a picture of a hardcover book called *The Seas*, with a brief caption: This one rearranged something in me.

He liked the way she used that word. *Rearranged.*

He opened up the chat window again, staring at the heart on his last message. It would be just past three in the morning on the East Coast, which meant there would be no chance of her actually seeing any message he sent in real time. He typed a couple of sentences, only to delete his first attempt and start over. But the second one was shit, so he deleted that, too.

"Whatchu drinking?" Randy said at his elbow, flagging down the bartender. "I'll get you another."

Chris' tumbler had a lot of drink left, and he took an obligatory sip just to show Randy he was still working on it. "I'm good," he said. "Let me buy yours."

Randy grinned at him. "Won't say no to that," he said, and Chris gestured to the bartender to let him know to put the drink on his tab.

"If we played in a big market like this," Randy said, "I bet we'd be getting surrounded by people here. Like everyone wanting our autographs and shit."

Chris shrugged. "Sure. If we played for LA, we'd be more recognizable in LA."

"No, but I mean, like *anywhere.* I go to clubs in Charleston and people barely know who I am. They come up to me about my tattoo, but half the time it's just because they're also from the D.R. or know someone who is. Which is cool, don't get me wrong. But you get it."

He slung back the tequila shot the bartender had set in front of him, the giant Dominican Republic flag tattoo on his forearm rippling. Chris had seen Randy get recognized plenty of times, so he knew he was exaggerating. Randy also lit up when interacting with anyone from his family's homeland, so Chris knew it wasn't something the younger player took for granted. At the same time, Randy was only a couple years into his career in the major leagues, and he was driven and passionate. He wanted a big career, wanted to be the guy on all the highlight reels, and he was seeming to understand that he might not have that chance playing with the Battery.

Chris tried to remember when he'd felt that way. He must have, at some point. He'd been like any other young guy, dreaming of making it to the big show, wanting to follow in the footsteps of the players he'd idolized as a kid. Even playing at Dodger Stadium the past three days, he couldn't deny it—there was something extra special in the air.

But now he couldn't imagine anything worse than the idea of being recognized every time he left the house, of having even more pressure on him than he already felt. The only good thing about that clip of him starting to cry was that his face was only visible for a second before it crumpled, his batting helmet helping to hide at least some of his identifiable features. As long as he stayed in this dark corner at the end of the bar, he should be able to get through the night without incident.

Back in Charleston, on the other hand . . .

Chris took a long swallow of his drink. It burned his throat a little bit, but in a pleasant way. He was starting to feel looser already. "I'm worried when we get home everyone will know *exactly* who I am."

Randy grimaced with a face like, *oh yeah, you* should *be worried.* "I don't know, man," he said. "I think people are on your side. That chick who was yelling at you, she's the one in the hot seat now."

This time the burn of the drink wasn't quite as smooth, and Chris coughed, his voice coming out a rasp. "What?"

"You didn't see the video?" Randy said, pulling his phone out of his back pocket. "It's kinda funny, actually. Hang on."

In a few seconds, a video filled the screen—**Carolina Battery heckler gets heckled, a breakdown**. This fucking guy. Chris had seen his videos before. Honestly, they had great analysis and were often pretty funny . . . unless you happened to be the subject of one for some error that had cost your team the game. Or unless you happened to be the guy who'd had an eight-second breakdown that could apparently be broken down into countless hours of content for days after.

He recognized her right away. She was slight, with reddish curly hair. She kept nervously tucking it behind her ear as she made her way out of the bar, her head down, until she seemed to realize that it would be better to let her hair cover her face. She pulled her purse in front of her body, as though she needed that extra shield before going into battle. The bar wasn't completely packed, but it had a decent crowd, and by the time she left they all seemed to be focused on her. The sound was a crackling mess of noise, but Chris could make out a few choice words, including a couple from whoever was filming the video. This particular YouTuber—who didn't film anything himself for these videos, just compiled footage and put his own commentary over it— started describing the whole situation, but Chris paused the video and handed Randy back his phone. He'd seen enough.

"Has she been identified?" he asked.

Randy scrolled through the comments, frowning down at his phone. "Not here. I think there was an article that named her, though."

Fuck. That was the last thing Chris wanted.

"It'll blow over," Randy said. "Seriously. Remember that dude a couple years ago, the football player who got called out for *taking a nap* in the locker room at halftime and being an absolute bear to wake up?"

The corner of Chris' mouth twitched. "No."

"Exactly." Randy clapped him on the back. "Now are you going to get your ass out here on the dance floor or what?"

Chris held up his drink. "Not enough of these in the world."

THEY DIDN'T HAVE TO POUR HIM ONTO THE PLANE THE NEXT morning, but he definitely felt a little worse for wear after his early wake-up call to load onto the bus to the airport. Randy, meanwhile, was bouncing on his toes and talking in rapid-fire Spanish to a few of the other Latin players. Fucking twenty-five-year-olds.

His brother Tim used to love throwing their three-year age gap in Chris' face. No matter what, it always seemed to come out in his favor. When *he* was Chris' age, he'd say, no way would Dad have let him go to Dorney Park alone with a friend. But then later he'd say when *he* was Chris' age, he was already mature enough to have his own after-school job.

He'd loved his brother, but sometimes it had been exhausting, that constant need Tim had had to compete. Their dad definitely hadn't helped. He loved to pit the two boys against each other, compare one to the other. And the metrics and standards always changed, so what earned you high marks at Christmas wouldn't always be impressive by Easter. Then again, Chris was rarely able to be around at Easter, or Memorial Day, or the Fourth of July. He hadn't meant to be in only sporadic touch with his brother, but his schedule had been so busy, and there'd been so much other stuff he needed to focus on.

Now he wondered if he'd known more about what was going on, if he'd have been able to do anything differently. He wished he'd paid more attention. That was a dangerous road to go down, one he traveled most nights when he couldn't fall asleep.

A morning flight when they didn't play until the next day was definitely a different experience than the late-night variety right after a game. They felt more businesslike, where guys were apt to keep to themselves or keep things low-key in smaller groups. Chris shoved his duffel bag in the overhead compartment and snagged a window seat, pulling out his phone like most of the other guys already seated had done.

He opened up Instagram again and scrolled through his feed quickly, not stopping to really see anything. Thinking about his brother made him type his name into the search bar, pulling up his old account that still sat there, last updated five months ago. It was one of the worst things he could possibly do and yet he couldn't seem to stop himself.

The last picture was from a couple weeks before Christmas. It was a picture of the tree in Tim's house, Tim's face slightly blurry in one corner as he tried to get a selfie with the decorations in the background. **How do lights always get tangled no matter what you do???** Comments underneath from various friends of Tim's had all basically been *Right?!* or suggestions for how to pack the lights next time.

Chris had seen Tim at Christmas. His brother had seemed like he was doing really well then. He'd talked about a new network engineer job he might apply for, that had better pay and a shorter commute than the job he had. He'd seemed hopeful.

Chris slid back to his own profile, just as a way to exit out of his brother's. He'd rarely commented on his brother's posts—not because he didn't love him or care about what was going on in his life, but just because he always thought it was silly to have these tiny, meaningless interactions publicly with people who you interacted with privately in a more meaningful way. But now he questioned that, too, wondered if those small gestures of reaching out were meaningless after all. If he could go back in time, he'd comment on every single one.

He started going through his own profile, deleting each post starting with the most recent and working his way down. He paused for only a second on one, a video clip of him hitting a home run he could still remember viscerally, the impact of the ball on the bat, the loud *crack* that he immediately knew meant it was out of the park. His agent hadn't had to post that one—he'd posted it himself, with a caption underneath. **This feeling**.

It made his chest clench just to see it, to think about who he'd been then and who he was now. He deleted that post, too, and kept going.

The plane had been in the air for twenty minutes by the time he finished. There had probably been a faster way to do that, some way to reset your whole account, but it had been oddly satisfying to go through it one by one. After those first few, he'd barely glanced at the picture itself, not really wanting to take a trip down memory lane. Now his feed was a blank black square.

He was about to delete Instagram entirely, but before he did he opened up his last message exchange with duckiesbooks one more time.

Sorry about that, he typed. **I'm not on here much. If you ever want to say hi, just text me.**

He sent it before he could talk himself out of it, adding his cell phone number to the bottom. Then he deleted the app from his phone.

EIGHT

DAPHNE WAS AT A COFFEE SHOP, TRYING TO GET SOME WORK done. She did this once a week or so—"treat" herself to an expensive chai latte and the chance to get out of her apartment, hoping that the change in scenery would somehow make the words come easier. Usually, it seemed to have the opposite effect. She found herself logging onto the Wi-Fi and then back off, telling herself that going off the grid would help her be more productive. But then two minutes later she'd have her phone out just to check one really quick thing, and the cursor on her blank document would keep blinking.

At least the coffee shop was a safe space. No one seemed to recognize her from TV or care anything about what might've happened at a baseball game, and she no longer took either of those things for granted.

Another notification popped up on her phone, but she was determined to ignore it. But then she thought about how much more distracting it would be if she *didn't* check it, and she needed her full focus to figure out how to write about digital media services and CDN strategy. Sometimes it felt like playing the driest possible game of Mad Libs.

It was another message from Chris. **If you ever want to say hi . . .** and his phone number.

What the hell? It seemed like a pretty straightforward message, but for the life of her she couldn't figure it out. He'd bailed on their last conversation, then three days later he'd sent . . . this?

Did he *want* her to say hi? He must, if he'd given her his number. She clicked on his profile picture to see what he might've posted lately, but there was nothing. Not the professional photos she'd seen uploaded before, not the brief bio that stated he played third base for the Carolina Battery. Nothing.

The message had been sent only a few minutes ago. She knew what Kim would say if she were here—she'd tell Daphne to play it a little cool, wait a full day at least before responding. She might even advise Daphne not to respond at all, if she knew the whole story. Nothing good could come of it.

But Kim wasn't there. And Daphne had felt a zip along her spine at seeing the digits on the screen. She'd spent the last few days thinking about their conversation, reading back through the messages. He must've thought about her, too, just a little, if he was messaging her now. The very idea put butterflies in her stomach. This was another open door, and she wanted to walk through.

hi

She started to text more, but then left it at that single word. She'd take his invitation literally and see where it went from there. If he came back with some *Who is this?* type of response, maybe she'd see it as a sign and give up, claim a wrong number.

But his response came back quickly, almost like he'd been waiting for her text.

Much better. Hi.

You never told me what kind of plane traveler you are.

She'd been at the coffee shop for an hour and had maybe three hundred words to show for it, but she closed her laptop while she leaned back in her chair.

D: Seat back: never (I worry it's rude??). Earbuds in: sometimes—

I love a good audiobook on a plane. Window: also preferably (sorry!)

C: Why sorry?

Daphne wished she could go back and delete that part. She tried to think of a way she could spin it, where it didn't seem like such an obvious slip, like if he'd said he preferred the right side of the bed and she'd said so did she. Not that she was thinking about what side of the bed he slept on.

She'd say she didn't want him to think she was copying his answer. That was reasonable. She was starting to type it out when another message came in.

C: I'd let you have the window seat.

She bit her lip, unable to stop herself from smiling at that. This felt like a perfect opportunity for her to try out those rusty flirting skills, say something clever back, but her mind was a blank. His words sat there on her phone an uncomfortably long time before he followed them up with another message. She was relieved that the conversation had been brought back to a place that didn't make her stomach flip; she was disappointed, too.

C: We just took off from LA twenty minutes ago.

So he was bored on a plane again. Maybe she should mind that he only seemed to text under those conditions, but she couldn't bring herself to.

D: That's an early flight. It's such a weird feeling, isn't it? Waking up in one state and then ending up 3,500 miles away by the end of the day. You're probably used to it.

C: Yes and no.

She rolled her eyes at his nonanswer. If he was going to go back to that, she didn't see the point in communicating at all. She thought about what Layla had said, about what a tough interview he was, but this wasn't an interview.

But then a block of text came in.

C: There is a lot of travel in baseball—at least it's by plane. In the minors, a lot of it is by bus, which could be a nightmare. The bus would break down, you'd never be able to get any sleep, etc. You adapt to whatever your current situation is. But there are always these little moments, where it all really hits you. Like now, the sky is streaked with orange and the clouds are so close. Yesterday, I was looking up from the field at Dodger Stadium, and I could barely see a strip of blue. Only rows and rows of people, going up so high it was like there was no sky at all.

As silly as it seemed, she'd never actually thought about what it would feel like, to be out there on the field in front of all those people. She supposed that was what had gotten her into trouble in the first place, heckling him at the game. She'd been like a toddler with her eyes closed, believing that if you can't see them then they can't see you. But the way he described it, she *felt* how big that experience could be, how small it must make you feel.

C: What's your name, by the way? I can't put you in my phone as duckiesbooks.

Daphne's fingers froze over her screen. There'd been a brief mention of her as the heckler in an article in the local paper—she didn't know if he'd seen it, but she couldn't give him her real name *now*. So far she'd been able to justify her lies as ones of omission, but a fake name would be clear, deliberate dishonesty. She didn't know if she wanted to take that step, but couldn't think of what else to say.

D: Why not? First name Duckie, last name Books. :)

C: What does the S. stand for?

D: That's a rather forward question. We barely know each other.

C: Duckie S. Books it is. Should I add Esq. to the end? Feels like a distinguished name like that deserves to be an esquire.

D: How do you know I'm not?

C: . . . Are you?

Daphne laughed. A lawyer! Her parents probably wished. Not because they'd ever been particularly pushy about education or high achievement—if anything, they'd been super laid-back when she was growing up, often forgetting to even ask to see a report card or progress report when she brought one home. But they'd like knowing that her job was more stable at least.

D: No, definitely not.

C: All I remember about your job is that you have to send invoices and sometimes it makes you cry.

That reminded her, she actually needed to follow up on another one. It had been a roundup of modern fairy-tale retellings for a popular book site, and had been so much fun to write she almost felt guilty for getting paid to do it. *Almost.* She was still going to get her fifty bucks.

D: That feels like an accurate summary tbh

D: Why did you delete your Instagram?

She was genuinely curious, but also the further they got away from discussing her identifying details, the better.

C: Social media felt like a distraction I don't need right now. That's the short answer, anyway.

D: And the long answer?

A pause, so long she thought maybe he really was typing out another block of text, some detailed explanation of how he was trying to prioritize in his life or rebrand or whatever else someone with a verified checkmark might say.

C: It made me sad.

A woman in a slouchy sweatshirt approached Daphne's table, asking if she could use the extra chair. Daphne smiled and said sure, no problem, watching as the woman dragged the chair over to a table where a couple other women were all talking and laughing. The woman had a stroller pulled up next to the table, and one of the other women had a baby strapped to her chest in a sling.

Daphne felt her smile droop a little as she thought, not for the first time, about what she might've given up by divorcing Justin. She didn't want to stay married to someone only because the timing was right to start a family together. At the same time, in her lowest moments she couldn't deny that sometimes she worried that he'd been her chance, and she wouldn't get another.

D: I get that.

C: I did see your post about that book you were reading—the one with the mermaid on the cover. It was good?

Daphne still had the book in her purse, actually. She took it out and set it on the table, as if she'd just arrived at a book club and was ready to discuss. With an apartment as small as hers, she tried really hard not to make false idols out of books as physical objects, but she couldn't deny that this was one of the most beautiful she owned. Hardcover with dreamy, watercolor art printed directly on the textured white of the cover.

D: It's one of those books that you'll think about for a while afterward. It's about a girl who thinks she's a mermaid, and the book's very metaphorical where you're not quite sure whether she's experiencing magic or madness. I love the way the author writes about language and words.

She hesitated before typing anything more. She didn't want to be the one to bring up his brother, but she also felt irresponsible not giving more explanation on the book.

D: Definitely a content warning for suicide, though.

She slid her fingernail along the book's spine, tracing the smooth letters of the title.

C: I appreciate that. I'll probably never read it—I was just interested in your thoughts. I can't remember the last time I read a book.

Maybe it was good that he'd said that. Because Daphne could feel herself starting to fall under the spell of these intimate conversations just a bit, get dangerously close to imagining what it would be like to meet in real life and talk face-to-face. She needed something to knock her back on her ass a little, and a revelation that he didn't like to read would definitely do it.

D: Try. What book do you think it was?

C: It was probably college. We had to read Catch-22 for a class on twentieth-century American literature. I remember liking it at the time but couldn't tell you anything about it now.

Daphne actually couldn't remember that book much, either. She thought she'd read it, but when she tried to conjure details about it she was pretty sure she was confusing it with Kurt Vonnegut novels she'd read around the same time.

The coffee shop was starting to get busier now, people hovering around the door looking for an empty seat. She felt bad about monopolizing a table when she clearly wasn't using it, so she started to pack up, shooting a quick text to Chris.

D: I have to get going. But I'm interested in your thoughts on books, too, so if you think of any others to share, I'm here!

C: Will do.

DAPHNE FORCED HERSELF TO FINISH HER DRAFT BLOG POST AND send it off to the client before she even checked her phone again. She also did the dishes that had stacked up in the sink and extricated some Easter grass from Milo that he somehow kept finding and chewing on. Next year she'd have to tell her parents that, no matter how much she appreciated them still sending her a basket even though she was a grown adult and they were on the road, maybe skip the plastic grass.

By the time she was finished, it was past lunchtime. She made herself a quick bowl of ramen and sat down at her counter to eat it.

At this point, she didn't know what exactly she'd call whatever this thing was with Chris Kepler. Were they friends? But surely friends didn't conceal their real identities from each other, so that didn't feel accurate. But she did like talking to him, got excited every time she saw a new message come in. She wondered if there was some way she could come clean at this point, explain how the misunderstanding had happened in the first place. Maybe if she brought up the heckling situation somehow, she could gauge how he felt about it, find an opening to identify herself.

D: Have you seen the video of your heckler being heckled?

Not the most elegant way to broach the subject, maybe, but it did the job.

C: Yeah.

Or . . . it didn't. Seriously, that was all she was going to get?

D: Alexa, play "Karma."

C: Eh. I think karma can take the day off on this one. I just want the whole thing to be over.

So all Daphne had managed to do was dog herself, make herself look catty doing it, and remind him of something he'd clearly rather forget. Well played.

C: You're really not going to tell me your name? Even just your first name? You've read my Wikipedia.

Daphne chewed on her lip. He had a point. She knew his middle name (Ray) and his zodiac sign (Taurus) and where he'd gone to high school (some place in Pennsylvania, it's not like she'd memorized it all). She hadn't gone so far as to seek out interviews or other sources of information, but she knew they were out there.

D: Duckie is my name. Well, a nickname.

That would be less of a lie if she were still four years old. Nobody *actually* called her that, except for her brother when he wanted to be obnoxious.

C: Like the guy in Pretty in Pink?

Daphne smiled. She wouldn't have pegged him for a John Hughes fan, but she was already realizing that there was a lot she would've gotten wrong about Chris Kepler.

D: Definitely not. That guy was the worst.

C: Are you Team Blane?!?

D: I'm Team Go-to-Prom-by-Yourself-and-Then-Leave-High-School-Behind. Also Team The-Dress-Looked-Better-Before, but I respect Molly Ringwald's singular artistic vision.

C: Who did you go to your high school prom with?

Her face fell as she remembered. She'd hoped Justin would take her, actually—the way it always seemed to happen in the movies. Your best friend's younger sister doesn't have a date, so you step in to be chivalrous, and when you see her coming down the stairs in her prom dress, it hits you, wait, I'm *in love* with her.

She'd read too many romance novels in high school.

Instead, Justin had taken one look at her in her dress and makeup and said, *What's wrong with your face?* Then he and Donovan had gone upstairs to get high and play video games, laughing the whole way, probably at her expense.

She'd brought up that moment one time with Justin after they'd gotten together—years later, after she'd graduated college—expecting maybe for him to shed some light on that night. Like maybe he really *did* like her even then and was playing it cool, or maybe he felt bad for the way he'd treated her sometimes as her brother's friend.

But instead he'd just laughed and said, *Oh yeah! You were wearing so much eye makeup. You looked like an alien.* Then, seeing her face, he'd pulled her in for a kiss. *You're prettier without makeup, babe. That's all I mean.*

He was good at those kinds of comments. They *seemed* like compliments, but they didn't leave you with the warm glow of a compliment.

D: I went by myself! So I know what I'm talking about re the Pretty in Pink situation. And don't think I was a wallflower in the corner with a book, either. I drank spiked punch and danced with friends and did all the stuff movies tell you you're supposed to do. Except for lose my virginity, I guess.

At least when she said something awkward in person, she could blame it on short-circuiting in the moment, her brain causing something to fly out of her mouth that she immediately wished she could take back. But those were typed words she'd just sent. To this person she barely knew.

C: Overrated.

She didn't know if he meant in general or from personal experience, and she definitely had enough social graces not to ask.

D: Let me guess—you were prom king?

C: Ha. No. You're thinking of the football quarterback. Honestly, my life revolved around baseball so much that I barely knew anyone outside of the team. I ended up asking a girl from my homeroom because I overheard her telling a friend she didn't have a date, so I felt pretty sure she'd say yes just to have someone to go with.

D: And what happened?

C: She did say yes. She was very nice, even when I got the wrong kind of corsage. I was supposed to ask her what color her dress was beforehand, I guess. I just liked the yellow rose so I picked that one. It also pinned to the dress and she'd wanted a wrist one. I had no clue.

D: There are a lot of rules. My friends all wanted to pick our dresses out of this one catalog some company paid to have distributed at the school. They thought it would help to make sure that none of us accidentally found ourselves in a "Who Wore It Better?" situation. But I didn't want to use the catalog, and you would've thought I was the only person refusing a blood oath or something.

C: Why didn't you want to use the catalog? Plans to make a Frankendress out of two perfectly good dresses?

That made Daphne snort-laugh.

D: The dresses just weren't cute, in my opinion. And I didn't like the company on principle. They advertised "plus sizes" that were just the same pictures as the smaller sizes, but stretched out with Photoshop.

C: No.

D: YES. Not even Photoshop—more like someone had pasted the picture in a Word document and then dragged the edge to widen it.

C: That's . . . I don't even have the words.

D: I may still have a copy of the catalog somewhere. It was bonkers.

C: I hope you do. It belongs in the Smithsonian.

Daphne started typing a response when she saw a new message come in.

C: Hey, we're about to land and head right into a team meeting. Will you be around later?

The beauty of texting was that you didn't need someone to be *around*. You could just send the message and then wait for them to get to it when they got to it. But Chris didn't seem to fully appreciate that, or maybe he just liked knowing that there was a person on the other end, reading and responding to his texts in real time. She could understand that, since it was an aspect of their conversations over the past few days that she'd really enjoyed, too.

C: I promise I won't go dark again.

He also didn't need to make any promises to her. But she found that she liked that he had, regardless.

D: I'll be around.

NINE

CHRIS DIDN'T KNOW WHY HE'D LIED TO DUCKIE. HE DID HAVE TO head into a meeting right after landing, but it wasn't one for the whole team. They were all going back to the clubhouse after the flight, and some guys had plans to work out together, some coaches were going to work with players on specific skills, but as far as Chris knew, he was the only one Marv had asked to come directly to his office.

"It'll only take a few minutes," Marv had said, his face as inscrutable as always. During a game, one of the only ways you could tell if Marv was upset in the dugout was by the way he spit out his sunflower seeds. He gave the gesture a bit more attitude after a bad call from the ump or an egregious error from one of his guys.

Chris had only been called into Marv's office twice before. Once, at the start of last season when he'd been traded to the team, and Marv had extended a welcome and explained a few things about the way he ran the clubhouse. The second time was when Chris' shoulder injury wasn't healing as quickly as they would've liked, and he'd been sent to a rehab assignment. Both times, at least he'd had some sense of what Marv wanted to talk to him about. Now, he had only vague ideas, and they were all bad.

"I want to get ahead of this heckler business," Marv said as soon as he'd sat down. Chris knew that his face could be as inscrutable as his manager's, and he hoped it wasn't betraying anything now. He was sick of hearing about it.

"It's an extra distraction," Marv said, "that we do not need. Would you agree?"

"Yes," Chris said. *So much yes.*

Marv gave him a cursory smile. "Good," he said. "Good."

Chris had known one outfielder a few years ago who'd gotten hit by a home run ball thrown back onto the field by an angry opposing fan. He hadn't been seriously hurt, thankfully, but the fan had gotten banned from all thirty ballparks and the whole incident had definitely been the subject of lots of talk on sports radio, ESPN, YouTube videos like that guy with the breakdowns, and on and on. Surely *his* incident didn't need to rise to that level. It wouldn't have if he hadn't started to cry at the worst possible moment, when the camera would be trained right at him. He wished he'd had his inscrutable face on then.

Marv picked up the phone and called someone else to join them, and from the short delay before the person arrived, it was obvious the whole thing had been prearranged. The new guy wore a team polo and had his graying hair gelled up into spikes, and he reached out to shake Chris' hand before Chris had even placed where he knew this guy from.

"Greg," he said. "Executive producer for the network. How are you doing?"

Chris knew that his answer didn't actually matter, so he just nodded. What was going on here?

"Listen," Greg said. "The good news is that the Battery is part of the national conversation now. The bad news . . ."

He shrugged, not needing to finish that sentence. The bad news was that it wasn't exactly for baseball.

"With Layla out, we're still working on filling content for home broadcasts, and we had one idea that we wanted to run by you."

Chris frowned. "Layla's out?"

Greg waved his hand, like that was the least of it. "Maternity leave," he said. "Or, what you call it before the baby is born. Point is, we'll be looking for someone to fill in for the rest of the season."

Chris hadn't even known Layla was pregnant, but he guessed there was no reason he should know. He generally liked Layla, but he didn't know her very well, and he wasn't one to volunteer for any interviews he didn't have to do.

It was starting to feel like that was what was happening here. He just couldn't figure out quite what the setup was yet.

"Uh-huh," he said.

"Here's the wild thing," Greg continued, his eyes lighting up. "That heckler? Turns out she's the sister of Donovan Brink, Layla's husband, who works for Guest Services. And, even wilder, turns out she actually has a background in broadcasting, studied it in college."

"So it was all a ploy to get on TV?" He wasn't sure he understood what Greg was trying to say. That sounded like a lot of coincidences all stacked up.

"No, no," Greg said, his gaze cutting over to Marv. "We have no reason to believe that. But the point is, that we think we could make something out of this. Do an All-Access pregame segment where she interviews you, where you talk a bit about what happened. Keep it light, show there's no hard feelings on either side, baseball's fun, that kind of thing."

Chris glanced at Marv, who was looking at him expectantly. They were framing it like he had a choice, but he really didn't.

"Layla said she already floated the idea," Greg said. "It would be good for the heckler, too, when you think about it. Cut down on some of the harassment she might be getting in the community, show that it's all good now."

Chris remembered the brief glimpse he'd gotten on that video of her in the bar, the hunted look on her face. He had no idea if that was the kind of thing she was facing on a daily basis, but he certainly didn't think it was right for people to make her life hell just because she'd yelled one thing at a sporting event.

If they even knew what she'd yelled, they'd probably find it funny. Now that he was out of the heat of the moment, he could admit that there was something kind of hilarious about her heckle. Who referenced Winnie the Pooh at a baseball game?

"Fine," he said. "Just tell me what you need from me, and I'll be there."

Greg pressed his hands together as if in prayer, making an obsequious half-bow gesture that irritated Chris. He stood up once Greg had left, figuring that was the end of the meeting, but Marv signaled for him to sit back down.

"Your walk-up song," he said. "Who's it by?"

Of all the questions Chris thought Marv would ever ask him, that had to be at the bottom of the list. If he tried to imagine Marv listening to music on his own time, it would be an old record of some 1960s classics or something. *Etta James, the wife's favorite,* he'd say.

"Glass Animals," Chris said slowly.

Marv nodded before picking up the phone at his desk and dialing a few numbers. "It's Marv," he said shortly to whoever must've picked up. "Tell the DJ to take that Glass Animals song out of the rotation. We'll get you Kepler's new walk-up song before his next at-bat. No, not tomorrow. Against McCullers."

He grunted once, some acknowledgment of something the other person had said, and then hung up.

"I'm sick of hearing that song," he said. "You're in a slump, fine. There's a lot of season left. Get focused, work on your swing, and for the love of Christ turn that dial to something else."

Chris opened his mouth to say something before he realized that a spirited defense of Glass Animals' repertoire was not in his best interests here, especially when Marv had casually dropped him out of tomorrow's lineup. "Okay," he said. "I'll find a new song."

"See that you do," Marv said, shuffling some papers on his desk in what was clearly a *now I'm done with you* gesture. "Or we'll pick one for you."

BY THE TIME CHRIS LET HIMSELF INTO HIS CONDO LATER THAT night, he was exhausted. He'd stayed at the clubhouse almost as late as he would've if he'd had a night game, and would have to turn around and head back there first thing when he woke up.

His dad called him while he was heating up some chicken in the microwave. Chris briefly thought about ignoring the call and answering it tomorrow, but he knew he'd already put off his dad a few times and it was better just to get it over with. He put the phone on speaker and set it on the counter so he could hear while fixing his dinner.

"Hey, Dad."

"Where are you? You sound like you're in a tunnel."

"I have you on speaker. How's it going?"

"You're asking me that question? That's what I'm asking you. You catch that foul ball yesterday, you end the inning, Dodgers wouldn't have scored, your team could've stayed in it."

This was typical for calls with his father, which was one reason why he dreaded them so much. Chris happened to know that his dad kept a notepad by the phone, and would make notes of things he wanted to talk about. Not that he needed any reminders—he had a memory like a steel trap.

The play his dad referred to now hadn't been a fuckup. It hadn't been an error. But it had been a missed opportunity, and this time last year, maybe he would've made that play. He knew it wouldn't help to go into any excuses.

"I know," he said, taking the wind out of his dad's sails. "I know."

His father was silent for a few moments. Chris always wondered what would happen if he filled that silence, if he said something like, *I miss Tim*. Or if he asked his dad something like, *Do you think about Tim, Dad?*

Chris knew that his father did. As a parent, he had to. But he also knew that his dad didn't want to talk about it.

"You in the lineup tomorrow?"

"Day after."

He was saved from having to explain by the microwave timer going off, and Chris leaned into the phone to make sure his dad heard him. "That's my dinner," he said. "I should let you go."

"You eating right?"

He was eating okay—trying to get lots of protein, still making smoothies every morning like he had been for years. But he was eating alone a lot, grabbing a quick meal at the clubhouse or eating leftovers at home like tonight. He was eating to fuel his body but to give any credit beyond that would be stretching it.

"Yeah," he said. "Chicken tonight. Love you, Dad."

His dad grunted something that could've been *You, too* before hanging up.

Chris pulled up a stool to the kitchen island to eat his meal there, like he did most nights. He'd bought the condo fully furnished—it had just seemed like less hassle that way—and the dining room table was this behemoth plank of raw concrete. It had *looked* badass, and definitely fit the whole masculine modern aesthetic of the place, but he'd quickly learned that the textured material was an absolute bitch to clean. So he rarely used it, just like he rarely used the open living room that they'd told him would be perfect for entertaining, and he rarely used the balcony that they told him had the best view of Charleston Harbor.

He didn't even want to think about how rarely he'd *used* the master bedroom. As in, never. He'd dated here and there, but never actually brought anyone back to his place.

He slid his phone closer, intending to open his music library and start scrolling through, trying to find a new walk-up song. But instead he opened his text messages, staring down at the last message from Duckie. I'll be around.

That couldn't be her real name—even a nickname. Who went by *Duckie*? It was a little weird that she wouldn't just tell him what her name was, but he'd heard horror stories about what it was like being a woman on the internet. Maybe she'd had a bad experience on a dating app or something.

Not that they were doing anything close to talking through a dating app. For all he knew, she was dating someone already. He frowned, trying to remember if she'd mentioned anything either way.

It was late, but he typed out a message anyway, just in case.

I need a new walk-up song, it said. Any suggestions?

He took a bite of his chicken, and by the time he glanced back at his phone her response had come in.

D: I take it you can't choose "The Way" or you'd be "breaking the rules."

He smiled, wiping his fingers on a napkin before picking up his phone.

C: That would be a flagrant disregard for the rules. You can't trick the universe by creating a situation in which you'd hear the song. This is why you're not even allowed to download it, lest it get shuffled onto some playlist.

D: Okay, okay. "Lest it get shuffled." Jeez, you're strict. What are the actual rules of walk-up songs? Like can they have lyrics, how long are they, etc.?

C: Typically they play only ten seconds or so, long enough for you to come up to the plate. You can tell them to cue up to any part of the song. Lyrics are fine, but games are family events so obviously nothing crude.

D: Well, there go all my suggestions.

He let out a short laugh, realizing he'd been grinning through their whole exchange so far.

D: Give me some examples of the genre. I need to know the parameters.

He thought about what most guys on the team used. Randy's was "Pa' Que la Pases Bien" by Arcángel, Beau had chosen "Heads Carolina, Tails California" as blatant pandering, and their Korean first baseman had gone back to his roots with "IDOL" by BTS. The song choice didn't have to be a big deal—lots of guys just picked something fun, something that got them pumped up. But given the way he'd been playing and the way Marv had instructed him to pick a new song, Chris was feeling a lot of pressure to make it something he'd live up to.

C: We didn't have them in high school, but in college my first walk-up song was "People of the Sun" by Rage Against the Machine.

He looked up the video for the song and dropped a link so she could take a listen.

D: Okay, hang on.

She came back a few minutes later with a new text.

D: This song is badass. It makes you want to punch stuff for sure, but, like, in a good way. Why not use it again?

He'd thought about it. It would be easier just to go back to something that had worked for him in the past. But part of him knew that it was dangerous to move backward, even for something as innocent as a song.

C: My brother Tim always wanted me to use "Eye of the Tiger."

D: A classic choice. Literally the whole point of that song is to get you pumped up.

C: We grew up near Philadelphia, so the Rocky movies were important in our house. I just could never do it. Too much hubris involved in choosing what is possibly one of the most inspirational songs in sports movie history.

D: "Get'cha Head in the Game" from High School Musical is RIGHT THERE.

She dropped a link, and he clicked to watch it, oddly mesmerized by the synchronized dance moves.

C: That one might be a little on-the-nose.

D: But it's about basketball, so no one will guess. Clever disguise.

Weirdly, he appreciated that she didn't try to say anything like, *You have your head in the game! You played great yesterday!* She simply accepted what he said without making a big deal about it, made a joke, and moved on.

C: What song gets you pumped up?

There was a delay in her response, while he assumed she was thinking about how to answer. He used the time to carry his dishes over to the sink, where he washed and dried them quickly before placing them back in the cabinet. He filled a glass with some ice water before picking his phone back up, reading her message while walking to his room.

D: Off the top of my head . . . "Roam" by The B-52's. Ever heard it? It's impossible to be in a bad mood while you listen to this song.

She'd posted a link, and he clicked to listen. He recognized the song immediately—he'd heard it a bunch of times on the radio without really registering who it was by.

You're right, he typed after the first few minutes. This song is catchy.

D: "Catchy"? No. That's too reductive. The song is pure joy in sonic form. And I don't have any rules limiting my ability to listen to it—the more the merrier, as far as I'm concerned. Be honest—did you dance while you played it?

Chris had slid into his bed, leaning back against his headboard with one knee up while he texted with her. Did he *dance*?

C: No. I don't dance.

D: Not even when no one's watching a la "Dance like no one is watching"?

C: No.

C: Do you?

D: When no one's watching? Sure.

There was zero reason for him to read any innuendo in that. They were talking about *dancing*. And yet he felt his body tighten in response to her words.

C: And what if someone is watching?

D: I mean, it helps if I have a drink in me. But I like to dance. I don't mind being watched.

They were still talking about dancing . . . right? Suddenly he wasn't sure. He had no idea what she looked like, so he couldn't picture her exactly, but something about the mere suggestion was enough to get him going. He thought about her hand in that picture, her graceful fingers. He thought about what those fingers could do while he watched.

Jesus.

D: I also belt it out in the shower, and I've already told you I have a terrible voice, so there ya go. Sing like no one is listening, etc.

Her mentioning being in the shower was *not* helping. But her tone was back to being lighthearted and joking, and he realized he must've been reading way more into what she was saying than she'd meant. He tried to think of the most deflating thing possible to get himself under control.

C: Live laugh love.

D: Exactly.

He was going to regret this, he just knew it, but he couldn't stop himself.

C: By the way, let me know if you ever wanted to come out to a game. I could get you two tickets so you could bring a friend or your significant other or whoever.

The minute it was sent, he groaned. He had absolutely zero game. If Randy were here, he would've coached him in a much slicker way to get at that information. Once, they'd been at a local bar during last season's All-Star break, and Randy had asked a woman if he could follow her, because his mother had always told him to follow his dreams. Chris had thought for sure he'd get his ass kicked with such an obvious pickup line, but then Randy turned on that charming smile. He and the woman had ended up dating for a few months after that.

It was several minutes before her response came in, during which time Chris imagined every single scenario. She *did* have a boyfriend and was trying to think of how to break it to him, she had a boyfriend and they were snuggling together right then and there, planning when they might want to take him up on the ticket offer, she had a girlfriend instead of a boyfriend, she didn't have either but was still incredibly weirded out by the obvious fish for information, and on and on.

But then when the new text finally popped up, it was maddeningly short on detail.

D: Thanks, I appreciate it.

Was it possible he'd actually been *too* slick, where she didn't know what he was really asking? He wasn't going to repeat himself. That would be too sad.

D: No boyfriend tho

He bit his lip to stop the smile from spreading across his face before realizing that no one was watching him. He could smile as wide as he wanted.

TEN

DAPHNE STARED AT THE GLOWING SCREEN OF HER PHONE. SHE'D already been in bed when he'd texted her, but since sleep regularly eluded her for hours after she lay down, she hadn't seen the harm in texting a little.

It had started out innocently enough, talking about music. She'd enjoyed listening to the song he'd sent her, and sharing a song with him. There'd been that brief moment, when they'd been talking about dancing, and she'd tried to turn it into something else. But he hadn't responded right away, and she'd felt silly . . . what was she trying to do, *sext* with him?

Then he'd made that comment about bringing her boyfriend to a game, and she'd started spinning out. Was that a sign that he was interested in her that way? Or maybe it was a sign that he wasn't . . . that he assumed she'd already have someone and wasn't bothered at all by that idea.

On top of that, she felt a weird guilt not explaining about the divorce, like she was withholding information when she said she was single. Kim had coached her through this already when they'd been signing her up on dating apps. It was nobody's business what was in her past, Kim had said, and she could choose to share that information whenever she felt comfortable and not a second before. And yet Daphne couldn't shake the feeling almost like she was doing something wrong, even though she wasn't with Justin anymore, hadn't been for a while, and knew she never would be again. That feeling went away eventually . . . right?

She was already lying to Chris about so much, she had a weird need to be brutally transparent about at least *one* major thing in her life. Maybe it would cool any interest he might feel toward her, but maybe that was a good thing. Maybe she didn't want him to be interested.

Actually, I'm divorced.

Oh, who was she kidding. She wanted him to be interested.

"Stupid, stupid, stupid," she muttered, pulling the covers over her head as if to trap herself in some kind of protective fort. Only her phone was in there, too, so really the call was still going to come from inside the house on this one.

C: Oh.

C: Sorry, I don't quite know what to say. My first instinct was to say, "Cool," but something tells me that's not it?

She huffed a laugh that fogged her phone screen in her little covers fort.

D: That's not bad, actually. A lot of people respond that they're sorry to hear it, which is nice, but awkward when you want to be like, "Don't be! I'm not!"

She hoped that wasn't too negative. She tried really hard not to shit-talk Justin openly . . . except to Kim, of course, who'd had a front-row seat to Daphne's feelings. She believed that Justin might make *someone* a decent husband one day. It just hadn't been her.

D: What about you?

C: I've never been married.

She rolled her eyes. That kind of information she would've expected his Wikipedia to cover. Whether he was currently dating anyone, on the other hand . . .

C: And no girlfriend right now.

Daphne felt something behind her rib cage lift, before dropping down into her stomach again. It was irresponsible to be talking to him at all, much less like this.

She *wanted* to keep talking to him. She wished she could go back in time, handle everything differently from that very first message. Maybe if she'd come clean right away . . . but then maybe he wouldn't be talking to her at all.

The best thing she could do now would be to either confess, or to break this off before it became something. Already it was starting to feel like *something*.

D: To be honest, the divorce did quite a number on me. I can't even imagine dating anyone again.

A particularly egregious lie, given that she'd only recently started to imagine it. But a necessary one. She needed to put some distance between her and Chris Kepler. Milo, on the other hand, wanted nothing to do with distance, and snuggled his warm body right over her chest, half blocking her view of the phone and practically smothering her under the blankets.

She threw off the covers and sat up, adjusting Milo into her lap while she checked the new text that had come in from Chris.

C: That's understandable. Did you want to talk about it?

Fuck, it made it worse when he was *nice* to her. Didn't he know she didn't deserve it?

D: I think I just need to go to bed. I appreciate it, though, seriously. More than you know.

She stroked Milo's head, giving him a few little scritches under his chin. She'd gotten him only a week after she'd moved into the apartment, stopping into an animal shelter on a whim one day as she'd driven by. She'd always wanted a cat, but Justin had said he didn't like the smell of a litter box, no matter how many times she'd promised she'd clean it out every day. Marriage was about compromise, that's what people always said, but you could keep compromising until suddenly you looked up and realized nothing about your life looked the way you wanted it to. Now, when she found herself feeling occasionally sad, Milo was a reminder—she wasn't lonely. She was free.

D: FWIW I think it's possible to do "Eye of the Tiger" in a tongue-in-cheek kind of way, not in a hubris way. Rocky's the underdog after all, right? But no matter what you pick, I bet it'll be great. 🖤

She put her phone on Do Not Disturb and resolved to *try* to get some sleep. But her mind kept churning all night, and it felt like hours before she finally drifted off.

DAPHNE SHOWED UP AT HER BROTHER'S HOUSE THE NEXT DAY with a half-dozen donuts and a giant tote bag filled with her stuff, out of breath from trying to juggle everything from the car. Layla had called her and asked her to bring over her makeup and a few of her most professional outfits, and Donovan had piped up in the background and requested the donuts. It was such a bizarre combination that Daphne couldn't figure out what was going on. They wanted to eat dessert together in style?

"Is everything okay with the baby?" she asked Donovan when he opened the door. It didn't really make any sense that there would be an emergency and they would call her over with these specific requests, but until Layla had safely delivered, her mind would always jump there first.

"Everything's fine," Donovan said around a mouthful of donut. He'd already opened the box and selected the jelly-filled one she'd gotten just for him, bringing the rest back to his and Layla's bedroom. Layla was lying back in their bed, a laptop propped up on a tray across her lap.

"So when they say bed rest, they mean literally," Daphne said, looking around at the mess her brother's normally neat bedroom had become.

"Oh, I can get up," Layla said. "I do little stuff around the house, nothing that would exert myself too hard. But this is my new home office right here."

"I call her Bed Lady," Donovan put in.

"Clever," Daphne said dryly. "So what's with the makeup and clothes? Are you guys renewing your vows or . . . ?"

Layla swatted at Donovan, who was standing far enough away to make the motion ineffectual. He probably knew the danger zone to avoid.

"I knew he wouldn't tell you," she said. "So, remember how I talked about you interviewing Chris Kepler? The network agreed it would be a great idea to film a pregame segment before tomorrow's game. It'll be a fluff piece, nothing hard, but you can address the heckling thing, show that it was all in good fun. They're having me script some questions for you, and I can get you all prepped up."

Daphne froze. Words were coming out of her sister-in-law's mouth, but they made no sense. Layla had been *serious* about that? And now they wanted her to be on TV?

"But I don't know anything," she said, then blinked, catching herself. "About baseball, I mean."

"Maybe you had it right the first time," Donovan said, a piece of donut tumbling out of his mouth and onto the carpet as he spoke. He scooped it up and put it back in his mouth. "Five-second rule."

Daphne ignored her brother. "I can't interview a baseball player on national television when I barely understand the sport in the first place."

"Regional, not national," Layla pointed out. "And that's what I'm here for. I'll tell you everything you need to know—which for this, honestly, isn't much. You're not going to be talking to him about his five-four-three triple play."

At Daphne's nonplussed expression, Layla leaned over her laptop and started typing something, as if trying to pull up video of the referenced play right then and there. "This was last season," she said. "The Marlins hit a line drive to Kepler, who gets the out at third, then turns it to second, who's able to throw the guy at first out in the *nick* of time—"

Daphne held up her hands. "Please," she said, "for the love of god, no more. See? This is exactly what I'm talking about. I'm so out of my depth here. Plus, I mean."

She gestured at herself, like, *look at me.*

Layla gave her an appraising glance, then asked Donovan to leave them alone for a bit. After her brother had closed the door behind him, Layla set her laptop to the side to study Daphne closely.

"You studied broadcasting," she said. "In college. You did like book reports for the university public access channel or something, didn't you?"

Daphne shrugged. "Technically, I majored in communications. Broadcasting was just a part of my degree. I've never had any real experience, outside of covering some local events and interviewing a couple authors for the eight people who actually watched that channel."

"Still," Layla said. "You have some experience, and at least at one point, this was something you wanted to do. So why didn't you?"

"I—" She thought about how many times Justin had told her that those kinds of jobs were nearly impossible to find, how she should think about where her talents were. *You can write up those little blog posts in an hour, and get fifty bucks a pop. Hell, that's more than I make.*

She'd tried to explain to him how the math didn't always work out in her favor—when they took more than an hour, when she was in between jobs, when she had to chase down payments or not get paid at all. But somehow Justin had managed to make her feel like her dreams were too big but also pathetic and small, all at the same time.

"I had a hard time finding a job," she said finally, opting for a neutral truth. "You know how it is."

Layla grimaced. She certainly *did* know how it was, which was no doubt why she was so keen to do anything to ensure stability in her current gig. And Daphne definitely didn't want to do anything to mess that up. If Layla wanted her to do this, and believed that she could, well . . . she still thought she might crash and burn, but she guessed she could give it a try.

"At least we have a while to get ready," Daphne said, trying to put a brave spin on it.

But to her surprise, Layla burst out laughing. "Oh, honey," she said. "It's the pregame segment they'll air tomorrow, which means you'll shoot it after the game tonight. That's why I asked you to bring all your stuff over. We're going to get you camera-ready in the next three hours."

Daphne clutched her duffel bag to her chest as if she were planning to make a run for it. *Today?* She was going to be on camera *today* and all they'd told her was to bring fucking donuts?

She was going to see Chris today. She would have to *talk* to him, and not behind a phone screen, not under a veil of anonymity, but as herself. The Heckler.

She couldn't do it.

Layla must've read the play of emotions over her face, because she gave her a gentle smile. "You've got this," she said. "We can role-play and I'll coach you through it. But first, let's figure out what you're going to wear."

CHAPTER

ELEVEN

IT WAS STRANGE, BEING AT THE BALLPARK AT NIGHT WHEN IT WAS almost empty. The game had finished an hour before, the stands had already been cleaned by the yellow-vested staff, and the grounds crew had come out and raked the red clay around the base path. Daphne had been greeted by a guy named Greg, who introduced himself as the executive producer and almost definitely had hair plugs to achieve the early-'00s boy band look of his hair.

"We have you set up in the bullpen," he'd said, leading her to two folding chairs set up across from each other in a little carved-out area to one side of the field. Greg appeared to be gesturing toward one of the chairs, so she started to sit, figuring that was where they wanted her for the interview. But Greg immediately gave a little laugh, grasping her by the elbow to bodily encourage her back up. She was so stunned by the physical contact that for a second she just froze, having no idea how to react.

"Not so fast," he said. "We need to get you miked up first. You can leave your notecards here."

Layla had typed up questions and talking points for her, printing them neatly on cardstock via a printer she'd set up on her nightstand. It had all been a whirlwind—Layla switching from giving her advice to asking her pointed questions (*You don't have a lipstick that's brighter?*)—and Daphne still wasn't confident that she could pull this off. She was nervous about appearing on camera in general, about looking at her cards too much, not looking at them enough and getting off track.

She was even more nervous just about seeing *him*.

He'd replied to her last text, about how she thought he could get away with using the *Rocky* theme, with a simple *Thanks*. She didn't know whether that was because no further response was required, or because he'd sensed her trying to close down the conversation, or because he wanted to close down the conversation. She was exhausted, trying to keep up with the dynamics at play every single time they texted.

That's your own fault, a voice inside her head whispered as the tech finished securing the small mic to the collar of her dress. *If you'd been straight with him from the start . . .*

Maybe there would be a chance to say something today, after the interview. Maybe it would be easier doing it face-to-face, where she could gauge his reaction and rush in with an explanation.

But then she approached the folding chairs again, slowing a little as she saw Chris already seated. He had her notecards in his hands and was staring down at one, spending so long on the question that he couldn't possibly be reading it. The hair at the back of his neck was trimmed with almost military precision, the edge straight and neat.

She knew with a sudden clarity that she wasn't going to say anything about being duckiesbooks.

"Sorry," she said, tucking her hair behind her ears as she took her seat. She'd only meant *sorry for any delay on my part*, but Greg cut in.

"Save that for once we're rolling," he said. "And we're going to edit this together into an eight-minute segment or so, include game clips, that kind of thing, so don't worry about stopping and starting if you mess up. Just go with the flow, have a conversation, and we can find the best bits to work with later. If we need you to do something again, we'll cut and ask you."

Chris murmured his agreement, even though the directives couldn't possibly be for him—he'd done this before, after all. She found that she couldn't physically make eye contact with him. He was still in his uniform, and she looked at his shoes, the clay streaked on his white pants, anywhere but at his face.

"I thought you didn't play today," she blurted. Layla had told her something to that effect, when they'd discussed the scheduling of the interview.

"Pinch runner," he said. "In the eighth inning."

His voice was even better in person. Not as smooth, maybe, a little more gravelly, like there was some texture that got lost on TV. She had a hard time even focusing on what he was saying for a minute, although she realized that it was more baseball-speak she probably would've missed anyway. Layla had tried to give her a quick primer on some of the terms she'd be dealing with in the interview, but Daphne still felt a little like when she'd had to give presentations in French class back in high school. She could memorize vocabulary words and correct conjugations, but she had to think very carefully about how to construct them together, to the point where they almost became meaningless units of sound.

Greg counted them in, and Daphne tried to smile, keeping her gaze trained somewhere over Chris' left shoulder. "It's not often a heckler has a chance to sit down one-on-one with the object of their a-attention," she started, stuttering a little on the introduction she'd rehearsed with Layla. "Chris, what—"

Greg called "Cut," which wasn't a surprise. She'd already messed up. She was supposed to use another word, not *attention*, although now she couldn't remember what it was. Abuse? Perhaps it was a fair characterization, but she didn't really want to think of it that way. Chris Kepler was definitely an object of her attention, in a way that hit a little too close to home to use *that* word, either. Layla had told her to use Chris' name liberally throughout—to build rapport but also to remind the viewer who they're watching, she'd said—but the word had sounded all strangled and unnatural coming out of Daphne's mouth.

"Let's do that again," Greg said. "This time with eye contact."

Daphne gave a self-conscious half laugh, puffing her cheeks out. Then she lifted her gaze to Chris', meeting his eyes for the first time since she'd sat down.

Their color was hard to determine. Green, she might've said if pressed. But there was some steely blue in there, too, some flecks of gold. Hazel, maybe. An entire color palette for a painting of a mountain landscape, all contained in the irises of his eyes. He wasn't wearing his hat or a batting helmet, as he had been most of the times she'd seen him on TV, and having such a clear view of his eyes felt almost uncomfortably intimate. She felt like she could count each individual eyelash at this distance. God, his eyelashes were beautiful.

They said eyes were the window to the soul, and maybe that's why she'd been so scared to look into his. Because for just a second, she felt something click into place. This was the same guy who'd bought a yellow rose corsage for his prom date, who'd lost his brother only a few months ago, who'd asked if she wanted to talk about her divorce and had seemed genuinely open to listen.

She wondered what he saw when he looked back at her. Probably nothing more than his heckler, someone he had to spend the next twenty minutes talking to even though he'd rather be doing anything else in the world.

An unbearable tension was rising in her chest, and she

dropped her gaze down, unable to sustain eye contact for another second. She stared at his hands, frowning.

"Um," she said.

"It's not often . . ." he prompted, like they were in a school play.

"No, uh." She gestured toward his hands. "You have my cards."

"Right. Sorry." He offered them back to her, and it seemed to Daphne that he went out of his way to make sure their fingers didn't touch in the exchange. Or maybe that was just her projecting. For her part, she was careful to grasp them by their farthest corner from where he held on.

Once the cameras were rolling again, she got back on track, getting through the intro and into a few easy questions about his career and his time with the Battery.

"I have to admit," she said, starting to settle in a little. "It's easy as a fan to feel like players are pretty removed from whatever's happening in the stands. How aware are you, down on the field, of what people are doing or saying?"

He made a face, a straight-lipped head bob that seemed to suggest a noncommittal *so-so* type of response.

Everything that used to be background is turned up so loud, I can't tune it out.

That's what he'd typed to her a few days ago. But now, he said, "We hear when the crowd gets loud, definitely. And sometimes individual comments get through—like yours."

He didn't say the words with any particular animosity, but she felt her face heating nonetheless. "I'm so—" she started, before Greg called cut.

"That's my bad," Greg said. "I should've been clearer at the beginning. We don't want to get too deep into the actual incident here, or the, uh, reaction. This is more about moving forward."

Daphne drew her brows together, trying to mesh that with

what Layla had told her. What was the point of them doing this interview? She hadn't planned to bring up exactly what she'd said, and she definitely hadn't wanted to harp on the crying thing the way the rest of the media had for the last week. But if she couldn't talk about it *at all*, not even to apologize . . . why bring her here?

She flipped through a couple cards, until she got to some of the "fluff" questions Layla had prepared for her. They were things like *What's your favorite postgame snack?* or *Who on the team is the biggest prankster?* But she felt like such a fraud. She couldn't sit here and ask those questions like this was a normal interview.

She glanced back up. She had no idea if the camera was rolling now or not, had lost track of whether they were taking an actual break from filming or just one of those pauses that Greg had told them to push through.

"I'm really sorry," she said, because she was going to get that out, at least once. "I shouldn't have heckled you. I—there's no excuse. I'm mortified that I did it. And *Christopher Robin*, god, it's just so stupid."

"It's fine," Chris said, but suddenly his gaze didn't seem fully focused on her anymore. The words had come out fast, almost before she was done speaking.

"No, really," she said. "I—"

"No, *really*," he said, his voice ringing with terse finality. "It's fine."

He stood up then, starting to unwind the microphone wire from around his back. "I actually need to get—" he said, then gave up on the wire, running his hand through his short hair. "I have an appointment. Are we done here?"

Even Greg seemed a little speechless. It was pretty clear that they weren't *done*—they had maybe two minutes of usable footage, if you took out all the stops-and-starts and bloopers. But it was also clear from Chris' tone of voice and the fact that he was already walking away, a wire still dangling off his belt, that it hadn't really been a question. Maybe Chris legitimately had an appointment, something that had to do with the team—physical therapy or practice or whatever they did when they weren't playing. Maybe he really did get his hair cut every day, and he was running late for his trim.

But even if it weren't highly unlikely that he had an actual appointment at ten o'clock at night, something told Daphne none of those were it. She'd managed to offend Chris Kepler *again*, only this time she had no idea how.

"We'll be in touch," Greg said, giving her a tight smile.

CHAPTER
TWELVE

CHRIS STOOD IN ONE OF THE SHOWERS, FULLY CLOTHED, LEANING against the tile wall and trying to catch his breath. He didn't know what had happened—one minute, he'd been in the middle of doing the interview. The next, he felt like he couldn't breathe.

The last few minutes of the interview were a blur. He could barely remember how he'd even gotten to the shower, although he must've had the presence of mind to consider that it was one of the few places he might get some privacy.

He'd known the interview would be a bad idea. His agent had called him earlier that day, wanting to give him some last-minute guidance on how to answer some of the questions. *People want to feel like they're part of the game,* she'd said, when she'd told him how to respond to the question they knew would be coming about the heckling. *But you're also a professional and people need to see that you're going to do your job regardless.*

The fact that he'd apparently gotten to the point where she felt like she *had* to remind him of that kind of thing was concerning by itself. He'd been giving interviews since high school, even more after he'd been picked in the sixth round of the draft after college. Of course he would do his job. Wasn't that all he'd been doing? Keeping his head down and playing baseball like everyone wanted him to?

Part of it had definitely been *her*. His heckler. Greg had said her name, he realized, but he hadn't caught it. He'd been too busy clocking various details about her appearance, things that surprised him even though he'd seen her at the game, and then later in the shaky cell phone footage of her getting booed out of the Charleston bar. Her reddish-brown hair was curly, and either she hated it in her face or it was a nervous habit, because she kept pushing it behind one ear while she'd been asking him questions. But the curls were stubborn, always springing back to brush her cheek when she glanced down again at one of her cards. Her bare arms had been covered in freckles, and there was a particular freckle right at the corner of her mouth that he'd been afraid to stare at too long, in case she thought he was coming on to her.

Then there had been that surreal moment, when she'd looked up at him for the first time. It couldn't have lasted any longer than a few seconds. And yet it felt like time had slowed down, stretched like taffy. Her eyes were brown but had glowed almost amber under the lights, and for a minute he'd forgotten why they were sitting across from each other in the first place.

So she was pretty. It didn't change anything, and it certainly wasn't the reason he was now hiding out in the bathroom, his heart still galloping in his chest.

He pulled his phone out of his pocket, idly clicking through a few apps while he tried to distract himself. Before he knew it, he'd pulled up the text exchange with Duckie again, his final *Thanks* sitting at the end like a stone.

Okay, so her divorce . . . how had she put it? *Did quite a number on me*. She wasn't ready for another relationship. He respected that, was grateful she'd been transparent about it. Now that the option was off the table, he could fully admit how far he'd let his imagination go down that path. That kind of thinking would've always been ridiculous, even if she hadn't put a stop to it—his career kept him way too busy, he needed to focus, he didn't even know her, and on and on.

At the same time, he really could use a friend. And right now, she was the only person he could think to text.

"Hit Me with Your Best Shot"? he typed. Not sure I want to issue that direct of a challenge, but could be funny.

Maybe he should start leaning into pitches more. It might improve his on-base percentage, at least.

Her response appeared almost immediately.

Don't judge me but I hate that song. I feel like you only ever hear it at a rowdy late-night bar or in the dentist chair.

And then, a few seconds later:

What are you up to?

He sank down to the floor of the shower, bringing his knees up so he could lean against the tile wall. It was probably disgusting, no matter how spotless the clubhouse crew kept everything, but he had to change out of his uniform anyway. And right then, he just couldn't bring himself to care.

C: Ever since we started talking, I've been thinking about something. It all started with a book, you know. This whole baseball thing.

D: Really? What book?

C: I don't remember the title, but it's probably still in a box at my dad's house. How Baseball Works, something like that.

D: So basically you . . . studied to be a baseball player?

He rubbed his hand over his chin, trying to remember what the cover had looked like. It *had* appeared almost like a textbook, he remembered that. Oversized and heavy, large blocky letters on a white background, a stock photo of an old baseball in the center. It had broken down the sport section by section—the history, the way the equipment had evolved over the years, rule changes, famous players, scandals and statistics, anything you could possibly want to know.

C: We lived really close to the public library, and my dad would let my brother and me walk there by ourselves. I was maybe six years old, he was nine. I'm pretty sure the copy I own is the same one from the library—I kept checking it out until eventually I never returned it. Which, come to think of it, might be why I don't have as many memories of going to the library when I was older. It was technically a grown-up book, but I could barely read most of the words. I just liked the pictures.

D: That's adorable.

C: By the time I stepped foot on a field, it felt like I'd been dreaming about baseball for so long. Every night in bed, I was turning those pages, running the bases in my mind.

His brother had loved the book, too. But it had been different for him—he truly *was* a student of the sport. He wanted to know all the players' names and their stats and how each team was doing. He could wow adults with his knowledge of iconic historical moments from decades before he'd been born. But when it came to playing, Tim's talent for the game had been average, and his motivation to keep going maybe below that. For a while, his dad had pushed both of them the same amount, enrolled them in the same travel leagues, and somehow managed to always seem like he was in the stands at both of their games even though Chris knew logistically there had to be times when he'd had to choose one over the other. And then, as they got older and the distance between their abilities became more and more stark, his dad had started focusing more of his energies on Chris.

It made Chris feel disloyal to his brother, to even have those thoughts. It made him feel worse when he thought about all the times when they'd been younger, when he'd *relished* the extra attention his playing had gotten from their dad. The way it had made him feel special.

C: I've also been thinking a lot about what you said last night. About your divorce, and how you're still hurting. I don't want to push you into anything you're not ready for. But Duckie, I could really use someone to talk to right now. And something tells me you could, too.

The wait for her response felt like ages. The shower had seemed mostly dry when he'd sat down, but by now a vague hint of dampness was starting to seep through his uniform pants. This was definitely disgusting. He had to get out of there.

D: You're right.

C: So you're in?

He was staring at his phone, waiting for her reply, when he heard Randy's voice outside the shower.

"Yo, Kep!" he said. "I know you're in here. You trying to save the planet or something?"

If Chris ignored him, he'd go away. How long did it take for someone to respond to a text?

"I'm as concerned about global warming as the next guy," Randy said. "But that shit's systemic, man. You're not gonna save enough with soap-only showers to make up for, like, the oil spills in the Gulf."

Chris saw Randy's hand reach around the shower curtain, feeling for the nozzle, but seconds too late to react. Suddenly cold water was streaming down on top of him, matting his hair against his head and soaking through his uniform.

"Holy shit!" Chris shouted, holding his phone out of the splash zone while he jumped out of the shower. "What the hell, Randy?"

Randy stepped back, his hand over his mouth in an exaggerated expression of shock. Or maybe he was just trying not to lose it laughing. It really could go either way.

"Why so decked out to take a shower? You're not"—now he was definitely laughing—"you're not one of those people, are you? Those never-nudes?"

Chris unbuttoned his jersey and took it off, wringing the water out of it back into the shower pan, more to make a point in front of Randy than for anything else. "You've seen me naked, Randy." It was a locker room. It was inevitable that they'd all seen each other in various stages of undress.

"I know, man, which is why I know you have nothing to be ashamed of," Randy said. "You probably get a complex, with me walking around here, but you're perfectly—"

Chris pulled a face, snapping Randy with his wet jersey. "Shut the fuck up," he said. "If you ruined my phone, you're going to pay for it."

"Oh, shit," Randy said, looking genuinely contrite for the first time. "Is it okay?"

Chris swiped to wake it back up, relieved when everything seemed to work without a hitch. And on his screen was a text from Duckie, her response to his question from before.

I'm in.

He grinned, only looking up when he heard Randy grunt from right next to his ear.

"I knew you had a girl," he said, not even trying to hide that he'd been reading over Chris' shoulder.

"She's just a friend," Chris said.

Randy made a face like, *sure she is*. He definitely didn't believe Chris for a minute, but that was okay. Chris didn't believe himself yet, either, but he would. He'd have to.

THIRTEEN

DAPHNE WAS STILL SITTING IN HER CAR IN THE VIP LOT NEXT TO THE stadium, staring down at her phone.

Good, Chris had texted, and then a smiley face.

A *smiley face*. He hadn't struck her as much of an emoji user, so the sight of it really threw her.

What exactly had happened in the last hour? She'd shown up for the interview and thought she was doing an okay job. Sure, she'd been a little nervous, had flubbed a few lines, but they were just starting to click when it had all gone south. She'd apologized, he'd shut down, and then he'd ended the interview so abruptly that even Greg hadn't bothered to try to smooth things over with her. He'd just left her alone with the techs to take care of her mic, stalking off with his cell phone pressed to his ear.

She'd only just had time to reach her car when she'd gotten that text from Chris. Where he wanted to talk about song choices and a book he'd read as a kid. It had felt like they were chatting about nothing, but she knew they were talking about *everything*, even if she didn't know what it all was.

And then he'd told her he wanted to be friends, keep talking. He'd asked her if she was in.

Her phone rang in her hand, startling her. It was Layla's

number on the screen, and she picked it up on the second ring, her heart already pounding.

"Is everything okay? Is it—"

"Oh my GOD," Layla said, the word so loud it crackled in Daphne's ear. "I'm going to purchase a toll-free number, something like 1-800-NOW-BABY, and if there's an emergency with the baby it'll be the *only* number I use. Okay? Otherwise, assume it's just a normal phone call because I'm still a normal person who's allowed to make normal phone calls. Is that clear?"

"Absolutely," Daphne said. "Crystal clear."

"It better be."

"You don't really need the number to be toll-free, though," Daphne said. "If you're only going to use it for outgoing calls."

On the other end, Layla was ominously silent.

"Also, 1-800-NOW-BABY sounds like a phone sex line. But, like, a charity one."

Daphne could practically see her sister-in-law drumming her perfect French-tipped nails on the little lap desk she'd set up to use in bed.

"Because it's toll-free—"

"Are you done?" Layla cut in. "Because I did actually call for a reason."

"Yes, of course," Daphne said, staring back toward the ballpark. She could guess what that reason was. No doubt Greg had already reached out to Layla, said something about what a disaster the interview had been. So now if she hadn't managed to get her sister-in-law in trouble by her disgraceful attendance at the game in the first place, she'd *definitely* managed it by blowing this opportunity her sister-in-law had set up for her. What a wonderful aunt she'd make.

"First of all, I'm sorry that the interview was cut short. That wasn't supposed to happen, but it's not your fault."

"Well—" Daphne started to say. She had a feeling it was at least a little bit her fault.

"No, I told you he was like that." Layla was quiet for a moment, as though reflecting on her past interviews with Chris Kepler, the way they'd gone. Daphne had watched a few of them, actually, over the last few days. Sure, Chris wasn't always the most *effusive* person—he seemed adept at giving you exactly what you needed out of him and no more—but he had sat in front of the logo-printed screen and taken questions from reporters, just like any other player on the team. Daphne's interview with him had definitely been special. And not in a good way.

"What did you think of him, by the way?"

"Chris Kepler?" Daphne asked, more to stall than anything else. It wasn't like Layla could be talking about Greg.

"Mmm."

"He was . . ." *He has beautiful eyes.* "He seemed nice. Polite, like you said. He wasn't rude to me or anything. He just . . ."

"Ended things early," Layla filled in. "I know. And like I said, that wasn't your fault, and Greg knows that wasn't your fault. He said you were a little shaky at the beginning but then really got into a groove."

"Oh," Daphne said. "Thank you."

She'd felt awkward the entire time, but she supposed there had come a point where her self-consciousness was more about the general situation and not so much about the cameras. She'd barely noticed that they were there.

"They're wondering if you'd like to take over as sideline reporter for the rest of the season."

Daphne had been blasting the air conditioning in her car, because between the humid South Carolina night and her nerves over the interview, she'd felt like she was boiling from the inside. But now she turned the knob down a few notches, certain she hadn't heard her sister-in-law clearly over the loud rush of air from the vents.

"They want *me* . . . to talk about baseball?"

"Listen," Layla said. "I'm going to be straight with you. *I'm* the one who wants you to talk about baseball. The network just agreed with me to give you a try. I think it would be good for you, I think you'd be good at it, and most importantly, I think it would allow me to stay involved and not worry about my job."

Daphne wasn't offended by Layla's self-centered approach. If anything, she was relieved. It made sense that Layla would want to still have a lot of pull behind the scenes, and with someone like Daphne in the position, she could. The chances that Daphne would do Layla's job better than Layla had been able to were very slim. She wasn't a threat.

No, the whole thing made sense from Layla's angle. But what about from her own?

"I have clients," she said. "Articles to write, deadlines . . ."

"Okay, but do you *like* any of your clients? Do you *want* to write any of those articles? What would happen if you, I don't know, got hit by a bus and couldn't do it for a few months?"

It was fortunate that Daphne knew her sister-in-law was like this. She hadn't been a bridesmaid in their wedding because Layla had two sisters and a whole drinking-comped-martinis-at-a-Vegas-bachelorette-party friend group from her college sorority, but she'd been in enough of those rooms to know Layla could be ruthless. One friend had dared to say that strapless dresses were cheesy and Layla had firmly, matter-of-factly told her that she could take that energy outside. After the friend had flounced off, the clerk had rushed in with several strapless samples, and Layla had taken a giant swig of her champagne and said in a withering tone, "She wasn't *wrong*. Bring me something with a cowl neck."

"I suppose in the unlikely event I got hit by a bus," Daphne said now, her voice dry, "they would have to find someone else to write their blog posts."

"So tell them to do that," Layla said. "Daphne, this is a real opportunity for you—you have to grab it. When will this kind of chance *ever* land in your lap again?"

Layla had a point there. Even though Daphne had given up the idea of doing anything in broadcasting years ago—hadn't even known if she'd *want* to—this would be the closest she'd probably ever get. Having this experience on her résumé might open up other doors that had previously been shut.

"Also, the money is good," Layla said. "I'll have to double-check on benefits but I think you could be eligible for at least part of the season. No travel at least at first, but they may ask you to start doing road games, too, depending on how it goes."

Hearing Layla lay everything out made it feel more *real*, more possible. Daphne already found herself running through her remaining assignments in her head, trying to figure out which ones she could extricate herself from versus which ones she could grind out before she transitioned to another job. She didn't even need to know Layla's definition of what constituted "good" money—she already knew it would be much higher than anything she was used to. But still she found herself hesitating, having a hard time picturing herself in this new role.

As if sensing that Daphne was on the edge, Layla softened her voice. "I know it's scary, upending your life for something temporary," she said. "But the way you've been living since Justin . . . you deserve more than that. And I'll be there to guide you every step of the way."

Maybe it was what her sister-in-law *hadn't* said that made the biggest difference. Because Daphne could easily fill in the blank, could see the ways that she'd been living a temporary life for the last year, in a weird limbo state where she didn't know what she wanted or how to go after it. If this gave her nothing more than a chance to reset, to reimagine what her life could look like . . . well, wasn't that exactly what she needed?

"Okay," Daphne said, "I'm in."

It wasn't lost on her that it was the second time that day—that *hour*—she'd committed to something outside her comfort zone. It also wasn't lost on her that those two things were connected.

How was she going to juggle texting with Chris Kepler as Duckie, while potentially working with him as Daphne?

BY THE TIME DAPHNE HAD GOTTEN HOME, LAYLA HAD EMAILED her a list of—well, it was tempting to think of them as a *list of demands*, like they were negotiating a hostage situation, but she knew that wasn't fair. Layla was trying to make sure she was ready to take over reporting duties by tomorrow's afternoon game, which was so fast it was making Daphne's head spin.

The first thing was an emergency hair appointment the next morning, which Layla had already texted her own stylist to arrange. *She won't do anything drastic*, Layla had promised, *just trim you up and give you some tips for how to maintain your look. And before you protest, yes, your hair looks fine but also you're going to be on TV! This is a different level of "fine"!*

"You can do this," Kim said, scanning over the list. Daphne had recruited her friend as logistical support for her day of preparations, but already it was clear that moral support was going to be just as important. "I mean, it's a *lot* . . . but you can do it."

"It's absolutely ridiculous," Daphne said, almost driving past the tucked-away salon with its discreet sign. She had to put her signal light on at the last minute and hit her brakes harder than she would like to make the turn. The car behind her honked, and she held up her hand in an apology.

"They're going too fast to see that," Kim remarked, and Daphne shot her friend a look.

"I think they saw," she said. "They made a gesture back."

"That . . . was not a wave."

Daphne ignored that, grateful that her car was compact enough to fit in the parking spot she was able to find around the back of the building next to the dumpster. Kim was already unbuckled and halfway out of the car when Daphne touched her arm.

"Sorry, I just need a minute," she said. "I hate driving to new places. I hate worrying about what the parking situation is going to be somewhere I've never been before. And I'm about to let this random person I've never met do god knows what to my hair, and—"

Kim laid her hand over Daphne's, giving a squeeze. "You hate change," she said. "And these are some major ones. But change isn't always bad. I mean, Exhibit A, you don't have to put up with Justin anymore. And by extension, that means I don't have to, which is a fun bonus."

And now I'm alone and live in a glorified dorm room, Daphne wanted to say, but she understood her friend's point, and was grateful for it.

"Now, can we go inside?" Kim said. "I bet this is one of those places that offer you a glass of wine when you walk through the door."

Kim was spot-on about the wine, even at that early hour. Daphne accepted a glass of water instead, since she was driving and way too nervous to be drinking on an empty stomach. Still, maybe Layla knew what she was doing when she had Daphne go to a hair appointment first, because within twenty minutes she felt so much more relaxed. The woman who was taking care of her was perfect, one of those hairstylists who can make friendly conversation but was also more than happy to just work silently, and

Daphne found herself sinking into the sensation of having her hair shampooed by someone else, the peacefulness of being left in a darkened room with some leave-in conditioner or who knows what other amazing-smelling products sitting on her head.

Her phone buzzed from her purse, and she leaned down to check it. It was a new text message from Chris.

C: I told you about one of my formative books. What about one of yours? That Milo one?

If he wanted to be friends, he couldn't have picked a better conversation topic. She could talk about this for hours.

D: The one I probably read the most was called Mandy, written by Julie Andrews Edwards, who I found out only later was THE Julie Andrews from The Sound of Music. It's about this orphan girl who finds a cottage in the woods and makes it her own. I was obsessed with reading about her sweeping out the cottage and decorating it with seashells and saving up to buy seeds for the garden.

C: The rituals of it.

Daphne actually hadn't put that together, how similar it was to the comfort she took in organizing her own bookshelves or making herself a cup of tea.

D: Exactly. Sometimes I think I read books to vet them to reread, you know?

C: I don't know if I do know, but I want to. Explain that to me.

It probably sounded strange. It wasn't that Daphne didn't like that thrill of opening up a new book, not knowing what jokes were going to land and what plot twist was going to take her by surprise and how it was all going to end up. But it was all about those books that burrowed their way into your heart, that you felt like you'd carry with you forever.

D: Like reading a book the first time is like a perfect first date. It's exciting, there are sparks, you're discovering new things about the other person and yourself, you end your night thinking, WOW, yes, this is something special. But the point of a good first date is to set yourself up for more dates. A lifetime together, maybe.

She wished she'd picked a different analogy. Suddenly this felt like walking a tightrope.

D: So I just love finding books I'd spend a lifetime with, I guess. If that makes sense.

C: It does. Thank you.

She wondered what he was doing right then. Layla told her that the players often arrived at the stadium hours before the game started, getting in their batting practice and stretches and other drills before playing. She'd never realized before how all-consuming baseball could be, and now she felt like she understood more about why he'd be feeling so out of it if this one thing that took up his time no longer felt like a safe place to land.

C: You won't be surprised to learn that most of my reading choices were made based on page count. If I had to write a paper on a book, I was going to pick the shortest one possible.

D: I don't know, Catch-22 is pretty thick.

C: Well, that one had a badass cover. I also wasn't above judging a book by its cover (which I seem to recall is something you're not supposed to do?)

That parenthetical was impossibly cute. She would really need to be careful, if she was expected to see him later that day and act like a normal, professional person. She had no idea how she was going to get through it without embarrassing herself.

D: It's human nature. We all do it.

C: True. I do feel at a disadvantage, though.

Daphne took a sip of her water. There were cucumbers in it, which was a nice touch and something she'd only ever seen in movies. She was trying to remember the last time she'd had her hair professionally cut anywhere that wasn't a Fantastic Sams.

D: How so?

C: You know exactly what I look like. Meanwhile, I have no idea about you.

Some of the water went down the wrong tube, the rest of it dribbling down her front as Daphne started coughing from the sip. Her hairstylist poked her head in to check if she was okay, and Daphne was too embarrassed to do anything but give a weak thumbs-up.

"Great!" the stylist chirped. "Let's give it a few more minutes."

D: Right now, my hair is wrapped in a giant towel on top of my head. Very Brigitte Bardot, but terry cloth.

C: Sounds chic. You know what I mean, though.

Yes, she did know what he meant. And suddenly, she went from being a little freaked out—he knew exactly what she looked like, after all, even if he didn't know it yet—to being irritated. Over and over on those dating apps she'd had to fill in this kind of pointless information, sometimes getting into such nitty-gritty details she felt like she was describing someone else, crafting a composite sketch of a person she'd seen once in passing rather than revealing anything meaningful about herself.

D: What does it matter? If I told you I had blond hair and blue eyes and a 36DD chest, would you like me more?

C: No.

C: To be honest, I would think it was a little strange that you'd included your bra size as one of three details to respond to that question. But I wouldn't like you any less for that, either.

Daphne bit her lower lip, trying not to smile. She was still annoyed, damn it.

C: I'm sorry, I wasn't trying to make it weird. It doesn't matter.

This wasn't fair, and she knew it. She constantly tried to picture him as they were texting back and forth, wondering if a joke had made him smile, if he was alone or surrounded by people, if he was casually checking his phone every once in a while or glued to the screen like she was when she thought a new text might come in. And that was all when she had a frame of reference to work from, a very clear idea of what he looked like.

D: No, I'm sorry. I'm being disingenuous. I just don't really like pictures of myself.

C: I get it. If you'd rather, I'd take a picture of Milo, too. Or a particularly nice sunset if you happen to see one. The book you're reading. Whatever.

So, basically, an Instagram feed. Daphne almost texted that to him, as a little joke, but then thought better of it. There was something different about sending a picture to one recipient rather than sharing it in a public post. It said, *Here, this is something I wanted to share with you.* It said, *I'm dying to know what you think of this.* It said, *This reminded me of you.*

She scrolled through her photos on her phone. She didn't have to go back very far, since seventy-five percent of her pictures were of her cat, twenty percent of books, and the remaining five percent were screenshots of memes she thought were funny. She found a picture of Milo she thought was particularly distinguished, where he was loafed up on the windowsill, framed by the bedraggled houseplant he loved to chew on and a sliver of sunlight coming through the blinds. She'd tried making a clicking noise at him to get him to look at her, but he'd kept his eyes in little slits, unbothered by the silly human disturbing his peace.

D: Here's Milo.

C: Oh. I thought he was going to be an orange striped cat, like the one in the movie. You're right; sometimes it's best to leave a little mystery.

D: NOT FUNNY.

The hairstylist poked her head in the door again. "I think you've been marinating long enough," she said. "Let's get you in that chair and see if we can shape your curls a bit. Follow me."

Daphne felt a little wobbly when she stood up, like she'd been sitting in that dim room so long she'd forgotten what it was like to move into the light. She glanced down at her phone, which she still had clutched in her hand.

C: Milo is even better than I could've imagined. Thanks for sending.

FOURTEEN

CHRIS KNEW THEY'D AIRED HIS PREGAME INTERVIEW ONLY BE-cause his phone blew up with notifications about it. Most were complimentary, although he knew they didn't mean much. They couldn't even be going off that many specifics, since, all told, he'd probably strung together no more than twenty words in a row.

He did feel a little bad for the interviewer. Sure, she'd heckled him at a game, but that already felt like a million years ago. He'd left the interview because he physically couldn't stand to be sitting in that chair, talking about himself, for a single minute longer. It hadn't been personal.

They'd won, and he was actually in a good mood, feeling relatively hopeful for the first time in a while. Gutierrez had hit a three-run homer to give them the lead in the seventh, and Beau had made an amazing play in center field for the last out. Now, he was anxious to get back to his phone, to see if Duckie had said anything else after he'd responded to her picture of Milo. He didn't know how to make her see that it was less about *how* she looked and more that he wanted to be able to put a face to their conversations. She was already starting to feel so *real* to him, but there was still a layer of distance that came from not being able to picture the person behind the words.

The field was clearing out, and he was about to head back to the clubhouse when something brought him up short. Randy, who'd been a step behind, made an exaggerated point of walking into his back.

"Come on, man," he said, laughing. "Keep it moving. Some of us have plans."

"Why is *she* here?"

"Who?" Randy glanced around when Chris pointed his chin over at the area near home plate, where a few bright lights and cameras were pointed toward a woman in a baby blue sheath dress. The dress looked vaguely familiar. The woman was *definitely* familiar.

"She's taking over for Layla," Randy said. "You didn't see her out there before the game? Wait, didn't you talk to her?"

The fact that Randy even knew about the pregame segment put a pit in Chris' stomach. It wasn't like they usually had the time—or frankly, the desire—to watch any of the extra broadcast stuff before a game started. Sometimes they played the pieces in the clubhouse, which always led to good-natured ribbing of whoever'd been in the hot seat that day, and if you were the focus of a segment, you'd watch it later with your family or friends no matter how many times you said you didn't care. But there was no reason for Randy to know about the interview he'd done—the interview he'd walked out of—yesterday unless it was already going around the clubhouse as another sign that he was losing it.

Or maybe he was being paranoid. He'd had a decent game today. Clean, at least—no errors, a walk, a single that had skipped right past the other team's second baseman.

"She's kinda cute," Randy said, tilting his head. "Not my usual type, but I could make an exception."

"Don't."

Chris only meant because obviously it would be a terrible idea to try to date someone you had to work with, but Randy gave him a little eyebrow raise. "You are a man on the move lately," he said, then held up his hands when Chris shot him a look. "Hey, much love, man. When the pitch is good, you gotta swing."

Chris started walking away, but Randy followed him, laughing. "*Pitch*, I said *pitch*. With a *p*. You want to go over there and talk to her? I'll back you up."

They'd wrapped up whatever segment they were filming—it looked like she'd interviewed Gutierrez, probably about that big home run. He was sure Gutierrez had given her much better sound bites than he had. The guy could be a low-key dick in the clubhouse, but he loved the spotlight.

"She shouldn't be here in the first place," Chris said. "Is that all it takes to get a job here now? Hell, get Piercing Whistle Guy an application."

Randy laughed, diffusing some of Chris' frustration. It was impossible not to laugh along with Randy when he got that expression on his face, like they were two cutups in after-school detention.

"That guy was the worst, man," he said.

"By the sixth inning I thought my head was going to explode," Chris said. "The sound just sliced right through. But hey, he got our attention, right? Make enough noise and you, too, can be on TV. I can film a segment with *that* guy where he asks me about what it's like to play through a debilitating headache."

"Yeah," Randy said, but his face had fallen slightly. "Kep—"

Chris mimed like he was holding a microphone. "I found it so inspiring how you achieved a frequency at the absolute highest range of human hearing. Fingers crossed, maybe tomorrow someone will spit on me. Then we can get all y'all out here for a round table—the whistler, the spitter, and my very own heckler."

"Kep—" Randy said again, and the expression on his face finally got Chris to turn around.

He'd had a sinking feeling before he saw her. It would be just his luck for her to be standing right behind him, and sure enough, there she was. She looked slightly different than the last time he'd seen her, he realized—something to do with her hair, which was a little less wild than when he'd talked with her before. Her mouth was also shinier, which confused him for a second until he remembered that lip gloss existed. Only after a beat did he realize he'd been staring at her mouth, looking at that freckle again, and he lifted his gaze to her eyes.

She'd definitely overheard what he'd said. Her face stayed perfectly still, but the light in those whiskey-colored eyes told him that she'd heard it all.

"I look forward to talking with Piercing Whistle Guy and Spitting Guy," she said. "Maybe they'll stay for the whole interview."

She spun on her heel and walked away before he could say anything else, sending something flying at his feet. He picked it up, frowning. A binder clip.

"Damn," Randy said. "That was hard to watch, not gonna lie. I tried to warn you."

"I didn't say anything that wasn't true," Chris said gruffly, but he knew he'd been out of line.

"Neither did she," Randy pointed out.

And with that parting shot, Randy was already disappearing into the dugout, heading back into the entrance to the clubhouse. Normally, Chris would do the same, start his usual postgame routine of getting in the ice tub if he was particularly sore, getting a workout in if he wasn't, taking a shower and grabbing something to eat. But instead he looked down at the binder clip, then up at the direction where she'd headed. He closed his fist around the clip, and crossed the field to follow her.

FIFTEEN

IT WOULD BE FITTING IF *SHE* CRIED BECAUSE OF SOMETHING *HE* said. It would be the moment she'd been waiting for, karma truly on her scent like a bounty hunter. But this was her first day on a new job, and Daphne didn't want to embarrass Layla, who she assumed had never cried a day in her life, much less while on the clock.

Luckily, there was a lot more work involved in this assignment than Daphne had even realized, and so she could focus on that instead. Layla had prepared her for today as best as she could, and outlined what the role would look like—Daphne would handle reports during the game about injuries, insights from the coaching staff, that kind of thing, and then do some pre- and postgame interviews with the players. Layla was still doing a lot of the prep work from home and handling the social media side of things. Between that and the fact that Daphne wasn't expected to travel yet, she knew she was only doing half of Layla's usual job.

It was still overwhelming. Daphne was wearing more makeup on her face than she was used to, which felt weird; trying to read PR sheets that she only half understood about various transactions—who'd been sent back down to Triple-A, who'd been recalled, so many names and words she didn't know; and couldn't help but feel a little starstruck when she was standing next to someone she'd been told only moments before was one of the greatest sluggers of his time. The name Gutierrez didn't even mean anything to her, and still she'd gotten flustered when he trained his perfect smile on her and started talking about the home run he'd hit that night.

And to top it all off, she was wearing a borrowed dress from Layla. Her sister-in-law had more of an hourglass shape than she did, so the dress puffed out weirdly around Daphne's chest with extra fabric. She'd followed Layla's advice to use a binder clip in the back to cinch it tighter—*On camera, no one will be able to see*, Layla had said with a dismissive hand wave—but she'd lost the clip somewhere along the way, and now the dress hung loose and baggy. It was such a small, stupid thing, but it immediately reminded her what an impostor she was. Even her fitted dress had been fake.

She was standing outside one of the employee-only doors, trying to get her bearings before entering, when she heard a voice behind her.

"I think you dropped this," Chris said, holding out her binder clip.

Daphne felt her face flame. Hopefully, he just thought she'd been using it to hold papers together. You know, like a normal person. The fact that she hadn't been *holding* any papers . . .

It was impossible for their fingers not to touch in the exchange, no matter how hard she tried. She felt the contact in a jolt, a sudden unwelcome reminder of what he'd said in one of his texts. *I like to feel the bat.*

She could *not* think about that right now.

"Thanks," she said stiffly.

He clenched his own fist at his side. "Look," he said. "I'm sorry. It's not about you. It's . . ." He paused, as if searching for the right words before resigning himself to whatever second-rate ones he could come up with. "I was frustrated, and I shouldn't have said what I did."

"I shouldn't have, either," she said. "That's why we're here in the first place."

He just looked at her, almost like he was working something out in his head. Maybe whether to confirm or deny what she'd said—the latter option would be more courteous, perhaps, but the former option more true.

"I have no illusions about why I'm here," Daphne said now in a low voice. "You're right—I'm hardly qualified. It's ludicrous, really, that they would've offered me the gig at all. But I'm—" She swallowed, thinking better of what she'd been about to say. Best not to get into the whole deal with Layla, how she was hoping to help out her sister-in-law. Better still not to get into the rest of it, how she'd been excited for the chance to make her life look completely different, even if she was scared of what that might mean.

"If you're not comfortable with me being here, I understand," she said. "Just say the word, and I'll quit. Seriously. No hard feelings."

He was staring down at his shoes now, but leaning in, and she knew he was listening closely even though his face betrayed no reaction. The first few buttons of his jersey were undone, revealing a thin gold chain over the athletic shirt he wore underneath. She thought back to that scab she'd seen on the back of his elbow that first fateful day, and had the wildest urge to check if it was still there or if it had completely healed.

"I don't want you to get spit on," she said somberly. "I wouldn't work with that guy."

The barest twitch at the corner of his mouth, so tiny she almost missed it. He dragged his hand over his jaw.

"Ah," he said. "The whistler's the one who really got under my skin. Probably just jealous."

She raised her eyebrows. "You can't whistle?"

He puckered his lips, blowing through them until a small tuneless note came out, more air than sound. He gave her a rueful smile.

"Don't quit," he said. "Not on my account."

And with that, he walked away.

THE HOURS OF THIS NEW JOB WERE GOING TO TAKE SOME GETTING used to. Even though it had been an afternoon game, by the time she did everything she had to and met everyone at the stadium, and then grabbed dinner, Daphne didn't get home until after eleven. She was bone-tired but also too keyed up to go right to sleep.

"My poor little Milo," she said, crouching down to pour a cup of food into his empty dish. He was going to have to adjust to this new schedule, too, because he was used to getting his dinnertime meal much earlier. She'd fed him before she'd had to leave for her hair appointment, but already that felt like ages ago. Before she'd texted a picture of Milo over to Chris as Duckie, before she'd overheard him talking about how unqualified she was for this job as Daphne.

It shouldn't hurt, maybe. He wasn't wrong. But it had definitely stung, that reminder that no matter how friendly they were through texts, it still didn't change how he felt about *her*.

She opened her text messages, hesitating for a second before starting to type.

What walk-up song did you end up going with?

Definitely disingenuous. She'd been at the game, after all—she'd heard the music pumped over the loudspeakers in the stadium. But she couldn't remember hearing anything before he came up to bat, and she didn't know if that's because there was no song or because she'd somehow spaced out and missed it each time. There had been a lot happening on the sidelines, notes to review, people constantly updating her with information or telling her the next cue for a segment. She hadn't been able to pay attention as much as she'd wanted to.

C: Still can't decide. Marv gave me the option of some instrumental track he'd found, or nothing. For now, I'm going with nothing.

C: (Marv's the team manager.)

Daphne knew that, of course. She'd even talked with him briefly today in the middle of the seventh inning, asking him questions about how he felt about the starting pitcher's performance.

D: I have a strategy.

C: Let's hear it.

D: Pick one of those songs that tells people what to do. Like the Cha Cha Slide or the Cupid Shuffle or whatever. Then while the opposing team is distracted—they're all to the left, to the left, walking it by themselves, that sort of thing—bam! You hit it out of the park.

She sat down on her bed, tucking her legs beneath her. She'd already changed into her pajamas and put her hair into a pineapple-looking bun on the top of her head like she usually did before going to sleep, but she knew it would be a bit before she'd even try to settle down.

C: There's only one problem.

It was a corny attempt at humor? And didn't even make any sense, because of course the song ended by the time the at-bat started, and if the pitcher was busy dancing, how could he throw the pitch for Chris to hit, and on and on.

C: Won't I also be afflicted by the Cupid Shuffle?

She grinned down at her phone.

D: I thought you said you don't dance.

C: I don't.

D: Then you should be immune. But I guess there's only one way to find out . . .

It was wrong, what she was doing here with Chris. It would be extra wrong if she used these texts as a way to glean information as Duckie that he probably wouldn't want Daphne to know. At the same time, what she most wanted to find out was how he really felt about his heckler working with the team, whether he'd meant it when he said he didn't want her to quit.

But just as she was reminding herself that there was no way she could ask, Chris surprised her by opening up the topic himself.

C: You ever say something you really regret?

D: Only every day of my life.

D: Seriously, though, I second-guess half the stuff I say. They always tell you that other people don't think about your words as much as you do, but then I think about how much I overthink EVERYTHING including other people's words so that doesn't always help.

D: And that . . . was probably not helpful at this exact moment. See, I've done it again.

C: No, that's exactly it. Like in high school they were always telling you that nobody else would notice a pimple on your face, but I always noticed other people's pimples.

D: Oh god. I'd be mortified if we'd gone to high school together. I always used to break out on my forehead, which is why I had bangs for so long.

C: I bet you were cute with bangs. And I don't necessarily mean notice in a bad way. If anything, it was endearing. When someone has a flaw you know they're self-conscious about, but you wish they could see themselves the way you see them.

Something about his words made her sad, but she didn't know

why. Maybe it was just the comedown from all the adrenaline of the day.

D: "Chris Kepler finds pimples endearing." I'm adding that to your Wikipedia.

C: Right next to "eschews batting gloves." I sound like a real weirdo.

D: You sound nice.

He *did* sound nice. And that was the part that was going to get her in trouble, because the pull of these conversations was just too strong, even when she knew that there was no way he'd be saying any of this to her if he knew who she was. Maybe especially if he knew who she was.

C: Well, I said something not very nice tonight. I think I was trying to be funny. Or I wasn't really thinking at all. And then afterward, I felt terrible.

Now that he was actually talking about it, she found that she didn't want him to. He'd already apologized to her in person—it felt wrong to collect his private guilt, too.

D: That's what got me in trouble recently. I thought I was being funny and instead I was just being mean. Maybe we're not funny people?

C: I think you're funny.

If only he knew.

D: And I bet if your joke hurt someone's feelings, they knew you didn't mean it. I'm sure you made it right.

C: We'll see.

Daphne worried at her lower lip, scrolling back up through their conversation before opening up the text box again. She snapped a picture of Milo, who was resting next to her leg, not purring but just providing a solid mass of warmth.

D: Milo thinks it'll be okay.

C: Well, then obviously it will be. Nice dinosaur pajamas, by the way.

They were her oldest, shabbiest pajama pants, lime green with hot pink T. rexes. She'd had them since college.

D: Send me a picture.

She was surprised when it came in. It was of a lanky guy, maybe in his early twenties or so, his hair long under a yellow baseball cap, his arm around a guy holding two thumbs up. It took a minute for her to realize that the guy in the yellow cap was a younger version of Chris, and the guy next to him must be his brother.

D: What's that from?

C: The first game Tim came to see me play in the minors after I'd been drafted. I made one of the stupidest base-running errors of my life—basically, I didn't actually touch second base when I was rounding it for a triple. Little League stuff. So the guy at third tagged me like no big deal, easy out. I was so embarrassed that my brother had seen that, but afterward we went to a diner for late-night pancakes and he just kept laughing, "How'd you miss the fucking bag, buddy?" Not in a harsh way, not how our dad would've said it. Just, "how'd you miss the fucking bag?"

C: For years afterward, he'd randomly say it. Over the most trivial stuff. If I spilled a bit of my drink at dinner. If I got a question wrong on Jeopardy if we were watching it with my dad. That kind of thing. It never failed to make me laugh.

C: I miss that.

He missed *Tim*. Daphne knew that's what he was saying, and she was suddenly profoundly grateful that he would tell her that story, that he would share that part of himself with her.

D: I love having those kinds of little inside jokes. And I love being brought into other peoples'.

C: Tim was always the funny one.

Daphne sat staring down at that message for a few minutes, just thinking about how hard it was to let go of someone—how impossible, really. How you might forever define yourself in relation to them, even after they were gone, how you might be afraid of losing those parts of your identity the way you'd lost them.

C: How would you feel about a phone call?

Now Daphne stared down at her screen for a very different reason, frozen by his question. She couldn't talk to him using her own human voice! That would be a disaster. At the same time, she couldn't deny the sharp pang of yearning she felt at the very idea, the way it shot right to her toes.

D: It's pretty late. I should get to bed.

C: Oh yeah. I didn't necessarily mean now.

C: (Although now would've been all right by me.)

C: But it's late. Sleep well!

The more she and Chris talked, the more of these threads appeared. The one where she wanted to tell him in person that she knew what he was going through, that she wanted to make his life easier, not harder. The one where she wanted to tell him over text that there was nothing more she craved than to hear his voice in her ear. She wished she could find a way to weave the threads together, but she couldn't. Not without everything falling apart.

D: You, too.

SIXTEEN

THE LAST TIME THAT CHRIS' AGENT HAD FLOWN DOWN TO CHARLES-
ton to visit him in person had been . . . well, never. So the fact that
she was there now was a little concerning, no matter how many
times she said she'd been "in the area" anyway to talk to a new
prospect.

He'd only met Suze a few times, in fact. She was in her early
fifties, although she'd never claim it, an absolute powerhouse who
was a partner at a small, boutique agency based out of New York.
He'd had another agent at the start of his career, but had liked
Suze as soon as he'd met her and made the switch after his former
agent started taking longer and longer in between phone calls and
emails. "With me, what you see is what you get," Suze had said,
and he'd actually believed her.

Suze's father still held Nippon Professional Baseball records in
Japan, and when it came to the sport itself Suze knew her shit.
Unfortunately, she also had a laser-sharp detector for when a cli-
ent was bullshitting her.

"What's going on?" she asked point-blank after the waiter dis-
creetly set their drinks in front of them. Chris knew this was one
of the nicest restaurants in Charleston—there was a steak that

cost fifteen dollars an *ounce*—although he'd never had any reason to go there. But he hadn't been at all surprised when Suze made the reservation and told him to meet her there before heading to the ballpark.

"I've just been in my head a little bit," he said. "I'm settling in. It's still early in the season."

"Well, keep in mind that you're playing out the last year of your contract," she said. "And the Battery could re-sign you, or . . ."

She gave an elegant shrug of one shoulder, not needing to finish that sentence. If Chris wanted to keep playing for the Battery—if he wanted a chance to continue playing in the major leagues, period—he'd need to show that he was an asset to a team. Right now, with his numbers . . . he wasn't *terrible*. But he definitely wasn't good, either.

"Maybe it's for the best if we put out feelers to other teams," she said. "You'd have more options in free agency."

Something must've flickered on his face, because she set her sparkling water back down on the table with a sudden keen look in her eye. "Unless you're set on trying to stay here."

Now it was his turn to shrug, a little more awkwardly than she'd managed it. "I like Marv and the guys I play with. But I understand it might not work out."

She narrowed her eyes. "Who's duckiesbooks?"

Of all the possible questions she could've asked, that would've been at the very bottom of his list. It was so strange to even hear the Instagram handle come out of her mouth that for a minute he just stared at her, blinking.

"What?" he said finally.

"You deleted all your Instagram photos," she said. "Thank you for that, by the way."

He really couldn't follow this conversation. "You're . . . welcome?"

For the first time, he saw a flash of genuine irritation on her face. "Of course I'm not actually *thanking you* for undoing years and years of my work. Assistants' work. Still. Do you think Coca-Cola would thank one of its employees for deleting all its branding files?"

"Well, in that scenario, I'd be the Coke."

She stared at him like he was talking gibberish. He could explain further, get her to see how flawed and frankly kind of fucked up that whole analogy even was. He wasn't a product engineered with some secret formula. He wasn't a brand ambassador. He was a person, and yeah, okay, he was a professional athlete and that meant he had to play a certain role, but he'd never *asked* her to maintain his social media accounts.

But he knew that was beside the point now, and getting away from the main topic at hand. "I should've asked you first," he conceded. "But I just need to get off social media for a bit. Take a hiatus. And when I do come back—*if* I do—I'll be changing the password and taking charge of my own accounts. I don't recall saying you could read my messages."

That was the only way she would've even known to ask about duckiesbooks.

If Suze was in any way chagrined at being called out, she didn't show it. "I didn't *read* anything in detail," she said. "I don't have time for that. But you granted me some control over your social media, and that means I *can* access everything, including your messages. In the last ten days, I've seen you become a *There's no crying in baseball* meme, had to talk to your manager about why you should do a special interview segment and then later why you walked out of said interview segment, seen you erase years of professional photographs from your feed, and then you have *one* new message chain and it's with someone who seems to have come out of nowhere. I'm your agent, Chris. I care about your career, and I care about you. Do you see why this would all seem concerning when put together?"

He did, actually. When she laid it out like that, it seemed obvious that he was on some kind of spiral. Who knew, a few days ago he might've even described it that way himself. And yet for some reason, he didn't feel that way about it now. He knew he had a lot of work to do, but at least he felt hopeful.

"Everything's fine," he said. "I'm working on my swing with the hitting coach. I've been fielding well. I'm sorry that interview didn't go the way anyone wanted it, but . . ."

He thought about her, the interviewer. His heckler. He realized he still didn't actually know her name. There'd been a single daisy doodled in the corner of one of her notecards the day of that interview, and he remembered staring down at it until his eyes unfocused. He'd been so in his own head, and then later so up his own ass that he'd decided to go on that whole riff she'd overheard. He should offer to sit down for another interview, prove that he could be cooperative and available. A part of him even *wanted* to. She seemed like she would be easy enough to talk to.

But he also couldn't trust himself not to fuck it up again.

"I just need to make sure we're on the same page," Suze said. "That we're both focused on the same goals. You're allowed to have a personal life. From a branding angle, I wish you *would* have more of a personal life." She held up her hand, as if anticipating his retort to that. "I'm not saying you're only a brand. I respect that you're rethinking your social media presence. I really do. I wish you would have *talked* to me about it first . . . but ultimately those are your decisions to make. What I *don't* need is to have to do a bunch of damage control because you've been sliding into some random person's DMs."

It sounded so sordid when she put it that way. Chris could feel the tips of his ears growing hot.

"It's not like that—" he started.

"Whatever it *is* like," she said. "Do your due diligence. And no dick pics."

She said it so matter-of-factly, looking up a second later to smile at the waiter who dropped off their food. She was already starting in on her filet, slicing off a neat sliver of a bite as though they'd been in the middle of talking about the weather.

"I wouldn't—" he said. "I mean, I've never—"

"Because they *will* be able to prove it's your dick," she said. "I'm running up against client confidentiality here, but let's just say that men love their dicks until they're in court against an expert witness who's holding up items for scale."

This was like having the birds-and-bees conversation with a parent all over again. Worse, even. All Chris' dad had done was bring home a pamphlet from the pediatrician's office about *Sex and Your Changing Body* and leave it on Chris' bed for when he got home from school. At least he hadn't had to sit across the table from his father at a fancy restaurant in the middle of the day and listen to him talk about the etiquette of sending personal photos of genitalia.

"Obviously, if they're unsolicited, that's harassment anyway," she continued. "Even solicited, it's just as dangerous for you. I can't think of a single reason why anyone would solicit a picture of that unless as a setup for blackmail or extortion."

She took another bite of steak, covering her mouth as she hastened to add, "Not *yours* specifically. I mean dicks as a genre."

"I have no plans to send any pictures of my dick," he said faintly, still unable to believe he was having this conversation.

"Good," she said. He could practically see her checking an item off her list in her head. "And the less you put in writing, the better. Stick to phone calls, in-person meetings."

He wondered what his agent would say if he told her he'd never communicated with this person any other way than through text.

If he told her he didn't even know Duckie's real *name*. She might choke on her steak.

God, he'd wanted so badly to talk to Duckie on the phone last night. He'd almost thought about just calling her, and seeing if she'd pick up. But she was so skittish around talking to him, and he didn't want to risk scaring her off.

"I appreciate you looking out for me," he said now to Suze. "But I hope I haven't done anything to give you the impression that I'm looking to harass anyone, via text or otherwise. I'm really not worried about this becoming a situation."

"No, no," Suze said. "Of course not. That wasn't even necessarily what I was thinking of. I meant more . . . if you had an argument with a teammate, if you're frustrated with your manager, if you're looking to make a move on any endorsement deals, if something is affecting your playing . . . those are the kinds of things you share with *me*. They're not anything you should share with a stranger, and especially not in writing."

For a second he wondered if she *had* read through that first message exchange with Duckie. If he didn't know any better, he'd almost think that Suze was chastising him for telling Duckie about his brother's death, when he hadn't even shared that with her as someone with a fiduciary duty toward him and a vested interest in his career. But being indirect wasn't Suze's style. It was far more likely that she sensed there was *something* going on with him, thought it was suspicious that he'd started talking to a new person right around the same time, and had connected some dots just as she'd said she had at the start of their conversation.

He briefly thought about telling her more. *Help me help you,* she'd said in one of their first meetings, unabashedly quoting from the most famous sports agent movie of all time.

He just didn't see how she *could* help him, or what difference it would make.

"I'm being careful," he said, picking up his fork to take his first bite of his food. It was one of the first meals he hadn't eaten in the clubhouse or alone in his condo in a while, and was undoubtedly of the highest quality. But he barely registered the taste while he managed a smile for Suze. "Don't worry about me."

WHEN CHRIS GOT TO THE CLUBHOUSE, HE SHOULD'VE HEADED straight to the exercise bikes. That was his usual routine, to warm up his muscles a bit before taking some batting practice. But something made him turn down the hallway, out of the clubhouse proper and toward where the station personnel usually hung out, planning their segments for the broadcast.

He waved to a couple guys in the war room, who sat up straighter before giving him a delayed greeting, obviously surprised to see him in their territory. Then he tried the room next door, which had groupings of monitors set up, various control panels, and other equipment. He almost kept walking, thinking that room was empty, but then he saw her. She was leaned forward in an office chair, scrawling notes in a spiral-bound notebook on her lap, glancing up at the screen in front of her every once in a while.

She had headphones on, and he didn't want to startle her. But he also felt weird, just standing there watching her. His gaze flickered to the screen she was studying, surprised to see himself on it. It was an at-bat from a game that he instantly recognized as one from last season, where he'd had that big walk-off home run against the Royals. He'd ended the season with decent numbers, including seventeen homers, but that one had been special.

He lifted his hand, rapping his knuckles lightly against the door, then harder when she didn't seem to hear the first time. That got her to jump a little, turning in her chair to face him.

"One second," she said, her voice pitched louder than it needed to be as she scrambled to pause the footage, then pull the head-phones off her head. They'd left an impression in her curls, and she clenched her fingers in the hair at her scalp, bunching it up and then releasing as if trying to reset it.

"I was just . . ." She gestured back toward the freeze-frame on the screen. "Watching old broadcasts. Trying to learn from what Layla would do."

The image happened to be him coming into home plate, his hand already raised for the teammates who were waiting to high-five him there. Even in the blurriness of the image, he could see that he was smiling. And he could press play on the memory in his own head, remember the way it had felt when Randy removed his batting helmet from his head, and Beau jumped up for a chest bump.

"Makes sense," he said quietly. "We study film all the time. Go ahead and play it."

She shot him a doubtful look before leaning forward to press play. She unplugged the headphones and turned a knob until sound started to fill the small room.

"I was really trying to cue up the postgame interview," she said with an embarrassed grimace. "See what kinds of questions Layla asked."

And there it was. A moment that he could watch happen in front of his eyes, and still feel in his body as though he were right back there on that field. That Chris hadn't known he would lose his brother months later, hadn't held a single molecule of fear. That Chris had lived in a completely different world, one that was captured there on that little screen for posterity, one that he could never go back to.

She was watching him watch himself, and for a moment there

was such compassion in her brown eyes that he almost thought she *knew*. But that was impossible. He was just paranoid, after that weird meeting with his agent only hours before.

"Did you need something?" she asked softly, almost tentatively, like the room had come under a spell and she was afraid to break it. It felt like it had.

He *had* sought her out for a reason, but he couldn't quite remember what it was.

"Uh," he said, scrambling to think. "Just that I wanted to let you know that I'm available."

Her eyes widened a little, and he realized what that had sounded like. That conversation with his agent must've *really* fucked with his head.

"I mean for another interview, if you needed one," he hastened to add. "Or to give you background on matchups, tips on how to approach some of the guys . . . whatever would be helpful."

On the screen, Last Year Chris was standing with Layla, his face covered in a sheen of sweat, still a little out of breath not from the home run but from the celebration afterward. Layla was turning to him and asking him if he knew when he saw that pitch that he was going to send it to the cheap seats, and he was grinning and starting to say something about *I had a pretty good idea, because* . . .

He'd been the one to tell her to go ahead and play the footage, but suddenly he didn't want to be in the same room as Last Year Chris anymore.

"So, yeah," he said, slapping the doorframe with the flat of his hand. "Let me know."

He turned to head back down the hallway, but then one last impulse had him turning back around.

"Oh, and one more thing," he said.

She still looked slightly shell-shocked. "Yeah?"

"What's your name? Sorry, I didn't catch it."

He could've asked around—*someone* had to know. Marv or other players who'd already talked to her at yesterday's game. Greg, the executive producer, if he could stomach the interaction. But for whatever reason he wanted to hear it directly from her.

"Daphne," she said finally, lifting her gaze to his.

"Daphne," he repeated. It was a pretty name. It suited her. "Nice to meet you. I'm Chris."

SEVENTEEN

IT WAS ALMOST A FULL WEEK BEFORE DAPHNE HAD ANY CHANCE to take Chris up on his offer. The days passed in a blur of prep work with Layla, more prep with the rest of the broadcast team, getting used to where to stand and how to dress and what to say. The Battery were playing a relatively uneventful afternoon game against the Rangers, and Chris was up to bat. Daphne paused in looking over her notes just because she always tried to catch his at-bats. If she could.

She still had to glance up at the scoreboard sometimes to confirm how many balls and strikes had been called, but at least she knew what to look for now. She was just glancing back to Chris when she saw the ball fly out of the pitcher's hand and hit Chris squarely in the side of the ribs.

He was on the ground so fast she barely had time to think about what she was doing. All she knew was that he wasn't getting up right away, and she couldn't stand to see him like that, clutching his side, twisting his body as he braced one leg against the dirt. She was halfway to home plate when she felt the cameraman's touch at the back of her elbow.

"If they want you to do an injury report, they'll tell you," he said. "For now, let the medical staff take a look."

"Right," she said. "I was just—"

But she realized there wasn't any explanation that would make more sense than the conclusion the cameraman had already jumped to, so she stopped herself before she made it worse. She watched as Chris got up under his own power—which she took as a good sign—and disappeared into the clubhouse for some imaging. It was another full inning before she got the report in her earpiece that he was fine, that he'd been pulled from the game as a precaution but was expected to be cleared to travel to Pittsburgh with the rest of the team. She hoped she delivered the news in a calm, matter-of-fact manner, but she supposed Layla would tell her later when she gave Daphne the rundown of her performance.

Of course, Chris coming out of the game had the side effect of putting him in the dugout for the rest of it, just watching. He spent some time leaning against the rail with a couple of the pitchers, but then eventually she looked up and saw that he'd taken a spot at the corner nearest the photographer's well where she normally stood. If she took two steps backward, his sleeve would brush her arm.

She leaned back a little. "Everything okay?"

He looked at her for a second, almost like he'd completely forgotten that only forty-five minutes before, he'd been hit by a baseball traveling over a hundred miles an hour.

"Your—" She made an awkward gesture toward her own rib area, and his gaze dropped for just a moment to where her hand lingered, then slid back up over her chest, her throat, her mouth, before landing somewhere near her ear.

A muscle in his jaw ticked. "Yeah," he said. "Just a bruise."

"It looked bad."

He'd taken off his jersey and was only wearing the athletic shirt he normally wore underneath. So it was a simple motion for him to peel the shirt up, showing a tanned expanse of skin over muscle until he reached the affected area, which was already turning an angry purple. Daphne swallowed, suddenly glad that there was the netting of the lower dugout between them, preventing her from doing something wild like reaching out to touch it. He seemed to realize then that he was showing her half his stomach, and he dropped his shirt again.

"I've had worse," he said.

Daphne was positive that it was *obvious* just how much she was leaning in to hear him over the noise of the game, how much she'd wanted to smooth her fingers over that bruise, how much she'd thought about how to make it better. There'd been that moment—the way his eyes had swept over her . . . but he'd just been tracking her own hand. If she wasn't careful, she was going to make a real fool of herself. She cast around for something to say, anything to bring their footing back to the professional.

"Why does Randy do that, with the batting helmets?"

Kendall had gotten a home run the previous inning, and Randy had done the same thing she'd seen him do on the tape and in other games, where he was waiting at the top of the dugout to lift the hitter's helmet off his head. He did it with a certain flourish, almost like a crowning, but in reverse.

"It's just a home run celebration," Chris said.

"Ah." Well, that much she'd figured.

The Battery's left fielder, Mitch, kept fouling off pitch after pitch, and both she and Chris watched the at-bat. Chris leaned over the railing, turning away from her to spit in the dirt. "Sorry."

"It's okay," she said, because she was used to it at this point, and they didn't usually bother to turn their heads. Or apologize. She'd noticed Chris liked to chew gum during games and would sometimes blow bubbles out at third base when nothing was happening, which she tried not to find cute.

She also noticed now that, after he'd leaned forward, he didn't return back to his former position as he picked up the thread about home run celebrations. "Lots of teams have even more elaborate ones. The Mariners have a six-foot-tall trident they parade around with." Mitch drew a walk, and they both watched him make his way to first base, giving the first base coach a fist bump. "Here's a tip for you—do *not* ask Mitch about the batting helmet thing."

That took Daphne by surprise. "Why not?"

Chris crossed his arms on the dugout railing, his elbow so close to her now that it brushed her arm. "He doesn't let Randy do it," he said. "He's sensitive. About his hair."

"Really?" Daphne had the impulse to laugh, which would surely be rude. It was just that it was unexpected, this big brawny man who played professional sports being that hung up on something like a receding hairline.

"One time he colored it in a team photo with a Sharpie."

That time Daphne couldn't help the small giggle that escaped her, although she immediately put her hand up to her mouth. When she glanced over at Chris, she thought she'd catch him smiling, but instead he was looking at her mouth again. Then his gaze lifted to hers and for a minute she was lost in his hazel eyes until he looked back toward the field.

"We all give him a hard time and he's a good sport about it," he said. "But yeah, it's a team thing and he does *not* want to be without a hat or batting helmet on TV if he can help it. Also, if you move a little to the left you'll be better protected from foul balls."

With that, Chris headed back toward the rest of the team in the dugout, stopping to fill a cup with some water before he took up another place farther down the rail. Daphne moved a few steps over like he'd suggested and glanced back up at the scoreboard, trying to reorient herself to what inning they were even in.

DAPHNE USED THE NEXT TRAVEL DAY TO MEET UP WITH KIM AGAIN, needing a bit of normalcy after the whirlwind of the last week. They met at a local pub they'd been to a few times before, with dark lighting and amazing chicken wings. They'd already spent an hour on breaking down Kim's latest Tinder disaster when Daphne's phone buzzed with a text. Before she could reach for it, Kim turned the phone toward her.

Kim raised her eyebrows. "*Chris* says he just got on the plane and it made him think of you. Are you *still* texting with that baseball player?"

Daphne grabbed for her phone, annoyed at her friend's nosiness even though she knew she had no right to be. They'd glanced at each other's phones countless times on nights out, laughing over a meme someone had sent or rolling their eyes at a last-minute request from one of Daphne's clients.

"Sometimes," she said. *Every day.* "Here and there."

"I would be the first person to tell you to climb that tree," Kim said. "You know I would. But doesn't it make it awkward now that you work together?"

Daphne took a sip of her drink, grimacing a little when the ice crashed against her teeth. "It's . . . complicated," she said.

"Complicated like . . . you're hooking up?"

"No!" Daphne said, a little too forcefully. People at a nearby table glanced over, trying to see what the commotion was about. "No," she repeated, quieter this time. "Nothing like that. We just, you know. Talk."

"Why does *getting on a plane* make him think of you?" The way Kim said it, it was almost like there was some innuendo in the question.

"The flights can be long, he gets bored, sometimes we text," Daphne said. "That's it."

"Ah," Kim said. "I'm starting to understand all those 'late nights' you've been working."

Now Daphne was legitimately annoyed. She didn't know how many times she had to repeat herself, but she was also conscious that the more she did, the more it sounded like she was hiding something. And she *was* hiding something. Just not that.

"He doesn't even know that I work there, actually," she said before she could think better of it.

Kim had been right in the middle of a big bite of chicken wing, and she still had some sauce on her face when she finally got the words out. "Come again?"

"I originally messaged Chris as duckiesbooks on Instagram," she said. "I mean, we moved it to text, but. He knows me as duckiesbooks."

Kim carefully wiped her face and each finger with her napkin, as though she needed the break to figure out what to say. "So he texts you as . . . what does he think your name is?"

Daphne felt her neck grow hot, and she knew it wasn't from the chicken wings. She was a total wimp and always ordered mild. "Duckie."

"But meanwhile you see him almost every day as . . . Daphne?"

"Yes," she said. "Obviously I go by my real name at work."

"I don't think you get to use the word *obvious* here," Kim said. "What were you thinking? This kind of dishonesty isn't like you, Daph."

She knew her friend was right. It was the reason she'd had a pit in her stomach for the past couple weeks, and it wasn't going away. At the same time, she didn't know how to explain herself without sounding pathetic. In so many ways, those text messages seemed like the most honest version of herself there was. She liked having someone to reveal herself to, someone who seemed to relish that reveal like each new detail was something special. She liked getting to know him on a deeper level than she probably ever could've if they'd met face-to-face first.

"I know," she said finally, pressing her fingers to her temples like this was a headache she could make go away. "God, I know."

"Listen, you know I'm pro you getting back out there," Kim said. "But, like, swiping right. Messing around. Dating even. Not *catfishing*. And not with some guy you have absolutely zero chance of a future with."

That got Daphne to lift her head. "What do you mean by that?"

"Come on," Kim said. "He's a professional athlete. He makes stupid money throwing a ball around and probably has just as many women throwing themselves at him. It's nothing against *you*. It's just . . . how's it going to be when the novelty wears off, you know? And you're stuck in another Justin situation where you worship the ground he walks on and he barely even thinks about you."

Kim signaled the waitress for a refill on her drink, like she hadn't just thrown a bomb in the middle of the table. And who knew. Maybe she was right. Maybe she saw the situation clearer than Daphne ever could.

THE MINUTE DAPHNE GOT BACK TO HER APARTMENT, SHE UN-hooked her bra from under her thin tank, slid off the skirt she'd put on to go out, and put back on her favorite dinosaur pajamas. She curled up on her bed, grateful when Milo immediately jumped up to lie next to her, even if he did go with the butthole-in-her-face orientation he seemed to vastly prefer.

She didn't like to think that the text conversations with Chris were just a novelty for him, but she supposed it was possible—that he was briefly taken with the idea of corresponding with someone who didn't want anything from him as a baseball player, and it would wear off. These texts felt so real to *her*, but of course, she had the benefit of knowing who she was talking to. She had no idea how they felt to him.

Daphne grabbed her cell phone off her nightstand, opening up Chris' last text. At this point, hours had passed since it had come in, and the words just sat there, seeming to have gained extra portent with the passing time.

Just got on the plane—made me think of you.

They were playing in Pittsburgh that week, so it wouldn't be too long of a flight. Probably he would've already landed by now, which would mean he'd be asleep in a hotel room. Or he'd be down at the hotel bar with some of the other guys, letting women lean in and ask suggestive questions about rounding the bases. She'd heard stories, especially about the other single guys like Randy and Beau. She hadn't heard any stories about Chris, but that didn't mean there weren't any. Kim had a point—he was a professional athlete. Daphne had no idea what that world looked like.

She was half-tempted to text him something suggestive herself, like *just got into bed—made me think of you*. She even started to type it, before deleting the words. Who was she kidding. She could never pull that kind of thing off.

Instead she texted, You still around?

His response came in quick, a single word. Yup.

Now that she knew she had him, she just had to think of what she wanted to say. She was feeling almost too many emotions to express them all. She wanted to tell him everything, from the very beginning. She wanted to beg his forgiveness and tell him how much it would cost her to lose his friendship. Because it *would* cost her, so much that she felt a physical ache in her stomach at the thought.

Maybe it was that ache that made her type, I wanted to let you know how much it's meant to me, to have someone to talk to. Not just someone—you. My days are easier to get through because I know you're on the other end of these messages.

There was more she could say, but already it was feeling like a lot, so she pressed send.

C: Same. And it's not just having someone for me, either. It's you.

Well, fuck. She felt that stir in her lower belly, a confusing sensation alongside the churn of guilt his words also caused. What would he actually think if he knew she was . . . *her*?

D: If you knew me in real life, you wouldn't say that.

C: I want to know you in real life. You have no idea how badly.

C: Last night, I actually dreamed about you.

Daphne thought back to the game yesterday, that purple bruise on his ribs, that stretch of stomach, the way he'd turned his head to spit. None of those things should take up so much space in her brain, and yet there they were, playing over and over . . .

Jesus, she'd had dreams about him, too.

D: How would you even know it was me?

C: What can I say, dream logic. But it was definitely you.

Daphne remembered once reading a theory that you could only see people you'd seen in real life in your dreams. That they were recorded memories—deeply subconscious, perhaps, but all based in fact, not fiction. But she also believed in the power of the human imagination, so she never knew if she subscribed to that theory or not.

The idea that Chris might connect this alter ego with the real her even in a dream, as if his subconscious was doing the investigative work for him . . . it had never even occurred to her. The idea terrified her but also filled her with a kind of relief.

D: What happened in the dream?

The dots appeared, then disappeared, before reappearing again. She assumed he was typing a long narrative, and waited patiently for it to come in, but when the text finally came it was a single line.

C: Can I call?

Daphne sat up so fast that Milo jumped off the bed, slinking off toward the bathroom in the most melodramatic put-upon manner. He slipped into the cabinet under the sink, which she couldn't use for its intended purpose for this very reason—it was his favorite hiding spot for when he was feeling his most emo, so she couldn't very well put all her cleaning products under there.

Just like she couldn't very well talk to Chris on the *phone*, when surely he'd recognize her voice from work.

D: It's not a good time, sorry.

She hated how dismissive that looked on her screen, so she rushed to think of a credible explanation.

D: My apartment walls are super thin—I try not to make any noise after ten.

It wasn't a *lie* . . . but it definitely sounded like one, even to her. If she had to listen to her neighbor blast entrepreneurial podcasts on speakerphone at six a.m., then he could stand to hear a murmured conversation once in a while.

C: No problem. My hand just hurts a little and it was a lot to type.

She hated that his hand was bothering him. That wasn't even an official injury or anything she'd been made aware of on the prep sheets, just something that obviously plagued him from time to time.

D: Do you want to call and tell me, and I'll just listen?

It was a risky proposition that she was already second-guessing when her phone lit up in her hand, vibrating with a call. She picked it up, biting back the automatic *hello* that almost came out of her mouth. She should've suggested he send voice notes instead. Why hadn't she thought of that?

Because she wanted the immediacy of having him right there, on the other side of the phone. Even when she knew it was dangerous.

"Hi," he said, that voice right in her ear. Then he laughed, low and intimate. It made her toes curl. "Can you at least say *hi* back? Just so I know someone's there? This is a little weird."

"Hi," she whispered, her voice sounding so rusty that she almost cleared her throat and tried again. But maybe it was better that she sounded as little like herself as possible.

"Hi," he said again. "So about this dream. First of all, I do want to warn you that it gets a little . . . I don't know what the right word is. Not sexual. *Sensual*, maybe. It gets a little sensual."

Daphne sank back down into the bed. For being silent, she suddenly felt like this was the loudest call she'd ever been on. She felt like he could probably hear her breathing and her heartbeat through the phone.

"I don't want to continue if that makes you uncomfortable," he said. "Can you confirm if you're okay for me to continue? Just say *yes* so I know."

It took every effort for her to keep her voice modulated. "Yes," she said, the single husky syllable vibrating in her throat.

"Okay," he said. "It starts with me walking through this forest, and it's beautiful—all sunlight coming through the trees, birds calling to each other, just this peaceful nature scene. I get the feeling I've been walking for a while, and I'm starting to get tired. I can't explain it, because I don't feel lost or afraid or anything like that, but the scenery never changes and after a while it doesn't seem as beautiful. It's just *there*."

She made a small sound of affirmation, just to show she was listening.

"And then I come to this clearing, and there you are. You're eating strawberries directly from your hands, and the juices are running through your fingers, down your chin."

Dream me has about the same table manners as real me, she almost joked, then bit her lip. She wanted so badly to ask what she looked like. What did a dream version of her look like, to him?

As if sensing her question, he laughed a little. "I don't know how your dreams are, but I don't always see every detail crystal clear. So like the pine needles beneath my feet felt so real, but you're a little blurrier. It was less about what you looked like and more about the feeling of you. Not unlike the way we've been talking, actually."

And how do I feel? she wanted to ask, but of course she couldn't.

"Anyway, you're eating strawberries," he continued. "And you hold out your hands, to offer me some. And I say, I'm allergic—I really am, by the way. My throat completely swells up. But you just say, *No you're not.* And then you kiss me."

Great. She was some kind of fruit assassin. *And then what happens?* she wanted to ask, and again he seemed to anticipate her question.

"And then I wake up. But the weirdest thing is that I felt like I could taste the strawberries, could feel that stickiness on my mouth. Even though I probably haven't had one since I was seven years old, for obvious reasons, so I don't see how I would even remember what they taste like."

He was quiet for a minute, and they just sat like that, on the phone together but not saying a word. It was surprisingly erotic.

She wondered if he was feeling the same way, or if all this tension was completely one-sided.

D: That dream is a little sexual.

There was a slight delay as he obviously had to check the text message, and when he came back his voice had a rasp to it that buzzed right down to her clit like a live wire. "Ah," he said. "Yeah. I definitely—sorry."

D: Why are you sorry?

"I didn't want to make you uncomfortable."

D: You didn't.

She thought about the pulse between her legs, how badly she wanted to touch herself, how badly she wished *he* would touch her. In the past two weeks, they'd flirted a bit, skated close— sometimes *so* close—to taking it over that edge. She'd always held back. She'd always had good reasons to, the same reasons that Kim had been warning her about earlier that night and still existed now. But suddenly she didn't want to hold back anymore.

D: I mean, you did make me uncomfortable. Just in a different way.

"Oh?" The way he said that word, she knew he understood what she was saying. She wanted to be bold enough to spell it out, to tell him what she wanted to do, to ask him if he'd woken up from that dream dying to come. But she couldn't imagine typing those words out, couldn't imagine saying them aloud even if she wasn't trying not to speak on this phone call. The best she could do was tell him she had to go.

D: Don't worry, I'll take care of it. Hanging up now.

"Wait," he said.

Daphne gripped the phone, her palm already slick.

"Don't hang up. Please."

She swallowed. She couldn't do what he was asking, for so many reasons. It was wrong. But then the very fact that it felt *wrong* only made it more exciting, and she was torn between what she knew she shouldn't do and what she really, desperately wanted to give in to.

"I'll tell you every way I've imagined this," Chris said, his voice barely above a whisper. "I'll tell you everything I want you to do. I know you have to be quiet—but I don't."

She kicked her covers off, suddenly way too warm with them draped over her. She wanted exactly what he was describing, could already imagine the things he could say in that voice of his that would make her come in a matter of seconds. But it also felt too vulnerable—both for her but also for *him*. What would he think if he knew who she was, who he was saying those things to?

D: No talking.

She hesitated before sending the next message.

D: But I won't hang up.

EIGHTEEN

DAPHNE SET HER PHONE NEXT TO HER ON HER PILLOW. IT WOULD be better if she could forget he was even there, that he could hear her.

The fact that he could hear her would be what got her off.

She slid her hand under the waistband of her pajama pants, into her underwear. She wasn't surprised to find herself already wet, sensitive to the tiniest pressure of her fingers. They hadn't explicitly talked about him taking care of himself, too, but she liked to think that he was—that he was hungry and aching on his side of the phone the way she was on hers. She turned her head, trying to listen for any sounds coming from him, when she rubbed the crest of her clit in a rough circle and let out a whimper.

"*Fuck*," he groaned, and she tilted her head back, lips parted as she applied more pressure to that same spot. He was definitely also getting off.

It should've shocked her, some of the images that flashed through her mind as she touched herself. Briefly, she thought about something else, *anything* else, so she didn't have to feel guilty later about all the ways she'd thought about him. She thought about that first night she'd started officially working for the Battery, when he'd handed her that clip. She imagined him being the one to tug her dress close to her body, fisting the fabric in his hand until he could look down and see every curve outlined through the material. She thought about him spitting, she imagined him spitting on *her*, right between her legs.

It was useless to resist these thoughts. She gave in to them, gave in to the heat building at the base of her spine, crying out when it finally exploded in a way that was decidedly *not* quiet.

Afterward, she lay on her back, breathing heavily, her hand still resting on her lower stomach as she recovered. Through the phone, she could hear Chris grunt his own release, and the sound sent a flutter through her that almost made her want to reach back down and go again. Then she heard him say her name —only it wasn't really her name.

"Duckie?"

She pushed off the bed, leaving her phone on the pillow while she headed into the bathroom to wash up. When she caught sight of herself in the mirror, her cheeks were flushed and her hair was tangled and wild around her face. She'd never even pulled her pants down or reached for one of the toys she'd started keeping in her nightstand drawer. The whole thing had taken, what, five minutes? It felt like a fever dream, and her body was still hot with fever.

By the time she got back to her phone, the call was still open but new text messages had come in.

C: That was . . . fuck.

C: You there?

C: Duckie?

Her hands were trembling slightly when she picked up the phone, reaching over to grab one of her earbuds to put in, which she probably should've done from the start.

D: Here, sorry.

C: Everything good?

That was almost too big a question to answer. But she knew he was referring specifically to what they'd just done, and she didn't want him to think she hadn't enjoyed herself there when she had. She definitely had.

D: Yeah, all good.

Over the phone, he cleared his throat. "Can you still hear me?"

Yeah.

She expected him to say something else, but there was such a long pause before he spoke again that it managed to surprise her a little. "Can I ask you a question?" he asked finally.

Okay.

"What's . . ." He stopped, as if needing to regroup before he got the question out. "What's actually going on here? What are we doing?"

It was basically what Kim had been asking her earlier that night, and Daphne didn't have an answer now any more than she had then. She knew she was getting in dangerously deep, where she might not be able to pull herself out. She also didn't know that she wanted out. It was a confusing place to be.

"I understand being cautious online," he said. "Believe me, I do. My agent doesn't think I should be talking to you at all . . ."

He'd talked to his *agent* about her?

"And Randy has some elaborate theory about how you're either some Russian mail-order bride or else a Russian bot trying to hack the election through my phone? It's honestly a little confusing and I don't know where he got Russia from in the first place."

He'd talked to *Randy Caminero* about her? She'd just interviewed the guy about an amazing double play he'd turned to end a game. She could actually hear him going off about Russian bots, and the idea made her smile. Then her smile dropped again, as she thought about the implications of this. Fuck, she was in so deep.

"The point is," Chris continued. "You won't tell me your name—a Googleable, verifiable version of your name. Meanwhile you know exactly who I am. We're on the phone right now and you won't *talk* to me. I just heard you come and I've barely heard your voice. I've offered to get you tickets to a game—I would *love* to get you tickets to a game. I would love to meet you, wherever or whenever that has to be. Even just as friends, although you know I'm interested in you as more than that. And sometimes I get the impression you're interested right back. I don't know what to do with what we just did if you're *not* interested back. Maybe I shouldn't have said any of this, maybe I'll feel stupid in the morning. But do you see where I'm coming from? Or am I completely off base here?"

She squeezed her eyes shut. Everything he was saying made perfect sense. It wasn't fair for her to keep playing these games with him when he'd been nothing but honest with her.

She could say it, right now. Speak into the phone and just say, *My name is Daphne* . . . and let that fall into place. Or she could say, *At first I didn't want you to know I was your heckler, but now I don't want you to know that we work together* . . .

But then she thought of him in real life. He was hard to read. She couldn't tell how he felt about *her*, the sideline reporter, Daphne Brink. He'd been kind to offer to help her out, and he'd seemed sincere. He'd given her a few legitimate pieces of information, from the Battery's home run celebration to where to stand to avoid getting hit by a foul ball. But it's not like he'd seemed *into* her. She was just a person he had to deal with as part of his job, and for all she knew, he still resented it.

I think I should tell you about my divorce, she typed. But it's probably easier if we're both just texting.

"Oh," he said, almost like an involuntary verbal tic, like if she hadn't happened to have him on the phone like this she wouldn't have known that was his first reaction at all. "Okay. I guess I'll . . . hang up now?"

She hung up first. But once she did, she still didn't know how to start. After a few minutes, a new message popped up on her screen.

C: Was it bad?

She thought she knew what he meant. Was her marriage abusive, maybe, or even just was the divorce messy. She wanted to answer *no*—it wasn't like Justin had hit her, and once she'd made the decision to end things it had been a fairly clean break, as far as the logistics went. But then she didn't know if *no* told the whole story, either. Being with Justin had made her feel claustrophobic and small, and she was still working through the aftermath of that.

D: He was my brother's best friend. Is my brother's best friend, I guess I should say.

C: That must be hard. Him still having a role in your life.

So far, Daphne had been able to largely avoid Justin, but she knew she wouldn't be able to forever. She'd go over to visit the new baby, and there he'd be. Cookouts at her brother's house, Thanksgivings when Justin didn't travel to see his own parents . . . she didn't relish the thought of having to deal with him in all those situations.

D: I had such a big crush on him, growing up. When we finally got together, it felt like a dream come true. Like something out of a movie.

This was the easy part to explain. Daphne was almost ashamed of how proud she'd been of her and Justin's "love story," how much she'd loved to tell it to people. It was what happened after that was harder to talk about.

D: Looking back, I think that's what drew him to me. He loved how much I loved him, if that makes sense. Like, have you ever seen Sixteen Candles?

C: It's been a long time. I don't remember it as well as Pretty in Pink. But yes, I've seen it.

D: Jake Ryan is SUCH a catch, right? He's so dreamy, and he spends the whole movie trying to find out more about Sam. But if you think about it, one of the only things he ever says about her is that it's kind of cool, how much she's always looking at him.

C: Doesn't he also send his actual girlfriend home drunk with a kid he just met?

D: Yeah, and says, "Have fun." Literally this guy is the worst. But the actor is beyond hot, so somehow Jake Ryan still gets to be a certified dreamboat even decades later.

C: I take it you're the Sam in this scenario.

D: Basically. And maybe that wasn't fair to him, either, maybe I loved a version of him I put on a pedestal rather than the real person. But at least I tried.

C: And he didn't.

D: I started to realize that we were always watching whatever new show he was into, or going out with his friends. Don't get me wrong, I don't mind doing either! But it was almost like he didn't care to be alone with me, except for, you know. And even that felt like it didn't matter that it was ME specifically, just that it was a warm body.

She couldn't believe she'd typed all that. She hadn't necessarily planned to get into the nitty-gritty of her sex life with Justin, but it had ended up being a big part of what went wrong. It had been one area where she couldn't deny she was unsatisfied, even to herself.

C: I hate that he made you feel that way. Did you ever talk to him about it?

D: A few times. We even tried one counseling session, but he got angry and said the therapist was a quack and we never returned for the second appointment. We didn't cancel it, either, so we still got charged two hundred dollars.

C: Ouch.

She felt like she was losing the thread of what she was trying to say. She could tell a thousand stories about all the little moments that had added up, like tiny paper cuts that you could shrug off until all of a sudden you were covered with them. The times she'd shared an idea of something she wanted to do, and he'd pointed out all the reasons why she wouldn't be able to. The times she'd worn a new outfit or gotten her hair styled, wanting to try a new look, and he'd made her feel self-conscious and stupid. The times she'd lain on her back, staring at the ceiling, while he'd fallen asleep next to her without seeming to notice or care that she was obviously not happy.

D: It was my fault. I recognize that. I felt misgivings about marrying him on our wedding day, on the day he proposed. But I kept thinking it would get better. That the more he got to know me, the more he'd eventually love me.

C: You wanted the relationship to work. That's nothing to beat yourself up about.

D: I feel like such a failure. Our last big fight came because of this board game we played over at one of his friends' houses. I can't remember the name, but it was one of those where you try to guess how someone else will answer a question, almost like a Newlyweds style game. It was us and two other couples, and I don't know, I guess they thought it would be fun.

C: Already the idea of this game is making me break out into stress hives, but go on.

D: Right? So much pressure, because no one wants to be the couple who doesn't know each other as well. And then he missed literally EVERY SINGLE QUESTION about me. My favorite color. My biggest fear. My least favorite place I've traveled. And okay, it's not like they make you take a survey to get your marriage license, but his answers were so off I actually thought he was trolling me.

C: But turned out he was just an oblivious prick?

Daphne snorted at that one. She shouldn't encourage the shit talking, probably, but damn. It felt good to see Chris lay it out like that.

D: We got into a huge argument in the car on the way home. Basically, it retreaded familiar ground about how I felt like he didn't care, he said I was being overly sensitive and reading too much into it, and on and on. Only this time we said stuff we couldn't take back. He said that maybe my problem was that I wasn't "interesting" or "charismatic." And I said I wanted a divorce.

The phone lit up with a call, vibrating in her hand, and Daphne automatically tapped the screen to accept the call before she could even question if she should.

"First of all," Chris said right away, not bothering with a hello. "Fuck that guy. Second of all—no, second, *fuck* that guy. That's a horrible thing to say to someone, much less your *wife*. Not to mention, it's categorically untrue."

Daphne had started to cry. She didn't want to—she hoped it wasn't obvious over the phone, although she had a feeling that her shaky breath was probably a dead giveaway. "Not completely untrue," she said in a ragged whisper.

She wasn't uncommonly beautiful. Her biggest hobby was to read, the most solitary of acts, and even her attempts to connect with people about books fell flat, if her weak social media presence was anything to go by. Until she'd had this incredible stroke of luck, her job had been solitary and boring, as well, and even now that her job was probably the most interesting thing about her, she felt like she didn't deserve it. She hadn't *earned* it.

She didn't even deserve this, right now. Talking to Chris, having him take her side and be kind to her. But it was also hard to deny herself, when it felt so good to hear.

"I've been drawn to you from that very first message," he said now. "I still remember what it said. You said you were having to stay aggressively in the present, and maybe that was what those yoga influencer accounts had been saying this whole time. I liked the way you phrased that—*aggressively in the present*—and the influencer part made me laugh. Actually laugh, out loud, on the plane. I couldn't remember the last thing that had made me laugh in the few months before that."

She gave a shaky laugh herself then, pressing the back of her hand to her nose, trying to stop it from running without getting snot all over herself. Eventually she had to reach for tissues she kept next to the bed, putting the phone on mute while she blew her nose. On the other end, Chris was quiet, too, almost like he could tell she needed a minute to get herself together.

"God," he said finally. "I hate that I'm not there. I hate that I can't really see you, and talk to you, and tell you what that message and all the others since have meant to me. Not *interesting* or *charismatic*? That guy is a troll. I hang on every single word you say. And more importantly, Duckie, you have a good *heart*. You reached out to me when you didn't even know me, just because you saw I was hurting."

Daphne closed her eyes. He couldn't have picked a worse thing to say.

"I have to go," she said, and hung up. She tossed the phone toward the end of the bed, where it bounced off her mattress and onto the floor. If she'd cracked the screen, it would only be fitting.

She couldn't do this. It was getting out of hand. So she'd developed a crush on Chris Kepler. She'd get over it. She could extricate herself from the online relationship, keep the in-person relationship strictly professional, and move on. Kim had been right—this was a complete disaster.

But when she retrieved her phone, she saw that there was a

new message in her texts. She knew it had probably hurt his hand to type it, and she felt terrible about that, too.

C: I'm sorry if anything I said made things worse for you. You're not a failure. You're the opposite, in fact, because you were able to see that you were unhappy and do something about it. That takes a lot of guts—guts I wish that I had sometimes. And I'm sorry if I'm moving too fast for you. I know things are a little complicated because of your divorce, my job, etc. I just really like you. I have from that first message.

Daphne couldn't just ghost him. That would be the easiest thing to do, but a true coward's way out. She had to figure out how to do things the right way, give him some closure. But she knew she wouldn't be able to figure it out tonight.

D: Good luck at your game tomorrow. Thanks for talking with me.
C: Anytime.

CHAPTER

NINETEEN

"SO WHAT DID SHE SOUND LIKE?" RANDY ASKED. THEY'D TAKEN five of the eight road series games they'd played and were back in their own clubhouse, lifting weights. Chris always felt such relief when he came back home after being away, but now it was even more acute. He was really hoping to get Duckie to agree to meet up with him.

He knew it was a long shot. They'd still barely spoken on the phone—and she'd been fairly distant the last week, actually, responding with quick little texts like *haha* or *I know, right?* but otherwise saying she was busy. He didn't know if that last phone call had made things weird somehow. For him, it had been one of the most erotic experiences of his life.

She *had* to be interested. What could be the harm in getting a cup of coffee? Or tea—he knew she preferred to drink that. It was tricky with his schedule, but he could make something work first thing before he had to head into the ballpark, or even super late if she was willing to meet up after a game. She seemed to stay up pretty late herself. In fact, she had a knack for texting him at almost the exact time he got home after a game, which made him wonder if she watched him on TV. She never said anything.

And now he was so conflicted about it all he'd resorted to

rehashing the whole situation for Randy—not only the anonymous texts but their brief one-sided phone conversation, too,
leaving out the whole mutual masturbation part—just trying to
get a read on it.

"She sounded . . ." Chris struggled to think of the word. The
only thing that popped into his head was *familiar*, but of course
that didn't make any sense. Maybe he'd heard her voice in his
dreams.

God, he was so cheesy he embarrassed himself.

"Squirrelly?" Randy supplied. "Look, man, I'm telling you.
It's *weird* that she won't give you any info. This is a catfishing situation for real. At the very least, she's married."

Chris frowned. "She's divorced."

He'd hated hearing about her ex-husband, but he'd been grateful that she'd trusted him with the story of what had gone wrong.
It had made some things make more sense, like the fact that she
seemed so unwilling to share too much of herself. She obviously
had some insecurities about whether anyone would be interested
in what she had to share, thanks to the shit her ex had said to her.

"Slow down," Randy said. "I can't spot you if you're up and
down like that."

Chris set the barbell back on the rack, pushing himself to a sitting position on the bench. "You think she could still be married?"

Randy shrugged. "She can text, but she can't talk? Sounds to
me like she's got someone already sleeping right next to her."

The idea made Chris feel sick to his stomach, but he forced
himself to consider it. *But it was almost like he didn't care to be
alone with me, except for, you know. And even that felt like it didn't
matter that it was ME specifically, just that it was a warm body.*

"Maybe she's in the process of getting a divorce," Chris said.
He didn't love the idea that she would've lied about that, but he
could understand if the relationship was already pretty much

over, if they'd talked about it and seen a counselor . . . who was he kidding. He hated that idea.

Randy made a face that clearly indicated what *he* thought of the suggestion. "Maybe," he said. "And maybe she does, and you get together, and a year from now you're on the road and she's got some other dude she's texting every day. Only you're not even home, so she can feel free to take his calls all she wants to."

Chris must've looked stricken, because Randy reached out to squeeze his shoulder. "Or maybe not, man. I could be totally off. I don't know this chick. But don't forget that *you* don't know her, either."

It wasn't lost on Chris that, if he'd been playing that stupid board game, he probably would've gotten those questions wrong, too. He didn't know her favorite color, or greatest fear, or least favorite place to travel. But he did know that she wore lime green pajama pants with bright pink dinosaurs on them, that she was a nervous driver, that she wanted to go to Prince Edward Island someday to see L. M. Montgomery's house. And she knew stuff about him, too, stuff he'd barely told anyone—about his brother, about the way he felt about playing baseball, about how lonely his life sometimes felt.

He pulled out his phone, typing out a new text.

C: I'm going to reserve two tickets for tonight's game for you. Just go to will call and ask for the tickets under "Duckie S. Books." If you can't make it or don't want to come, I understand—but I hope you do.

There. He'd made a move, given her an opening. What she did with it would be totally up to her.

HE RARELY REQUESTED TICKETS BEYOND THE ONES HE USED TO bring his dad out to occasional games, so the front office was very accommodating. He'd asked for two seats right by third base, so he had a chance of finding her in the crowd when he was out on the field.

An hour into the game, he was starting to question whether that had been the smartest move. He knew better than to glance up into the stands between every play. This wasn't Little League, where he'd once waved to his brother from first base and gotten picked off by the pitcher.

But by the eighth inning, the seats were still empty. Worse, he'd even taken a brief bathroom break when the top of the Battery's order was up to bat, not because he'd particularly had to go but because he wanted to check his phone to see if she'd texted. He'd never done that during a game before.

She hadn't.

They were down by one run in the bottom of the ninth, two outs, nobody on. The best thing Chris could do would be to hit a home run, obviously, and tie up the game with one swing of the bat. But he knew that the other team's closer hadn't given up too many of those, so the second-best thing he could do would be to just get on base, however he had to do it. Beau was in the batting order behind him, and he hadn't had a lot of luck against the closer, either, but at least it would give them a shot.

Chris had it in his head that he was going to watch the first pitch almost no matter what, show the guy that he wasn't trigger-happy, that he wasn't going to chase. Then the pitcher would have to tighten up, throw one in the zone to get back in the count.

But that first pitch was an absolute beauty, a sinker that dropped right in over the middle of the plate. The umpire called, "*Strike.*" Chris was so rattled that he took an aggressive swing on the second pitch, one that ended up almost in the dirt with Chris pivoting down to one knee from the force of his swing. He could practically hear the collective disappointment from the crowd, the expectation as he stepped out of the batter's box, tapping his bat against his cleats, before stepping back in and getting set.

He watched a ball, then fouled off two in a row to stay alive. He could *feel* himself getting closer, could feel the pitcher's frustration as he shook off two suggestions from his catcher before finally nodding his head. When the fastball came, it was a little outside, but Chris found himself reaching for it anyway. He was almost surprised when he felt the bat vibrate from the contact beneath his fingertips, when the ball went flying toward the back corner of right field. It wasn't enough to be a home run, he could tell that, but he could also tell that the right fielder wasn't going to get it in time to be an automatic out.

He took off, rounding first base and heading into second, where he allowed himself a quick sideways glance out to right field. That guy was an All-Star, with multiple Gold Gloves and an absolute rocket of an arm. But he was still fumbling with the ball, hadn't fielded it cleanly, and Chris knew that if he could get on third base, the chance that Beau could score him would be that much greater. He put his head down and pushed through, his lungs burning as he booked it toward third, sliding into the base only a split second before he felt the third baseman's glove brush his leg.

He popped up, keeping his foot on the bag, looking to the third base umpire who called him . . .

"*Out!*" the ump shouted, clenching his fist with what seemed like unnecessary emphasis.

"I was safe," Chris said. "I beat the tag."

The other team had already started to trot off the field, giving each other celebratory high-fives and pats on the back, and Chris looked to the Battery dugout. Marv was on the phone, indicating a call to see if a review would be necessary, but when he hung up he just waved at Chris to come in. The game was over. Chris was out.

"I was safe," he said again, but even the ump had walked away.

Chris crouched down on the base, his forearms resting on his knees. He would've had a double standing up if he'd just stopped at second. He hadn't even looked at the third base coach to see if he was waving him on or not—a cardinal sin. He also didn't need to look up into the stands to know that she'd never come, and he bet if he checked his phone she wouldn't have texted, either.

"*Fuck.*"

He stood up, brushing the clay off his pants, although he needn't have bothered. As he headed toward the dugout, he saw just about the last person he wanted to see.

Daphne. Waiting with her microphone to talk to him. He knew it was part of her job, but he'd rather walk over a bed of nails than give an interview right in that moment. But there was something about her face that made him slow down, head toward her with his shoulders set in a resigned line.

"Chris, tough loss," she said. Was he imagining things, or was she looking over his shoulder again instead of directly at him? He thought they'd gotten past that. "What did you see that made you go for the extra base?"

"I thought I had it," he said. "Turns out I didn't."

It was a complete nonanswer, which she'd probably thought they were past, too.

"You were playing the game the right way," she said. "Taking a risk. Can't fault you for that."

That surprised him. Normally, sideline reporters didn't say much that could be deemed a judgment on the game—it was more relaying an event and then asking how you felt about it, maybe sharing someone else's judgment and asking you to react to it. But her comment felt almost . . . personal.

She didn't look so good, actually. Her face was pale, and there were circles under her eyes visible even through her makeup.

"Yeah, well," he said. And then just stopped. For a moment they stared at each other, a beat of completely dead airtime before finally she seemed to shake herself out of it, turning back toward the camera.

"Tomorrow's pitching matchup is confirmed . . ." she started to say, and Chris peeled off, heading through the dugout back into the clubhouse. Randy was there, sitting on one of the benches and typing something on his phone. Chris rummaged in the duffel at the top of his locker for his own phone, scrolling through a few notifications before putting it back. Just as he'd thought. There was nothing.

For the first time, he started to feel a little worried. It wasn't like Duckie, not to be in contact at all for so long. What if something had happened? She was so paranoid about car accidents . . .

"I can't believe Marv didn't even challenge the call," he said to Randy, trying to distract his heartbeat back to a normal rate.

"Dude," Randy said without even looking up. "You were out."

TWENTY

OF ALL NIGHTS FOR HER CAR NOT TO START, IT HAD TO CHOOSE that night. When she was at her most bone-tired and desperate to get as far away from the ballpark as she possibly could.

"Perfect," she muttered, trying to turn it over again. It made a sickening rattle before shutting back off, which meant . . . what? She tried to remember what her dad had taught her. If it was the battery it wouldn't start at all, right?

It didn't matter. Either way, she was looking at calling roadside assistance at best, giving up and paying for an expensive rideshare home at worst. The second option actually didn't sound that bad, if it meant she could get out of there.

She held her phone in her hand, finger hovering over the app, wondering if she should just bite the bullet. But she hated wasting all that money she didn't really have, when she paid an annual fee to get help in a situation exactly like this one. She opened up her roadside assistance app instead, opening a new service ticket to fill out all the information they needed.

She'd only gotten through two fields when a text popped up on her screen.

C: Hey, everything okay?

Oh yeah, everything was great. Only I've been stringing you along and feeling increasingly terrible about it.

C: I just got worried when I didn't hear from you.

And as if she needed any more proof that she was a terrible person, *that* had never even occurred to her. She typed a quick response into the text message box.

D: Sorry, everything's fine. I couldn't make it to the game, but I do appreciate the thought.

C: Okay.

Just when she thought that was all she would get—that single terse word, with the period after it, which *felt* sinister even though she'd already noticed that Chris largely respected punctuation and capitalization in his texts—he texted again.

C: I know I said I'd understand if you didn't come to the game tonight, but I realized I don't. Not because I'm mad, but just because I don't understand any of it. Are you still married?

Her first reaction was an incredulous denial—hadn't they talked in detail about her divorce just a few nights ago? But then when she thought about it, she realized that would make a lot of sense from his end. It was almost such a neat explanation that she briefly thought about just saying *yes*, and using that as her excuse to end things. But telling a lie to get out of another lie didn't feel like the right answer.

D: No.

She left it at that single word, figuring that any long-winded explanations would only get her in more trouble, or make him question her credibility. She expected him to challenge her further, but she didn't expect the text she got instead.

C: I don't think I can do this. Whatever "this" is.

She knew she had no right to be angry, but she also couldn't stop herself.

D: So everything you've said—about being okay to just be friends,

about understanding if I wanted to take things slow—was just bull-
shit? Because I can't make it out to a game on short notice, that's it?
I have a life, Chris. I might have plans that preclude me from being
able to come to a ballgame at 7pm in the middle of the week. Ever
think of that?

C: I get that you have a life. But you won't share that life with me,
at all. If you had plans tonight, you could've texted back and just said,
sorry, won't be able to make it. You didn't.

The fact that he had a point only perversely made her more
upset. She should've responded to his text—it had been cruel not
to. She'd just been so unsure of what to say, and then she'd gotten
so wrapped up in her actual job covering the Battery that she
hadn't been able to explain why she wasn't at the game . . . that she
was, in fact, at.

C: I don't want to fight with you. I do understand if you're not ready
for anything beyond anonymous texting. But it turns out that the
anonymous texting thing is starting to be hard for me to keep up, so
where does that leave us?

This was what she had wanted. Better, in a way, because he
was the one calling it quits and she didn't have to feel guilty about
being the one to pull away. So why did it feel so awful?

D: I guess nowhere.

C: Fair enough.

How could he say that, when nothing about this felt fair? And
it was all her fault. She'd made a mess of this whole thing, and in
that moment, her yearning to go back in time and do it all differently was a physical ache. Hot tears were sliding down her cheeks,
but she didn't bother to wipe them away as she texted her response.

D: Take care, Chris.

The three dots bouncing up on the screen, then disappearing.
He was typing. It was several minutes before the reply came in.

C: You, too.

Daphne was leaning against her steering wheel, no longer actively crying but still sniffling a little, when a knock came at her window and scared the shit out of her. Her elbow hit her car horn, making it bleat just as she let out a little scream. She looked up to see Chris taking a step back from the car, his hands in his pockets.

She rolled down her window.

"Sorry," he said. "I didn't mean to startle you. Everything okay?"

It was the same question he'd asked her only half an hour ago via text. Or rather, he'd asked *Duckie*. Her alter ego that he was no longer speaking to.

"Fine," she said, resisting the urge to wipe at her eyes. She knew they were probably red and swollen, but she hoped that the parking lot was dark enough to conceal the evidence of her crying. "Just waiting on roadside assistance."

That was a lie, since technically she'd never submitted that service ticket. But she would, as soon as he left.

He shifted his weight to one foot, squinting out toward the other cars in the lot. There were still other people at the ballpark. She recognized Randy's sleek new sports car, Marv's giant SUV.

"Why don't you wait in the clubhouse?" he asked. "I can walk you over there and let you in."

"Oh," Daphne said, trying for a smile and hoping it came across as natural. "That's okay, but thank you. They'll be here any minute."

"I'll wait with you."

The absolute last thing Daphne wanted, especially given that it would probably be half an hour *after* she put in the ticket, if past experience was anything to go by.

"That's really not—"

"I'll just be over here." He gestured toward the space next to hers before walking away, leaning against one of the streetlamps as he pulled his phone out of his pocket. He checked it briefly before putting it away. His expression didn't betray anything that he might be thinking, and she was left wondering if their conversation had affected him as much as it had affected her.

She wanted him to care as much as she did.

She didn't want to have hurt him. Again.

It was all too confusing, and having him standing only a few feet away wasn't helping matters.

She started filling out the assistance form in the app, then got frustrated and decided just to call. After the technician had established that she was safe, she heard the clicking of a keyboard and then he came back on the line.

"We don't have any drivers in your area at the moment," he said. "It's going to be at least forty-five minutes, more likely an hour or so. Do you still want to request service?"

"What's my other option?"

She'd meant it as a rhetorical question, but the technician jumped in to explain. "If you're going to have the car towed to a service center, you can schedule that for tomorrow and someone can meet you out there. We can help arrange a rideshare if needed, although you will be responsible for any charges through that company. We can—"

"Okay," Daphne said, interrupting. "Never mind. I can figure it out."

"Are you sure? Because—"

"Yes," she said. "Thank you so much. You've been very helpful."

It wasn't his fault there were apparently no drivers in the entire Charleston area, after all. She hung up, taking another glance out the window. Chris was still there, leaning against the streetlamp.

When he'd removed himself like that she'd thought maybe that was how little he wanted to spend any time with her—that some chivalrous impulse wouldn't allow him to walk away, but he'd be damned if he'd actually stick around to *talk* to her.

Only now did it occur to her that maybe he'd done it specifically to give her some space, to not crowd her.

She rolled down her window.

"I'm calling a rideshare," she said. "It should only be a few minutes."

"No worries." He hesitated. "Do you need a ride?"

That brief pause told her everything. She didn't particularly want to spend time in an enclosed vehicle with him, and she *really* didn't want to as some kind of obligation. "No, no," she said. "I got it."

She lived half an hour away from the stadium, which normally she didn't think of as *that* big of a deal. But when she put her destination into the rideshare app, all of a sudden the little car icons disappeared until there was only one, fifteen minutes away. Whatever. It was still better than waiting for roadside assistance, right, if it meant that she was home by the same time she would've still been waiting in the parking lot?

"Let me give you a ride," Chris said. While she'd been looking at the app, he'd come closer to her car, near enough that she could smell the faint scent of his soap when the wind blew the right way. It smelled like fresh aloe and summer, and she wondered randomly whether players brought their own soap or if they used whatever the clubhouse provided. This scent was very *Chris* in some way she couldn't define.

"It's kind of far," she said.

He took his car keys out of his pocket, seeming to sense that she was capitulating. "That's okay," he said. "I could use a drive."

FOR THE FIRST TEN MINUTES, THEY DIDN'T SPEAK, EXCEPT FOR Chris to ask where they were going. His car wasn't what she'd expected, not that she'd known *what* to expect. But maybe flashier, like what Randy had, or more luxurious, like Marv's. Chris' car was very clean, and obviously fairly new, but other than that it was just a regular car.

Once he'd merged onto the highway, he glanced over at her. "Are you cold?"

"Oh, no," she said, pulling at the hem of her skirt to hide the goose bumps that had broken out over her knees. "I'm fine."

But he reached over to turn the dial for the AC down a notch anyway.

"You're doing a good job, you know," he said.

"Sorry?"

He cleared his throat. "With the reporter gig. It's not easy . . . absorbing all that information, getting ready on the fly, knowing how to talk to everyone. You're doing a good job with it."

"Thank you," she said, a little surprised. "I know it came from ignominious beginnings."

The corner of his mouth twitched. "Ignominious," he said. "Yeah."

And for a while, that's all she thought they were going to say. He seemed content to just drive, and she had to admit that there was something almost peaceful about being in the car with him. He drove easily, one hand resting on top of the steering wheel, the other resting on the gearshift almost as though he were used to driving a manual. He used his signal light and didn't follow too closely or speed too much. She found herself staring out the window, watching the passing streetlamps and trying not to think about the way things had just ended with the very same man who was sitting so close she could feel the body heat coming off his arm.

"Why did you say that comment, about Christopher Robin?"

It actually took a second for her to catch up to what he was talking about. The incident that had started it all, and it seemed so long ago now. Like that had been another version of her entirely. She was so sick of all the different versions of herself.

"I don't know. I was drunk. I was trying to get into the game, and the guy next to me was shouting different stuff, but I didn't know much about baseball so I could only riff on people's names, and your name is Chris and the guy said you hadn't been hitting well, so . . ."

She shrugged awkwardly. A circle of hell should definitely be having to re-explain your unfunniest joke again and again until the end of time, because it was its own excruciating torture.

But he laughed, the sound low and husky and a little sudden, as though he'd surprised himself with it. "*Your name should be Christopher Robin, 'cause you're hitting like Pooh,*" he said. "That's pretty good. Who says that at a baseball game?"

"To the home team, no less?" She groaned. "God, I wanted to die."

His smile fell, and she only thought about what she'd said after it was already out there. Her excuse for the heckling might've been the drinks she had, but there was no excuse now. She'd just been thoughtless and insensitive.

"I used to watch that movie so much as a kid," Chris said. "*Winnie the Pooh.*"

"Really?"

"My brother called me Christopher Robin when we were young," he said.

"Aw," she said, hoping she didn't sound too strangled. "That's cute."

So *that* was the reason he'd cried. It made so much sense now. It made her heart hurt. She waited for him to say more about his brother, hoping that maybe he would open up to her—Daphne, not just Duckie—but he just signaled for the next exit and kept driving. She was conscious of the fact that they only had ten minutes left in the drive, and suddenly she was anxious to get him to keep talking.

"I'm sorry I had to ask you about that last play tonight," she said. She could tell he really hadn't wanted to talk to her, even more than normal—but it was to his credit that he'd stopped and done so anyway.

"It's your job," he said. "It's fine. I haven't had the best night."

"Neither have I," she said, more to the window than to him. Out of the corner of her eye, she could see him glance at her, but she didn't turn her head. He pulled up to a red light, drumming his fingers on the steering wheel.

"Just the car troubles, or something else?"

She did turn to look at him then, and was surprised to find him looking right at her. She had another one of those paranoid frissons up her spine, the sudden certainty that he *knew*. But of course that was ridiculous.

"You looked a little upset earlier," he clarified. "After the game."

"Did I?" she asked faintly. She hoped it hadn't come through on camera, but from what little footage of herself she'd actually watched, it probably had. She was still getting used to seeing herself in high definition.

She was still getting used to seeing *him* this close. If she really thought about it, it was wild, how only a month ago she wouldn't have known who Chris Kepler was. She wouldn't have cared. Once, only a couple months before she'd said she wanted a divorce, Justin had dragged her to some fan event, where a bunch of

Battery players had been signing autographs. For all she knew, Chris had been there—she'd mostly stayed to the back of the crowd, fanning herself with a small paperback she'd pulled out of her purse. It had been unseasonably hot, and she'd gone home with a sunburn on her bare shoulders that had bothered her for a few days afterward.

"It's cool if you don't want to talk about it," he said. "I don't particularly want to talk about my night, either."

"Look at us, the life of the party," she said, then wondered if that was presumptuous somehow, putting them together in the same sentence like that. But he just glanced over at her, giving her a quick smile that didn't reach his eyes. The light turned green, and he turned his focus back to the road.

"You don't like giving interviews, do you," she said. It wasn't really a question, since the answer was already extremely obvious.

He shrugged. "I know I have to," he said. "And it's not always so bad. I like talking about baseball."

"Just not about yourself."

"I know it's a privilege to have this job, and to *get* to talk about baseball as part of it."

"Easy now," she said. "I don't have a microphone in my hand this very second. You don't have to give me any sound bites."

This time when he smiled, it did crinkle the corners of his eyes just a little bit. "I didn't use to be this bad," he said, then quickly looked over at her, as though he realized how that sounded. "It has nothing to do with *you*. Like I said, you're doing a good job. But suddenly I feel attention on me and I just . . . clam up. When we were sitting down to do that first pregame segment, everything was fine. And then out of nowhere, my heart started racing, I couldn't breathe. I felt like I was underwater, running out of air, and I just knew I had to get out of that interview and back to the surface."

His Adam's apple bobbed a few times, as if he was having trouble swallowing. "Like I said, nothing personal to you."

That definitely put that whole incident in context. She'd thought he hadn't wanted to be in the same space with the woman who'd heckled him, or that he'd been frustrated by her amateurish stumbling over the scripted questions. She hadn't known he'd been feeling trapped.

"It sounds like you had a panic attack," she said gently.

He glanced at her. "I've never had anything like that happen to me before. I even had the trainers check me out."

"What'd they say?"

"They said everything looked fine." He pulled a face. "They said it was probably stress. But who *isn't* stressed?"

Ain't that the truth. "Who would you talk to, though, about stress? Like, does the team have a sports psychologist or, I don't know, a counselor or something?"

It wasn't lost on her that she was basically re-creating the first conversation she'd had with him by text, after he'd told her about his brother. But she hadn't gotten a satisfactory answer then, and she couldn't help but bring it up again now.

"I'm sure," he said, then tightened his grip on the steering wheel. "We're off the record, right?"

The whole time they'd been talking, she'd barely remembered her role as a reporter, even though they'd literally referenced it several times. "Of course," she said, then gestured at her window. "It's a right at this next street, by the way. Then your second left into the complex with the palms strung with Christmas lights."

"'Tis the season all year round, huh?"

She shrugged. "Makes it easier to give directions at least."

After he'd made those turns, she had to remind him of the apartment number and show him where to park in front of her duplex. She knew they'd lost the train of what they were talking about, which was a shame, because she'd thought maybe she was getting somewhere with him. But then she also thought about those last text messages, the finality to them, and reminded herself that actually they were going nowhere.

"This is me," she said unnecessarily once he'd parked, gesturing toward her front door. At least the outside of her apartment looked clean and inviting, even if the inside was tiny and perpetually a little messier than she would like. She'd lined her front step with some potted plants, and put out a welcome mat with a giant sunflower on it. Not that you could see much of it in the dark, but it made her feel good to know they were there.

She hesitated, wishing suddenly that she could ask him in for that cup of tea. But of course that was impossible, for so many reasons.

"You have a cat," he said, as if reading her mind.

Yes, Milo was definitely one of the reasons she couldn't invite him in. She'd sent him so many pictures of her pet that he could probably pick him out of a lineup. But how did he . . . ?

Chris pointed toward her window, where Milo was clearly silhouetted, loafing on the sill and crinkling the blinds again.

"Yup, that's my cat." She gave him what she hoped was a brilliant, distracting smile. "Well, thanks for the ride. I guess I'll see you tomorrow?"

She asked it like a question, but of course they *would* see each other tomorrow. The Battery were playing an afternoon game, and she was supposed to arrive at the ballpark by eleven o'clock for all her prep. She knew the players often got there even earlier, for batting practice and other warm-ups. Chris was usually one of the first ones to arrive.

She got out of the car before she could embarrass herself by saying anything else, but she heard him call her name once she'd reached her front step.

"Daphne!"

She slowed, turning around. "Yeah?"

His window was down, his forearm resting on the edge. He was messing with his side mirror, not looking at her even though he'd been the one to call for her.

"Do you need a ride in the morning?"

"Oh, that's . . ." *A really nice offer.* Her apartment had to be so far out of his way, especially since she was pretty sure just from a few things he'd said in his texts to her as Duckie that he lived relatively close to the stadium.

But they'd closed the book on the text relationship. She'd known they'd still see each other in person, obviously, but she had resolved to be careful, to make sure there was no chance he ever connected her with her online alter ego.

"You'd have to be ready around nine," he said. "For us to get there by nine thirty."

"Okay," she said. "I'll be ready."

BY THE TIME CHRIS GOT BACK TO HIS CONDO THAT NIGHT, HE WAS barely aware of making the drive. It was almost scary, how on autopilot he'd been, merging back onto the highway and navigating the streets until he'd parked in his reserved space and gotten on the elevator.

His thoughts were on a loop. First, he'd thought about Daphne, what a surprise she'd turned out to be. *Ignominious beginnings.* The phrase had made him laugh, but she wasn't wrong. For two people who'd gotten off on such publicly awful footing, he found that he actually liked her. She was easy to talk to, which was a dangerous quality in a reporter, but somehow he trusted her. He knew she wouldn't tell anyone else about the panic thing, or put him on the spot about it in an interview. He didn't know how he knew that, but he did.

Then that made him think about Duckie, who he *had* opened up to, time and again. He'd thought it had been reciprocal, that she was letting him in, too, but apparently not. Apparently she had her limits. And he had to respect those, even if he didn't understand them. As much as he wanted to text her again right now, tell her that anonymous messages were completely fine and he'd wait as long as it took, he knew it was only a matter of time before they found themselves right back in this situation. It was fucking with his head.

That led him to think about the loss that night. He'd missed two calls from his father, and one of the first things he did when he got home was to pull up the game replay on his TV, something he almost never did. Of course, they watched film of specific at-bats, pitching matchups, fielding plays . . . it was just rare for him to watch the actual broadcast for a game he'd played in. He fast-forwarded to the last inning, grabbing a beer from the fridge as he watched his last at-bat. The strike looking, the swing on the ball at his shins.

But finally he got that hit. It had looked great, hard and to the back-right corner, where the fielder had to scramble after it. He rounded second, and the guy had the ball in his hand. He threw it in and Chris was already down, sliding into third, and . . .

Sure as shit. He'd been out. He should've stayed at second base.

Then the postgame interview. He'd had the sound turned down, but turned it back up in time to hear Daphne telling him that he'd played the game the right way. He took another swig of his beer, smiling a little even though he had no real reason to. The end of that game had been embarrassing, from that last play to his interview, where he'd just stared at her for three painfully long seconds before walking away.

He should probably get up and do something. He had laundry he'd been putting off. He'd have to go to bed a little earlier than usual, since he'd have an earlier wake-up time. But instead he just sat on his couch for the full length of the postgame show on the replay. Hell, maybe he'd learn something.

DAPHNE WAS STANDING OUTSIDE HER APARTMENT WHEN HE pulled up. She tucked her hair behind her ears, bending down to look through his window like she doubted it was him. When she finally opened the passenger door, he held out his arm, almost as if blocking her.

"Whoa," he said. "Normally customers ride in the back seat."

Her tentative smile dropped a little. "I can ride in the back," she said. "That's not a problem."

Now he had to hold out his arm to stop her from closing the door all the way. "No, no," he said. "That was a joke. A bad one. Sorry, get in."

She did, her body language still a little uncertain.

"It was because you were peering in like I was an Uber driver," he said. "You know, the classic, *is this Andrew's black sedan?* type of look. Like I said, bad joke."

"Oh," she said, relaxing into the seat. "I just wasn't sure if you'd remember how to get here. I realized—"

She broke off suddenly, biting her lower lip. Somehow, though, he thought he knew what she was about to say. "We should've exchanged numbers," he said, grabbing his phone from the cup holder next to him, unlocking it, and handing it to her without taking his eyes from the road. "Go ahead and text yourself and then we'll have each other's."

"That's okay," she said, a little stiffly. She was looking at his phone like it was a snake. "I don't think I'll need a ride again after today."

He could've pointed out that it might not hurt to have each other's numbers anyway, but he wasn't going to push it. She pressed her hands between her thighs, almost as if she needed to stop herself from touching anything. Or maybe she was just cold again—he'd noticed the goose bumps on her skin last night even though she'd insisted she was fine.

He'd noticed a lot about her, actually, despite his best efforts not to. Like now, the smooth strip of thigh from where her dress had ridden up an inch, the hollow curve behind her knees. He cleared his throat, suddenly wishing he could blast the AC a little higher.

"Music?" he asked.

"Sure."

He put on a playlist he'd made a while back with enough variety on it that he figured it'd be relatively inoffensive no matter what her musical tastes were. But then it opened with an older Rage Against the Machine song, and he almost skipped to the next track, not sure if that was a little heavy for what she'd be into.

"Did you ever figure out your walk-up song?" she asked, then immediately tensed up. He was keeping his eyes on the road, so he couldn't see her expression, but he could tell her entire body language had stiffened in the seat next to him.

"No . . ." he said slowly. "Marv keeps threatening to pick one for me, but so far I've been getting away with just not having one. Why do you ask?"

"No reason," she said, her voice tight. "I just noticed you didn't have one."

"This was one of my walk-up songs in college, actually," he said, gesturing toward the radio. "I don't know, maybe I should use it again. Do you have any suggestions?"

"Nope," she said. "I don't really like music."

Any music? Now he was wondering why she'd agreed to him putting on his playlist in the car. Maybe that explained why she'd suddenly gotten so tense and awkward. He reached over to turn the volume down.

"Sorry," he said. "We don't have to listen to anything. Or do you prefer talk radio, a podcast? Anything but sports, that's all I ask."

She rubbed her hands on her dress, and even though the fabric was a perfectly modest barrier between her palms and the bare skin of her thighs, he still found himself tracking the motion out of the corner of his eye. *Why* was he having all these thoughts about the team sideline reporter, of all people? No way would he ever act on anything with her, even if he wanted to.

Did he want to?

He thought back to that moment after he'd gotten nailed by a pitch and come out of the game. It had been second nature to show her the bruise—he was used to it, having physical therapists and trainers and teammates inspect his body, put their hands on it, and figure out where he hurt, how to stretch a muscle. But the minute he'd lifted up his shirt for her, it had felt . . . different. Thrilling. He'd felt her gaze on him like it was a physical touch, and then he'd felt self-conscious about feeling that way. Vaguely guilty, too. In the end, he'd stuck around long enough to make sure she didn't get hit with a foul ball off Mitch's bat, and then he'd removed himself from the situation.

Either way, it didn't matter now. A reporter for the team was definitely off-limits no matter what.

"I don't actually *hate* music," she said. "I don't know why I said that. This song is nice."

He didn't challenge that, even though *nice* was a bland word for a song that in his opinion was anything but.

"What would you think about letting the fans pick your walk-up song?" she suggested suddenly. "We could advertise it on the broadcast, run a poll on social media, let people fill out cards when they come to the ballpark. I don't have all the logistics figured out, but it could be fun."

He winced. "I don't know. It could really bring out the trolls. The write-in opportunities alone."

"What do you mean?"

He held up his hand, counting off even though he quickly ran out of fingers. "Smash Mouth's 'All Star,' to show how I'm *not* an

All-Star. Smash Mouth in general. Anything with the words *slump, weak, choke, wimp, crybaby, loser, pussy,* other homophobic or transphobic options I'm not even creative enough to think of . . ."

He probably shouldn't have said *pussy* out loud like that, even in a different context. Now it felt like the word reverberated through the car, and he wished he could turn the music back up without it being obvious.

Daphne, thankfully, seemed too focused on the song issue to worry about the awkwardness of that word. "We could give them options," she said. "That way it would be a vote, no chance for write-ins. Marv could make one of the suggestions if he wants his song choice represented on the ballot. We could even ask your teammates for options—it would be a really fun thing to bring up in interviews. What do you think?"

He still wasn't sure, but she was smiling at him, looking excited and happy for the first time since . . . well, at least since before last night. He didn't have the heart to burst her bubble now.

"Why not," he said. "I trust you."

CHAPTER
TWENTY-TWO

I TRUST YOU. IT HAD BEEN TWO WEEKS SINCE CHRIS HAD SPOKEN those words, and still they echoed in Daphne's head. They put a pit in her stomach if she thought about them too hard, but she was determined to earn his trust with this walk-up song idea at least. She'd talked it through with Layla and Greg, and they'd figured out how the voting would work and the various segments they'd film to promote the poll and showcase the result after the All-Star break. She also didn't know if the two things were connected, but Greg had told her that she'd been cleared to start traveling with the team for their next road trip.

Since first suggesting the walk-up song idea, she'd had minimal interactions with Chris on the project. She'd gotten her car fixed, so there'd been no need for any more rides, and although she'd seen him around the ballpark, she'd gone out of her way to avoid him except for when on camera. For his part, he'd asked her a few polite questions about the car repairs and once about her cat, but he seemed just fine with not talking to her beyond that. She tried not to let it hurt—*she* was avoiding *him*, after all, so she couldn't be upset if he was doing the same, any more than she could be upset that he was no longer talking to Duckie after making his position on the whole anonymous thing clear. But that was the problem about feelings. You couldn't just will them away with logic.

There had been way too many close calls that last day when he'd driven her to the ballpark. The more time they spent together in person, the more she questioned what she'd told him as Duckie, what she'd told him as Daphne, what he'd told her, when she'd mess up and say something that would give the whole thing away. So the less they interacted, the better.

She missed it, though. She missed his texts. She missed *him*.

It didn't help that all she'd been doing for this segment was *talking* about him. Now she was in the clubhouse with the camera crew, sitting down to talk to Randy Caminero about the song he'd choose for Chris.

"What kind of guy is Chris Kepler?" she asked, a question she'd tossed out to all his teammates she'd interviewed so far. The answers had mostly been variants of "quiet," "thoughtful," "steady." They'd talked about his work ethic, how seriously he took the game. He was generally well thought of by the team. She wondered if he knew that.

"Chris!" Randy said now, his eyes lighting up. "That's my boy, for real. He's . . . what can I say about Chris, man. When the benches cleared last week, he was the first one there and the only one who could've held me back from a fight. He's a good friend. Sometimes he comes across as reserved, but he's kind of an open book, you know?"

She actually wasn't sure she *did* know. In her experience, Chris seemed to keep large parts of his life to himself. "What do you mean?"

"I've just never met anyone who cares more than Chris Kepler. About the game, about other people, you name it, he genuinely cares. Unfortunately, he apparently doesn't care enough about his dignity to pick his own walk-up song, so I gotta go with—"

They had to cut Randy's first choice. And second. And third.

"This will air at *twelve thirty* on a Sunday afternoon," Daphne said, laughing so hard she could barely get the words out. "Kids could have a mouthful of peanut butter and jelly, asking, 'Dad, what does WAP mean?'"

"So we're promoting bonding and communication," Randy said. "What's the problem?"

"And sex ed, apparently," Daphne said, wiping the tears out of her eyes.

Just then, Chris walked in the clubhouse, glancing between the two of them before looking at the camera guy.

"Sorry," he said. "I can come back."

"No, no," she said. "Stay. Randy and I were just talking about—"

She'd been about to say *your walk-up song*, but Randy cut in before she could finish.

"—Sexual pleasure," he said, giving Daphne a wink. "Hers, in this case."

"Not *mine* specifically," Daphne said, aware of how that sounded. "Just the woman's in general."

That didn't sound much better. She didn't know how Randy got away with saying such outrageous things, but somehow he did. Even now, she didn't feel threatened or uncomfortable with his blatant innuendo. There was a friendly vibe to it, like they were just joking around, not that there was anything *actually* sexual about what they were talking about.

The minute Chris had walked in, on the other hand . . . suddenly the whole topic felt charged. She couldn't forget the time they'd both come while on the phone together. And she still hadn't forgotten the way it had sounded when he'd said that word in his car. *Pussy.* Just thinking about his voice wrapped around those two syllables . . . well, she'd barely had to use her vibrator for more than a couple minutes.

"We're almost done here," she said now, hoping her voice sounded crisp and normal. "I've already spoken to several other Batteries players and staff. After that, we'll get off a quick interview with you and then . . ."

She noticed both guys were staring at her. Randy seemed like he was trying to hold back a grin but doing a terrible job of it, and finally he stood up, slapping the camera guy on the back. "Let's leave them to get off that interview," Randy said, the almost imperceptible pause he put before the last two words still ringing in the room after he and the camera guy left.

"What?" she asked.

Chris' cheeks were streaked with a noticeable slash of pink.

"Uh, you said *Batteries*." He cleared his throat, his gaze lifting to hers. "Instead of *Battery*."

Now it was her turn for her cheeks to heat. Any other time, she could've played it off as a minor flub, an error that she knew happened all the time to Battery players and they'd learned to take with good-natured humor. *That's what we get for being the only team without a plural s name*, she'd heard the outfielder Beau say, to which catcher Kendall would say, *What about the Red Sox? The White Sox?* and Beau would hiss, *Red socksssssss, come on, you hear it, same difference.*

It would've been a little embarrassing, given that she was the team reporter and shouldn't make such an obvious error, but whatever. She'd live with it.

But given how red her face probably was, the way she was only now hearing the way she'd said *we'll get off a quick* . . . No wonder Randy had left with that parting comment.

"Whoops," she said faintly.

"It happens," he said. "One guest commentator got through two whole innings on *Sunday Night Baseball* before anyone thought to correct him."

With that, he signaled that he was going to treat her mistake like it *had* been a run-of-the-mill verbal mix-up, which she appreciated. She should've taken that as her cue to shut up, but for some reason, she couldn't stop the words coming out of her mouth even as her brain looked on in aghast horror.

"Obviously I wouldn't use anything with *batteries*," she said. "I live in the modern era. All my toys are rechargeable with USB." That made it sound like she ran a veritable sex shop out of her tiny apartment. "Not *all* like I have a million or anything like that. I mean like a couple. That are rechargeable. And then, um, one that's . . ."

She trailed off. Her brain had completely given up on her, gotten a new identity and was somewhere down in Mexico.

". . . analog."

He took a step closer to her. "Why are you telling me this?"

"That's a great question," she said. A prickling heat had started to spread over her limbs, making her want to sink back down into one of the chairs, but something made her stand her ground. "I have no idea."

His fingers brushed her skirt, causing the gauzy fabric to flutter against her skin. She could imagine the pressure of his hand at her waist, the firm way he'd hold her, and she swayed slightly toward him.

But the kiss never came. Instead, he pulled back, shoving his hands in his pockets.

"I, uh." His hazel eyes were dark as they briefly met hers, before he looked away. "I gotta go."

And she was left standing there in the clubhouse by herself, wondering what the hell had just happened.

CHAPTER
TWENTY-THREE

CHRIS ACTED TOTALLY NORMAL WITH DAPHNE IN THE DAYS AFTER what she started to think of in her head as, alternately, *the day I made a complete ass of myself* or *the day Chris Kepler almost kissed me I'm positive of it*, depending on what time of night she was lying awake thinking about it. He was professional; he answered her interview questions; he gave her a smile and a nod if they passed by each other in the clubhouse. Really, she could have no complaints.

She had complaints.

Something had happened . . . right? The air around them had been so charged she'd been surprised she didn't get a static shock when he'd touched her. But then his touch had been so light, a mere whisper of his fingertips on her skirt, that sometimes she wondered if she'd imagined it. Sometimes she felt like she was walking around still waiting for that electricity to neutralize.

And she thought there had been something else building between them, something close to friendship. But was that real, a genuine rapport that developed in the, what, two times he'd given her a ride? Or was that just her projecting because she *had* been friends with him back when she was texting him as Duckie, a friendship that she'd completely fucked up?

A friendship that had definitely been more than that. A friend-ship that she missed.

Now, they were on the road in Minnesota. It was Daphne's first time traveling with the team, and her duties were lighter on the road, because she still reported on injury updates and did postgame interviews with the players, but she didn't have as much to do with the main broadcast. Today's game had ended by late afternoon and tomorrow's didn't start until almost twenty-four hours later. It would've been the perfect opportunity to go out and explore a little, take advantage of this rare chance she had to travel to all these cities she'd never been to.

Instead, she'd stayed in her hotel room all day, reading, until finally she realized she'd barely eaten. She pulled on an old college sweatshirt to disguise the fact that she wasn't wearing a bra, slid her feet into some flip-flops, and made her way down to the hotel bar to see if it was still serving appetizers.

She stopped short when she got there. She had no idea what the players did during any downtime in between games—bench-press more? Look at a clipboard with some *x*'s and *o*'s scribbled on it and talk strategy? Go out and try to find a way to blow off steam?

She'd imagined Chris doing all of those things—okay, she was pretty sure the *x*'s and *o*'s thing was more football, and she didn't *like* to think of the ways he might be blowing off steam, but the bench-press fantasy wasn't too bad. Still, in all her speculation she'd never thought he'd just be . . . sitting at the bar. Alone.

He seemed to be reading something on his phone, his elbow on the counter, his cheek against his fist as he scrolled through the phone with his other hand. Once whatever he was reading made the corner of his mouth twitch slightly, and that was when she realized she'd just been standing there, staring at his profile like a weirdo. She slid onto a barstool at the counter perpendicular to his—if he looked up, he'd surely see her, but she wasn't about to take the seat next to him or disrupt whatever solitude he was looking for.

"Get you anything?" the bartender asked, sliding a napkin and a bowl of nuts toward her.

"Oh," she said, realizing she'd barely had time to think about what she wanted. "Just a Coke to drink. Do you have, like, chips and hummus, anything like that?"

"We have spinach dip."

"Okay," she said. "That's fine. I'll take one order of that, please."

The bartender reached over to snag the paper menu that had been sitting right in front of Daphne the whole time. She didn't know how she hadn't noticed it, and wondered now if there was something else she should've ordered, something more filling than chips and dip, but she also knew she wasn't about to call the bartender back. She was chewing on her lower lip, trying to think about what to do, when she glanced up.

Chris was looking right at her.

She lifted her hand in an uncertain wave, feeling like a massive dork the minute she did it. She really hoped he didn't think she'd come to the bar specifically because of him—how was she to have known he'd be down here? But he just stood up from his stool and picked up his glass, gesturing toward the seat next to her with a *do you mind?* type of expression. She shook her head before worrying that made it look like *no, don't sit here* instead of *no, I don't mind,* so she patted the seat next to her in a move she knew would haunt her until the end of time. *Such a dork.*

"You're up late," he said.

"Ten? That's not that late."

He made a noncommittal noise, replacing the soggy napkin that had stuck to the bottom of his drink glass with a new one. A

highlight from the game earlier that day briefly popped up on
SportsCenter on the TV above the bar, and Chris watched it, a
slight tic in his jaw the only sign that he had any reaction at all to
the image of Beau face-planting in the middle of centerfield trying
to make a catch that had cost them two runs. The program headed
into a commercial break, and still Chris only sat there, idly stroking the condensation on the side of his glass with his right middle
finger.

"Who's your best friend on the team?" she blurted before she
even knew what she was saying. "Randy?"

"My best friend." He laughed, running his hand over his jaw,
but there didn't seem to be a lot of humor in it. She couldn't tell if
he was laughing at the idea that he had a best friend at all, or that
she'd phrased the question in such a middle school kind of way.
"Yeah, it would probably be Randy. He's a good guy. When he's
not pranking people or saying inappropriate things to the sideline
reporter."

So he *did* remember that brief incident in the clubhouse. Maybe
that knowledge was what emboldened her, or maybe she was just
at her absolute breaking point with Chris Kepler and his monosyllabic answers and polite little smiles, because she said, "Is there
any rule against players and staff dating?"

That got Chris' hand to still on his drink. "Why do you ask?"

She wished she hadn't. It wasn't like her, to be so *obvious*. She'd
been sincere when she told Chris during their text conversations
that she wasn't sure if she was ready to date again after her divorce. She knew she was fragile, that whatever capacity she might've
had to withstand being hurt had been depleted by the whole experience, and it might not refill again for a while. Maybe ever.
How did you rebuild your reserves against being hurt?

But then Chris had made his own feelings clear over text—he
was interested. In *her*. He'd wanted to meet her. And although

Daphne knew all the reasons that shouldn't happen, all the reasons it *couldn't* without her revealing who she was and the way she'd deceived him, she couldn't stop thinking about it. She hadn't felt as close with another person in a long time as the way she'd felt while she was texting with Chris. She missed that. She *craved* it.

The bartender brought her food, and she welcomed the interruption to busy herself scooping spinach dip onto a chip, taking a bite. Maybe she could get through the entire basket before she'd have to answer his question.

Chris cleared his throat. "As far as I know, it's technically allowed. You'd probably have to formally disclose it to someone. And you're not team staff, technically—you work for the network. But there are unwritten rules."

"Unwritten rules?"

He looked over at her, his expression as serious as if they were talking about a career-ending injury. "They're very important in baseball. Don't mention a no-hitter while it's happening. Don't steal bases if you're ahead by a lot. Don't watch a home run too long, *especially* if you're ahead by a lot."

"Don't date a member of the staff or broadcast team?"

"I'm sure that's in there."

Okay, so he wasn't interested in her. At least not this version of her, sitting right in front of him. And could she really be surprised? She was wearing her rattiest old clothes, her hair was probably a mess, and there was still the fact of their first meeting between them, where she'd heckled him and made him cry. She went to pop another chip in her mouth and dribbled some spinach dip on her leggings. So, yeah, she couldn't be surprised.

"Maybe it's different because you're only filling in on a temporary basis," Chris said. "I don't know. If you asked Randy to grab a drink after a game or something, I'm sure he'd be thrilled."

Daphne swallowed too fast, causing a sharp corner of chip to catch in her throat. She tried to wash it down with a big gulp of her Coke, but that only made it worse, and it was a couple excruciating minutes of coughing in between taking smaller sips before she was able to recover enough to say, *"Randy?"*

She'd given him the thumbs-up during her coughing fit to let him know she was okay, but he still looked concerned. "Yeah," he said. "He told me once he thinks you're cute. If that helps."

And she thought Randy was objectively adorable, but she would no sooner think of asking him out than of dating her brother. "I'm not interested in Randy."

His middle finger was back to doing circles on his drink, and he was staring at the glass like he could put a hole in it. "No?"

She had the sudden urge to laugh, and she tried to hold it back, knowing it was an inappropriate response to the situation. But turns out ten *was* kind of late, she was exhausted, she was in a brand-new city where she'd only seen the inside of a ballpark and this hotel, and now she was propositioning a guy at a bar—not just any guy, but *Chris Kepler*—which she'd never done before in her life and would never do again after making such a mess of it this time. She needed to go. Take her chips and dip back up to her room, or leave them, whatever, anything to get out of the awkwardness of this moment.

"I should probably—" she started to say, at the same time as Chris said, "There should—"

She paused, waited for him to continue. But he seemed to be doing the same for her, so finally she prompted him to go on. "There should what?"

He looked over at her, his gaze dragging over her face, her mouth, down her throat to her chest, where suddenly she was positive he could tell she wasn't wearing a bra. She felt her nipples tighten in response to that single sweeping look, and instead of her usual instinct to cross her arms over her chest, to hide away from the attention, she found herself sitting up a little straighter. Let him look. She wanted him to.

His eyes when they met hers again were hot, like he knew exactly what she was doing. "There should probably be some actual ground rules, if a player was with someone who worked with the team. Not just unwritten ones."

Daphne licked her lips. "Actual ground rules. Okay. Such as?"

"Probably easier if it's not made public," he said. "At least to start. Minimize any potential impact on either person's job."

"That makes sense," she said. "When it's work time, focus on work. Set some boundaries."

"Boundaries are good."

She thought about the actual logistics of sneaking around with him, the way her brother and Layla would react if they found out. Probably not well. Kim would reiterate all of her concerns about Daphne putting too much on the possibility of a relationship with Chris, which Daphne really didn't want to hear. It would be better if she didn't have to worry about that part of things, at least for now.

"Like maybe they should only be together when the team is on the road," she said. "So there's a clearer line."

"Exclusive?"

She snuck a sidelong look at him, trying to figure out how he meant the question. Was he asking because he *wanted* to be exclusive? Or because he didn't?

"Yes," she said finally. "But with an easy out clause. If either met someone else or the arrangement wasn't working anymore, they could end it. No questions asked. No strings."

When she'd entered the bar, she'd seen the light golden color of his drink and thought maybe it was some type of liquor. But now that she was up close on it, she could see the bubbles. She was pretty sure it was ginger ale. Whatever else you could say, they were both stone-cold sober while they were having this conversation.

"So just sex?"

Once again she wished she could decipher *how* he meant the question. She'd never had a casual relationship before. She didn't know if she'd know how to even have one. But Kim's words also echoed in her head, and she was scared by the idea of trying to make more out of it than it was. She didn't want to be the person face-planting in centerfield thinking she was going to make the catch.

"That's probably easiest," she said slowly, still thinking it through. "Friends with benefits."

She hoped he understood that it was as much about the friendship as it was about the benefits.

He scrubbed his hand over his face. "Don't get me wrong," he said. "I want to. God, do I want to—"

Daphne was so surprised by him breaking their little game, by that explosive use of *I*, that she almost missed what he was actually saying. But once she caught up, realized he was *rejecting* her, she felt her face heat and her heart speed up. Fight or flight kicked in and who was she kidding, she'd always choose flight. She wanted to be out of there as fast as possible. The only problem was she hadn't settled her bill yet.

"No, right." She tried to snag the bartender's attention, but he'd turned away to take another customer's order. "It would be extremely irresponsible. There's a reason it's frowned upon."

"It's not that, it—"

Finally the bartender turned around and Daphne was able to give him the tight smile and eye contact that hopefully was universal body language for *check, please!* Because thinking that Chris just didn't want to break any rules—unwritten or otherwise—

was vastly preferable to the alternative that he just didn't think she was worth breaking those rules for. She really didn't need him to *say* it.

She thanked the bartender as she added the tip and signed the receipt. There were still about half of her chips left in the basket, and it felt like a damn shame to walk away from them, but she didn't have much of an appetite anyway.

"Wait." He reached out to touch her arm, before drawing back, his hand clenched. "It's nothing to do with you. It's me. I'm all f—" He swallowed whatever he was about to say, then set his hand next to hers on the counter, their pinkies almost touching. "There's someone else."

Whatever she'd expected him to say, it wasn't that. "You're seeing someone else?"

"Not exactly," he said. "No. I'm not. It's over. Or it wasn't anything. I don't know."

He ran an agitated hand through his hair, leaving it sticking up a little in the back. It was so rare to see him ruffled in that way; she almost wanted to run her own hands through it, smooth it back into place. If the whole thing wasn't so sad, it would almost be hilarious. He was turning her down because he was still hung up on someone else— only that someone else was *also* her. She was touched that he would be so loyal to someone he'd never even met, someone who'd ended it almost a month ago. She was sick inside from what she'd done, this impossible situation she'd created with her own deception.

"It's fine," she said. "You're right, it's late, I'm tired, I guess I was—" The word *lonely* stuck in her throat, too pathetic to speak out loud. It also would make it sound like that was the only reason she'd wanted him, as some last-ditch companionship, when there was more to it than that. More that she couldn't even express, because he didn't know.

She gave him a smile that she hoped came across as genuine. "I'll see you tomorrow at the game. And don't worry, I won't—" She started to say that she wouldn't make it weird during any interview, but that should go without saying, surely? Eventually she'd get over the mortification of this night. She needed to just finish out the season, keep Layla's seat warm, and then go back to her regular life where she didn't have to think about the rules of baseball, unwritten or otherwise.

"Daphne—" he said, but she was already turning away, hoping she could make it out of there before she did something to make it even worse, like start to cry.

CHAPTER
TWENTY-FOUR

FUCK. THAT HAD NOT GONE ANY WAY THAT CHRIS WANTED IT TO.

When he'd spotted Daphne in the bar, his first instinct had been that he wanted to talk to her. She had a way about her that was easy to talk to—she had kind eyes, an open and honest face. But then when he'd actually sat next to her, he found himself all tongue-tied, barely able to come up with the blandest thing to say, something about what time it was.

He'd thought she was interested in Randy at first, and that's why she was asking him about dating policies. The very idea had sent a jolt through him so strong it had taken him aback. Something like jealousy. Something like *mine.*

Which was unexpected on so many levels. For one, Chris couldn't remember feeling that way even about women he'd been actively dating. He'd always been laid-back in relationships—he knew his schedule didn't leave a lot of time for someone else in his life, and he'd always been careful not to promise anything he couldn't deliver.

And then there was the matter of Duckie. She lived in his phone, in a text message exchange that was already time-stamped over three weeks ago. For all he knew, she wanted nothing to do with him. Meanwhile, Daphne was *right there*, standing in front of him, and he'd turned her down. He'd hurt her.

"Another?" the bartender asked, gesturing to Chris' glass, which was now more melted ice than ginger ale.

Chris stood, grabbing a few bills out of his wallet and laying them down without even looking at them. From the bartender's expression, he could tell it was way too much, but he didn't care. He'd once rounded the bases for an in-the-park home run in less than fifteen seconds. He had to hope it was enough to catch Daphne before it was too late.

CHAPTER
TWENTY-FIVE

THE DIAMOND-PATTERNED CARPET WAS SWIMMING IN FRONT OF Daphne's vision, and she angrily swiped at her eyes before any tears could fall. She just couldn't believe she'd been so *stupid*. She never put herself out there like that. Never. And now she remembered why.

She stepped into the elevator, frustrated when it took her several tries to get the door panel to light up from scanning her room key card. The doors were starting to close when she saw a blur of motion outside, and normally she would've hit the *door open* button, tried to hold the elevator for whoever needed on, but tonight she wasn't in the mood to share space with anyone. She tucked herself into the corner, hoping they wouldn't see her, but then a hand shot out to stop the doors from closing.

It was Chris. He was breathing hard, his chest rising and falling, a single lock of his hair stuck to his forehead with sweat.

"What—" she started to say, but she didn't get the words out before he took her face in his hands and kissed her.

And oh, did he *kiss* her. It was a toe-curling kiss. A just-got-back-from-war kiss. His fingertips were at her jaw, and he tilted her face up to claim her mouth, his tongue sliding along the seam of her lips until she opened up for him. He backed her against the mirrored wall of the elevator, and she was only dimly aware of the door closing behind them, cocooning them inside the small space. She gripped his biceps like she was about to fall over, even though there was no fear of that, not with the way he was holding her. His hands slid down, grasping her waist as he leaned into her ear.

"I *do* want you," he said. "I think I've wanted you from the first moment I saw you."

"Not the *first* moment," she said, her voice coming out a little breathless.

"During that first interview, then," he said, palms warm on her rib cage, skimming the undersides of her breasts. "The way you tucked your hair behind your ear." His large hands were fully cupping her under her sweatshirt now, and he groaned as he rubbed his calloused fingers over the taut buds of her nipples. "*Fuck.* I knew you weren't wearing a bra."

"I knew you were looking." She pulled him back down for another kiss, her tongue swirling with his in a hot, wet joining before he moved to press openmouthed kisses to her throat. Briefly she got a glimpse of herself over his shoulder in the mirrored wall of the elevator, and she barely recognized herself—her eyes glazed, her curls sticking up in every direction, her mouth swollen and raw.

They were still entangled with each other when the door opened on her floor, then closed again when they didn't move apart. He reached around her to push another button. "My room," he said.

She didn't care where they ended up. Despite the fact that they'd just discussed the need to keep any relationship private, despite the fact that there were almost certainly cameras in the hotel elevators, she found she couldn't think straight enough to worry about any of that.

Except—

"Won't there be a lot more traffic with the team all hanging around?"

He considered that for a second before reaching around her again to press the original button for her floor. He didn't have to crowd her to do that, but he seemed to want to stay as close as possible, one hand still under her shirt, the other pulling her back for a quick, hard kiss before the doors finally opened again.

"I don't know who else has rooms on this floor," she said against his mouth. "But what if—"

She gave a little squeak as he scooped her up, one arm under her knees and the other wrapped tight around her shoulders. "We'll say you rolled your ankle," he said.

"Wait, really?"

He grinned down at her, and it was such a happy, open expression. She didn't think she'd ever seen it on his face before—in pictures, maybe, but never in person. It made something tighten in her chest.

"No, not really. They'd see right through that. We'll just have to be fast."

And with that, the doors opened, and he started heading right before she'd had a chance to tell him her room number, laughing when she corrected him and he turned around toward the correct door. She reached down into the side pocket of her leggings, extracting her key card and waving it in front of the door until she saw the green light come on.

They were barely in the room before he'd laid her down on the bed, pushing her sweatshirt up so he could kiss her bare stomach, run his tongue along where her lower breast started to curve, take her nipple in his mouth. She gasped, arching up into him as she pulled him closer, her hands finding their way to the bunched muscles under his shirt.

"I want to worship you," he groaned against her breasts, the day's worth of beard on his jaw abrading the sensitive skin in a way that made every nerve ending fire.

"Worship me next time," she said. "Tonight I just want you to fuck me."

He had her leggings and underwear off in record time, and she pulled her sweatshirt over her head while he dealt with his own clothes. She should've felt self-conscious about being fully naked in front of him, so starkly, so suddenly, but she could only focus on *his* body, the flat planes of his chest and stomach, his thick muscular thighs. She'd already felt the hard jut of him when he'd slid her down his body, but now that she was seeing his erection up close, she couldn't help it. She was a little intimidated. It had been a long time.

"Wait," she said, the word coming out instinctively, before she even had the chance to think about what she was saying.

He kneeled down by the bed, settling between her knees. "We don't have to do anything," he said. "We can stop."

"I'm sorry," she said. "I—"

"Don't apologize." He squeezed her thighs, and even that— more of a comforting gesture than a sexual one—made her tremble. "What do you need?"

She gave a little laugh, throwing her arm over her eyes so she could temporarily block everything out, pretend she hadn't just delivered one of the hottest lines she'd ever said and then immediately ruined it. Not that they *had* to have sex—she knew that. But she genuinely wanted to. She wanted it so much that she'd now well and fully freaked herself out.

"I think I talked a big game," she said. "I've never—ah, I know this is *such* a line, but I've never done anything like this before. I just need a minute."

"Daphne, we can take all the time in the world. It doesn't have to be tonight. Or it doesn't have to be at all, if you want to back out of our deal. No strings, remember?"

Of course she remembered. She'd been the one to suggest it, and she was also the one who didn't even know how that would work. She was already proving herself singularly terrible at it.

Chris leaned forward to grab something off the bed, and the way his body heat suddenly overwhelmed her, the close proximity of him to where she lay splayed and open . . . when he held up her sweatshirt, she just blinked at it for a second, unable to compute what she was even looking at.

"Did you want this?" he asked. "Or to get under the covers?"

He must've seen that she was feeling vulnerable, and wanted to help her. It was such a sweet gesture that Daphne felt the brief sting of tears at the back corners of her eyes, but she really didn't want to cry. She knew if she cried, it would *definitely* be over, and she wasn't ready for it to be over.

She shook her head. "I like when you look at me. I like when you touch me."

Something flared in his eyes, and he gave her thighs another squeeze, this one decidedly more sexual. "I like to look at you," he said, and she felt a pulse between her legs as his hot gaze landed right on the core of her. His hands were higher now, his thumbs pressing into her hip bones as he nudged her legs a little wider. "I like to touch you."

"That's good," she said, her voice coming out a little choked. "It's always good when interests align."

"Mmm," he said. "Can I taste you?"

Even the way he asked the question had Daphne wanting to clench her thighs together with the sudden desire that shot down her spine. Oral sex wasn't something she'd ever gotten particularly comfortable with—it always made her feel self-conscious, and since she'd never come that way it felt like a lot of embarrassment for nothing.

"Let's save that," she said, guiding his hands up to her breasts. She left her hands on his even after he'd cupped both soft mounds, liking the way it felt, that contact. "For now, this is enough. I've gotten off to thinking about you looking at me like this."

"Really?" He looked adorably surprised, and she almost laughed.

"The last time I used my vibrator," she said, "I imagined you watching me."

"I have given a *lot* of thought to your vibrator." He rolled her nipples under the pads of his thumbs, causing her to moan. "And what did you mean by one being *analog*?"

"Ah," she said, squirming a little under the delicious pressure of his fingers. She couldn't help but think of the way he'd stroked circles on his glass down at the bar, wonder what it would feel like if he did that to her clit. "A dildo. It's—"

She started to say it wasn't very big, that she'd barely used it, but she couldn't believe she was talking about her sex toys at all.

"Christ," he said, sounding genuinely pained as he pressed his face into her stomach, breathing her in. "I'll definitely be getting off to thinking about *that*."

She bit her lower lip, running her hands through his hair. Maybe she couldn't believe they were *talking* about her sex toys when they could be doing something else. "I brought my vibrator with me," she said. "It's in my suitcase under some of my clothes, in a black drawstring bag."

He looked up at her, as if confirming what she wanted him to do, before crossing the room to lean down over her open suitcase. It wasn't fair, how good his body was. She knew he was an athlete, that at some point working for that body was his literal job, but she still thought an ass shouldn't be allowed to be that tight. And at the same time, there was something almost vulnerable in the curve of his spine as he carefully moved piles of clothes to the side, something that reminded her that it was a privilege to see him this way.

And then he turned, holding up the black bag, and she got an eyeful of the front of him, too. It should definitely be illegal.

She pushed herself up so she was leaning against the headboard in the middle of the bed, reaching out for the vibrator. It was one she'd bought on a whim after seeing it in some themed listicle online for Valentine's Day, the first one when she'd been single. It was hot pink and had multiple settings she never bothered with, because she'd found a combo that worked for her and figured why reinvent the wheel.

"So what would you do," he said, turning the desk chair so it was facing the bed, and taking a seat. "If you were here alone."

She hadn't expected him to do that. She didn't know what she'd expected. She was so turned on she thought she might come the second she touched the vibrator to her clit.

"I usually start slow . . ." she said, switching it on and skimming it lightly over her most sensitive spot, her hips jerking automatically from the sensation. When she looked up at Chris, she saw his throat bob with a hard swallow.

"Yeah?" he said, his voice a rasp.

"Mmm," she said, pressing the vibrator against herself with more pressure, canting to the side to get a better angle. She hit a spot that she knew she had to back off from, or she'd definitely be done for.

He'd started stroking himself, and the sight of him doing *that*, his focused attention on her . . . it was better than any fantasy she ever could've had. But suddenly she didn't want him so far away.

"Come here," she said.

He slid onto the bed next to her, and she put her hand over his on the vibrator, guiding it exactly where she wanted it. "Oh, fuck," she said. "Right there."

"You like that?"

She tried to say *yes*, but it came out more like a whimper, and then he was holding her calf, pressing against her leg while he kept the head of the vibrator pulsing against her clit.

You have to be quiet—but I don't. She'd thought about him saying that on the phone so many times. She'd thought about what he would've said, if she'd let him talk. She didn't want to think about it now, didn't want to let the Duckie memories interfere, but it was impossible. It was all wrapped up together in her mind.

He took the vibrator away for a second, and she gave a frustrated sound that made him squeeze her calf, pull her toward him until he'd slung her leg over his shoulder, his hand sliding farther up her thigh.

"You have to let me worship you a *little*," he said, rubbing his thumb over her clit. She felt like every nerve ending down there was still buzzing from the vibrator, and the pressure of his touch almost sent her over the edge.

"Not yet," he said, sliding a finger inside her. "*Fuck*, you're so wet."

It wasn't long before he was using two fingers, then three, as he stroked her in slow, almost *maddeningly* slow, movements of his hand. Just when she thought she'd die if she didn't come, he reached around with the vibrator, his other hand still inside her as he pressed the buzzing sex toy to her clit. She tried to hold back, but she couldn't, and a ragged moan tore out of her throat as the wave that had been washing down her spine crested and broke, and she trembled and spasmed against him.

"That's it," he said, his breath hot on her ear. "Come for me, baby. Good girl. Come hard for me."

She felt like she was still coming, that heat in her body still sending off new sparks, but eventually she was able to get her breath back. He'd turned off the vibrator and stowed it next to the bed, and for a minute they just lay like that, him propped over her on his elbows, her holding on to his biceps and staring up into his hazel eyes and knowing that she didn't want to let him go, not just yet.

"Do you have a condom?" she asked.

"In my wallet," he said. "But do you—"

She didn't need rest. She didn't need to stop and think. Her body felt languid and golden and beautiful, and she wanted to live in the feeling as long as possible. She wrapped her hand around the back of his neck and pulled him down for a kiss. "Go get it."

Daphne barely had time to miss his body heat before he was back in the bed, his hard cock sheathed in a condom.

"Let me make sure you're ready first," he said against her mouth, kissing her as he slipped a finger inside her body. She was so wet, she could feel it—that heat, that easy slide. He had to know she would be, but he didn't seem to mind the excuse to touch her one more time.

And then he was pushing into her with his cock, filling her up inch by agonizing inch, until she couldn't stand it. She slanted her hips, wanting to take him deeper, faster.

"I can take it," she said. "Please."

He let out a harsh breath that almost sounded like a laugh. "*I can't*," he said. "Give me just a second. You feel so fucking good, Dee."

She didn't know if he was aware of it, the way he'd just shortened her name. She liked it. She liked it so much that she wrapped her legs around his strong thighs, rocking him against her until she could feel that he was all the way inside. And then she clenched those inner muscles, squeezing around him until he let out a hiss.

"That's how it's gonna be, huh?" He retreated enough that she felt bereft, but only for a moment, before he drove into her again and again, clutching her to him as he fucked her the way she'd asked to be fucked at the very beginning. That thin gold chain he always wore dangled down between them, and even that got her hot, the way it sometimes slapped against her chin as he moved inside her. She clung to his back, her fingers digging into the bunched muscles there in a way she knew would probably leave marks, but she didn't care. She hoped they would.

"Now I want you to come for *me*," she said, and that was all it took. Chris bit out a final curse as his body shuddered in her arms, and then his weight was heavy and hot on her as they lay still entwined, panting together.

Why did this part feel more intimate? Even after all that they'd done before? They were both covered in a sheen of sweat, her breasts flattened against his chest, and she was so close to his face she felt like she could count every individual eyelash. It wasn't fair, how long his eyelashes were. Chris Kepler as a physical specimen wasn't fair.

He seemed to be taking her in the same way, looking down at where their bodies were still pressed together, then glancing back up at her. She could've sworn she saw a streak of pink across his cheekbones, almost like he was blushing.

"I wondered," he said. "How far the freckles went."

Daphne looked down at her own body, which, yes, was covered in freckles. They were more faded and spaced out the more she got to the areas covered by a bikini, but they were still there.

"I could only see to right about"—he traced the tops of her

breasts with one finger, stopping at a point a couple inches above one nipple—"here."

"You're still inside me," she whispered. *And getting hard again.*

It wasn't a complaint, but he seemed to take it as one. "Sorry," he said, giving her a quick kiss on the forehead before rolling off her, leaving her feeling suddenly cold and empty. He grabbed the vibrator, holding it up like it wasn't still the most earth-shattering thing that had ever happened to her, this night in a hotel room with Chris and a sex toy.

"Soap and water?" he asked, and somehow she managed to nod.

He disappeared into the bathroom, presumably to take care of that and the condom. She knew she should use it directly after him, but she suddenly felt shy and exposed, still lying naked in the middle of the bed. Panic was starting to make her heart beat faster, and she tried to talk herself down from it, tried to tell herself that everything was going to be okay. So they'd just had sex. She'd wanted it. He'd wanted it. The sex itself had been amazing.

But *fuck* if it hadn't complicated things even more. She'd known that going in, but had ignored the little warning voice in her head, had convinced herself that whatever relationship they'd had via text was over so what was the harm in acting on the tension that was building between them in real life?

She slid in between the sheets, wishing she could get instantly warm.

TWENTY-SIX

THE ENERGY HAD CHANGED WHEN CHRIS STEPPED BACK OUT INTO Daphne's hotel room. He couldn't explain how or why, but suddenly any ideas he'd had about climbing into bed with her, going for another round either before or after they fell asleep, all seemed wrong to even think about, much less bring up. He supposed that was what they had talked about—a clear arrangement, on the road only, just two people who were obviously attracted to each other blowing off some steam.

"I should get going," he said, picking his clothes up off the floor. "BP is early tomorrow."

Daphne looked so small in the huge bed, the sheet pulled up to her armpits. "Of course," she said. "I'll see you then."

He yanked his T-shirt down over his head, shooting her a look. He was fully dressed now, but the way she was staring at him was like he was still stark naked. If he didn't get out of that room in the next two minutes, he didn't know that he'd have the strength to leave.

She flushed, as if realizing she'd been caught out. "I mean, I won't see you at batting practice. But after. When the game starts."

He had his hand on the door handle before he paused, turning back. "You know, we're in Chicago next."

"I saw that."

"Still on the road, technically."

She bit the corner of her lip, as if holding back a smile. He didn't know until then how much he'd needed that—some sign that things were okay between them, that they hadn't ruined whatever tentative friendship they might have by sleeping together.

"I've always heard Chicago is a really cool city," she said.

"It is."

She did smile then, her entire face lit up in an expression that took his breath away.

"Too bad we won't get to see much of it," she said.

BY THE TIME THE BATTERY HEADED BACK TO CHARLESTON, THEY were on a three-game winning streak, which would've been a normal sweep for another team but which felt pretty momentous for them after their season up to that point. Chris had never felt so amped up in his life, not just during the games but *after*, when he thought about how much time he had to spend doing the typical postgame routine of interviews, workouts, and food before he could show up at Daphne's hotel room door.

They'd had sex in the bed multiple times, on a chair, in the shower, against the wall. She'd given him a blow job in front of the mirror and just the image of her on her knees, his hand lost in the wild curls at the back of her head, had been enough to make him have to take care of himself the next morning, too. He never slept over, or even mentioned it—after that impulse the first night they'd been together, he'd figured that their arrangement couldn't be clearer. She seemed to want to keep it to sex only, like they'd discussed, and he . . .

He didn't know what he wanted.

The players jumped on a charter plane directly after their last night game in Chicago, while the broadcast team caught their own flights on a different schedule, which meant he never got the chance to say goodbye to Daphne before they left. He didn't know why that bothered him—it wasn't like they wouldn't see each other again, in less than twenty-four hours. But it did.

He checked his phone automatically once he was seated on the plane, although he didn't know who he'd be expecting a text from. He hadn't heard from his father in days—weird, how he heard more from the man when he was doing *badly* than when he was doing *well*—and of course Duckie had gone radio silent a while ago. It only just now occurred to him that he and Daphne had never exchanged numbers, which seemed like a colossal oversight.

Randy crashed into the seat next to Chris, jostling his shoulder as Randy leaned over to peek at Chris' phone screen. "Still talking to your girl?" he asked. "She sent nudes yet?"

Chris slid his phone into the front pocket of his backpack at his feet. "If you're not careful people will take you seriously and think you're an asshole," he said.

Randy let out that staccato-fire laugh he gave when someone in the clubhouse had come up with a particularly good roast, and Chris couldn't help it. It was hard to stay mad at Randy, even in a playful way, when he laughed like that. "Nah, but seriously, man. You're, like." He made some gesture with his fingers around Chris' face, which against all odds Chris actually understood. "Brillante."

Talking to Randy about any of it would be the worst possible idea. The man had all the discretion of a Times Square billboard. And yet.

"Have you ever had feelings for more than one person at the same time?"

"Hell yeah," Randy said. "When I was in the minors and

bumming around El Paso, I met these two chicks at the county fair and—"

"Never mind," Chris said. "Forget I asked."

Randy sobered up, like he finally understood that Chris was trying to have a serious conversation. "So you got your texting lady, and then you got . . . ?"

"I met someone else." Chris knew he had to be careful about what exactly he said. "In . . . real life, I guess. Not just over the phone."

Randy's eyebrows rose. "Do they know about each other?"

"I don't talk to the text one anymore."

"Oh." Randy pursed his lips, his eyes moving around the plane like he was literally searching for an answer. "So . . . no problema. Move on."

Right. When Randy put it like that, it seemed easy. And wasn't that what Chris had done? He'd moved on approximately nine separate times.

"Look," Randy said, gesturing at Chris' face again. "Whoever has you like *this*? That's the one."

Then he punched Chris in the arm, which took him by surprise more than actually hurt, but still Chris made a show of rubbing his bicep. Randy let out that staccato laugh again.

"Plus," he said. "You're actually hitting the ball for once in your sorry life. Whatever—or *whoever*—you're doing? Keep doing it."

TWENTY-SEVEN

DAPHNE KNEW SHE OWED HER FRIEND MORE THAN JUST A COFFEE for checking in on Milo while she was out of town, but that was all Kim would accept. "I'd say you could buy me a book," she added. "But you know I'm a Kindle Unlimited girl."

Daphne also knew that her friend would *die* for all the Kindle Unlimited–worthy highlights from her trip, but Kim's last words about Chris still rang in Daphne's head. *And you're stuck in another Justin situation where you worship the ground he walks on and he barely even thinks about you.*

She had to make sure she didn't let herself get too deep with Chris, that she didn't mistake it for more than what it was. They had agreed to have some fun together, hook up on the road only, no strings, that was it.

"We should be able to find you something here," Kim said, placing her coffee on a shelf while she crouched down to check out the Dating & Relationships section of the bookstore. "Jesus, they still sell *Men Are from Mars . . .*?"

"I think I'm good," Daphne said. She felt a twinge of guilt at not being more forthcoming with her friend. Normally she'd tell Kim everything. "Didn't you want to look at the stationery?"

Kim was a sucker for cute stationery, and so they spent almost an hour looking through the fancy notebooks, testing out fancy pens on scratch pads, and marveling at how much money it all cost. Daphne was trying to see if she could smell a Scratch 'n Sniff sticker set through the packaging when Kim held up a notecard set, looking suddenly shy.

"I'm thinking of trying to design this kind of stuff," Kim said. "Open an Etsy shop or something. You know I would've studied art if my mom had let me."

They'd been communications majors together in college, Daphne because she thought it was one way to get at what she wanted to do, and Kim because her mom had thought it would be more prudent to study something marketing-adjacent rather than artistic. But Kim had always had a knack for simple, eye-catching design. One of the casualties of Daphne's marriage had been a beautiful print Kim had made them as a wedding present, featuring the details of the day with a border of vines.

"I think that's an awesome idea," Daphne said. "You should one hundred percent go for it."

"Yeah?" Kim still looked a little uncertain, which was so unlike her normal brashness that Daphne rushed to assure her.

"*Hell* yeah," she said. "I'll be your first customer, but definitely not your last."

"You've inspired me, you know. The way you've really gone for it with this reporting gig. It's so cool to watch you do something you've always wanted to do, and kick ass at it."

Daphne didn't know if she'd go *that* far. "It's temporary."

"But you're making the most of it. Isn't that all you can do?"

A blue cover on the shelf had caught Daphne's eye as they walked by, and she stopped to pick up the book and turn it over to read the back. **Set in Italy during World War II, this is the story of the incomparable, malingering bombardier, Yossarian . . .**

"It's just an interim job," Daphne said, placing the book back on the shelf. "I can't get too attached to it."

ONE PART OF HER NEW JOB THAT DAPHNE *DIDN'T* LOVE WAS THAT Layla now wanted her to come over any night the team was off so they could run through film together.

She knew on the one hand she should be grateful. Layla had been reporting from the sideline for years and was a total pro. She had genuine insights into Daphne's performance that were helpful, not only for her current gig with the Battery but down the line, for any potential broadcasting job Daphne might want in the future. Which was the primary reason Layla gave for wanting to run through the film in the first place, although Daphne understood that Layla was also having a hard time giving up control, was bored and unsatisfied with just running the social media and feeding Daphne press briefings to inform upcoming broadcasts. All of that made sense. But some nights Daphne was just *tired*, and wanted a single day where she didn't have to think about baseball.

And this time, she had an extra layer of anxiety, because even though she thought she and Chris had done a good job so far of keeping their secret, somehow she worried that laser-eyed Layla would take one look at the two of them standing together in a postgame interview and just . . . know.

"See," Layla said, sitting forward in her bed and rewinding back over an interview Daphne had done with one of the Battery's starting pitchers. "You asked him how it felt to have command over the strike zone. But you'd already asked him how it felt to record season-high strikeout numbers. It's basically the same question."

"I know," Daphne said. "The minute I asked it I knew it was

stupid. I was just trying to look at the sheet and I think I saw *strike* twice and so . . . yeah, it was bad. At least no third strike, I'm out?"

Layla also never laughed at any of Daphne's jokes. To be fair, Daphne still wasn't sure if she'd hit her baseball humor stride. Look at how she'd gotten into this mess in the first place.

"You did a good job with this one, though," Layla said, trying to fast-forward the broadcast but struggling to get the TV to recognize the remote. Daphne was sitting in Layla's desk chair next to the bed, and she felt like she was on the edge of her seat while she waited to see what she'd done to actually warrant her sister-in-law's praise. Finally Layla held the remote over her head, moving it around until she'd scrubbed the footage to Chris walking over to Daphne on the sideline. She pressed play right as he stopped, his hands on his hips, looking over at Daphne.

He was so handsome in his dark blue Battery jersey, eye black still smeared on his cheeks, his hair damp with sweat. She could still *smell* him like he was right there next to her in the room. Somehow it was never a bad smell, even when he was at his grimiest after three hours of hard play. He just smelled earthy and real and like *Chris*, hints of the same scent she could roll over in the middle of the night and still smell on the hotel pillows. He smelled like *hers*. She couldn't think of any other way to describe it.

"Chris," on-screen Daphne said now, "you went three for four tonight. Describe what was going through your mind when you were up to bat there in the top of the ninth."

"Well," he said, grinning down at her, "my goal is always four for four. But yeah, after I struck out earlier I knew they might try to attack me the same way, high and inside—"

Daphne hoped Layla couldn't tell that she was blushing. The *four for four* bit had been a joke meant just for her, a reference to how many times he'd made her come the previous night. She'd meant to tell him afterward that he couldn't *do* that, that he was playing fast and loose with the keep-work-separate rule, but all the players had gotten an earlier flight and so she'd never had the chance. And the truth was, she wasn't sure she did want him to stop. She liked seeing that side of Chris, the one who joked and smiled at her like she was the only person who could make his eyes light up in that way.

Layla apparently agreed, because she jabbed the remote toward the TV. "*That* is good stuff," she said. "That's what I'm talking about. I don't know how you got him to open up more— god, he was always such a *robot* with me—but keep doing it. Seems like everything is cool after the whole heckling thing?"

"Um." Daphne didn't quite know how to respond to that. "Yeah, it's cool."

"And engagement is up with the walk-up song poll." Layla tapped something into her phone before frowning down at it. "Do you know why he deleted all his Instagram photos, though? It would be nice to have him posting some of this stuff."

It made me sad. That's what he'd told her when she asked. Or what he'd told Duckie, at least. She wondered suddenly what he'd tell *her*—Daphne, the sideline reporter, the woman he was hooking up with. Something told her it wouldn't be that.

"I don't know," Daphne said. "I don't really ask them about that kind of stuff."

"Well, see if you can get some info," Layla said. "Not on camera or anything—just mention it casually. You can tell him I was wondering since I was going to tag him in a few things, if that makes it easier."

"I'll try," Daphne said, which wasn't even her first lie of the night. It was starting to really bother her, how many lies she was telling. They were getting harder and harder to separate from the truth.

SHE WAS STILL REFLECTING ON ALL OF THAT WHEN SHE SHOWED up at the stadium the next day before the game, planning to clarify a few things on the press sheet with the announcers. But as she walked by the video room, she was surprised when she felt a hand at the small of her back, and Chris guided her inside before shutting the door behind them.

"What—" she started to say, before he spun her around, catching her at the waist as he pressed a long, hot kiss against her mouth.

Her knees felt like Jell-O by the time he pulled away, touching his forehead to hers. "Hi."

"Hi," she said, her voice a little shaky. "I thought—"

"I know," he said. "Road games only. I just never got to say goodbye to you in Chicago, so I figured . . ."

"You'd say hello to me in Charleston?" She tried to sound chiding, but it was hard when she was smiling.

He pulled his phone out of his back pocket, starting to type something in. "I also realized we never had the chance to exchange numbers, so—"

She took a step back, unable to hide her visceral reaction to the idea. From the way his brows knit together, she could tell he'd clocked it.

"Unless you don't want to?"

She could get a new number. That was literally her first thought—that she could go all the way down to the kiosk in the mall and get an entirely new phone. Or maybe she could get a burner from a gas station, wasn't that a thing people did? Or she could get one of those free internet numbers, where it rang through to her phone but had a completely different set of digits from the one she'd already given him as Duckie.

Those were all decent ideas, and she wished she'd thought of them before now. But as it was, it was too late to act on any of them—he was already looking away, sliding his phone back into pocket.

"It's not that I don't want to . . ." she said.

"It's cool," he said. "You're probably right. We don't need to—we'll always be at the same hotel. A *u up?* text would be redundant."

He started to open the door, and she stopped him with her hand on his forearm, blurting out the question before she could think any better of it. "Why did you delete all the pictures off your Instagram?"

He blinked at her. "What?"

"Sorry," she said. "I just—Layla was asking. Because she wanted to tag you in some stuff."

He stared down at her, and she almost kept rambling, unsure if he was even following what she was trying to say. But then he cleared his throat. "Social media is a distraction," he said. "I needed to focus."

And with that, he left.

TWENTY-EIGHT

"YOU'RE STILL IN YOUR HEAD," CHRIS' DAD SAID, REACHING TO grab the bat out of his hand. He got into his stance, demonstrating a slight hesitation before taking a big swing. "You see that? The hitch? You've still got a hitch."

Chris had about fifty different responses to that. He was a thirty-two-year-old man. He'd been playing in the major leagues for eight years. He'd been hitting *better* the last few games. There was an entire coaching staff whose job it was to advise him on his swing; they were aware of the "hitch" and had been working with him on it. A hitch wasn't always a bad thing. Lots of power hitters had a hitch. Pujols had had a hitch. And regardless, Chris wasn't a Little Leaguer who needed his dad to teach him how to coil.

But of course, his dad *had* been the one to teach him everything he knew about baseball. It was the reason Chris, who was right-handed, batted left. His dad was a leftie and it had been easier for him to demonstrate that way, so that was how Chris had learned.

His brother Tim had batted better from the right, actually, had been a viable switch-hitter all through high school. For some reason, Chris had never gotten the hang of batting from that side, even when it should've been more natural for him.

"It's a mental game," his dad said now, taking another swing. "You know that. It's *mental*. You gotta stop thinking, let your body do what it knows how to do."

If Chris had it in him to respond to *that*, he would've asked how exactly his dad recommended he just "stop thinking." He would've asked if that's what he'd done, if that's how he got through his days without thinking about Tim at all. But instead Chris just pulled the collar of his shirt up to wipe sweat off his chin, stepping out of the box in the makeshift batting cage his dad had constructed in his backyard.

"I'm going to grab a Gatorade from the fridge," he said. "Want anything?"

"Nah," his dad said, still taking another big hack with the bat at an invisible ball. He tapped the bat in the dirt, getting set again. "Actually, get me a beer."

The screen door leading onto the back porch squeaked a bit, the door with its own hitch before it closed all the way, and Chris made a note to fix that. His major league salary had bought this house, and that salary had also funded the back addition on it including this porch and the batting cage. He had no issues giving his father anything he wanted, money-wise. The man had raised him, had shaped him into the man and baseball player he was. He'd give him the last shirt off his back if he needed it.

But it was becoming increasingly difficult to feel like he was giving his father anything else that he wanted. Chris felt like he couldn't be as devoted a son; couldn't be as good a ballplayer; had obviously failed at being a brother.

There was a magnet on the fridge with the team's schedule on it, and Chris paused in front of it, finding that day's date on the calendar. He lived his life from series to series, week to week. Sometimes his dad was more on top of what he'd be doing a month from now than he was. It would be six days until the next road series.

Six days until he could be with Daphne again.

He couldn't deny it had stung when she didn't even want to exchange numbers. Admittedly, he'd never done a friends-with-benefits type thing before, but didn't that mean they could at least be friends? Friends texted each other sometimes. If he wanted to see if it was a good time to head over, if he wanted to check if he should order any food to bring with him, if he left something behind in her room. If he saw something that reminded him of her or that he thought might make her laugh.

Chris was still staring at the magnet, his eyes unfocused, when his dad came up behind him. "It's one of those old-fashioned fridges with a handle you pull with your hands," he said, reaching around to open the fridge and extracting their drinks.

"Sorry," Chris said. "I got . . ." He didn't want to say *distracted*. It would give his dad more fodder for the same broken record he'd already been playing all day.

Chris took a big gulp of the Gatorade, feeling the cool liquid slide down his throat without really tasting it. "Do you remember when Tim cut my hair that time?" he asked his dad. "I was what—three? Four?"

His dad used a bottle opener stuck to the side of the fridge to pop the top off his beer, taking a sip without making eye contact with Chris.

"We were playing with some kids down the street," Chris said. "They were chasing me. And Tim said if we cut my hair they wouldn't recognize me, that it would be a perfect disguise. That seemed so brilliant to me at the time. I thought, how lucky am I to have a big brother who knows how to hide me."

"He was messing with you," his dad said gruffly. "He did that when you were kids."

It was true. Chris could remember lots of times when Tim had played some trick on him, gotten him to believe that he was playing a video game no-handed when it was a recording, made him freak out that there was a frog in his bed when it was a toy. But that wasn't how he remembered this particular incident. It had really felt like it was him and his big brother against those kids, against the world. He would've done anything Tim said.

"Sometimes I feel like I'm still hiding," he said.

His dad grunted, tipping his beer bottle toward Chris. "You just gotta find your drive for the game again," he said. "It's gotten you this far. It can take you the rest of the way."

But that was the problem, Chris thought. The rest of the way *where*? To what?

BY THE TIME THE BATTERY WAS ON THE ROAD AGAIN, CHRIS HAD made several decisions. First, he couldn't do batting practice at his dad's anymore. It wasn't helping him; it hadn't helped him for a while. It was more for his dad than for him, and it wasn't a sacrifice he was willing to keep making.

He also realized he *did* care where he ended up next year. He knew the Battery wasn't the best team in the league, knew it was possible he was just prioritizing what was comfortable over what was best for his career. But he was invested in this team. He respected his manager. He liked living in Charleston, wanted a chance to really be a part of something in this community. "You're not giving me much to negotiate with," his agent had said when he called to tell her that he really wanted to stay out of free agency next year. "I trust you to help convince the Battery that I'm still an asset," he'd said. "Just do anything you can to keep me here."

The final thing he decided was that it was fine if Daphne didn't want to give him her number yet. He'd just have to earn it.

"Hey," he said, leaning into Daphne's hotel room once she'd

opened the door. She'd just gotten out of the shower, her hair still wet and smelling like vanilla, her cheeks all pink. She was wearing the hotel's fluffy white robe, her bare toes sticking out from underneath. She looked adorable, and he immediately wanted to kiss her.

She gestured him into the room, closing the door behind him, but she was backing away, holding the lapels of the robe tight at her chest. "Bad news," she said, and his heart dropped into his stomach. Was she okay? She didn't *look* sick, but . . . you couldn't always tell. Or was it something about *this*, about their relationship? Someone had found out, she didn't want to do it anymore, she'd met someone else.

She pulled a face. "The Red Sox are in town."

Automatically, he ran through his mental Rolodex of matchups and schedules, remembering that Boston had a big divisional matchup this weekend. "They're in Tampa," he said. And why would that be bad news either way?

Daphne rubbed her eyes with one hand, giving a self-deprecating little laugh. "Sorry," she said. "Trying out my baseball humor again. I just meant I have my period."

"Oh." It still took a minute for Chris to catch up. The only reason he could think of why that would be *bad* news was if they were trying to get pregnant, which . . . suddenly he had a flash of images of Daphne, her belly swollen, Daphne, holding a baby. His chest clenched with a sudden ache, and he felt almost desperate to think about something else, anything else. It was outrageous, to have those kinds of thoughts about someone he wasn't even in a relationship with. It was surprisingly painful, and he didn't know why.

She was looking at him now, and he wondered how long he'd been standing there, silent in the doorway. "I'm feeling kind of crampy and tired anyway," she said. "So it's not going to be a great night to get up to anything. This whole series, probably. Sorry."

Chris wanted to tell her that she didn't have to apologize. That despite whatever ground rules they'd established around hooking up, it had never had to be only physical for him. But he still didn't know how she felt about all of it, so he figured it was better to play this one with soft hands.

"Want to watch a movie?" he asked. "We could see what's on TV."

She hesitated for a moment before giving him a nod. "Sure. I have to finish with my hair, if you want to find something."

He settled in on the bed, grabbing the remote to start to flip through channels, but he kept getting distracted by her movements out of the corner of his eye. The room had one of those setups where the counter and sink were outside of the bathroom, and she had several products all laid out, spritzing her hair with a spray bottle before she put a dollop of cream in her hand and started spreading it through her curls.

"What's all that?" he asked.

Daphne turned toward him. Her robe was gaping a little bit now, showing him the soft swell of one breast, almost exposing the nipple. He meant it when he said he was fine with not doing anything that night. If he was being honest, he was pretty exhausted himself, his body achy from the late game the night before and the flight today. But what could he say, none of it turned off the way he reacted to her.

"It's the problem with curly hair," she said. "If I don't use the right shampoo, condition and moisturize it properly, get all the tangles out, it's a nightmare."

Chris loved her hair. He loved it when it was big and perfectly styled during the broadcasts. He loved it when she pulled it up in a loose bun on the top of her head with one of those elastic bands she always wore around one wrist. He loved it when it was sweaty and stuck to her neck while he was still buried inside her.

He tried to turn his attention back to the TV, flipping through channels without registering much of what he was seeing. "That must take a lot of time," he said.

"It can," she said. "But I kind of like that part. I didn't use to take care of my hair like this—I just used whatever products were on sale and sometimes I blow-dried it for a special occasion and that was about it. It was one of the things that made me the most nervous about being on television. I didn't really feel camera-ready, you know?"

Chris realized he'd never even thought about that part of this new job for her, how jarring it must've been to suddenly have to worry more about her appearance. He fixated on how he was playing, whether his glove had actually tagged an opposing player out at third before he touched the bag, whether he'd been stupid to take a big hack at a ball obviously in the dirt, ending up on one knee. He didn't give a lot of thought to how he *looked* on camera.

"You're always camera-ready to me," he said. "If it makes any difference."

He could see her smile at him in the mirror. "It's been a benefit to the job, when you think about it. I used to feel like spending too much time on your appearance was vanity, or just a waste when you could be doing other things. But now I see the ways that it can be really good, actually. To take a little extra care with yourself, to give yourself something that's just for you. After my div—"

She broke off, her fingers still caught in her hair where she'd been combing the cream through. Her eyes met his in the mirror, and she looked almost stricken.

"Go on," he said.

She gave a brittle laugh, scrunching her curls with one hand before she finally started putting the products back in a clear plastic pouch propped up on the counter. "I feel like I'm in an infomercial," she said. "Like I should be telling you all these products can be yours for the low price of nineteen ninety-five a month for twelve months. Sorry, this is so boring. Did you find anything good on TV?"

He turned his attention back to the television. Commercials, commercials, some religious programming. Then he stopped on a channel that was showing *Pretty in Pink*. The movie was almost over, Molly Ringwald already in her prom dress. *I'm Team The-Dress-Looked-Better-Before.* He changed the channel, letting it sit on a commercial for talking to your kids about drug and alcohol abuse, the child actor's *Love you, too, Dad* voice-over plugged in where his lips didn't even move.

"It's not boring," he said. "I'm interested. I don't know that much about you."

Once again, he had the impression that his comment somehow bothered her. She just gave a jerky shrug, then disappeared for a second before coming back wearing a white T-shirt, *Carolina Battery* across the front in script letters.

"I forgot to pack my pajamas," she said. "And so I grabbed the first thing I could find to use as a nightshirt while I was at the airport. You have to promise you won't laugh. Or get a big head about it."

"Why would I get a big head?" he asked. "You work for the team. You're allowed to wear the merch. Some might say you're encouraged to wear it."

She turned around, and he had to swallow at the way the hem of the T-shirt hit her at the thighs, her shapely legs bare beneath it. When she lifted her arms up to scoop her hair over one shoulder, he saw the briefest flash of her black panties. He was so distracted by that image that it took a second for him to register what she was trying to show him—his number 15 on the back of the

T-shirt in screen-printed numbers, his name across her shoulder blades.

He really shouldn't feel a possessive surge at seeing her wearing his T-shirt. But *fuck* if he didn't like it. Suddenly he found he was having all sorts of fantasies about just how much he liked it.

"Surprised you didn't get Caminero," he said when she turned back around. "We sell a lot more shirts with his name on it than mine."

"I know," she said. "I had to really dig through the racks for this one."

She was grinning at him, and he supposed maybe he should care about this reminder of his place in the organization, especially given his current contract negotiations where he was hoping to stay. But it wasn't anything new to him. And he found that he liked the idea that she didn't just pick up the *first* thing—that she'd gone through the piles of shirts until she'd found the one with his name on it.

"Come here," he said, not even waiting for her to fully climb in the bed before he grasped her around the waist and brought her onto his lap. He pressed a quick kiss to her temple before he started laughing, leaning his head against hers.

"You promised you wouldn't laugh," she said.

"The *Red Sox* are in town," he said. "Christ. Took me a minute, but that one's killing me."

CHAPTER
TWENTY-NINE

THEY ENDED UP WATCHING AN EPISODE OF *SEINFELD* AND THE LATter half of a movie where the whole premise was apparently that the two actors were the victim of some magic that switched their bodies, which was an extremely confusing scenario to come in the middle of. Chris had taken his shirt off at some point, and Daphne kept thinking about getting up to put some leggings on, but then she felt warm enough from snuggling up against his hard chest, his arm around her and resting on her bare thigh.

The credits to the movie were rolling, and she was in that blurry, half-awake state where she felt like everything was a little underwater. She thought she might've fallen asleep during the last ten minutes of the movie, which was fine—it wasn't like she'd been able to follow it anyway. So her reaction time wasn't super-fast when Chris suddenly asked, "Earlier you said *after my*, and then you never finished. After your divorce?"

Her heart was hammering in her chest. "My divorce?"

"That's what it sounded like you were about to say," he said. "Or something else?"

She supposed it couldn't hurt to reveal that one detail about herself. Lots of people got divorced, after all. It didn't have to connect her back to Duckie. "Yeah," she said. "I was just saying I tried to find better ways to take care of myself. After my divorce."

He was quiet for a minute, and she wished she could read his mind, know if he was even thinking of Duckie at all in that moment. "Why didn't you want me to know about that? I don't care if you've been married before."

"I know." Daphne pushed herself off him, scooting back against the pillows. "Or, I mean, I *should* know. But it still feels like an awkward thing to bring up. Sometimes it makes me feel like . . ." She caught his gaze, his eyes sympathetic but also very, very serious. She swallowed the word *failure.* "It's just awkward to bring up."

"Do you still have feelings for him? Your ex?"

His voice was matter-of-fact when he asked the question. For all she knew, he didn't care about her answer either way. But then he rubbed his hands along his thighs, almost like his palms were sweaty, and she thought maybe he did care. At least a little.

"No," she said.

He nodded, his Adam's apple bobbing as he swallowed. She should really leave well enough alone, because nothing good would come of bringing it up, running the risk of him connecting the dots, but suddenly it was bursting in her chest and she had to get it out. "What about you?" she asked. "Your someone else?"

Chris shook his head, giving her a smile that she thought was almost sad. "I told you, it wasn't really anything. Just someone I was talking to for a little bit."

Daphne hated that it hurt to hear him say that. She should be happy. The last thing she wanted was to know he was thinking about another woman while he was with her. But when *she* was also that other woman . . . she couldn't help it. It hurt to hear their relationship dismissed that way.

"I think maybe people come into your life at different times, for different reasons," Chris said, then smiled when he saw the dubious look on her face. "I know that sounds cheesy. But I mean it. I think I was meant to have someone to talk to at that time. I needed that. But it was a fantasy, you know? It ended up not being real. And now I'm grateful to have you in my life, and if it meant that you had to get divorced first, well, I'm sorry you had to go through that but I'm grateful it brought you here."

"You barely know me," she whispered. "You said it yourself."

He leaned back against the headboard, turning to look at her, his hazel eyes dark and sleepy as they traveled over her face. "I'd like to know more," he said. "But in the meantime, I know enough. I know that you're a hard worker. It's not easy, jumping into Layla's job and having to figure out the player personalities and how to convey so much detailed information in a short amount of time. I know that you care. You didn't have to help me with my walk-up song, or interview the team about me, but you did. Not just for a segment but because . . ."

This time when he swallowed, it looked almost painful, like he had something stuck in his throat. "My brother died at the beginning of this year," he said. "Just after New Year's. It was suicide. He—"

Daphne only realized tears were streaming down her face when Chris reached out to wipe one off her cheek. "Ah," he said. "Don't cry. It's okay."

She shook her head, wishing she could say something, wishing she could just *tell* him. Because right now she felt just about the most awful she'd ever felt in her life. She felt awful for him, for what he'd lost. And she felt awful about the fact that this wasn't even the first time he'd opened up to her about it, and of course he didn't know that. "It's not okay," she said finally.

He still had his hand on her cheek, stroking her skin with his thumb. "No," he said. "It's not."

"I'm so sorry," she said. "I'm so, so sorry."

"I've been thinking about him a lot lately," he said. "With the All-Star Game coming up. It wasn't a surprise when I didn't see my name on the ballot. I'm lucky I got my average up above the Mendoza Line, but it's hardly All-Star level. But I realized I'd always had this dream of going one day, not even for the game but for after the game. You know, when they show all the players on the field with their families?"

Daphne nodded, even though she didn't think she'd ever seen an All-Star Game in her life. She only knew what it was from press briefings she'd gotten about the one pitcher from the Battery who'd been picked to go.

"I always had this vision of being out there, having my dad with me, my brother Tim. And maybe Tim would have a kid. Maybe *I'd* have a kid. Tim was so funny, he could make anyone laugh, he would've made a great—"

Chris' face crumpled briefly, and his eyes were shiny, but he was holding his jaw very rigid, like he was willing himself not to cry. "Some people say suicide is selfish, but then I thought, how fucking selfish am *I*, that this is what I'm thinking about? A fucking All-Star Game. I don't care about a fucking game. What was all of this for? The World Series? Some stats? Money? I don't give a fuck."

He was so tense Daphne worried he'd break. She wrapped her arms around his shoulders, pulling him toward her. And when she felt his body start to rack with silent sobs, she tightened her grip, holding him as he clung to her like he was drowning and she was the only one who could save him.

"I should've been there more," he said. His voice was thick and muffled against her shirt, but she understood every word.

"He was obviously in a lot of pain," she said. "You couldn't have fixed that all by yourself."

"I should've tried harder."

She had to swallow against the lump in her own throat, not wanting to break down herself. "You try, Chris," she said. "You try so hard. It's who you are. But that's a lot to carry."

She held him until she could tell he was all cried out, stroking his hair and murmuring occasional responses to anything he said. By the time he drew back, his eyes were swollen and red, and there was a damp circle on her shirt.

"Sorry," he said, running his thumb over her taut nipple where the fabric was wettest. "Chris Kepler cried again, this time on the heckler's Chris Kepler shirt, a breakdown."

He smiled at her, and she returned it, although the expression felt shaky and false on her face. Why should it upset her, that he referred to her as the heckler? That's what she was. And there was a time when she thought she'd never be able to look at Chris Kepler without thinking about that moment, and feeling terrible about the fact that she'd made him cry, however unintentionally. But now she looked at him and saw so much more. She saw the man she was falling in love with. She saw the man she knew she was going to hurt, much worse than she could ever have done by shouting an insult at a baseball game.

"I'm tired," she said. "And I know you must be exhausted. Do you want to just sleep here? We can set an alarm for early in the morning for you to head back to your room."

"*Yes,*" he said, pressing an emphatic kiss to her forehead. "I thought you'd never ask."

THIS TIME, WHEN DAPHNE ENDED UP AT LAYLA'S HOUSE AFTER the road series, she barely let her sister-in-law queue up any footage from her interviews. She already knew what they'd be. She'd asked all the questions she was supposed to, there'd been a funny moment when Randy photobombed her postgame interview with the winning pitcher, Chris had looked a little tired, dark circles under his eyes that weren't just from the eye black but probably didn't even register on camera.

After that first night, he'd spent the next night in her hotel room, too. They'd managed to catch a replay of the exact same movie, only this time from the beginning so they spent most of the movie marveling at how much more sense it made now that they knew the actors were supposed to be playing each other. They ordered room service and found ways to work around her period and stayed up late talking. And by the time Daphne was on her flight home, she knew things couldn't keep going the way they were.

"I fucked up," she told Layla now. "I really, really fucked up and I know you're going to be mad at me but I need you to first just listen to me and tell me what to do."

Layla, uncharacteristically, looked so startled that she didn't say a word. She only stared at Daphne as she paced back and forth in front of Layla's bed, outlining what had happened from the night she DMed Chris to the night she ended things with him to the relationship they had now. She left out the salacious details—no need to fill Layla in on *everything*—and also kept Chris' revelations about his brother private. Otherwise, she laid it all out. When she was done, she was almost out of breath, both from the pacing and from the onslaught of words.

"Don't worry," she said, catching sight of Layla's shocked face. "I'm going to tell him. I have to. My plan is—"

Layla sat up in the bed then, clutching her belly even though she was only just starting to show. It occurred to Daphne that maybe she should've cleared Layla's health before she went into this whole saga. Her sister-in-law's face was all red.

"You absolutely will *not* tell him," Layla said. "Not until the season is over, at least."

Now it was Daphne's turn to look shocked. "But that's months away." They were barely into July—there were practically three full months left to go.

"And it's going to come a lot sooner if you tell him. For *you*, because honestly, you'll be lucky if you don't get fired. And for *him* and the rest of the team, because any long shot they might have at making the playoffs will be toast if he's all distracted and upset and bringing it into the clubhouse every day."

"But wouldn't it be better—"

"No." Layla cut her off without even letting her finish. "It would *not* be better. Look, what you did was—I don't even know. I don't know what would possess you to stay anonymous in the first place, and then I really don't know what would possess you to start a real-life relationship with the same person you catfished. That's some Theranos-level shit."

Daphne opened her mouth to protest—she didn't know if she deserved to be compared to a company that had defrauded investors out of millions of dollars—but she shut it again when she could see that Layla wasn't going to be interrupted.

"But you did it," Layla continued. "Damage is done. You can't undo that, but what you can do is *mitigate* it. Which means, for example, not fucking up the Battery's playoff chances because you're suddenly having a crisis of conscience."

Daphne knew from her reporting that the Battery was currently fourth in their division, but in a tight race. They'd have to improve their record post-All-Star break quite a bit from their record pre-All-Star break, and considering they hadn't gone to the playoffs in . . . Daphne didn't know the exact year, but it had been a long time. She had to admit that in anything she'd considered while figuring out what to do, she'd never once factored in the *playoffs*. She heard Chris' voice in her head, saying it was just a fucking game, that he didn't care.

But he did care. She knew that. And Layla had a point—any harm that had been done was already done. The last thing Daphne wanted was to make things *worse*.

She sat down on the edge of the bed, burying her face in her hands. "I never meant to hurt anybody," she said. "Not you, with your job, not the team, definitely not Chris."

Layla leaned forward to give Daphne's shoulder a squeeze. Coming from her, it was an unprecedented gesture of comfort, and Daphne almost lost it right there. But then Layla spoke, and brought Daphne right back down to earth. "I know you didn't, honey," she said. "But intention doesn't really matter in situations like this. It's only about the *impact*, and right now the best thing you could do is nothing. Let this meteor hit in the off-season, when he can deal with it. And in the meantime, he seems happy, he's hitting better, he hasn't made an error in weeks . . . is that such a bad place to be?"

Daphne shook her head, but the pit in her stomach said otherwise. It said it was absolutely the worst place to be. Sure, the meteor hadn't hit yet, to use Layla's metaphor. But she didn't know how you were supposed to just live your life, knowing that it was going to. Knowing it would destroy everything.

THIRTY

THE ENERGY IN THE CLUBHOUSE WAS RELAXED AFTER THE BAT-
tery's last game before the All-Star break. They'd won at home in
decisive fashion, which was always a good way to head into the
break, the team was at .500, which felt almost like a winning record, and everyone was excited to have a few days off.

Chris was trying to sneak out of the clubhouse early enough to
find Daphne before she left for the night, but Randy grabbed him
before he made it. "Hey, man," Randy said. "Cookout at my place
Tuesday for the game. Food's gonna be lit—I'm making my ma-
mi's mangú. You in?"

"Sure," Chris said. "Sounds good. What can I bring?"

"Just a case of whatever you like to drink," Randy said. "And
bring your girl, if you want. It's a family-friendly affair."

Chris wondered suddenly what it would be like to actually
bring Daphne. He knew he couldn't. But he already knew she
would get along well with all the guys—they seemed to have accepted her completely after she'd slid into Layla's role temporarily. He knew a few of the other players' wives and girlfriends,
Kendall's boyfriend, all who he thought would be good friends
with Daphne if they knew each other.

And it would be nice. To have someone to laugh in the corner with when Randy inevitably got a little toasted and started making outrageous predictions of what would happen in the game. To be able to casually touch her, a hand at the small of her back, a kiss on the cheek. To watch her across the room and know that at the end of the night, she'd go home with him.

But since that was impossible, he just grunted without responding to Randy either way. And then he grabbed his duffel bag and went in search of Daphne.

When he found her she was already in the parking lot, fumbling through her purse for her car keys. Other than their interactions on the sideline during the games, he hadn't gotten much chance to talk to her after the last road stand nearly ten days ago. If the situation were different, he almost would've thought she was avoiding him. But this had always been their deal—road games only, then back to keeping professional distance at home. He just hoped she was open to the idea of changing their deal.

"Hey," he said, catching up to Daphne just as she'd opened her car door. "What're your plans for the break?"

"Oh." She blew some strands of hair out of her eyes, giving a little laugh. "Sleep, probably. Lots of sleep. You?"

She did look tired. She was still beautiful—she was always beautiful—but now that she wasn't wearing all the makeup she wore for the camera, he could see that her eyes were shadowed, that there was something a little subdued about her.

"Come over," he said. He hadn't meant to blurt it out like that. He'd given a lot of thought to the most casual way to ask, and this had not been on the list. But he also found that he didn't want to play any games. He just wanted to spend time with her.

She hesitated, and he couldn't tell if it was an *I'm thinking of how to say no* type of hesitation or an *I really want to say yes* type of hesitation. He tried to channel all the casualness he'd lost from his opening gambit now, not wanting to scare her off.

"I got the stuff to make chicken carbonara," he said. "Don't make me go through all that trouble just to cook for myself."

She smiled. "There's always leftovers."

"You're right. We could probably eat it for lunch tomorrow, too."

This time when she looked at him, she seemed completely serious. Much more serious than a discussion about chicken carbonara warranted, that was for sure. Chris didn't know why, but he suddenly had the feeling that he was standing on some sort of precipice, and he could keep his feet planted on the ground or he could tip right over the edge. He held his breath, waiting to see which one it would be.

"Okay," she said finally. "Give me your address and I'll be there by eight. I just have to head home and take care of a few things first."

THAT TIME GAVE CHRIS THE OPPORTUNITY TO STOP BY THE STORE and grab the ingredients the online recipe he'd found told him he needed to make chicken carbonara. It had been described as "easy," "delicious," and "date-night worthy," so he certainly hoped all that was true.

The recipe also advised that you cut up the chicken and bacon beforehand, especially if cooking for the first time or for guests. "Thank you," Chris muttered to himself as he laid out everything on his counter. "That is exactly what I need to know."

He just barely had time to prep everything the recipe called for and to quickly wipe down the surfaces in the bathroom before he heard the buzz from the lobby that let him know Daphne had arrived. He buzzed her in and was waiting for her in the open doorway when she came up the elevator.

"Hi," she said, looking a little shy. She had a tote bag on one shoulder, the logo on it advertising the Charleston County Public Library. It was stuffed pretty full, a cardigan he recognized as one she'd worn before sticking out from the top. He hoped that meant she was definitely staying the night.

"Hey," he said, leaning in to give her a kiss. "Come on in. I'll give you the very brief tour."

She followed him from room to room as he showed her the dining area with the concrete table monstrosity, the bathroom, the spare room where he kept a stationary bike and some weights, his bedroom. Her gaze seemed to take in every detail of that last one, even though she only lingered in the doorway without coming all the way in. He tried to see it through her eyes. It probably looked really plain, with not much more personality than in the hotel rooms they'd been in over the past month. He'd left a pile of his stuff on the dresser—his wallet, his keys, his phone. There were a few books on his nightstand that he was still trying to make his way through. He wasn't the fastest reader. The art was better than a hotel room's, but it didn't say much about him, either—he hadn't picked it.

Her eyes landed on the king-size bed, and suddenly he couldn't take the silence.

"It came furnished," he said. "It just seemed easier at the time."

"It's nice," she said. "Much bigger than the shoebox I live in."

He thought back to what he'd seen of her apartment, that night he'd dropped her off and then the next morning when he'd picked her up. She'd lined her porch with potted plants, and he'd liked that cheerful, homey little touch. His place might be bigger, but something told him that hers *felt* better.

But she was here now, and he had a meal to hopefully not fuck up. "Make yourself comfortable," he said. "I'm going to get dinner started."

THIRTY-ONE

IT WAS STRANGE, TO BE IN HIS BEDROOM. DAPHNE HAD BEEN LOW-key avoiding him since they got back from the last road trip, still trying to figure out what to do about the whole double-identity mess. And now she was here, and all she could do was picture him reclining back in that same bed, texting with her.

There were a few books on his nightstand, and she let her tote slide off her shoulder, crossing the room to get a closer look. They were stacked in the opposite way from how she would've done it, the top book a heavy hardback covering a slimmer volume and then a book so small she couldn't see its edges peeking out at all. The hardcover was exactly what she might've expected from an athlete—a sports biography that seemed half-journalistic, half-inspirational. Underneath was a book called *The Tender Land: A Family Love Story*, a haunting black-and-white image of a boy in a striped shirt standing in a kitchen on the cover. Daphne went to turn it over, to read the back, but then she saw the book at the bottom of the stack and her heart stopped.

It was *Mandy* by Julie Edwards. The cover was so familiar to Daphne, she felt like it was engraved on her soul—that swing of chestnut hair, the hat hanging down the girl's back from a satiny black ribbon, that vibrant garden carpeted with clover and violets and daffodils.

She was sitting down on his bed, holding the book in her hand, when he came back into the room. "I just put the garlic bread in," he said. "So maybe a couple minutes. Did you want some wine or anything like that? I can't promise how well it'll pair with the meal. I don't know dick about wine."

"I have to talk to you," she said.

He gave her a crooked smile that made her chest clench. "You take your wine seriously."

"Chris."

His smile faded, and he came to crouch at her feet, fitting his body between her legs in a way that reminded her of that first night after the elevator kiss. It was hard to believe that had been only a month ago. It felt like a million years had passed since then. It felt like no time at all.

"Before you say anything," he said. "I just want to say that I *know* this goes against our deal. I know that we're breaking our own ground rules here. But we don't have to overthink it. We have a few days off, we're both together in the same city, I don't know about you but I could use the time to decompress. I don't want to think about the team's record, about my dad or my brother or a single bad thing in the world. I just want to hang out with you, laugh sometimes, have some fun, the showerhead actually has *great* pressure, that's it. Okay? It's as chill as you want it to be."

Everything he said seemed to confirm what Layla had told Daphne. The last thing he needed right now was some huge discussion that would derail this break, the rest of the season, who knew.

She smelled something acrid, and it took her a second to realize what it was. "The garlic bread," she said.

"What?"

She sprang up from the bed. "Chris, the garlic bread is burning."

"Oh, shit." He ran back into the kitchen, grabbing the oven mitt off the counter before reaching in to take the bread out. Sure enough, the tops were charred black.

"Did you have the broiler on high?" she asked, finding the button to turn off the oven.

"I thought that's how you got it crispy on the top but soft on the bottom."

He started trying to scrape the black bits off the bread, little flakes of char going everywhere, and Daphne couldn't help but laugh. "I think it's done for," she said, wrapping her arms around his waist and giving him a squeeze. He was warm and strong and smelled so *good*, and she realized that this was maybe the first time she'd ever made the first move to touch him this way, just a casual embrace out of nowhere. From the way he stilled for a moment, pausing for an almost imperceptible beat before bringing his arm around to rub her back, she felt like he'd noticed it, too. She could hear him swallow as he rested his chin on the top of her head.

"You wanted to talk," he said.

Right now, that was the last thing she wanted to do. "It's not important," she said. "Dinner looks delicious, and I would love a glass of whatever wine you've got."

AFTER DINNER, THEY SETTLED IN ON THE COUCH, AND CHRIS handed Daphne the remote. "I think I have most of the streaming services on here," he said. "I don't really know, to be honest. I'm not home that much."

She'd kind of figured that. The condo was really nice—he'd taken her out to the balcony, to appreciate the view, and the inside was light and airy and modern and she bet he'd never had to put a mixing bowl under the bathroom sink to catch leaks the way she did at her place. But it didn't feel very *lived* in. The part that felt the most *him* was the open Battery duffel bag she'd seen on the floor of his bedroom, and that was the same as what he would've had in any hotel room.

"You said your dad lives nearby?"

"A little further out in the suburbs," he said. "But yeah, not too far."

"Do you see him a lot?"

Chris didn't answer that right away. He was rubbing his right hand, something she'd noticed he did if they were idly watching a movie or otherwise relaxing. She'd thought maybe he did it because it was hard for him to keep his body completely still, but she remembered now what he'd texted her once, about how his hand hurt. She wondered how many different ways he hurt every day that he just didn't tell anyone about. She reached over to take his hand in hers, pressing her thumbs into his palm.

"Is this okay?" she asked.

He leaned his head back against the couch. "Mmmm. Feels good."

Daphne liked being able to watch him like this—his eyes closed, his lashes against his cheekbones. The sharp angle of his jaw, the exposed line of his throat. He'd taken off his shirt right after dinner, and now he was only wearing his necklace and a pair of gray sweatpants, which were somehow the sexiest item of clothing she'd ever seen.

She dragged her thumbs hard over the lifeline in his hand, and saw a tic in his jaw. "Sorry," she said. "I don't want to hurt you."

He opened his eyes then, looking over at her. "You couldn't hurt me."

There was something in his hazel eyes, not a flicker or a spark, but something steady and true that was almost painful to look at directly. She had to drop her gaze, giving an awkward little laugh to cover the moment. "I mean, I *could*," she said. "I'm not a professional hand masseuse."

"You're perfect."

She knew he probably just meant that she was doing a decent amateur job of it, but the sentiment still made her uncomfortable. "Oh, I have flaws," she said. "Lots of them."

"Sure," he said. "Everyone does. What do you see as yours?"

Dishonesty? Self-sabotage? She didn't know. "I can be incredibly stubborn," she said. "And not always in a good you-don't-give-up kind of way. Sometimes I just get something in my head and it's hard to let it go, even when I know I should."

He seemed to think about that one. "You're self-aware about it, though," he said. "Which means you can notice when you're doing it and course correct. Or if someone called you on it, you wouldn't be as defensive. I don't think that one's so bad. What else you got?"

"I have a tendency to idealize people," she said. "Maybe that goes hand in hand with being stubborn. I see what I want to see, and that's not always the healthiest way to be in a relationship."

"You're looking for the best in people," Chris said. "I think that's a generous way to be."

She paused in her ministrations to his hand, pulling a face. "One of *your* flaws is that you're shooting down all my flaws."

"Well, it's good to know you're not idealizing *me*," he said, then made an exaggerated expression of injury when she swatted his arm. "Whatever happened to *do no harm*?"

"I told you I'm not a professional," she said. "I signed no oath."

He laughed, watching her as she brought his hand back into her lap and continued her massage. "Was that what happened with your ex?" he asked. "You idealized him?"

That was *exactly* what had happened. Their split had been inevitable, and she knew it was as much her fault as his. For however dismissive he'd been of her, however casually cruel, she'd married a person who didn't really exist. And on some level she'd known it, and wanted whatever dream of a marriage and home and children she'd built up in her head so bad that she hadn't allowed herself to look at the way things actually were. She'd basically told him all of that already, as Duckie.

"We married really young," she said. "I just think we didn't know ourselves very well."

He was quiet for a moment. It was summer, the sun didn't set until late. When Daphne had arrived, it had still been bright outside, but now it was well and fully night, and probably had been for some time. She realized she hadn't even noticed the transition.

"One of my flaws is I get tunnel vision," he said. "I used to think it was a strength, actually. I can really focus. Take every at-bat pitch by pitch, start fresh every single play. You can't throw two balls at once, you know?"

Daphne frowned, not quite sure she *did* know. On a literal level, she understood. He seemed to register her confusion, and flexed his hand, giving hers a squeeze.

"It's a saying," he said. "Applies more to pitchers, really, but the idea is the same. If you throw a bad pitch, let it hang right over the plate, the guy hits it out of the park . . . that sucks, right? It's the last thing you want. But you can't throw that ball again. You can only throw the next ball, and if you try to throw both of them at once you'll only fuck up that next pitch, too."

"So you're good at getting rid of the first ball," she said. "Putting it out of your mind. That's what you want, right?"

"I used to think so," Chris said. "Or maybe I still do. I don't know. I feel like my tunnel vision used to be *too* narrow, that it shut everything out when I should've been paying more attention.

And now I've calibrated too far the other way, and I'm trying to throw about a million balls all at once."

They were talking about his brother, Daphne knew. But she also knew that Chris didn't really want to get into it, was already thinking of how to edge the conversation onto another topic. It was shocking sometimes, how good she felt like she was getting at being able to read his tells, to figure out when to push and when to let something go.

"One of my flaws is sports metaphors," he said. "Sorry. Part of the territory."

This was a time to let it go. "I think I'm learning to keep up."

"Oh, you're a *very* quick study." He grinned at her. "A baseball savant. Although I've been thinking about it, and why the Red Sox? Why not the Reds?"

"Are you workshopping my period joke from *weeks* ago? Count this as a fatal flaw."

"*Fatal?* Come on. I think about you a lot. That can't be a flaw."

That brought Daphne up short. For some reason, she'd never considered that Chris might spend as much time daydreaming about her as she did about him. Even as they'd been texting, even once they hooked up in real life, she'd just assumed . . . she didn't know. There wasn't much to think about when it came to her. *Not interesting or charismatic.* It stuck in her head, even if she knew Justin had been being an asshole. The most cocktail-party-story-fodder thing that had ever happened to her was when she'd been on *SportsCenter* for heckling Chris, which he'd be the last person to be impressed by.

Daphne wanted to commission an essay from him about that one sentence—*I think about you a lot.* She wanted to know every specific detail. But she also didn't want to come across as needy or desperate or insecure, even if she was feeling like all of those things. So she had to let that one go, too.

"Okay," she said. "You got me. You want to know your *real* fatal flaw?"

"I'm on the edge of my seat," he said.

She leaned closer to him, not intentionally brushing his hand against her breasts, but not mad about it, either. From the way his gaze dropped to her mouth, she knew he was as affected by that brief touch as she was.

"You can't do this," she whispered. He was still watching her mouth as she pursed her lips, letting out a bright, clear whistle.

A smile cracked over his face. "Oh, thank god," he said. "I thought you were going to say my abs."

"How can your *abs* be a flaw?"

"That they're so intimidating," he said. "Or so hot. I don't know, I'm insecure about my abs."

She ran her hand over the flat, hard plane of his stomach. "Sure," she said. "That's why you're always keeping your shirt on. You're obviously plagued with self-doubt."

"It feels good to be so seen."

"They could use a *little* more definition, you know," she said, tracing the outline of his muscle, liking the way he automatically clenched beneath even that light touch. "You should see some of the covers of my romance novels. Washboard stomachs, the lot of them."

"Is that so?"

"Mmm-hmm," she said. "Just trying to give you something to aspire to."

He leaned forward, grabbing something off the coffee table. She saw what it was only after he'd uncapped it and held it out to her—a black Sharpie.

"Show me," he said. "Draw me like one of your romance covers."

Daphne gave him a dubious look, like *are you serious?* But he was grinning at her, and she took the marker from him, surveying his body like it was her canvas. "Okay, I don't know what crunches or burpees or whatever are going to get you these results—that's not my area of expertise. But if you want a glimpse of the final product, you'll want it to look something . . ." She started drawing wobbly squares on his stomach in a rough approximation of a six-pack. ". . . like . . ." This was fun, actually, she was really getting into her artist's rendition. ". . . this."

She tried adding some shading in the lower corner of each square, but Chris almost doubled over laughing, sending the marker line shooting sideways across his skin. She frowned at him in admonishment.

"I can't be held responsible for what you'll look like if you mess up my blueprint."

"Sorry," he said, but spasmed in a sudden laugh again when she went back to her shading. "I'm ticklish there."

"I thought you were an athlete," she said. "I thought you took your conditioning seriously."

"I do, I do," he said. "Keep going. I don't want uneven abs."

She managed to shade all six squares, even though there were a few jagged places where the marker had skipped as he tried to hold back a laugh. When she finished, she reached for the cap, but he grasped her wrist to stop her.

"I should get to draw something on you," he said. "It's only fair."

THIRTY-TWO

CHRIS COULD FEEL DAPHNE'S PULSE JUMP BENEATH HIS FINGERS.

"I don't know how you're going to draw bigger tits for me," she said.

"Your tits are perfect," he said. "But if you're ever struggling with your self-confidence, try walking around shirtless like I do. It really helps."

She reached down to the hem of her shirt, her arms crossed as she pulled it over her head, the action mussing up her curls. He smoothed them out, giving one a tug as he dragged his finger down her cheek, her throat, the top swells of her breasts over her lacy red bra.

"You'll probably need to remove this, too," he said. "To give me more to work with."

She rolled her eyes, like he was being ridiculous, but he heard the ragged hitch in her breath after she'd unclasped her bra and let it fall to the floor. For a minute he just allowed himself to look at her.

Her skin was flawless. He could already hear her protest, if he told her that. She'd point to every single freckle and say *flaw, flaw, flaw*. But he loved her freckles. He loved the way her nipples tilted up, the faint stretch marks at the sides of her breasts, the way she fit his hands perfectly. Sometimes when he touched her he felt like he could die, and that would be all right.

"Now let's see," he said, assessing her with an exaggerated expression of intense concentration. "I think if I . . ." He braced one hand against her rib cage, using the marker to drag a curved line from one freckle to another on her breast. ". . . can just . . ." He connected two more freckles, then went outside the lines a little bit to preserve the shape he was creating. ". . . There we go."

He capped the marker up, sitting back to survey his work, and she looked down at herself to check it out. "It's a heart," she said.

A slightly lopsided heart. He'd been trying to stay as true to the freckle map as he could. Suddenly he felt self-conscious, like that was *his* heart he'd drawn right on her skin.

"It'll wash off," he said.

Daphne leaned forward to press a kiss against his lips. "I love it."

She'd clearly meant it to be quick, more a punctuation mark to her approval than anything else, but he slid his hand along her jaw and up into her hair, holding her there while he deepened the kiss. She opened her mouth with a little moan, a hungry sound that shot straight to his cock. Suddenly if he didn't touch her, he *would* die.

He pulled her onto his lap so she was straddling him, holding her hips down to grind her against his erection. He knew she could feel it, even through the fabric of their clothes, because he heard her sharp intake of breath when he thrust his own hips up into her.

"I could come just from this," he said, kissing down her throat.

"This?" she teased, rubbing against him back and forth, back and forth, until he bit out a curse, cupping his hands beneath her ass and lifting her up to her knees. From that vantage point, her breasts were right in his face, and he rubbed his cheek against her nipple, feeling it rub and drag beneath his skin. He caught her nipple in his mouth, sucking, scraping his teeth along that tight little bud until her fingers dug into his shoulders.

Even that little heart was erotic to him, the black outline a reminder of the secret privilege of seeing her like this, her head thrown back, her lips parted, her nipples wet from where he'd had them in his mouth.

"Let's get you out of these," he said, rolling her shorts down her hips, picking up one knee, then the other, to tug them down her calves. She had to finish the job herself in an awkward contortion of her body, and she came back to him, laughing.

God, I love you. It was an odd moment for him to have that thought, maybe, but it shot through him with a jolt. It left him stunned, caught out, temporarily incapable of speech or movement.

Daphne hitched her thumbs into her underwear, starting to drag them down, too, but he recovered sufficiently to shake his head. "Leave it," he said. "I want you just like this."

Her panties were red, clearly a matching set with the bra, and he liked the idea that maybe she'd worn them just for him. That she'd gotten ready to come over tonight knowing full well that at some point they'd be stripped down just like this, exploring each other's bodies, and he'd like what he saw. He did like it. He wanted to let her know how much, even as he swallowed down any declaration of love that was building up in his chest. There would be a time for that, but it wasn't now.

He ran his hands down her back, all the way down until he hooked his fingers inside her underwear to squeeze right where the bottom of her ass met the tops of her thighs. He already knew it was a sensitive spot for her, and he was rewarded by the way she arched her back, her sternum pressing into his nose. Even the smell of her got him impossibly hard.

He kissed her belly, then licked, wanting to taste the salt of her skin. He wanted to taste her everywhere.

"Daphne," he breathed against her stomach. "Please."

She held his face in her hands, holding him in place. "Please what?"

"Please let me taste you. I want to feel you come on my tongue."

THIRTY-THREE

DAPHNE HESITATED, ONLY FOR A MOMENT, BUT HE MUST'VE REG-istered it because his hands tightened on her back.

"Why don't you want me to, sweetheart?"

If you'd asked her only a second ago, she would've said she wasn't much of an endearment person. But suddenly, she was very partial to *sweetheart*. There was something almost charmingly old-fashioned about it, and the way Chris said it, it was like he didn't have any hang-ups about it at all. It was just a word he thought of when he thought about her.

"It's not that I don't *want* you to," she said. "It's more . . ."

She tried to think of how to phrase it in a way that wouldn't make her sound pathetic, or risk inadvertently insulting him. "I've never gotten off that way. It just seems . . ." She gave an awkward shrug of one shoulder, her hands still in his hair. "Like a lot of trouble for nothing."

He frowned, and for a minute she thought that was it, she'd killed the vibe, just like she had been afraid of doing. But then he brought her back down on his lap, so she was nestled against him, and she could feel how hard he still was, how he made her core pulse just from that single sensation.

"What do you mean by *trouble*?" he asked. "For you, or for me?"

"Both, I guess."

"Okay," he said. His hand skimmed down her side, clutching briefly at her thigh, like he wanted to ground them both, before he pressed one finger against where she was most throbbing through her underwear. "Let's get me out of the way first. It is absolutely no trouble for me. It is the opposite of trouble. Do you want to hear just how *not* trouble it is?"

He'd started to rub slow circles over her clit, and she swallowed hard, wanting to say *yes* but unable to get the word past the lump in her throat.

"I've literally dreamed about burying my face in you," he said. "Of my tongue in your pussy, as far as it can go. If you're worried about your smell, don't. I love the way you smell. If you're worried about your taste, *please* don't."

He'd slipped a finger inside her before she even realized he'd moved her underwear aside, and she gasped, sinking down on him for one brief, delicious moment before he left her empty again. He brought his finger to his mouth, sucking on the tip.

"I fucking love the way you taste."

The rasp in his voice crackled all the way down her spine. She couldn't help but believe him, when he looked at her like that.

He took her hand, guided it to the hard length of him through his sweatpants. "If you're worried whether it'll be good for *me*," he said, "I can promise you that it will. I would spend all night down there if you'd let me."

She pressed the heel of her hand against him, stroking up in one firm motion, and he briefly closed his eyes, his head falling back as he took a shuddering breath. She was able to wrap her fingers around him enough to get a rhythm going of stroking him through the soft fabric, feeling him swell underneath her even when she'd thought he couldn't possibly get any harder.

Finally he lifted her off him by her hips, depositing her on the couch while he came to kneel in front of her in one fluid motion. "Don't change the subject," he said. "Tell me how I can make this good for *you*."

She didn't even know. That was the problem. She was sure that oral sex could be great—if everyone hated it, you wouldn't hear about it anymore, right? It would've been phased out a long time ago, okay, we tried that, didn't work, moving on. And when Chris talked about what he wanted to do to her, that felt good by itself. Maybe they could just keep talking, simulate the act without having to worry about the act itself.

But she craved his mouth on her. It wasn't enough to talk about it, she wanted to *feel* it.

"How about this," he said. "I'm going to touch you, and I'll ask how I'm doing. Okay? You just tell me how it feels, if you want me to keep going, if you need me to do anything different. Your only goal here is to enjoy it, so don't feel pressured to come. If you've had enough, just tell me, and I'll stop. There's lots of other stuff we can do."

He looked up at her, and she could've gotten lost in those eyes. She nodded to let him know she'd heard him, that she agreed, and he hooked his fingers into her underwear, giving them a tug as she lifted off the couch to accommodate him. Even that slide of fabric created a sort of static spark down her legs, and she was trembling when he pulled her closer to him, pressed a kiss to the inside of her thigh.

"How's this?" he murmured against her skin, continuing his openmouthed journey up her thighs, nudging at her center with his nose.

She'd never thought of noses as particularly erotic before, but there was something about Chris', strong and a little sharp and applying a teasing amount of pressure against her. She braced her hands on either side of her body, her fingers digging into the couch.

"That's fine," she said, her voice choked.

"Fine," he repeated with a quiet laugh, like he knew what an understatement that was. She felt the warm burst of his breath against her, and couldn't help but squirm. "Okay. We can do better than fine."

He touched her with his tongue then, a quick, darting slide, like he was sneaking a taste. Her hips jerked in response, and he slid his hands up to press his thumbs against her hip bones, holding her in place as he went back in. This time his tongue was slow, exploratory, as he licked and sucked. *I've literally dreamed about burying my face in you.*

"Ah," she hissed as he hit one particular spot, trying to retreat, but she had nowhere to go.

"There?" he said, his tongue pressing against it once again, until she felt heat pool in her belly. "If it feels good, tell me. Don't hide from it."

"I—" She clutched at his shoulders, not sure if she was trying to push him away or draw him closer. Her first instinct *was* to hide—the better it felt, the more she wanted to escape from it, like she was at the top of a roller coaster and scared of the drop.

But then he gave her clit a hard suck, and she couldn't help it. She shuddered against him, releasing a low, throaty moan that turned into a whimper when he did it again.

"You like that."

It wasn't really a question, but she felt compelled to answer anyway, panting as she looked down at him between her thighs. "Fuck," she said. *"Yes."*

He lifted his head to look at her, his pupils blown out, his lips wet. "Tell me," he said. "Tell me how it feels."

"God," she said, clenching his hair as he continued his agonizing rhythm. "It feels so good. Don't stop."

"Stop?" He gave her a wicked grin, and she pushed his head
down, her hand at the nape of his neck as she guided him back
to her.

"*Don't* stop," she said. "Please, Chris, don't—"

He didn't stop, but he did slide his whole tongue inside her,
and something about that, the memory of the way he'd said *my
tongue in your pussy, as far as it can go*, was all she needed. She
exploded in a thousand tiny pinpricks of light, her body tensing
up with the orgasm and then releasing slowly, slowly, until she felt
the last of the aftershocks ripple through her.

He leaned forward to rest his head on her stomach. She ran her
fingers through his hair, her chest still heaving, her breathing a
little ragged. "I thought," she said, "that wasn't the goal."

"For *you*," he said. "It was absolutely *my* goal to make you
come. And I'm very goal-oriented."

She laughed. "Get up here. And take your pants off."

"Someone's bossy." But it took him only a second to comply,
his sweats on the floor, his dick jutting out. The hand-drawn abs
were ridiculous, they should've taken her right out, but somehow
they didn't. She'd had no idea that sex could be so intense but also
so . . . fun. She was having a great time.

"You know," she said, straddling his lap once he'd joined her
on the couch. "I'm on birth control."

"Yeah?"

She figured he probably knew that—she hadn't hidden her pill
container when she left it on the bathroom counter in her hotel
room. But she wasn't just giving her medical history, and she figured he knew that, too.

"We could . . ." She slid against him, grinding her pelvis into
his erection. She was still extra sensitive from her orgasm before,

and even that slight friction made her vision go a little blurry. "Without a condom. Do you want to?"

"Fuck, you have no idea." He was holding himself so taut she could see the corded muscles in his neck, the veins in his forearms ridged as he gripped her thighs.

"I bet it would feel really . . ." She pressed against him harder, deliberately teasing. ". . . *really* good."

Chris gave a groan, his fingers digging into her as he lifted her up and settled her right on his dick. That feeling of being suddenly *full*, of being stretched around him, was so exquisite that another orgasm rolled through her body, taking her by surprise. He held her through it, letting her put all her weight on him, her cheek flattened against his shoulder. It wasn't until she'd stopped trembling that he started to move under her.

"Meet me here, Dee," he said. "Come on, baby."

She bracketed his body with her knees, taking him even deeper as she pumped her hips once.

"That's it," he said. "Ride me."

She felt boneless and wrung out, but humming with enough adrenaline that she could fuck him hard, barely noticing when she was moving on her own versus when he was lifting her hips and bringing her down on him again and again. She knew he was going to come a second before he did, the way his body tightened, the choked growl he let out from his throat. And then she could feel him filling her up, the warm rush of it.

They stayed like that for a few moments, whether because they were too spent to move or because they were afraid of whatever mess they'd make when they did, she didn't know. Probably both.

"You might need a new couch," she said.

"Mmm," he said. "I have a steam cleaner."

"Industrial?"

He laughed, lifting her off him finally and setting her down on the couch. "Wait here just a minute."

She thought maybe he meant to go get the steam cleaner right there and then, but when he came back, he was holding a wet washcloth. He knelt in front of her, using the warm cloth to wipe the stickiness off her inner thighs.

"Oh," she said, suddenly embarrassed. "I can do that. You don't—"

"I want to," he said.

He washed her carefully, then pressed a kiss to her knee before offering her his hand. "Need some help up?"

"I'm going to stay here," she said. "I can't move."

"Don't make me sleep in that giant bed all alone."

"That wouldn't make me a very good guest," she said.

"No," he said, his eyes sparking. "It wouldn't."

THIRTY-FOUR

AND BECAUSE CHRIS WAS A GOOD HOST, HE SHARED HIS BED AND showed Daphne the next morning that he wasn't lying about the great showerhead pressure. He even offered her one of his smoothies for breakfast, but she wrinkled her nose at the spinach he added to his, letting him make her a fruit-and-yogurt-only version instead.

"So what's the plan today?" he asked, leaning over the kitchen island counter.

"I actually had an idea for something we could go do," she said. "I was going to make it a surprise, but I think it's better if I tell you ahead of time to make sure you'd be into it. There's this—"

He cut her off. "Keep it a surprise," he said. "I like the sound of that."

She bit her lip, grabbing her phone out of her pocket to check something. It lit up with a brief glimpse of her lock screen, and he only caught a flash of the image, but it reminded him of something. He couldn't think what. The urge to ask her again to exchange numbers was so strong, but he'd already told himself he wouldn't bring it back up, that he'd wait for her to make the first move in that regard.

He just wished she would.

"Are you sure?" she asked. "It's . . . I mean, I hope it will be fun. But it's also kinda work, too. I can't explain it without giving it away."

Chris tried to think what it could even be. Maybe she wanted him to take her to some batting cages and teach her how to hit. Maybe an errand she had to run. She'd mentioned a couple issues with her apartment last night; maybe she needed him to change a lightbulb.

They all sounded fine to him.

"Let's do it," he said. "Should I dress any particular way?"

She hesitated. "Just in whatever you'd normally wear in public on a weekend, I guess. And bring your glove."

THE GLOVE THING WAS AT LEAST A HINT, SO CHRIS DRESSED CASU-ally in a T-shirt and gym shorts, an old baseball cap from his minor league days. When he and Daphne were both at the door, ready to go, he saw she was wearing her Battery T-shirt again with his name and number on the back. Briefly, he thought about warning her—if she didn't *want* their relationship to be public, maybe it wasn't the best idea to wear his shirt. But then she turned to smile at him, and he found he personally didn't care if the whole world knew.

He walked them out to his car, holding up the keys. "Want to drive?"

She seemed as taken aback as if he'd asked her if she wanted to pilot a fighter jet. "Oh, no, that's okay. You can do it."

He didn't mind either way—he'd just thought it made sense if she knew where they were going and it was meant to be a surprise. But the extremity of her reaction needled at something inside him, and he found he wanted to know what was behind it.

"We can also take your car, if you don't feel comfortable driving a car you're not as familiar with."

"Yours is fine," she said, giving a nervous laugh. "I would be so tense driving you around. I would hate to be responsible if anything happened. Your body is probably insured for more than my life is worth."

Something about that *really* didn't sit right with him. He didn't know if it was being reduced to a highly valued body, if it was her devaluing what *she* was worth, or if it was that, if he was being honest, he usually didn't get into a vehicle automatically thinking about the chances of a car accident and now he was a little unsettled.

"All right," he said. "Not a big deal."

He went to cross over to the driver's side, but she'd already moved in front of the door. "You really wouldn't mind?"

Chris had been the one to suggest it in the first place. He didn't see why he'd have any reason to mind. But he supposed some people were pickier about their cars—he doubted Randy would let anyone else drive his sports car, Chris included. So maybe that's all Daphne had been responding to. "I'm cool either way," he said. "I thought you'd want to since you picked the location. But if you plug it into my phone GPS I can get us there."

"I'll drive," she said, taking the keys from his hand.

For all that, Daphne wasn't a bad driver. A little more cautious than he was, maybe—she drove with her hands almost adorably at a perfect ten-and-two, whereas he was more likely to have just one hand rest lightly on top of the steering wheel. She stopped for a couple yellow lights he would've pushed through, but all that probably just meant she was a *better* driver than him, by the book at least. Randy texted him more about the All-Star Game watch party tomorrow night, and he took a few minutes to text back, looking up only when he felt the car slow down and heard the crunch of gravel under its tires.

The sign was old, brick with a white wooden placard that had an outline picture of a baseball player and WENDLE LITTLE LEAGUES printed in block letters. There were a few cars in the parking lot already, and one of the fields was currently in use, groups of kids wearing bright red shirts out there running drills. He turned to see Daphne watching him uncertainly, like she was trying to gauge his reaction.

"We don't have to," she said. "But I checked their website, and they're running this special baseball summer camp right now. Half the kids are here through some sort of scholarship that helps families who can't afford it. I thought we could stop in for a half hour or so, it doesn't have to be long—you could throw a couple balls with them, give them some tips, sign a couple autographs, and then we're out of here."

He looked back out toward the field. There was a group of kids in the outfield, doing the same practice he remembered so clearly from when he was that age. It was a simple pop-fly drill, the coach hitting a ball out into center field, the first kid in line running to field it, throwing it back before the next kid took his place to do the same.

He did stuff with kids for the Battery all the time. Little League groups who got special passes to games, kids through charitable foundations who got to throw a first pitch, occasional school visits. After Sunday afternoon games the Battery let kids come out and run the bases and sometimes Chris ran them, too. It was one of his favorite parts of being a professional athlete, actually, that he had an opportunity to make a kid's day by something as simple as tossing a ball up into the stands, that he could maybe be a mentor or role model in some small way.

But that was another thing he'd gotten farther away from this season. He realized that, other than the official things he'd done as part of the team, he hadn't really made an effort to do anything with the community at all. It had been yet another casualty of his tunnel vision, his lack thereof, whatever. It was so much easier just to keep to himself.

"Sorry," Daphne said. "This was a stupid idea. We can go."

"No," Chris said. "This is perfect. Do they know I'm coming?"

She winced a little, like she knew she was about to give the wrong answer. "No? I thought it would be a fun surprise."

He grinned at her, unbuckling his seat belt. "Even better. I love surprises."

He allowed himself only the briefest touch at the small of Daphne's back as they walked through the parking lot, dropping his hand the moment they came in view of the fields. There was a ripple effect as he approached—it only took the first kid who clearly recognized him to point him out to a friend, and then the word spread until he heard some kid say *Chris KEPLER!* in an annoyed tone that suggested he'd already said it a couple times. For a few minutes there was a lot of commotion, with kids who were at other parts of the field running over and everyone trying to talk to Chris at once. He did what he could to say hello and respond to questions that were being shouted at him—*Did he really play baseball? Was Gutierrez coming? Had he ever met Shohei Ohtani?*—but it was overwhelming.

He was grateful when he saw the adult on the field heading over to him, hand outstretched to shake.

"Hi," Chris said. "Sorry to just drop in like this. I'm Chris—"

"We know who you are, son," the coach said. "I'm Coach Mike, and over there—"

"But who *is* Chris Kepler?" a kid said from behind Coach Mike, and the coach turned, the universal expression of *could you not?* on his face, but Chris just laughed and held his hand out to the kid, too.

"Third baseman for the Carolina Battery," he said. "And this is Daphne Brink, the sideline reporter for the team. We saw y'all practicing and couldn't help but stop in to see what you were up to. You guys were looking good out there."

"We don't have any cameras with us or anything," Daphne rushed in to clarify, giving Coach Mike a friendly smile. "This isn't an official visit. Just a drop-by."

"Well, we're honored to have you," Coach Mike said. "We were just about to head to the batting cage, if you wanted to come show the kids how it's done."

He'd already started moving with the group over to a chain-link box built over to the side of the field, and Chris and Daphne fell into step next to him.

"He's batting .218," one kid from the back said, not in a disdainful way but just in a matter-of-fact way. Chris turned to look at the kid, who had straggly long hair to his shoulders and was all gangly legs and bony elbows. If he had to guess, he'd put the kids at about nine or ten years old.

"Shut *up*, Jonas." This from a kid with curly hair poking out from under his baseball cap. Just from the way he held himself, the confident way he walked, Chris could already tell that he was a serious player. Probably a coach's kid, or at least had a dad like Chris', who expected him to give it his all every time he was out there whether it was batting practice or a Saturday-morning game or a championship. "You're such a weirdo."

"I'm impressed," Chris said, addressing Jonas like the curly-haired kid hadn't even spoken. "That's my *exact* batting average as of yesterday. You know your stats, Jonas."

"You draw the second-most walks of anyone on the team and last year you led the team in steals," Jonas said, before frowning, like he was thinking about something. "This year you've barely stolen at all."

"I steal at least one base every single game," the curly-haired kid piped in. Chris just bet he did. Little League was lawless—the kids weren't adept enough yet to make quick judgment calls or accurate throws, so if you got on base you could almost always get an extra one at some point with fairly little effort. Chris had always been more of a contact hitter than a home run guy, but he was fast, and so he'd carried some of that mentality with him all through his playing career. If you got on base, you had to start thinking about how you might be able to stretch it.

"That's awesome," he said to the curly-haired kid, because even though he hadn't particularly liked the way he talked to Jonas, he wasn't about to be rude to a child. He met Daphne's gaze over the kid's head, and she smiled slightly, like she knew exactly what he was doing.

"Why haven't you stolen more bases this year?" Jonas asked.

"Let's lay off Mr. Kepler," Coach Mike said. "He's taking time out of his busy schedule to be here today, and—"

Chris waved him off. "No, it's okay. And please, call me Chris. It's a good question. I don't really know why I haven't attempted more steals this year, Jonas. Some of it is just opportunity—I haven't been getting on base as much, so I haven't had the chance. And when you have fewer chances, sometimes you take fewer risks. Sometimes you just don't like the timing with that particular pitcher. Sometimes your coaches don't want you to go for it. And sometimes . . ."

He locked eyes with Daphne again, suddenly sure that she knew exactly what he was thinking, that she could probably figure out a way to phrase it for an audience of children better than he could. Because although he'd never explicitly thought about it this way until now, wouldn't have even made the connection if he hadn't been talking about it, the truth was that stealing a base required a certain amount of full-steam-ahead confidence. A belief that you would make it to the next bag safely, and if you didn't, well, it had been worth it to try. He hadn't felt that way in some time.

"Sometimes you just need the right motivation," Chris said.

THIRTY-FIVE

CHRIS ENDED UP SPENDING TWO HOURS WORKING WITH THE KIDS at the summer camp, running all the way up through lunchtime. Daphne didn't know how he did it—after about half an hour, she got too hot to be out in the sun any longer, even though she'd just been standing there while Chris had been the one to throw balls for kids to hit during BP, hit balls for them to field. He'd paired with Jonas in a long-toss drill when Daphne begged off, going to sit in the dugout, where she could get some shade.

Coach Mike and the kids had split off to go eat lunch at the picnic tables over by the concession area. The summer camp provided a hot dog and chips, apparently, but Chris had paid for a round of Popsicles for the kids, and he brought one to Daphne in the dugout.

"I figured you for a red girl," he said, handing it to her.

"You figured right."

Chris had his own blue Popsicle, and he took a full bite out of the top of it in a way that made her shiver.

"The kids were so excited to have you out there with them," she said. "It was really fun to watch. You've just made their entire summer."

"*You* did that," Chris said. "Seriously. This was—"

He broke off, just looking at her. Something about that expression made her stomach swoop, but then it kept falling, and she was struck by an overwhelming dread she couldn't explain. She rushed to find something to bring the lighthearted mood back.

"Jonas sure was grilling you," she said. "Hard to believe a kid that young could know so much. He should have my job."

Chris sucked a bit of Popsicle juice off the side of his hand. It was so hot that the Popsicles wouldn't last long; Daphne knew they better eat them quickly before they both became sticky messes.

"He was funny," Chris said. "Tim used to be the same way when we were kids. He knew everything there was to know about baseball."

"Really?"

"Oh yeah. Once we went to a Phillies game when we were kids—I was probably eight, so Tim would've been eleven or so. And there was this guy in the stands behind us, just mouthing off, talking all this shit to his friends. You could tell he was showing off, like he was some kind of baseball expert. The Phillies fucked up this basic play at first to get the final out, the other team ended up scoring, and the loudmouth behind us started in about how the Phillies had the worst record in our division blah blah blah."

Chris laughed to himself, obviously remembering the moment.

"And then Tim—his mouth *full* of ice cream, he used to eat himself literally sick on that stuff, later he found out he was lactose intolerant and he *still* ate it without taking his Lactaid first—just goes, 'Expos.' He said it exactly like that, totally deadpan. He didn't even look back. And I could tell the guy heard him, because he got really quiet after that. For years after that, Tim and I would just say that to each other to shut down a debate. 'Expos.' I thought he was a god when he said that."

Daphne was in serious danger of wearing more of her Popsicle

than she got in her mouth if she wasn't careful. She had been trying to stay perfectly still, like a butterfly had landed on her and
she didn't want to risk it flying away. She really didn't want to
interrupt Chris or take him out of his story, but she also wanted
to understand it, and she didn't fully.

"What does 'Expos' mean?" she said. "Is that a baseball term?"

"Yeah, sorry. I guess that's pretty niche. It used to be a team—
the Montreal Expos. They're the Nationals now." Chris finished
the last of his Popsicle, tossing the stick in a perfect arc into the
trash can in the corner of the dugout. "And come to think of it,
I'm pretty sure the Phillies *did* end that season with the worst record in our division."

"I just don't know how you guys remember all this stuff," she
said. "Like I could ask you about an at-bat from two months ago
and I bet you'd remember what pitches he threw, what the count
was, whether you struck out or not. It's wild."

Chris shrugged. "Random noise, probably. Do you like the
reporting gig? Will you try to find that kind of job somewhere else
when the season is over?"

She hadn't really let herself think that far ahead. She'd been
taking it game by game just like the rest of them. What *did* she
want? There had been unexpected benefits to this sideline reporting gig. She felt challenged, she felt more confident, she felt like
she was part of something bigger than herself. But she also didn't
know that she wanted to be on camera all the time, despite having
grown more comfortable than she thought she would've at the beginning. So far, any public encounters with people who recognized her from the broadcasts had been largely positive, but still.
She'd never aspired to that.

"I don't know," she said slowly, turning the question over in
her mind. "I used to want—"

She broke off, not sure why the thought had even come to her mind. It had been so long since she'd even considered it. Maybe it had been being around all those kids today, watching Chris and Coach Mike teach them and make a difference, no matter how small.

"You used to want what?"

Daphne smiled at him. "I started off majoring in early-childhood education," she said. "But then I switched to communication and broadcasting, and at the time I thought I would *still* do something with reading and literacy. I don't even remember what—even just something like working on children's programming or helping a nonprofit spread its message or whatever. But then suddenly I was taking all these classes in production and digital media and I lost the thread somewhere in there."

"Hmm."

"That probably sounds stupid."

"The opposite," he said. "And I don't think the thread's lost. You can pick it up again whenever you're ready. Maybe even after the season is over."

"Maybe," she said. She didn't really want to think about the season ending. It made her feel impossibly melancholy.

Her Popsicle was seriously melting now, and she did her best to try to catch the drips with her tongue, but they were already splashing on her fingers, dribbling down her chin.

"I'm a mess," she said, laughing.

Chris' hand was on her bare thigh as he leaned over, slanting his mouth on hers. His breath instantly warmed her lips, still cool from the Popsicle, and she could taste the blue raspberry flavor he'd chosen on his tongue. He kissed her chin, then touched his tongue to the sensitive skin at her jaw. Even though it was at least ninety degrees outside, she felt goose bumps rise on her nape as he pushed her hair aside to lick another rivulet of juice that had slid down the side of her neck.

"You're sweet," he said, swirling his tongue in the hollow at the base of her throat.

"And *we're* still at a ballpark filled with children," she said. "Should we get out of here?"

"Yes," he said. "Emphatically yes."

IT TOOK A LITTLE MORE TIME TO LEAVE THAN THEY'D EXPECTED, because when Chris went back to say goodbye to the kids he ended up getting roped into another round of pictures and autographs, a few parents who'd arrived wanting to talk to him about how the Battery were doing this year. By the time they finally made it back to the car, it felt like they'd escaped a bank heist, like they'd really gotten away with something.

Daphne had already given Chris back his keys, and he held them up, dangling them from his finger. "I'll drive this time."

She was only too relieved—it had been stressful enough driving the both of them out here, although she really couldn't put any of that on him. He hadn't even berated her for stopping at a few yellow lights she *knew* she could've made it through.

The blast of air conditioning was welcome when Chris started up the car, and he turned it up. "Feel free to adjust the air however you want it," he said. "And the radio."

Daphne didn't really care what they listened to, but she knew he liked music, and it would be nice to have something on in the car. She pressed the preset buttons, trying to find a good station, before clicking up one digit at a time until she heard something decent.

Where were they going without ever knowing the way . . .

The song was vaguely familiar, and suddenly it hit her. "Oh my god," she said. "Isn't this your song?"

He turned to look at her, a crease between his brows. "My song?"

"Your double rainbow. You said that I'd know it—"

And then it really hit her. She wasn't supposed to know about that. He'd told *Duckie* about the song; he'd never told her. Panic clenched her stomach, and she knew it was written all over her face— her eyes wide, her breath coming shallow and fast as she sat, frozen in the passenger seat of his car, unable to say anything.

For a moment it was like Chris couldn't speak, either. He'd already pulled out of the parking space but had stopped now at the exit of the Little League field, the car idling as they looked at each other, that fucking *song* playing on in the background. He had the most awful, still expression on his face, and when he spoke it was barely above a whisper.

"Duckie?"

CHAPTER
THIRTY-SIX

"I CAN EXPLAIN," DAPHNE SAID, THEN WINCED AT HOW CLICHÉ that sounded. "I mean, it's not what—"

"Holy shit," he said. "Holy shit."

Any slight hope Daphne had clung to that maybe it wouldn't be so bad, maybe he'd be *happy* even, died with the way he said those two words.

"Chris—"

"What *is* this?" he asked. "Like what is even going on?"

She could do this. This was what she'd wanted—a chance to lay it all out for him, to plead her case. She knew it looked bad, but if he only heard her out, she was positive she could make him see that none of it had been intentional, that she hadn't meant for it to go this far.

"It started with that DM, right? I was trying to say I was sorry for heckling you. Only I accidentally left out the part where I actually said I was the heckler, and then you *replied*, which I hadn't expected, and we started talking and—"

"I don't give a fuck about that part," he said. "I know what happened with that part. But then you met me—as Daphne— knowing full well that you were also Duckie. We've been talking for *months*, we've been—" He broke off, taking a hard swallow. "And the whole time, you knew."

Behind them, someone honked, and Chris startled like he'd forgotten where they were. *Daphne* had forgotten where they were—already the Little League park and the kids and the Popsicles seemed so far away. He bit out a curse under his breath as he eased the car into traffic, heading back in the direction of his condo. She didn't know what she'd thought—she certainly hadn't expected he'd leave her on the side of the road right there—but she tried to take it as an encouraging sign that he was heading back to his place.

Then again, the brief pause didn't seem to do anything to make things better. If anything, when he spoke again, his words came out harder and colder than before.

"From the very start, you've known all of it—about my brother, about what I was going through. You sat across from me to ask softball questions about that one stupid incident, and the whole time you knew *exactly* why you'd made me cry."

He'd never phrased it that way, she realized. *She* had, in her guilt over it all, but he'd always brushed away any of her attempts to apologize for it, or made a sideways reference or joke without outright calling it what it was. She hadn't known if it was because he didn't see the incident that way, or because he just didn't want to make her feel bad about it. She supposed now she had her answer.

"That interview was the first time I met you. I thought about saying something, but I couldn't—I had a job to do, you had a job to do, it would've been—"

"Is that what it was about? The job?"

"*No.*" God, she was fucking this all up. "I didn't even know about the sideline reporter gig then. And when Layla told me, I didn't even know if I *wanted* it. I was nervous about working that closely with you. But I think that's also why I did want it, why I ended up taking it."

His mouth twisted in a poor imitation of a smile. "You took the job to be closer to me. And just didn't tell me that's what you were doing."

Okay, yes, when he put it like *that* she could see how it sounded absolutely deranged. "Subconsciously, you were definitely a big reason why I took the job. But at the time, I wasn't thinking of it that way. I *tried* to keep my distance. I thought I could cut off the chat as Duckie, and you'd never have to know. I thought I could just ask you a few questions after a game, keep it professional, and it wouldn't have to affect anything."

Ahead, the light changed and Chris slammed on the brakes to stop at the intersection. His knuckles on the steering wheel were white from how tightly he was holding it. "You must think I'm a real idiot."

"No, I—"

"Of course you couldn't use those tickets for the game," he said. "You were *at* the game. Of course you couldn't give me your number. *I already had your number.* And you know the worst fucking thing? This whole time, I've felt bad. I've felt terrible. I felt somehow disloyal to Duckie—which, Jesus, what a joke—and then anytime I thought about Duckie I felt disloyal to *you.*"

He gave a harsh laugh that shredded something inside her. "Duckie," he said. "Daphne. Daffy Duck. Come on, admit it. That had to make you laugh that I couldn't figure that one out."

"*No,*" she said. "It wasn't a joke. Please, if you believe nothing else—"

"How can I believe anything you say? You've been lying to me this *whole time.*"

They'd reached his building, and he pulled the car into his space, shutting it off but still just sitting there, like he couldn't bring himself to move yet. "That first night, when I told you in the hotel bar that there was someone else. You already knew about that—you *were* the someone else."

"I know," she said. She wasn't going to try to minimize or hide behind most of her lies being ones of omission. It was just as bad, and she knew that. "You have every right to be angry. If I were you, I would be. All—"

"But it *wouldn't* be you," he said. "Because I would've never done this to you."

He got out of the car then, shutting the door behind him. Daphne had to fumble with her seat belt several times to get it to unbuckle, and by the time she followed him, he was already halfway to the elevator. She had so much she wanted to say, but her throat was closed up. They rode all the way to his floor in tense silence, Chris with his arms crossed over his chest, leaning against the wall of the elevator like he physically wanted to be as far from her as possible.

"Chris," she said once they were in his condo. He still hadn't turned to look at her, taking the time to put his wallet and keys on the dresser in the bedroom like it required his full attention. "Please, listen to me. I know I fucked up. I know I let this get out of control. I did lie to you, and I am so, so sorry—you have no idea how sorry. But I swear to you, none of the important parts were lies. The things I said, the way I feel, those have all been true."

"The important parts." He snorted, like he found something about that funny, but his expression when he finally turned to face her had no trace of humor in it. "Do you know how shitty it felt, to have Duckie just disappear on me like that? How many times I read back through our conversations, trying to see where I'd gone wrong, if there was something I could've said or done differently to make her want to meet up, to share more of herself?"

Daphne didn't know what to say. Of course she'd thought

about how Chris might be affected by the way she ended their text relationship. But she'd also thought . . . well, it sounded so stupid now. She'd thought it couldn't have mattered *that* much to him, that he'd move past it pretty quickly. It would be a minor disappointment, a blip, but it wasn't like they'd ever called what they were doing a relationship, and he hadn't even known her real name. How serious could it be?

But of course it had been serious. It had been serious for *her*— enough that she'd wanted to end things via text to give herself a chance to be with him in real life. She could see that now. And it had been foolish and cruel for her to not see how serious it had been for *him*. He'd told her. She just hadn't believed him.

"Except one night when we shared quite a lot of ourselves," Chris said. "Do you remember?"

He had to know she did. The question had to be a way to twist the knife just a bit more, although his tone had been almost crushingly matter-of-fact. He was standing in the doorway to his bedroom, like he didn't know if he wanted to be in there or out in the main living area with her. Behind him, she could see his bed, the covers still rumpled from the way they'd left them that morning. She stepped closer, wanting to go to him, but she felt repelled away like there was an actual force field around his body.

"And then do you know how shitty it felt, to have my—well, whatever we were to each other—not even want to give me her *number*? What do you think I made of that?"

Whatever we were. She'd known it was coming, but still the past tense gutted her more than anything else.

"I never meant for it to go this far," she said, her voice shaking. Her eyes were filling with tears, her vision going blurry, but she willed them not to fall. Not because she cared if he saw her cry, but because she knew she didn't deserve to be the one breaking down right now.

"How far was it supposed to go? You *fucked* with me, Daphne, and I'm already—" The words sounded wrenched from some deep place inside him, like they scraped against his throat on the way out, and he seemed to forcibly swallow the rest of them down. "Were you ever going to tell me? What was the plan? We keep fucking but I just never get to meet your cat?"

That made her flinch. "I wanted to tell you," she said. "I almost did so many times. But then Layla told me to wait until the season was over, that it would be a distraction you didn't need . . ."

She knew that was a mistake the minute the words left her mouth. For one, it wasn't exactly a mark in her favor to acknowledge what she'd planned. For another, she hadn't meant to get Layla involved, or throw her under the bus in any way. She was just trying to convey that she *had* thought about it, that she'd consulted with someone whose advice she valued especially when it came to how something might affect Chris as a player or a teammate.

"Wow," he said. "Well, thank you. For considering my mental health. I can't tell you how much I appreciate it."

Daphne had seen Chris stoic and reserved, she'd seen him upset, but she'd never seen him sarcastic like this before. And even though she knew she deserved it, that he wasn't even saying half the things he *could* say to her, the contempt in his voice still caught her raw.

"I wish *you* would consider your mental health," she said before she could think about it.

He paused. When he spoke, his voice was low. "What is that supposed to mean?"

She'd said it; there was no taking it back. "Just that you can't white-knuckle your way through the whole season," she said. "You suffered a devastating loss, Chris. You're grieving. And if it helps you to play baseball through it, that's fine, if it would help you to take some time off, that would be fine, too, but either way

I think you should *talk* about it with someone, Marvin or Randy or one of the trainers, I don't even know, but someone who could—"

"I told *you*," he said. "Twice. I trusted you, and I told you. Twice."

She could see instantly that this was the most unforgivable part of what she'd done. She tried to reach for him, more out of an automatic impulse than anything else—tears were streaking down her face, she needed comfort and he *was* her comfort—but he flinched away. She realized he wouldn't be that for her ever again.

"I'm so sorry," she said. "I know those words don't mean much, coming from me. I know I could say it until I'm blue in the face and you wouldn't forgive me. You probably shouldn't. But I do want you to know that I really do care about you, Chris. None of that was fake. None of that *is* fake. I love you. I fell in love with you in our texts, and I fell in love with you in real life, and the only reason I wasn't more honest with you was because I was so afraid of messing it all up. Which, ironically of course, I did worse than I ever could've by being honest from the beginning. I know what I did was wrong, and I don't expect or deserve your forgiveness. But I did want you at least to know that I love you."

When he looked over at her, it was hard to believe the way he'd looked at her only an hour before, like she was something precious to him. "You're right, those words don't mean much," he said. "They don't mean shit to me. I don't even know who you are."

She felt her face crumple. "You *do*," she said. "I'm the same—"

"You're not." He shook his head, backing away from her. "I'll tell you one thing, though, you're not boring. Whatever else this was, it was a hell of a ride. A twist a minute. You can feel great about that part."

Feel *great*? This felt *awful*. And it felt even worse for all the memories she had of how happy they'd been right here in this same space only hours before. When they'd had the whole day ahead of them and were looking forward to spending it with each other. Daphne knew they'd said what they were doing was just a fun, no-strings arrangement—she'd been the one to use the phrase *friends with benefits,* but she'd been fooling herself. That had never been all it was. And now it might never have the chance to be anything at all.

"Please," she said. "Just—"

"I gotta go," Chris said, pressing his hand to his chest. "I can't—I gotta go."

He picked up his keys from the dresser, passing by her carefully in the bedroom doorway to avoid even the barest touch. "Just lock up after yourself when you leave," he said. He was talking fast, looking somewhere over her shoulder. "And from here on out, I'll answer any baseball questions you ask me in front of a camera, but I think it's probably best if we don't interact beyond that."

A broken, silent sob racked her body, but she didn't respond. He hesitated only a second at the front door, like maybe he wanted to say something else, but her vision was too blurry for her to see the expression on his face. And then, with a quiet *click* of the door, he was gone.

CHAPTER
THIRTY-SEVEN

CHRIS WAS GETTING BETTER AT RECOGNIZING WHEN A PANIC attack was coming on. It was the adrenaline spike, as if a line drive was heading straight for him, the way he suddenly got real focused on his breathing. In, out. In, out. It seemed impossible that his body just knew how to do that by itself, that it wouldn't fuck it up somehow.

He'd grabbed his keys without really knowing where he was going, but he didn't want to drive. He didn't want to be in the car at all, not when it still contained the echoes of some of what they'd said to each other. He pulled his baseball cap lower over his eyes, and started walking down the sidewalk.

Daphne was Duckie. He was still reeling from the revelation. She'd *lied* to him. He couldn't even think about all the times she'd asked him a question she probably already knew the answer to, or carefully meted out what she told him about her own life.

God, he felt so *stupid.* The clues had all been there, if he'd just stopped to pay attention. There were so many commonalities— the divorce, the cat, even her nervousness around driving. But none of those things by itself was that unusual, right? Lots of people got divorced, or had a cat. He never connected her to Duckie because it had never occurred to him that she'd have any reason to keep some secret identity from him.

Every single moment they'd spent together was now tainted with this extra layer, this knowledge that she'd had and kept from him. Even when they'd sat down for that first interview, *she had already been talking with him for almost a week*. He'd sat across from her saying banal shit about how he felt about the game and the crowd, and she'd already known exactly what was going on with him. She probably hadn't been surprised when he'd walked off.

And then afterward, *she* was who he'd turned to. He'd texted all that shit about needing a friend, about wanting to keep talking to her. She must've gotten a real kick out of that. When he wouldn't talk to her in person, she had him on her phone. And when she was ready to be with him in person, she could just ditch him through her text alter ego, leave him wondering what the hell had happened even as she propositioned him in real life.

He was out of breath, way more out of breath than he should've been just from walking. He needed to stop, he needed to sit down, but there was nowhere to sit. Eventually he came to a space between two buildings that was too narrow to be a proper alleyway, but enough room that he could lean his back against the wall, his hands on his knees while he tried to breathe more deeply. In, out. In, out.

You can't white-knuckle your way through the whole season. He could do whatever the fuck he put his mind to. He'd devoted his life to baseball. He'd been a middle schooler who'd spent every night at the ballpark, doing his homework in the dugout while he waited for his turn to hit. He'd barely had a life in high school or college, because he knew that every minute he spent away from training could mean the difference between a scholarship or not, getting drafted or not. He'd taken up running, biking, Pilates, he'd lifted weights, he'd eaten a more plant-based diet, a high-protein diet, he'd had surgeries, he'd rehabbed injuries, he'd done anything they told him to do, all in the name of baseball. And it was worth it. He could let his team down, could let *himself* down, but the sport was always there. The stitches on the ball felt the same, you knew exactly where to stand and what your job was, and you had twenty-seven outs to make your case, no matter what.

Put your faith in people, and you were bound to get hurt. Put your faith in the game—not even the people, not your teammates or your manager or anyone else, but the *game*—and you couldn't go wrong.

When Chris finally got going again, he automatically turned down a few streets until he realized he was making his way to Randy's place. The All-Star Game wasn't until tomorrow night, but he couldn't think where else to go.

CHAPTER
THIRTY-EIGHT

SOMEHOW DAPHNE MADE IT BACK TO HER APARTMENT IN ONE piece, physically at least, but once she was alone she let it all out. She cried so much that Milo hid under the bed, less interested in comforting her in her time of need than in removing himself from the tense situation.

On the one hand, she'd known this was coming. She'd been dreading it all these months, and it was almost a relief to have it out in the open, to not have to worry anymore about keeping secrets. But on the other hand, it had taken her by complete surprise, the way it had all happened and just how badly it had hurt. She couldn't shake that image of Chris' face, when he'd first realized. He'd looked betrayed. He'd looked *devastated*.

She heard a key working in her lock, and she sat up in bed, so thrown by the sound that she couldn't even process who it could be. Her first thought was Chris—which was of course ridiculous, and true wishful thinking. She'd never given him a key. She'd done everything to keep him as far away from her apartment as possible, actually, which was part of the problem with the subterfuge she'd been running. And even if he *did* have a key, there was no way he'd be coming over now. Those days were over.

It was only when Kim shoved her way in, the door sticking in its frame the way it did during the humid summer months, that Daphne remembered. She'd texted Kim earlier that morning, asking if she could stop by to feed Milo and check in on him. Back when she'd thought maybe she'd still be at Chris' place. Back when she'd been feeling hopeful, and happy, and like maybe she deserved it.

God, she hated herself for having felt that way.

"Oh!" Kim said, her hand flying to her chest as she was clearly surprised by Daphne's presence. "I'm sorry, I thought you said tonight?"

"I did," Daphne said. "*I'm* sorry. I should've texted you that I'd be home after all."

"Plans fall through?"

Daphne tried to respond, but she only ended up crying again. To her credit, Kim didn't ask any more questions for a few minutes. She just kicked off her shoes and climbed into bed with Daphne, holding her until the last of her sobs died down.

"Have you been hydrating?" Kim said. "Because I think that was most of your seventy percent."

Daphne let out a choked laugh, gesturing toward an untouched glass of water on her nightstand. "I've been meaning to."

Kim grabbed the glass and dumped the remainder of it in Milo's water bowl, then refilled it before handing it back to Daphne. "Nice and fresh," she said. "Take a few big sips for me and then tell me everything."

Daphne followed her friend's directions, and if Kim hit her with an *I told you so*, well . . . she knew she'd earned it. Kim had warned her from the beginning that none of this would end well—not chatting anonymously with Chris over DMs and texts, not hooking up with him in real life, none of it. But Kim just listened, wincing at a few of the worst parts and rubbing Daphne's knee sympathetically when she got to the end.

"I'm sorry, honey," she said. "What are you going to do?"

"*Do?*" Daphne blinked in genuine confusion. "There's nothing for me *to* do. It all blew up. He made his feelings perfectly clear."

"But did you explain? How it was all an accident at first, why you didn't tell him later?"

She'd tried to explain. She didn't know how coherent it had all been, or how much of it he'd heard. But she also knew that there was no explanation, no excuse that would negate what she'd done. She *had* lied to him. That part was undeniable.

"You didn't see the way he looked at me," Daphne said.

"Well, what are you going to do about the job? You can't show up every day and interview him like nothing happened. It'll be too painful. It'll be impossible."

Daphne buried her face in her hands, jamming the heels of her hands against her swollen eyes. She was so tired. She never wanted to think about walking into that ballpark again, never wanted to have to put on makeup and smile and ask surface-level questions about a specific play. But at the same time, she knew she couldn't quit. It would leave the team in the lurch and be a real shit move to do to Layla, who hadn't had to advocate for Daphne in the first place but who had, trying to support her every step of the way. Not only that, but she knew she couldn't quit for *herself.* This was something she needed to see through.

"I'll take it one day at a time," Daphne said. It wasn't lost on her that it was the very same sound bite players were always giving her. *One pitch at a time. Three outs to end the game.* Tunnel vision.

Kim was silent for a few minutes, just rubbing Daphne's back. "I still think you should try to talk to him again," she said. "When he's calmed down. It sounds like he really cared about you."

She knew what her friend meant, but that past tense still hit her right where she most hurt. *Whatever we were to each other,* Chris had said. She'd told him she loved him, and he'd said the words were empty, that he didn't know her at all.

The problem was that Chris *had* cared about her. She didn't know if she'd even appreciated how much, if she'd allowed herself to feel it. Maybe she could only feel it now because of its stark absence, the way that the clouds came out to cover the sky, and all of a sudden you missed the sun.

CHRIS HAD TOLD HER THAT THERE WAS A NEW ENERGY AMONG THE team, the first game back after the All-Star break. It was only three days, but when you were used to grinding the way they did six days a week, afternoon games, night games, doubleheaders, road trips, press events, fan events . . . those three days meant a lot. And there was always a renewed hope, he'd said. Like even though your record still carried over into the second part of the season, you could imagine certain slates wiped clean if you wanted to, a chance to have a new start.

Daphne didn't feel any of that. And from what she could tell, unfortunately Chris didn't, either.

The Battery were up by one in the seventh inning when the opposing team hit what should have been an easy grab at third base, thrown across to get the out at first. Daphne had seen Chris make the play a thousand times. It was one of her favorites to watch, actually, because it was basic enough that she didn't really sweat it, didn't feel her adrenaline spike as the ball headed toward him. He always fielded it cleanly. And then sometimes he held on to it for a second—it would *feel* like a second too long to her, she'd start to sweat it then, wondering if he'd be able to make the throw in time—or sometimes he had to throw right away, on the run or twisting his body, slinging the ball over to first in this straight spear that she could hear from her place by the dugout hit the first baseman's glove with a satisfying *thwack*.

It was during those kinds of moments when she thought, *I like baseball, actually.* There was a rhythm to it, a flow. And she watched Chris make that same play over and over enough that she could see there were nuances to it, too. *I think Chris would like Mary Oliver,* she'd thought once, a thought which had seemed to come out of nowhere, but which she understood more as she watched him play. How could you not be poetic about baseball?

But this time, the ball came right toward Chris, and he put his glove down, ready to make the same casual pickup he'd done so many times before, and instead the ball just skipped right off the end of his glove. There was an awful moment, where he obviously thought he already had it, reaching in to make the throw. When he realized he didn't, he spun around, looking for the ball on the grass.

"Come on," Daphne whispered. "Come on, come on."

There was still time to make the throw. The runner was still not quite to first base—it would be tight, but there was time. Chris finally scooped up the ball, turning to throw it almost over his shoulder, the ball landing with a bounce in front of the first baseman's outstretched glove and rolling all the way out to foul territory. By the time it was over, New York had scored to tie the game, and Chris had been charged with two errors on the same play.

"That's a rare one," one of the photographers muttered from behind her. "What's with him?"

Daphne knew it was a rhetorical question, so she didn't bother to answer. But it wasn't lost on her that she was maybe the only person in that entire stadium who knew *exactly* what was wrong with him, ranging from everything he'd told her to everything she'd done. When the inning was over, she watched as he came into the dugout, completely stone-faced, tossing his glove into the garbage can before disappearing down the steps into the club-house.

"Did he just—" the photographer asked, and this time Daphne knew the question *was* directed toward her.

"Yeah," she said. "He did."

ANY MINUTE, DAPHNE HAD EXPECTED TO GET A NOTE FOR AN UP-date to announce, something about how third baseman Chris Kepler had been replaced on the field, or even that Chris Kepler had been taken out of the game on some injury pretext. But it never came, and by the top of the eighth inning he was back out there again with another glove to finish the game. She should've known that wasn't his style, to just leave like that. At least not when it came to his job. With her, he'd left *exactly* like that.

After the loss, she also headed to the clubhouse for a quick interview with the starting pitcher. Several of the players jostled her as they went by—not in a rude way, but just in the inevitable way when everyone is headed to the same place. For the first time, it occurred to her to wonder if Chris had told anyone about what had happened between them. Randy, at the very least, probably knew. And if Randy knew, that meant the entire team knew. She hadn't gotten a weird vibe off anyone yet, but it slowed her steps a little bit, made her less confident as she moved toward the dugout.

But even after a few minutes among everyone else, she knew he hadn't said anything. For one thing, why would he? As far as she could tell, he was doing a bang-up job of pretending like it had never happened. He was back to his old stoic self, his face not giving away any hint as to what he might be feeling. Then for another thing, a word from him could be enough to poison the entire team against her, and somehow she just knew he wouldn't do that.

Still, if this was how the rest of the season was going to be—the tense silence, the way her heart seemed to live permanently in her throat—it was going to be a long one.

With everything else, it had completely slipped Daphne's mind that tonight was when Chris had unveiled the new walk-up song after the fan vote. Her own initiative, and she'd barely paid attention to what the selection had ended up being or even whether it had played during the game. She had notes from Greg that she was supposed to get a quick quote from Chris about the song, what he thought about the choice, how he thought it was going to help pump him up, that kind of thing. She could think of nothing she wanted to do less.

By the time she got to him in the clubhouse, he'd already taken off his jersey, was only wearing the navy athletic shirt he wore underneath. He was sitting on the bench, messing with his glove in some way, and it was only when she got closer that she realized he was cleaning it with a paper towel and a bottle of hand sanitizer. He must've retrieved it from the trash can.

She cleared her throat from behind him, and he turned, looking over his shoulder at the sound. There was a split second when his face was open and waiting—just ready to talk to whoever had come up to him—but then it quickly shuttered again when he realized it was her. He set the glove a little away from himself on the bench, like he didn't even want her looking at it, and stood up.

God, he was tall. She knew that already, of course. But he seemed extra tall now, looking down at her with those hazel eyes and those eyelashes and that mouth that once again was back to looking like it had never known a smile a day in its life.

"I'm supposed to talk to you about the walk-up song thing," she said.

He just looked at her, and for a moment she almost imagined he was taking her in the same way she'd been taking him in. That he was cataloging every detail about her face, that he couldn't help staring at her mouth. But then he glanced away, and she realized she'd been silly to even imagine it. He hated her now. If he'd been looking at her at all, it was probably just to remember how angry he was with her, how much he resented having to talk to her.

"Okay."

That was all she was going to get out of him, she realized, so she waved the cameraman over and waited until he'd framed the shot before she pasted on the brightest smile of her own that she could muster. "I'm here with Chris Kepler, who had the chance to unveil a new walk-up song tonight, chosen by *you* at home in a fan vote that got quite heated in the last round of voting. Chris, how do you feel about what the fans chose for you?"

"It's great," he said, and he was *good* at this. He switched into Chris Kepler, Professional Athlete so well that for a moment she was only relieved that he wasn't looking at her the way he had before. He was neutral, a vaguely positive shade of neutral, and even that was like taking a long drink of water after being in the desert all night. He said two words and she wanted to cry.

"I'm not that surprised 'Eye of the Tiger' won," he said. "It's a classic for a reason."

Wait. What? Daphne wished she had her notes in front of her, but she'd started handing them off to the cameraman in situations where she knew her hands would be in the shot. She'd been feeling more confident lately, more able to think on the fly if she needed to. But now she was struck speechless. *That* had been the song that won? It had been one that Chris had thrown out there as one of his picks, and he'd told her that it was only because he was having such a hard time thinking of anything else, so why not.

It was her turn to speak, to ask some question that would garner one more sound bite about how the song really fired him up, or thanking the fans for their input. But she didn't know what to say.

Chris was definitely looking at her now. She was sure it was in a *what's wrong with you?* kind of way, but she couldn't even make eye contact. She gave a helpless glance to the cameraman, like *can we just start over?*

"I was worried about this song," Chris said finally. "Not going to lie. It's so iconic, and when you go out and have a night like I had tonight . . . but then I remembered that the whole point of the first *Rocky* movie wasn't that he won, but that he went the distance. I think this team has a lot of fight in it."

Daphne tried to say *I agree*, but what came out of her mouth was more of a choked guttural sound than actual words.

"Although the song wasn't used until *Rocky III*," Chris continued after a pause. "I grew up in Philadelphia watching those movies with my brother and he would've had my ass if I didn't correct the record on that point." Now it was Chris' turn to glance at the cameraman. "Sorry. He would've wanted me to correct the record on that point, is what I meant to say."

Daphne tried to pull it together enough to do her job at least. If he was able to be professional and talk about the song like none of the past few days even mattered, then surely she could do the same. "Well," she said, addressing the camera. "A little appreciation for his new song and a movie history lesson all at once. Thank you, Chris."

If she had any fantasy that he'd be different with her now, that the interview indicated a softening of his attitude toward her, she was quickly disabused of that notion once the camera was off. He scooped up his glove from the bench and, without even a glance in her direction, headed out of the locker room and toward the hallway where all the training facilities are. Daphne had never been back that far—she'd never had any reason to.

I still think you should try to talk to him again, Kim had said, but Daphne didn't see how she'd crack through his reserve even to set up a time to talk, much less get through the whole conversation. Maybe if she could interview him, if there were a microphone and a camera between them. Even then, all she'd get would be that same polite Interview Chris from when she'd taken the job. And if it came to a staring contest, she knew she'd blink first.

But it kept her up that night, after she finally got home and fed Milo, crawled into bed, and put on an old sitcom with the volume low just to try to tune out her thoughts. When she looked back on that horrible scene in his condo, she didn't know that she *had* been able to fully explain everything. Despite the fact that she'd been waiting for months for the other shoe to drop, when it finally did, she'd been taken completely by surprise. She'd barely been able to *think*, much less get the words out that would help him to understand where she'd been coming from, why she'd done what she'd done.

Maybe there was no explanation. She knew that. Maybe anything she said would just be an excuse, maybe it would make Chris even angrier, if he bothered to listen at all. But she didn't want to leave it without at least *trying*. Even if it didn't change anything about the way he felt about her, maybe it would help to answer some questions. If she could give that kind of closure at the very least, she wanted to do it. For him, but also for herself.

She reached out to grab her phone off her nightstand, closing her eyes momentarily against the harsh bright light of the screen. It was already three thirty a.m., but she sat up, switching on the lamp so she could settle in. She knew she had a lot to say.

CHAPTER
THIRTY-NINE

WALKING AWAY FROM DAPHNE AFTER THAT INTERVIEW HAD BEEN one of the hardest things Chris had ever done. He didn't *want* to walk away. There was a yearning, desperate part of him that wanted the complete opposite. It had been hard to even stand that close to her, the smell of her hair, the map of freckles on her skin. He felt like he could still see the imprint of his hands everywhere they'd touched. He saw her frowning down at her notes and wondered if it was anything he could help her with; he saw her smile at the cameraman and wondered if she was already past their relationship. When she'd stumbled during her questions, something in his chest had clenched, and suddenly he was rambling about *Rocky* movies just to try to bail her out. She was still Daphne.

But she was also *Duckie*. There was a time when he would've wanted nothing more than to be standing next to her—to know what she looked like, to be able to see her in person and get to know her better in a real way that went beyond text exchanges. But that was before. Now he didn't know how to feel—about Duckie *or* Daphne. He was angry.

He was hurt.

After getting wasted at Randy's house that night after he'd found out, Chris had ended up crashing at Randy's place for the next couple of days. He hadn't intended to do that, but the idea of going back to his empty condo after Daphne left made something twist in his gut, and so he'd passed out on Randy's couch and then overstayed his welcome. Not that Randy had seemed to mind— he'd even asked Chris at one point what was going on, but Chris had waved him off, slurring something about how he just needed to unwind a bit. Or at least that's what Chris hoped he'd said. He didn't fully remember all of it.

When he stepped into his condo after the game, it felt . . . the same. It was the same place he'd lived for the last year, with the gorgeous view and that stupid fucking concrete table and the open-concept the broker had sold him on as perfect for entertaining. There wasn't a single sign that Daphne had ever been there— which, what had he expected? A note? She'd even made the bed.

His phone buzzed in his pocket, and he was absurdly grateful for the interruption to his thoughts, grateful just not to be alone. Maybe it was Randy. If a bunch of the guys were doing something tonight, he'd meet them wherever, he didn't care if it was late and he was tired or how early he had to be up the next day.

But it was his dad calling. Chris almost declined—turned out there *was* something he dreaded more than the silence—but he knew he'd only be putting off the inevitable.

He barely got his greeting out before his dad started in on him about the errors. "You're not providing value offensively right now," his dad said. "You *know* that, Chris. Your defense is all you have. Nobody gives a shit about your two Gold Gloves if you're dropping the ball like that. Come by this weekend, we'll—"

"No, Dad." Chris cut him off before he could go any further. "I'm not running any drills with you. I run drills every day. I take batting practice every day. I need a *break*, not a—"

"A *break*?" his dad repeated, like the very word was foreign to him. It probably was. Chris' dad could be a hard-ass, but it was only because he'd been a roofing contractor for Chris' entire life, and in that whole time Chris couldn't remember a single time he'd called out sick or missed a job. His dad had had walking pneumonia for two months back when Chris was a kid, and *still* he didn't remember his dad doing anything differently other than the way he'd fallen asleep on the couch in front of the TV instead of making it to his room.

"Not a break from baseball," Chris clarified. "I'm still starting almost every single game. I just meant a break from everything else, from extra drills or practices or—"

"You think when you're fucking up is a time to take a *break?*" This time when his dad said the word, it was less like it was unfamiliar and more like it was unsavory, like he couldn't stand even the taste of it. "Now's the time to do *more*. You should be fitting in a workout right now. Or if your shoulder is hurting again, at least some fielding exercises. You know it's all muscle memory, Chris, the more you do it the more you—"

"It's not my muscle memory!" Chris had meant to say it firmly enough that his dad would hear him, that he'd stop talking, but still the words came out harsher and louder than he intended. He took a breath, trying to settle down in the wake of his dad's stunned silence. "It's not my muscle memory. It's not my shoulder. It's my *head*, Dad. And I've been trying to do any drill I can think of, trying to get *away* from memory, but it's not working. I miss Tim. I miss him so bad I don't even know what to do with it. And you *never* talk about him and I need to talk about him. Nobody knew him the way we did, nobody knows what this feels like, and I can't—"

Chris swallowed past the lump in his throat, only then realizing he was holding the phone so tightly his hand had actually seized up. He forced himself to loosen his grip, tried to take a deep breath. He knew this was a lot to put on his father. He knew that the man didn't *mean* to be so critical, truly thought he was doing the best for his son. *Would you rather hit balls for the good money or do* this *twelve hours a day in the sun?* his dad had asked one summer when he'd brought Chris to work a few roofing jobs with him. *I want better than my life for you,* his dad had always said, and it took a while for Chris to see what an expression of love that was. He hadn't thought his dad's life seemed that bad.

Tim had been a little bit of an outsider during those years. He'd had other interests, hadn't played baseball past high school, had zero interest in being tapped to help out on roofing jobs even as a life lesson. Chris felt his own guilt about that now, but he didn't want him and his father to just close up around Tim's absence. He was scared to feel it. He *needed* to feel it.

But his dad was grieving in his own way. And maybe Chris couldn't force this, any more than he could force a home run when he just wasn't timing the ball right.

"Sorry," he said. "It's been a rough night. The game, and—I was seeing someone. Kind of. Anyway, that ended, and it's just been . . . a rough night."

His dad was silent for so long that Chris held the phone away from his face, checking if he'd dropped the call. But finally he heard his dad clear his throat.

"The reporter woman?" his dad said. "Daphne something?"

Chris couldn't have been more surprised if his dad started calling out winning lottery numbers. "Yeah," he said. "How did you know that?"

"I didn't," his dad said almost gruffly, like he was embarrassed. "But you had this way of looking at her. Anyway, I'm sorry it didn't work out."

"Me, too."

They sat in silence for a bit, but it wasn't a strained one. It felt oddly comfortable, actually. Chris was just thinking maybe he should beg off, let his father get to bed, when his dad spoke again.

"I do miss him," he said. "I miss him so much I have a hard time even saying his name. But I haven't been fair to you, and I'm sorry. I just want you to be happy. That's really all I've ever wanted, for you, and for . . . for Tim. I did right by you, didn't I?"

"You did, Dad."

"It wasn't easy, after your mom left."

"I know," Chris said. "I know."

THE CALL ONLY ENDED BECAUSE CHRIS' PHONE DIED AROUND one in the morning. They mostly discussed other stuff—not Tim, not Daphne, and not how Chris was doing on the team—but at one point Chris did say he was going to find someone to talk to and he recommended his dad did, too. He knew it was a long shot, but he almost thought his dad might do it.

For his part, Chris scheduled a meeting with Marv and asked that the mental skills coach be present, too. That had to signal to Marv that something was up, but he was a veteran manager, and so he took it all in stride. It was almost embarrassing to Chris, how much he took it all in stride. *Of course* he didn't even blink when Chris said that he knew his issues that season were mental, that he thought he would benefit from regular therapy. The only emotion Marv showed was when Chris revealed that his brother had died before the season started, and Marv reached out to give Chris a firm, compassionate hand squeeze. Chris could've broken down right then, but he kept it together. He realized that was what he'd been afraid of all along—not his manager's frustration or impatience or irritation, but his compassion.

"Do you need time off?" Marv asked. "Because we can do

that. You can take personal bereavement leave. We can even put you on the IL for mental health reasons, if you'd rather do it that way. And I do mean the injured list, not the restricted list—which would let you continue to get paid and accrue service time."

"No," Chris said. "I mean, thank you. If I do need that I'll let you know. But for now, I really think I can keep playing. I want to keep playing."

"Well, just say the word," Marv said. "You think you're out here to support the team, but don't forget that we're out here to support *you*. That's the definition of a team, Kepler."

After he left Marv's office, he found himself wandering around, saying a brief hello to a couple guys who were running drills out on the field, dipping into the clubhouse to grab himself a Gatorade, then heading up to where the broadcast booths were. He realized he was looking for Daphne. He hadn't liked it when she'd told him she thought he needed to talk to someone. He'd seen it as an attack. He'd seen it as a jab that he wasn't holding it together as well as he thought he was.

Turns out, maybe he wasn't holding it together as well as he thought he was.

He hung a left in the hallway, away from the video room instead of toward it. Looking for Daphne was pointless, its own agonizing form of muscle memory that he would have to work to actively rewrite. Eventually he'd get to where something happened and he wouldn't immediately want to share it with her. Eventually he wouldn't *miss* her with an ache that made him want to forget his anger, forget his hurt, forget anything if it just meant he could have her back.

It would take time, that was all.

FORTY

FOR WEEKS, DAPHNE HAD CHECKED HER INSTAGRAM DMS EVERY day, waiting to see if Chris had responded to her message. But not only had he not responded—he apparently hadn't even checked it, because the little grayed-out Sent never changed to Seen.

There had seemed something fitting about returning back to the original communication method they'd used. More important, she'd thought a DM had less of a chance of waking him up in the middle of the night than a text, gave him the opportunity to consciously check the message instead of being surprised by it at some point when maybe he wouldn't want to receive it.

The only problem was now she didn't know what to do. Should she delete the message, hope he never saw it? Should she resend it as a text instead? What if he was ignoring her on purpose, though—what if he'd seen the message come in and had left it to sit in his inbox, unread?

She tried to gauge his attitude toward her in person, but he was impossible to read. Sometimes she thought he'd softened toward her. Once, she tripped a bit on a wire stretched across the field, and he'd reached out to steady her even though she'd been in no danger of falling. Another time, she'd been laughing at something Beau Bummer had said after an interview and she'd looked up to catch Chris watching her, a momentary bleakness around the eyes until he blinked it away.

But for the most part, he treated her exactly the way he'd said he would that last day in his condo. He answered her baseball questions on camera, and other than that he had no interaction with her at all.

So she stopped checking her messages. And then eventually, she deleted the app from her phone entirely, sick of that twist in her gut every time she saw its icon on her phone screen.

It was mid-September when Layla went into labor. Daphne got the phone call from Donovan two hours before a game was supposed to start, and she'd anxiously filled Greg and the rest of the production team in on what was going on, saying why she wouldn't be able to do the broadcast that night. She didn't even know if she'd fully made sense, but they seemed to understand enough to tell her not to worry about it, to go be with her brother, to give their best to Layla. She drove faster than she ever had before to get to the hospital and barely had time to freak out about how stressful it was to have to cross four lanes of traffic to make a last-minute turn.

"You know these things take hours," Donovan said once she got there. He was watching the game on his phone, casually eating a bag of Flamin' Hot Cheetos, and then frowning down at the cheese dust he was getting all over the phone screen.

Even Layla looked calm and unbothered. "Epidural," she explained. "I can't feel anything below my waist and I don't want to. Who's filling in for you?"

"That guy Preston," Daphne said.

Layla made a face. "Ugh, I hate him," she said. "He talks like he has marbles in his mouth. And is it just me, or is his neck weirdly saggy for him being so small?"

"I don't know that I've ever noticed his neck." Daphne looked at her brother for help, but he was pumping his fist.

"Kepler with a two-RBI double," he said. "Man, I actually think they could do it. Cleveland is also fighting for a Wild Card spot but their ace pitcher just went out with an oblique strain."

The energy around the team had been pretty electric in the last few weeks. Against all odds, they'd had an *amazing* August when a couple other teams in their division had started to slide, setting the Battery up with a viable shot at making the playoffs.

"He's had a great couple months," Layla said. "I told you it was the right decision not to tell him."

Daphne cut her gaze over to her brother. She'd never known for sure if Layla had told him everything that went down with Chris Kepler. On the one hand, they were married, which brought with it its own code. She couldn't blame her sister-in-law if she *did* tell Donovan. On the other, the only thing more embarrassing than Donovan finding out she'd been hooking up with a baseball player would be Donovan finding out that she'd been dumped by the same baseball player for catfishing him.

Layla seemed to catch Daphne's look, and waved her hand. "Of course he knows," she said. "And he told me I was out of line for my Theranos comment. What you did was not the same as defrauding investors out of millions of dollars and average citizens out of accurate and safely obtained medical data. And you're not the Yoko Ono of the Battery."

"You . . . never called me that," Daphne said.

"Oh," Layla said, her tan skin coloring slightly. "Well, good."

At least not to my face, Daphne should've clarified. But whatever. It was over. "Yoko Ono wasn't even the Yoko Ono of the Beatles," she said. "If you're meaning it the way I think you are. We love to say John Lennon is a genius until apparently when it comes time to making his own decisions about—"

"I like that 'Imagine' song," Donovan cut in. "That's the Beatles, right?"

"I'm just saying," Layla said, blatantly talking over her husband. "It was obviously the right call not to tell him. Look at how well he's been doing."

Daphne should just let that go. She didn't want to air her dirty laundry now, here in a hospital room with the imminent (or not-so-imminent, apparently) arrival of her nephew. And what did it matter, if Layla was right or wrong or if all of it had spiraled into some gray area where Daphne didn't even know what was right or wrong anymore.

But.

"He found out, actually," Daphne said. "It really sucked and everything exploded and I guess you could say we broke up if you could even have said we were together in the first place, and now I get to ask him questions after the game about how awesome it is now that his batting average is up and pretend I don't want to cry."

Donovan looked up from his phone, his mouth open in slack-jawed shock. Layla popped a handful of ice chips, crunching them noisily with her teeth until eventually she swallowed.

"Well," she said. "I did not know that."

In the corner, there was a stack of luggage that Layla had referred to as her *baby bag*. When Donovan had pointed out that it was singular for a reason, Layla had said that she had three separate birth plans and she needed to bring different items for each potential eventuality and if other people were as prepared as her, they'd have an entire luggage set, too. It was wild to Daphne, to think that in a couple of days her brother and sister-in-law would be going home with a *baby*, an actual human they'd take care of and who would bond them together for the rest of their lives.

"I didn't want you to know," Daphne said. "I couldn't believe that there I was, barely a year after splitting with Justin, fucking up yet another relationship. And I really didn't want *you* to know."

Donovan pointed at his chest, like he was playing to the back-of-house in a school play. "Me? Why me?"

"You already think I'm such a failure for not making it work with Justin," she said. "I know you took his side, and—"

"Whoa, whoa, whoa." Donovan put the phone down and wiped his hands on his jeans before he held them up like he was actually trying to stop her words from hitting him. "I didn't take Justin's side. I mean, he's my friend, yeah, but—"

"I know he's your friend," Daphne said. "And I don't want to have ruined that, too. Believe me. But you've *always* taken his side. When you guys would hog the video game controllers. When you laughed at me the night of my prom. When I wanted to go on a honeymoon and Justin said we could use the money to buy into that flex Panthers tickets scheme and go to four home games as our honeymoon."

"That was a good deal," Donovan said. "And technically, *four* weekends in Charlotte instead of just one week somewhere else."

Daphne shrugged, like *see*. He was still doing it.

"And laughed at you the night of your prom?" Donovan said. "I don't remember that . . ."

But she could see the moment when he *did* remember the way he and Justin had reacted when she came out in her dress and makeup. It was oddly satisfying, having that validation that it had really happened, that it wasn't just something she'd made into a bigger deal over the years.

"I had no idea," he said finally. "I didn't know that was how you saw it. I'm sorry, Daphne."

She was conscious suddenly of the setting, of the fact that they were sitting in a hospital room where Layla was hooked up to all kinds of monitors that beeped and spiked, and nurses kept coming and going outside the hallway. It wasn't the time or place to adjudicate all her past insecurities. She could let Donovan off the hook.

"It's fine," she said.

"No," he said. Donovan looked genuinely stricken. "I'm so sorry. I never meant to make you feel that way. When we were younger . . . sure, I was probably a dick sometimes. I saw it as typical big-brother stuff, just giving you a hard time. He was my friend and you were the annoying little sister, you know?"

"I know," she said. "I'm sure I *was* annoying, always wanting to be underfoot. And it had to be painfully obvious what a crush I had on Justin."

"Well, yeah," Donovan said. "And if you want the truth, I didn't like it at first. Not because I didn't think *you* were good enough for *him*, but because I knew damn well that *he* wasn't good enough for *you*. But once you guys got together, it seemed to make you both happy, so I had to make my peace with it. You're your own person, you know? You can make your own decisions. And you'd decided you wanted him."

"For better or worse," Daphne muttered.

Donovan leaned forward on his chair, pressing his hands together almost like he was praying, like he was pleading with Daphne to hear him. "I was so close to saying something on your wedding day. Justin was *such* a prick at the bachelor party"—here Layla made a face and nodded, as if it was important that she confirm that Justin was, in fact, a prick—"and I could just *tell* that you were having second thoughts about it that morning. But you looked so beautiful in your dress, and there was that whole thing where they got the flowers wrong, and I couldn't. When you told me you were getting a divorce, my first thought was *thank god*. But I felt disloyal, because Justin *is* still my best friend, for all his faults as a brother-in-law, and you're my sister and I want you to be happy and you seemed miserable. So yeah, I tried to encourage you to get back together because I didn't know what you wanted and I never wanted to be the one who was standing in the way of it."

That was maybe the most Daphne had ever heard her brother say to her at once. He wasn't the touchy-feely type, generally—if he signed a birthday card to her, he'd write *Love, Your Big Brother*, but he wasn't big on saying *I love you* per se. But somehow that speech, the part where he'd said she looked beautiful in her wedding dress. It had felt damn close.

"Why is he still your best friend if he's such a prick?" She realized that was the question she most wanted the answer to.

Donovan sighed. "I don't know. It's hard to make friends as an adult."

"Well, join a book club or something. Take up archery."

"That's not a bad idea," Donovan said, brightening. Then, to make sure she understood: "The archery one, I mean."

Daphne rolled her eyes. "I don't know if you can be trusted with a bow and arrow. But I'd pay money to see you at a book club. A Nicholas Sparks one, maybe."

"That reminds me," Layla said from the bed. "What are your plans after the season, when you're done with this sideline reporter gig?"

Briefly, Daphne thought back to a time when Chris had asked her the same question. When she'd thought he was asking because he saw a future with her in it, and he was trying to see if she saw it the same way. It hadn't even occurred to her then to consider moving to take a similar job with another team, but who knew. Maybe that would be the best option for her. "I'm open to whatever," she said. "Why? Do you know a similar job in another market that might take me?"

"What?" Layla said, so sharply Daphne briefly thought she must've said something wildly out of line. Like of *course* she wasn't just going to land the equivalent of Layla's job somewhere else. That was a lot of hubris after she'd only been doing half duty for the past four months. She started to backpedal, say something about how she was only kidding, but just then a nurse came in.

"Hello!" she said in a chirpy voice that Daphne immediately knew Layla was inwardly flinching from. "Just here to check Mom's dilation."

It was weird to Daphne, to hear Layla referred to as "Mom," but she guessed she'd have to get used to it.

"Should I—" she started to say, sure she didn't need to be present for this part.

"You're not going to another market," Layla said. "We're about to have a *baby* and we're not looking to have his aunt move thousands of miles away. I was going to ask if you would want to be involved with the Battery on its charitable foundation side. They've been wanting to put something together for a while to do with books or reading or something like that, and I know that's kinda your thing."

Daphne's first thought was that it sounded incredible. Even without any more details, she was already really excited about the idea.

But her second thought was that she didn't know if she'd want to be involved with the team, even doing something like this, where she doubted she'd have much reason to run into Chris at all. Maybe it would be better to have a clean break.

"Can I think about it?" she asked.

"Of course," Layla said as the nurse put her surgical gloves on. "Now could you both *please* get the fuck out of here so I can have some privacy? I know birth is a beautiful natural part of life but I don't need an audience when there's a stranger's hand in my cervix."

It was practically a race to the door to see whether Donovan or Daphne could get out of there faster, and they stood out in the hallway, close enough to know when to go back in but far enough away that Layla couldn't accuse them of trying to eavesdrop on her cervix check or whatever.

"You know," Donovan said. "I bet I would make a *great* best friend for Chris Kepler. Maybe that's how you get him back."

Daphne shot him a sharp look. The sad truth was, he probably *would* make a great friend for Chris. She could picture it. Except she knew that, if anything, it would be Chris making Donovan give her a turn at a video game she was admittedly terrible at, while Donovan whined about how she was wrecking his stats. And then Chris would've let her play on his profile instead, and he'd try to coach her through but she'd be hopeless, except he wouldn't care about how much she was fucking up his stats, he'd just be laughing and then he'd squeeze the back of her neck in the way that let her know he was thinking about what he'd do to her later that night when they were alone.

She could get through whole hours without having these kinds of thoughts now, which was an improvement over a couple months ago. But they still haunted her, especially when she couldn't sleep.

"I'm sorry," Donovan said. "I was trying to make a joke, but too soon, huh?"

"Yeah," she said.

"The thing with Kepler, it was serious?"

Daphne had had *this* conversation with herself a thousand times, too, about how it hadn't been serious and that was the whole point, she really had no right to feel this way. But she was only trying to fool herself, and there was no fooling herself anymore. The way she felt about Chris was different from the way she'd felt about anyone else; the way it had ended had wrecked her more than anything else. Even her divorce.

"Yeah," she said.

The nurse poked her head out of the door, beaming. "Get ready, Dad," she said. "We're about to have a baby."

FORTY-ONE

"MAGIC NUMBER'S *THREE*, YO!" RANDY CAME FROM BEHIND CHRIS to pinch the tendons between his neck and his shoulder, right where he knew it would make Chris squirm.

"Don't tell me the number, man, I don't want to know the number."

"Ah, you *know* the number."

Randy had a point. It was impossible not to—the Battery had four games left in the season, and if they won three of them, they'd have a Wild Card spot. They didn't have to wait to see if another team lost, they didn't have to hope a favored team choked at the last minute, they could just win three out of four and they'd be in. The fact that they'd made it that far *was* wild, especially when you looked back on how badly they'd been playing in the early part of the season.

Most guys had cleared out of the clubhouse, but Chris had started sticking around later and later, wanting to put off going home as long as possible. Sometimes Randy invited him to do something, go out with other guys or just back to his place to play video games, and Chris was always grateful for those gestures. At his lowest moments, he thought about inviting himself over, but he hadn't gotten that desperate just yet.

"Did you see Layla had her baby?" Randy asked, taking his phone out of his pocket and scrolling through until he reached the picture he wanted, turning to show Chris. He *had* already seen that one—it had made the rounds in several group chats. It showed Layla in a hospital bed, somehow looking just as perfectly coiffed as she always was, holding a little bundle of blankets he had to assume was the baby, although there was only a sliver of a forehead peeking out from the swaddle. There was another one with Layla and Donovan together that showed the baby a little better.

"Yeah, that's awesome." Chris cleared his throat. "Are there any other pictures?"

Randy clicked through a few things, handing his phone to Chris. "Scroll up to see all of 'em."

Chris gave the first couple pictures a few long beats of his attention, even though those were the ones he'd already seen. There was another picture of just the baby, lying in the bassinet with BRINK-DEMIR written on an index card taped to the front, stars hand-drawn in blue highlighter to apparently indicate *boy*. Chris scrolled up one more and stopped.

It was a picture of Daphne holding the baby in her arms. He recognized the dress she was wearing as one she wore for the broadcast, and he remembered the night when she'd left early to go to the hospital. He'd been on his way to the dugout after a quick one-two-three top of the first, and his gaze had automatically slid over to the spot where she usually stood, surprised when he didn't see her. It wasn't until the seventh inning when he finally got out of someone that she was just at the hospital because her nephew was being born, and he was so relieved, he'd come *so close* to texting her. It wasn't the first time he'd had that impulse. He'd typed and deleted so many things into that text box, ranging from hey to you looked beautiful tonight to u up? to I miss you.

In the picture, she was looking down at her nephew and smiling, and something about the way her hand cradled the back of his head . . . He returned the phone to Randy. "Cute," he said.

"The baby, or Daphne?"

"Come on, man."

Randy made occasional comments like that, which Chris tried to respond to in the casual way he would if it were just a teammate teasing him about a crush on the sideline reporter with nothing else behind it. Normally that was enough to get Randy to drop it, until a week or so later when he'd hit him with another one.

But this time, Randy apparently didn't feel like letting up. "You were pretty worried about her that night," he said. "Kept asking where she was."

"It was unusual," Chris said. "That's all."

Randy gave him a long, considering look. "When are you just gonna forgive her, man?"

That comment wasn't easy to form a casual response to. Chris racked his brain to figure out what Randy could even mean by it. Did he know? But how could he know? Had Daphne said something? He couldn't imagine her having that kind of conversation with him.

Randy reached up into his locker for some lotion, applying it to the new ink on his forearm. Chris had gone with him as he got a tattoo of his mother's initials when they'd had a little extra time in San Francisco, and for the first time Chris had wondered if he should do the same thing for Tim. Get his initials, an image that reminded him of his brother, something.

Randy seemed to understand Chris' silence, because he capped the lotion back up and said, "You told me all about it that night you came over. You were pretty drunk, it didn't always make sense, but I think I pieced it together. Something about how your text girl and your real girl were the same girl? And then there was a bit about Daffy Duck. It wasn't hard to figure out that you were talking about Daphne. Anyway, you were *never* in your hotel room anymore, and you might think you have game, but you don't have woman-in-every-city type of game. Unless it's the same woman in every city."

He tapped his head, like he was Sherlock Holmes for cracking that one. Chris could only stare at him, completely taken aback.

"Why didn't you say anything?" he asked.

"Why didn't *you*?" Randy shot back. "Look, clearly you were going through it. I know you don't always like to talk about stuff, like your brother, and the game. I figured you'd come to me with it when you were ready."

Once Chris had talked to Marv, it was easier to slowly open up more with the rest of his teammates, let them know what had been going on with him. They'd all been supportive and cool about it, which wasn't really a surprise. His reticence to share before hadn't really ever been about *them*. Several actually shared their own stories of losing family members or friends to suicide, and he had been a little surprised by that part, just how much more common it was than he'd ever realized.

He'd shared even more with Randy, generally about how his weekly therapy sessions were going, how much better his relationship with his dad had been lately. But he'd never talked about Daphne, because she worked with the team still, and he didn't want to risk making anything awkward or uncomfortable.

At least, he thought he hadn't talked about her. Apparently that wasn't true.

"What exactly did I say?" he asked. "When I was drunk."

"Like I said, it was all garbled. But basically, that she'd lied to you and you didn't know who she was." Randy paused, as if considering his next words. "And that you really, really loved her. You said it hurt, how much you loved her."

Chris closed his eyes. He wished he could say that didn't sound like him, but . . . he still loved her.

"I just couldn't believe it," he said. "I mean, I was *all in*. And then I found out that she had all this information that I didn't have, that she hadn't seen fit to share with me. If I'm being honest, I was embarrassed. I felt like such a fool for not seeing it before."

"I get that," Randy said. "But isn't it just as foolish to throw it all away, just because you're mad? If you love her, then you should be with her. This isn't reason enough not to be."

"I'm not even mad anymore," Chris said. He hadn't fully realized it until he said it aloud, but it was true. He hadn't felt true anger about the situation in some time—weeks, maybe months. Maybe not since those first few days after. "I'm just . . . I keep thinking about what her plan could've possibly been. You know? Eventually the truth was going to come out. We couldn't have dated forever without me ever getting to see her place, or know her phone number. How far would it have gone? Would she have gotten a brand-new number, just so I never had to know? What about her cat? She wasn't about to rename her cat, or get a new one. So what's the only other option? Maybe she never thought we'd make it that far. We'd break up before any of it had to come to light, and she could walk away with a nice text relationship that lasted for a while and a nice friends-with-benefits arrangement that lasted a little while longer."

"Or maybe she didn't have a plan," Randy said. "Maybe it wasn't that deep."

Chris sat slumped over, his forearms resting on his knees, while he thought about that. Maybe it wasn't that deep. Maybe she'd just made an error, a series of errors on the same play. Maybe he'd fucked some stuff up, too. He thought of the way she'd told him she loved him, how open and vulnerable her face had been, the way it had crumpled when he'd thrown the words back at her. He'd made her cry, and god, he hated seeing her cry.

He'd told her then that they were done, not to talk to him except inasmuch as she had to as the sideline reporter for the team. She'd helped lay out the ground rules for their arrangement, and she'd been flawless in following the ground rules he'd set for their breakup. So then why, perversely, was he bothered that she *hadn't* fought it a little harder? Why did it make him worry that one of his fears was right, that it was just a sign that she hadn't been that invested to begin with, that she'd been playing by the rules that they'd set for themselves while he'd gone completely rogue?

"Just think about it," Randy said. "You don't have to make any big decisions tonight. Or even before the end of the season." He leaned down to whisper in Chris' ear. *"Magic number is three."*

Chris laughed, flinching at the way that tickled as he swatted Randy away. "Get outta here with that shit," he said. "I told you, I don't want to know."

THAT NIGHT, CHRIS SAT OUT ON HIS BALCONY WITH A BEER, LOOK-ing out over the water. When he'd told Daphne that he barely used his balcony, she'd been appalled. "If I had a view like this, I'd be out here every single morning," she said when he'd shown it to her that one time she'd stayed over. "And every night. Maybe sometimes in the middle of the day, too, except if it was super hot."

"And when," he'd said, pulling her onto his lap, "would you be with *me?*"

Now, he wasn't around during the early or middle parts of the day much, but he found that he did like sitting out there at night. And most of those times, he thought about what Daphne had said. He thought about Daphne.

One moment he kept going back to, for whatever reason: the way she'd looked fixing her hair in that hotel room. Wrapped in the white robe that was a little too big on her, her bare feet peeping out, the way she'd had her hands in her hair while she talked about taking more care with her appearance as a way to take more care of herself. There had been something so domestic about that moment, so *tender*, that he just couldn't get it out of his head.

He'd read through their text message chain so many times by now, he felt like he could quote parts of it word for word. It was almost unthinkable to him now, that he hadn't known she was Duckie. Sometimes he wondered if on some level he *had* known, although he knew that was a stretch. He just could hear her voice so clearly in those messages, could fill in all the blanks from both sides of her that he'd wondered about at the time. Her dickhead ex had made her feel insignificant and unworthy of his notice, and she still carried that with her. And then Chris had thrown that back in her face, too, telling her *I'll tell you one thing, though, you're not boring. Whatever else this was, it was a hell of a ride.* He felt sick to his stomach when he thought about saying that to her.

He got to the beginning of the text chain again, and this time he wanted to keep going, all the way to that very first message that had started it all. So he redownloaded the Instagram app on his phone, barely waiting for it to finish updating before he opened it up to check his DMs.

There were a bunch since the last time he'd been on, and he didn't even bother to delete them, just scrolled through until he reached the bottom of the unread ones to find her message. When he didn't see it, he scrolled back up, stopping when he saw her little profile picture of the rubber duckie on top of a stack of books.

There was a new message. He sat up straighter, reaching to put his beer on the table next to him without even looking, which was probably why it immediately wobbled and fell to the ground, the bottle miraculously intact but cold amber liquid puddling on the concrete.

The little gray words under her profile name said Sent 9w. Did that mean it had been sent *nine weeks* ago?

He was almost afraid to open it up. He couldn't believe these words had been sitting here all this time and he hadn't known; he couldn't believe in only a few minutes he would be done reading them. He clicked to open the message.

I had a chance to do this once before, but I made a mess of it. So, I'm going to try again. I hope you read all the way through to the end, but if you don't, I understand.

My name is Daphne Brink, and I am your heckler.

First, I want to clarify a few things. I didn't know anything about baseball. Literally nothing. So the idea of me heckling you . . . I mean, it's ludicrous. It would be like me heckling the world's greatest opera singer about their vibrato. It would be like you heckling a champion whistler.

Chris snorted.

I was also incredibly drunk. Which is not an excuse, I know, but let's just say I was not in a great place emotionally. I'd signed my divorce papers a couple days before, and I was at the game with my best friend, sitting in seats that my brother had originally intended to use to try to get me and my ex back together. That's a long story, I won't bore you with it.

Chris had spent so long thinking about all the connections between Duckie and Daphne, all the little points where she'd lied to him or where he should have figured it out, that he hadn't thought about all the near misses. All the ways that he might never have met her at all—if she hadn't been at that game, if she hadn't heckled him, if she hadn't DMed him in the first place. How could he fault her for all the bad parts, when he wouldn't go back to have it any other way?

When we started talking, it felt so good. Maybe it was just that I was lonely. Maybe it was just that it had been a long time since I felt like I really wanted to know a person, to have them know me. Maybe it had nothing at all to do with you at first. But I think I fell for you at least a little bit from that first message about your pug Otis. That is objectively a very cute dog and dog name, so you knew what you had there—but also I loved that you immediately made that connection, that you'd be texting a stranger about your childhood dog at eleven thirty at night.

I only realized after we'd been talking for a bit that I'd left out the most important paragraph of my initial message, the one that explained who I was and why I was contacting you. The whole point had been for me to apologize about heckling you at the game. I'd only added the rest of it to try to make it more interesting, to show you that I was a person, too, and was just responding to my own pressures and acting out in a way that had nothing to do with you. But I'd deleted that opening bit and hadn't added it back in, so now you just seemed to think that I was a really kind person who cared enough to reach out to you because I saw that you were upset on TV.

I know I should've just told you then. But I thought, what's the harm? It'll be better for him to think some kind stranger reached out to him than to have to think about his heckler again. And selfishly, I liked talking to you. I didn't want our conversation to end. We'd chat this one night, and that'd be it.

Except we kept talking. And Chris, when I tell you how much those conversations meant to me, I really mean it. They brought me back into myself in a way I don't even know that I can fully explain. And that was probably selfish, too, that I allowed them to keep happening even though I knew I was only getting in deeper and making things worse. By now, I really didn't want you to know I was the heckler, because I worried

I'd lose you. So when you asked me my name, I couldn't give it to you, in case you were able to connect the dots.

(Duckie is a nickname my brother called me when we were kids, by the way. And although the handle is supposed to be like Duckie's Books, I can tell you that the "S" stands for Sarah.)

Daphne Sarah. It made him feel almost dizzy, suddenly having all this information he'd wanted for so long. He'd wanted her name and a picture when he'd been texting with her anonymously; he'd wanted to ask her more about her divorce when they'd been together in person but didn't know if that was breaking their rules.

Chris tried to imagine how he would've reacted if, somehow, Daphne *had* just come clean with him when he'd asked for her name. No doubt he would've thought it was weird that she'd taken so long to clarify that point. He might've been embarrassed, clammed up a bit, worried that she was acting in bad faith and trying to catch him out in some way. Maybe it would've ended their relationship right there, another near miss.

Then you can start to piece together the rest of it. I didn't set up the interview, or the sideline job . . . but yes, I took them both partly because they gave me a chance to see you. Only then it got even more complicated, and I felt like everything was so tangled up I'd never get the knot undone. You asked me if I remembered the night we talked on the phone—of course I remember that night. I knew it was dangerous, I knew it was wrong, and still I wanted it so badly that I convinced myself it was okay.

Once he'd gotten past his initial reaction, the knowledge that *she* was the one on the phone that night had only made the memory ten times better. He could also see how vulnerable it must've made her feel, could understand why it had made her pull back the way she had. Especially when they'd started working together more.

I really didn't want to stop texting with you, but I knew it was for the best to try to make as clean a break as possible once I took over the sideline reporting duties. And then I thought I could keep it professional between us as the reporter, and you'd never have to know that we'd had this whole other relationship beyond that.

I recognize how shitty that sounds now. I see how it was always destined to blow up. But at the time, I didn't know what else to do.

And maybe it could've been okay—not great, but at least okay—if I'd left it right there. You'd briefly wonder about this anonymous person you'd chatted with for a few days, but you'd move on. I'd do my job as the Battery reporter until Layla got back, and then I'd move on.

But I couldn't leave well enough alone. I couldn't leave YOU well enough alone. I shouldn't have propositioned you in that bar, I shouldn't have let you take me back to my room, I shouldn't have let any of that happen.

He remembered the way she'd been after that first time. He'd come out of the bathroom and she'd been subdued, clearly retreating back into herself in a way that closed him out. At the time, he'd just worried that she regretted sleeping with him, that she was worried about her job or already second-guessing the rules they'd set for themselves. Now, of course, her reaction made a lot more sense.

From there it was easy to tell myself that the damage had been done, so what was the harm in just one more time? One more day, one more chance to be with you. And maybe I fooled myself along the way that I was somehow making the right choice for you, too, because if I could make you happy, it couldn't all be bad, right?

Then there was that night that you told me about Tim. It meant so much to me that you trusted me with that, that you would share memories of him with me. When you talk about him, I can see how much pain you're in, but I can also see the way your face lights up when you tell a story about who he was. I can tell how important he still is to you.

Chris realized he'd been holding his breath, and when he let it out, it came out shallow and shaky.

But it also felt so wrong—that you were telling me something I already knew, that I was having to pretend I didn't already know. That's the part I'm the most sorry about, the part that I don't know if I can forgive myself for. I certainly can't blame you if you don't forgive me. I said in that very first message that I don't pretend to know what you might be going through, and even now, when you've told both versions of me, I can't pretend to know. It's devastating.

You hold yourself in such tight control. You keep so much locked inside. And maybe I did use both the text messaging and our real-life relationship as a way to try to crack you open a bit, and that was wrong of me. I just wish you could see what I see when you let go of that control, when you're laughing with Randy in the dugout or when you're showing a kid how to field a ground ball on a bounce or when you can't sit still for five seconds while I draw perfectly shaded abs on you. Sometimes I think you believe you don't deserve that joy, but you do.

This time when Chris snorted at the *perfectly shaded abs* part, it sounded phlegmy and disgusting, and only when he reached up to wipe at his nose did he notice there were tears on his cheeks.

(btw I love that your new walk-up song is "Eye of the Tiger." And I love that your brother would've had your ass if you didn't clarify the correct Rocky movie that used the song. Is now a bad time to tell you I've never seen those movies?)

Anyway, I'm rambling again. Maybe you haven't read through this far, and so this is the worst possible place for me to put the most important parts. I really am sorry. I never meant to hurt you. And I really do love you. Those words might not mean shit to you, but they mean a lot to me. I understand if you never want to talk to me again. But if you do, just know I'm always here.

That was the end of the first long message bubble, but there was another one directly underneath it.

Oh, and—please don't let me have ruined any of the magic of "The Way" for you. I've been losing a lot of sleep over all of this, but you might be surprised by how much I'm haunted by the idea that I could've ruined that song.

Chris didn't know why that made him smile, but it did. Truthfully, he hadn't even given a second of thought to the song.

He clicked over to her profile, and there were a few new pictures from the last time he'd checked, but they were still all older. The newest one was from back in May, when she'd shown off a fanned array of library books on top of a patchwork quilt he recognized from pictures she'd sent him of Milo. Doesn't it always happen that all your library holds come in at once? her caption said.

Chris stared back out at the dark night, the barest reflections of light that demarcated what was water and what was sky. *If you love her, then you should be with her*, Randy had said. Like it was that simple.

And suddenly, Chris felt like it was.

FORTY-TWO

THE GAME HAD BEEN AN ABSOLUTE ROLLER COASTER. THE BREW-
ers had taken an early lead, but then a two-run homer by Gutierrez had put the Battery ahead. The Brewers had scored again, but
the Battery had had an incredible seventh inning, bringing home
four runs on some two-out magic. Daphne always worried about
games—had trouble believing that *any* of them were in hand, no
matter what kind of lead was on the scoreboard—but for once she
was feeling good about this one. It felt like destiny.

Or maybe she was just feeling good because Chris had smiled
at her. It hadn't been much of an interaction—he was on his way
to the on-deck circle, a reminder of that first time she'd ever met
him. She'd been standing near the photography well, looking
down at her notecards while she received a few instructions for
her next segment in her earpiece. She'd seen some motion out of
the corner of her eye, and she'd glanced up just in time to see
Chris walk by. And he'd smiled at her.

It had probably just been a polite smile, the kind you automatically give anyone as you pass by them. Probably Chris hadn't
even fully clocked that it was her he was smiling at, thought he
was acknowledging some random person, a photographer or the
batgirl or whoever, she didn't know.

But it hadn't felt like that. It had felt personal, special, a little secret. It had sent tingles from the base of her spine all the way down to her toes. It felt like the kind of smile that guaranteed some kind of ninth-inning heroics, which was why she wasn't even concerned when the Battery's closing pitcher walked two guys in a row and then hit the third to load the bases. It was the kind of smile that she could cling to even when the inning got completely out of control, with a wild pitch and a double and a two-run homer to end up putting the Brewers back on top. It was the kind of smile that she felt sure would send any ball that connected with a Battery bat sailing four hundred feet over the outfield fence. It was the kind of smile that she started to worry she'd imagined like some sort of mirage when the game ended on the Battery's final out, Randy Caminero swinging and missing on a curveball at the knees.

One of her least favorite parts of her job was talking to players after a loss, and this one hurt more because she knew it was an important one. They weren't out of playoff contention, but they'd made things that much harder. They'd have to be perfect from here on out, and they still had one more series against the Padres coming up, who'd been on a winning streak.

"Randy," she said, stopping him on the way to the dugout with her microphone. "What was going through your mind during that last at-bat?"

She'd asked Layla once, Why do we ask these kinds of questions when the answer has to be clear? Like, obviously the guy is hoping to get a home run, or at least a base hit; obviously he's hoping to score the runner on base and help his team take the lead. She'd heard so many versions of these same answers before that she could almost script their answers herself.

Of course it's filler, Layla had said. She'd said that half of what they did was filler, and that was okay, that was part of sports.

There was a patter to it, the speculation and observation and reflection. Being good at your job didn't always mean providing the most incisive analysis or the most unique answer although, sure, those were great when they happened. It was also just coloring in the background around the game, helping it to feel like a complete experience.

Now, Randy gave her the exact answer she'd expected, and Daphne tried to focus on active listening instead of looking around to see if Chris was still in the dugout or if he'd already left. She knew she was supposed to ask Randy about the upcoming series, so she pivoted to that question once he'd finished.

"I feel good about it," he said. "My boy Kepler has a saying—he says baseball is being endlessly optimistic in the face of math. I'm feeling optimistic. And I think he is, too."

And then Randy *winked* at her, heading to join the rest of the players disappearing into the clubhouse. She threw it back to the anchors who handled the postgame show, and once the camera was off her, she unclipped her microphone and handed it to the production assistant.

What had that wink been about? And why had he brought up Chris—was that on purpose? Players mentioned other players all the time, especially if they'd had a particularly good game and deserved a shout-out. Chris had played well that night, and had stolen a base in the ninth inning to set himself up to be the potential winning run if Randy had been able to bat him in. But Randy hadn't mentioned any of that. So what could that mean?

Daphne retrieved her purse from where she stowed it while she was doing broadcasts, withdrawing her phone to check it for any new messages. There was one from Donovan—apparently the first three nights of perfectly blissful full-night sleeps in the hospital had been some weird fluke, or a bait and switch, because now he said the baby was up every two hours and it was driving him and Layla out of their minds. The phrase 'sleeps like a baby' is a crock, he said.

She smiled. Send me a picture of my nephew and I'll give you my opinion.

A picture came in right away, and she saved it to the album on her phone she'd created of baby pictures before typing her response. Sorry, looks pretty legit to me. (When the season is over, I can come over and watch him for a few hours so you can nap?)

The grounds crew were already at work repairing the pitcher's mound, and there was no one in the stands save for a couple people in yellow vests still cleaning up around the seats. This transition always felt a little dreamlike to Daphne, the way the stadium could go from loud and crackling with energy to quiet and deserted only a short time later. Tonight it was making her feel especially melancholy, but she supposed the whole night had been filled with its ups and downs. The smile, the loss, the wink, and now it was time to go home, and she knew there were only a few games left before the season might be over for good.

She was halfway out one of the exits when she heard it. It sounded like a radio being tuned, little clips of voices and songs, some static underneath. Then the music started, and a man's voice singing—

They made up their minds and they started packing . . .

She recognized the song even quicker this time than she had the last time. She'd been primed to, maybe. She hadn't been able to get those few lines she'd heard out of her head, playing them on a loop with the memory of that look on Chris' face.

She glanced toward the field automatically, her gaze going up to where she knew the music came from during games. But of course she couldn't see anything from all the way down there, and so she turned around, facing the dugout.

Chris was coming toward her, still in his uniform, clay

streaked across his chest and down one leg of his pants. He stopped when he was right in front of her, and she waited for him to smile again, waited for some sign that this was really happening. But he looked quietly serious as he held out a hand.

"Dance with me?" he said.

But you don't dance, she wanted to say. Or, *Here? Now? To this song?* But the moment felt big and fragile all at once, and she didn't want to risk it. She put her hand in his, and just the feel of his strong fingers wrapping around hers, his other hand gripping her waist . . . it felt like that first time back in your own bed after spending nights in a hotel.

"I got your message," he said. "Sorry it took so long. I'd deleted Instagram off my phone."

"That's okay," she said faintly.

"Have you really never seen the *Rocky* movies?"

Of everything she'd said in that message, *that* was what he wanted to talk to her about? "No," she admitted. "But I mean, I know the gist."

"Hmm."

They were barely swaying to the music, the merest hint of dancing. He still held her hand in his, rubbing the back of her hand with his thumb. He wasn't wearing his hat, so there was nothing hiding his face from her, but his eyes were hooded as he looked down at their joined hands. She was about to break the silence when he spoke again.

"I wanted to thank you," he said. "For telling me all that. I don't know that I needed it—I'd already started thinking about how I could convince you to give me another chance. But there was still a lot in there that I did need to hear."

She craned her neck to look up at him. "*Me* give *you* a second chance? I think you have that backward."

His gaze flickered to hers. "I said some things that day that I really regret," he said. "And I didn't say some other ones that I regret even more. I do love you, Daphne. I fell in love with you twice—first with your words and your kindness and the way talking to you always felt like the best surprise and the greatest comfort all at the same time. Then I fell in love with *you*—with your laugh and your generosity and the way you make everything else brighter. You're the book I want to reread. For the rest of my life."

Her eyes had filled with tears, threatening to fall, and he cupped her face in his hands. "Ah," he said. "Please don't cry. I never meant to make you cry."

"These are good tears," she said. "I promise."

He swiped his thumbs across her cheeks, still holding her face. "Feel your feelings," he said, then gave her a crooked smile. "That's what my therapist says. I see her once a week now."

That surprised her. "Has it been helpful?"

"You know . . . yeah. It has." He sounded almost surprised himself. "She told me that my goal couldn't be not to have regrets, or not to feel sad, or not to ever experience any bad emotion ever. Those are all inevitable. My goal has to be to find ways to live my life even with those feelings in it, to leave space in my life for those feelings even."

"And that resonated for you?"

"It did," Chris said. "I mean, I immediately translated it into a sports metaphor to make it resonate *more*. But yeah, I can see how I was trying to make my grief as small as possible, and that just wasn't going to work. And then even when it came to you— any feelings I had about finding out you were Duckie, I should've stuck around to express them, to process them *with* you. But instead I just shut down again."

"I don't blame you for that," Daphne said. "What I did—"

Chris shook his head, sliding his thumb down to press against her mouth. "It's okay," he said. "You said everything you needed to already. I understand how it happened. In a weird way, I'm grateful it all happened the way it did. I can't imagine a world where I didn't get to have those conversations with you, where I didn't get to know you in all the ways that I did."

"I'm really sorry I stood you up for the game," she said, her voice a hoarse whisper.

He looked up, glancing around the empty stadium. He dropped his hands from her face, and she missed their warmth, but then he was drawing her closer to him by wrapping his arms around her waist. "I don't know," he said, starting to move to the music until she twined her own arms around his neck. "This would've been how I'd hoped that night might end up. I'd have spotted you in the seats, and when the game was over I would've caught your eye, gestured for you to come down to the field. Not to brag, but I know the woman who works that gate over there."

He nodded toward the gate that opened from the stands out onto the field, and Daphne glanced over at it before looking back at Chris, raising her eyebrows incredulously. "You *know* her?" she said.

"Her name's Edna," he said. "Very nice lady, but normally pretty strict about letting random people through that gate."

"But I'm not random."

His gaze ran over her face, from her forehead down to her mouth. "No," he said finally. "You're Duckie. And I would've convinced Edna to let you through."

She slid her fingers into the hair at the nape of his neck. It was a little longer than he usually kept it. She liked it. "And then what? You would've convinced me to dance with you on the field?"

Chris laughed. "I wish," he said. "I would not have had that level of game."

"Don't sell yourself short."

"I would've really wanted to kiss you, though."

She raised her eyebrows again at that. "But you wouldn't have?"

He tilted his head, like he was really thinking about that one. "If the moment was right," he said. "I like to think I would've gone for it. But I was trying to be so careful."

"This was back when you weren't stealing any bases."

He smiled at that. "Definitely not," he said. "But I was trying to be so careful with *you*. You said your divorce had done a number on you, that you weren't sure if you were ready for a relationship. I wanted to respect that, but I also couldn't stop thinking about you."

"Well, who's to say I wouldn't have made the first move?"

"Would you have?" He had that expression on his face again, the one she'd seen before. The one that still seemed a little surprised and flattered—*touched* almost—when she expressed how much she wanted him. Sometimes he treated her like she was so far out of his league, and even though she knew she wasn't, knew that she didn't *want* to be, knew that the idea of leagues at all was silly and borderline offensive . . . she still liked it when he looked at her like that.

"You probably would've been walking me around the field," she said. "Saying something about baseball that I was *trying* to pay attention to, but I would've been too focused on your mouth the whole time."

His hands tightened at her waist. "I see no issue with that."

"Tell me something," she said.

"Like what?"

"Anything. Talk baseball to me."

He squinted up at the sky, clearly trying to come up with something. "Uh," he said. "Every infield is the same. The pitcher's mound is sixty feet, six inches away from home plate, for example, in every single ballpark. But the outfield dimensions can be different, and that's one thing that makes baseball so special, because each stadium—"

She pulled him down toward her by the back of his neck, pressing her lips against his in what was an emphatic, if not particularly elegant, kiss. It was how their first kiss probably would've gone if she'd been in charge of it—all wanting and yearning and raw emotion without any finesse.

"Something like that," she said. "But, you know. Better."

"It was perfect," he said. "I'm already looking forward to the second one."

"Oh," she said. "In that case . . ."

She stood up on her tiptoes, her body pressed against his as she brought him down for another kiss. This time she slanted her mouth against his, shivering a little when his tongue stroked her lower lip, invaded the warm invitation of her mouth. His hands were firm at the small of her back, drawing her even closer before they slid down to cup her ass. Daphne moaned—she couldn't help it. Everything disappeared except for the crackling nerve endings wherever her body touched his.

That was when a loud *whoop* went up from the stands, followed by a smattering of applause. She broke away to see that there were still a few workers cleaning up trash around the seats, and they'd stopped to watch her and Chris down on the field. They were grinning and clapping, and Daphne could only give a sheepish wave.

"I guess the secret is out, huh?"

He smiled down at her. "Let's give 'em a show," he said. He took her hands in his, starting to move more to the music, swinging her arms out and then back in as he brought her closer to him and then away. For all that he talked about never dancing, he wasn't bad at it, even though they were just goofing around. He twirled her once, then spun her into his arms, swaying a little with her until spinning her again. She was laughing and half off-balance when he picked her up by the waist, lifting her as she instinctively wrapped her legs around him.

She enjoyed this rare perspective of being taller, where she could hold his face in her hands and kiss him like she was the one sheltering him instead of the other way around. He shifted her weight to get a better grip, but didn't seem in any hurry to let her go.

She realized that the same song had been playing on a loop at least a few times now. "I'm glad I didn't ruin this song for you," she whispered.

"Daphne, you *gave* it to me," he said. "You were right. If you love something, there's no reason to deprive yourself of it. Love's not a superstition. It's not a game of failure. It's . . ."

He swallowed, his gaze searching her face like he wanted her to understand what he was trying to say. And she did. Love was *this*. It was him, and it was her, and it was the future stretching out ahead of them in a million different possibilities.

"Do you want to get out of here?" she asked. "Go back to my place? I normally wouldn't do that on a first date, but . . ."

He grinned. "I thought you'd never ask."

EPILOGUE

THE BATTERY ENDED UP WINNING THEIR LAST GAME TO SECURE A Wild Card spot in dramatic fashion, featuring a Randy Caminero grand slam and Chris making an incredible bare-handed line drive catch at third, then he'd tagged the other base runner out in an unassisted double play. The celebration had been intense, and even months later Daphne sometimes felt like she could still smell the champagne on her from when it had been sprayed all over the clubhouse. Chris had been very diligent later that night in licking every last trace of it off her skin.

But then the Battery ended up losing in the Wild Card in the opposite of dramatic fashion, in a game that stayed tied at zero through fifteen innings until the Mariners hit a walk-off homer to move on to the next round. That was baseball.

They'd spent a few lazy months just hanging out, splitting their time between Chris' place and hers. His was without a doubt nicer, but hers had Milo in it, and he seemed to like spending time there. He filled her small apartment with his body, crouching down in front of her short bookcase of books, tilting his head to read the spines, crowding her in the kitchen when she was trying to fix them some tea, reaching up to get the extra jar of honey she'd stashed at the back of a top cabinet. He told her he didn't mind staying quiet at her place, as long as they could make up for it at his.

Her lease was up in March, right around when he was supposed to leave for Spring Training, and it made sense for her to just move in with him, so . . . that's what she did. He had a whole list of stuff he was hoping to get done before he had to fly out to Florida, including moving the last of her things in and helping his dad install a sprinkler system at his house. And she was hoping to get settled enough that she could join him down there in the next few weeks.

"Aren't there always those commercials about *the official movers of the Battery?*" Daphne asked, collapsing on the couch after they'd brought the final boxes in from the car. It had been chilly outside, but she felt overheated in her sweatshirt and leggings, so she pulled the sweatshirt over her head, depositing it on the cushion next to her. Chris had picked up Milo, and was giving him scratches under his chin the way he liked. Somehow Chris had the ability to hold Milo like a baby and get the cat to stretch out his front paws in a display of submission that Daphne had never been able to achieve. She mostly thought it was adorable, until she sometimes called Milo a traitor. "Where were they today? Could've really used their help with those boxes of books."

Chris could've pointed out that *he'd* mostly carried those, or that the fact that the company bought ad space during the games didn't mean that they just magically knew to show up when a player was moving. But his gaze had dipped to her chest, where the loose neckline of her shirt had shifted to show part of her bra. She almost thought he hadn't heard her at all, until his gaze snapped back to hers.

"Speaking of books," he said, letting Milo jump back to the floor. "I have something to show you."

He reached out his hand to pull her up off the couch, leading her toward the closed door of the spare room.

"Okay," he said. "So this is a work in progress, but . . ."

When he opened the door, the first thing she saw was a bunch of the artwork she'd had in her apartment hanging on one wall, arranged in a gallery display with all her mismatched frames. There were some new things mixed in there, too—a couple pictures of Milo that she recognized as ones she'd texted him, a picture of her holding her nephew, a lineup card from a Battery game. There was a desk in one corner with a bright yellow chair and a vase with a single gerbera daisy stuck in it, her laptop plugged in and charging from a power strip resting on the floor.

And when she turned, there was a whole wall of bookshelves. Just plain white shelves, waiting to be filled.

Except they weren't completely empty. There was a stack of books already on one shelf, which she recognized as some of Chris'. The library copy of the baseball book he'd retrieved from his dad's house. That sports biography, that book *The Tender Land*, a copy of *Catch-22*, his copy of *Mandy*, which they'd finished together, her reading parts of it aloud to him in bed. And on top of the stack, a little rubber duck, just like in her old profile picture.

"Chris, I—" She didn't even know what to say. She was overcome. She blurted the first thing that popped into her head. "I don't even own this many books."

"But you will," he said. "And you'll need space to work from home. You can rearrange anything you need to, or change it completely. It's yours."

Daphne was officially heading up Books with the Battery, a charitable initiative by the team to promote literacy by offering incentives for reading like free tickets to games, scheduling players to visit schools for story time events, and generally working to put more books of all types into the hands of kids and teens in the

Charleston area. It was still the early days of getting it off the ground, but she loved that it combined her love of reading with a bit of the marketing and public-facing parts of her previous job she'd actually liked. Plus, it would make it a lot easier to spend more time with Chris during the busy baseball season, since he'd been re-signed to the team.

She crossed over to the art wall, taking it all in. The lineup card was from April 28, the fateful game where she'd heckled Chris. There he was, listed in the number seven spot.

"It's incredible," she said, turning to face him. "I don't even know how . . . but are you sure you won't want this room for something else? Like your workout room or whatever it was before?"

"Oh, you mean my sad little bike and a stack of dumbbells? No. Besides, there's a gym downstairs, and training facilities at the ballpark. I can always use those."

"A guest room, then," she said.

He glanced around, as if taking in the room's dimensions. "We can get an air mattress in here if we really needed to."

She didn't know why she was having such a hard time accepting this. It just seemed like so *much*. She'd been excited to move in with Chris, she really had—it would be nice not to constantly be going back and forth, she wanted the domesticity of sharing a bathroom sink and having their laundry mixed up together, and of course, she loved spending time with him. But she had to admit that a tiny part of her had mourned the loss of this space that solely belonged to *her*. She'd really made that apartment her own, however small it had been. And now here was Chris, giving her a piece of that here. It meant more than she could say. She almost couldn't believe it was real, had to keep poking at it to make sure it was.

"A man cave," she said. "A crafting room. A craft beer brewing room."

He laughed. "No, no, and I wouldn't even know where to start, so no."

"A trophy room," she said. Surely professional athletes needed space to display all their memorabilia from over the years. Old college jerseys, signed baseball cards from players he admired, she had no idea. Chris had been featured in the latest issue of *Sports Illustrated*, part of a cover story about mental health in baseball that had included him talking about grief, together with other interviews from an outfielder who'd missed a whole season due to anxiety and a top minor league prospect who'd walked away to focus on life outside of baseball and the love he'd found with a teammate. Daphne had bought ten copies, so if she kept that up they'd need a whole room for that alone.

"My dad has all that stuff," he said. "And I don't think he'd give it up."

She had one more idea, but almost didn't want to say it, in case she was getting way ahead of herself. But once it was in her brain it took root, and she couldn't help but blurt it out. "A nursery?"

Chris froze, his face going very still for a moment before he lifted his gaze to hers. There was a shine in his eyes, like he'd been suddenly lit from something within. "Are you . . . ?"

Daphne realized her mistake and rushed to correct it. "No, no," she said. "I'm still on the pill, and obviously I would've talked to you before—and I know it can happen, but—I mean, no. I'm not."

"Ah," he said, leaning against the doorframe, like he needed something to take a bit of his weight. "Sorry. I guess I thought—"

He thought she'd been hinting at something. That made total sense, and she was embarrassed that it hadn't occurred to her. "Is that . . . something you want?" she asked.

"Do you?"

She could've pointed out that she'd asked him first, but she could already figure out his answer based on that one split second when he'd thought for a moment that she was telling him she was pregnant. It hadn't even been joy—that was too simplistic. It had been deeper, more profound than that.

"I would love to have a baby with you," she said. "Not necessarily right now—I like having it just be us. But in a year or two? Sure. I could see it."

He reached over to tug on her shirt, bringing her flush up against his body. She was definitely feeling overheated. "I like us, too."

"We're probably going to want to practice," she said. "To make sure we know how to do it when the time comes."

His hand was already under her shirt, pushing up her bra so he could palm her bare breast. "I'm a big believer in practice."

She twined her arms around his neck as he nuzzled against her, pressing an openmouthed kiss to the dip of skin where her shirt had slid off her shoulder. "I've heard it makes perfect," she said, the words coming out a little breathy as he continued his path to her jaw.

"Mmm. That probably takes a *lot* of practice, though."

"Well," she said. "What are we waiting for?"

ACKNOWLEDGMENTS

If you've ever followed a baseball team—like, if you've ever white-knuckled your way through extra innings, been brokenhearted by the trade deadline, hugged total strangers after the last strikeout to end the game, *followed* a baseball team—then congratulations. You already know a bit about the ups and downs of writing a book.

So I have to say thank you first to my starting lineup: Laura Bradford, Hannah Andrade, Taryn Fagerness, Kristine Swartz, Mary Baker, Kristin Cipolla, Stephanie Felty, Hannah Engler, Nick Martorelli, Christine Legon, and Jennifer Lynes.

And then, with a Call to the Bullpen brought to you by the Florida Lottery,[1] thank you to writing friends who supported me through it all: Carmen Alvarez (I think you're undefeated at the Trop??), Mae Bennett (your IG Live with Jessica helped unlock my epilogue!), Regina Black (you always ground me), Erin Connor (the wall to my spaghetti), Rosie Danan (the bunt scene in *The Intimacy Experiment* is my favorite, no surprise), Lindsay Grossman (for hustling out the box aka doing writing sprints with me), Sarah Grunder-Ruiz and Sarah Hogle (I KNEW you would both know which Glass Animals song would make great walk-up music), Julie Hamilton (thank god for deep dish and long emails),

1. Nobody actually sponsored these acknowledgments, although I'd be open to it.

Hailey Harlow (the way you stood up for Chris being safe at third), KT Hoffman (king of the ampersand, the most honest and beautiful writer about baseball, the truest friend), Kristin Hoyer (thank you for telling me I took my time with certain scenes in this one, meant a lot), Jessica Cook (thank you for being one of the first to get romantic about Chris Kepler with me), Jessica Joyce (my third base coach waving me around, for real), Kim Karalius (how long have we been doing this together!!), Rachel Runya Katz (will forever have Arcángel in my head now), Anita Kelly (your spirit is like a constant bucket of gum being turned over on my head in celebration and I promise that's a good thing), Jessica Martin (the flowers you sent were one of the kindest things that's ever happened to me—I mean it), Tracey/Tori Martin (our emails keep me sane!), Bridget Morrissey (you are as bright as an LA Fitness sunset), Maggie North (you ALWAYS have some insight or perspective that spins my head around a bit), Hannah Olsen (my accountabilibuddy!), Rachel Lynn Solomon (you inspire me in every way possible), Catherine Tinker (with all my heart, LFG), Julie Tieu (I treasure our friendship!), Emily Wibberley and Austin Siegemund-Broka (go listen to Phoebe Bridgers and touch grass), Ava Wilder (sorry I didn't make him talk, but Chihuahua-biting-down-on-a-laptop meme forever), and the Berkletes (aka the Instagram Sugar Baby DM Union).

The Allstate Good Hands Play of the Game goes to artist Jenifer Prince and art director Colleen Reinhart, who always hit it out of the park with their impeccable eye for design and their ability to bring my characters to life in their beautiful covers. They take my breath away.

The Heart & Hustle Award goes to my Baseball Lunch group chat. When I saw only one set of footprints in the clay, it was then that you carried me. I love you very much and I literally could not have done this without you.

Some Toyota Keys to the Game: "Cinnamon" by Hayley Williams; the Ab-Abber 2000; "for your information, he's a Little Leaguer"; Korn whatever that guy's name is for giving me the "not interesting nor charismatic" petty fodder I needed; Joey Wendle digging for third against Hunter Renfroe's throwing arm; whoever initially wrote "eschew" into Joey's Wikipedia entry, sorry about the sock-puppet account that removed it and said nobody uses that word—I love that word!; the KIND comments on Austin Meadows' Instagram page; "#1 Crush" by Garbage; Matt Antonelli's videos about playing in the MLB; the baseball scene in *Twilight*; "love you, too, Dad"; Jomboy breakdowns; I love that Bryce Harper reads romance; haroldsboomstick; remember when Stephanie Tanner struck out her crush?; the Savannah Bananas; those kids who Cupid Shuffled their way into a Raising Cane's and then Cupid Shuffled their way right out, I think about you every day; the IRS agent who recommended *The Art of Fielding* to me over the phone; the four right chords CAN make me cry; Tombolo Books in St. Pete; the Physicality (IYKYK); the Reading with the Rays initiative; the list of top Dewayne and BA bon mots I keep in my Notes app; Tricia, I promise I don't think just *anyone* could step in and do your job but I had to take some poetic license!

And the New Teeth Now Game Summary . . . of some favorite baseball friends and their team affiliations: Brandon M. (Yankees but also here for the memes); Catherine T. (Rays/Dodgers); Danielle S. (Mets); Hannah aka fringebookreviews (Twins); Heather H. (Diamondbacks); Jennifer Iacopelli (Yankees); Jessica Joyce (A's); Julie K. (Charlie Morton); Kat G. (chaos always); KD Casey (Nationals; the teams in the *Unwritten Rules* universe); KT Hoffman (Mariners; the teams in the *Prospects* universe); Kelsey B. aka myblogisgreat (Phillies); Megan Cousins (Tigers; the teams in the *Wild Pitches* universe).

Today's defense is brought to you by the Gold & Diamond Source, which is basically my cue to thank all my family and friends who have supported me in this endeavor. And to the readers and bookstagrammers and people who love books—thank you!! You were a huge inspiration for Daphne's character in particular.

Finally, I have to give it up for my All Stars: Ryan, August, and Kara. Kids, I love you and also I would lovingly remind you that the last call for Dippin' Dots is BEFORE the seventh inning. Ryan, I love sharing my life and baseball with you. Here's to many more years on the Chris Rose party deck, watching games and pulling up stats on our phones and coming up with creative riffs on players' names.

Ryan gave me the line "Baseball is being endlessly optimistic in the face of math," by the way. And I can't think of a truer sentence—about baseball, about publishing, about life. You ride the highs and the lows and then you have to treat it like a sand mandala and blow it all away. There's always next year.

Keep reading for an excerpt of

WITH LOVE, FROM COLD WORLD

from Berkley Romance!

LAUREN FOX HAD THE MOST BORING JOB AT THE COOLEST place. Literally, the coolest—it said it on the website and everything. If you felt the sudden urge to build a snowman or ice skate in Central Florida, Cold World was the place to do it. Lauren was Cold World's bookkeeper, meaning that she was mostly holed up in her office, which was kept just as frigid as the rest of the place, reconciling bank records and paying vendor invoices and making sure the Zamboni didn't get repossessed.

She loved her job, though. There was something so satisfying about entering numbers into spreadsheets, sorting the data into different permutations, and keeping her filing cabinet like a finely manicured garden of color-coded folders. And there was something just a little magic about stepping into a blast of winter every Monday through Friday, no matter how humid and gross the Florida air was outside.

Like today, the first day of December, clocking in at a muggy eighty-three degrees. Lauren had dressed in her usual uniform of skirt, tights, button-up, and cardigan, holding her arms slightly away from her body in hopes of staving off the sweat until she could reach the relief of a central air-conditioning system that set Cold World back four figures a month in the dead of summer.

It hit her in a wave as she walked through the front door, the air frigid with a slight whiff of cinnamon. They'd been decorating for Christmas since before Thanksgiving, because it was obviously their biggest holiday. The front ticket counter was draped with garlands, and giant ornaments hung from the ceiling. Life-sized reindeer statues, spray-painted with glittery silver and gold, stood watch in one corner, and the finishing touches had almost been put on the twelve-foot tree they put out in front of the gift shop every year.

The converted warehouse building opened up to the right of the ticket counter, holding the Snow Globe, an enclosed area kept even colder with real, actual snow on the ground. (It was a little icier than people expected, and not the *best* for snow angels, but hey, it felt miraculous when you could drive an hour away and be at the beach.) Then there was the small ice skating rink, and Wonderland Walk, a lane flanked by stands selling hot chocolate, warm cookies, and various artisanal goods.

Lauren didn't have much reason to go right. The administrative space was to the left—the Chalet, as they called it for the decorative faux ski-cottage front that hid the entrance to the offices, the break room, and the storage space. That was where she spent most of her day, and thank god, because it was at least moderately warmer than the rest of Cold World.

It could never get *too* warm, though, or it threw the whole balance of the building off, hence Lauren's ubiquitous cardigan. Even thinking about it made Lauren superstitious that the unit would fail, and as she entered the break room she kissed her fingers and pointed at the ceiling, a tribute to the air-conditioning gods.

"You find Jesus last night?"

Lauren startled in the act of reaching for coffee, dropping the K-cup on the floor. Normally, she had a couple hours to herself before most of her coworkers showed up to begin their shifts. But from the low, sardonic voice behind her, at least one person had decided to make an early morning of it.

"If Jesus is certified for commercial HVAC work," she said, bending to pick up the small container filled with lifesaving coffee grounds. "Then yes."

She liked the people she worked with. She genuinely did. Except . . .

Asa Williamson just got under her skin for some reason. Like now, he was leaning casually against the supply closet door, his eyes crinkle-smiling at her over his coffee mug, and she knew, she just *knew* that he was laughing at her.

He was tall and lean, lanky in a way that should make him seem awkward. But instead he always seemed easy, effortless, and comfortable in his own skin. His arms were covered in tattoos, which she couldn't help but notice because he wore short-sleeved shirts even when everyone else on the floor layered long sleeves under their baby blue Cold World polos. He was always doing something different with his hair—it had been long when she'd started two years before, down to his shoulders, and now it was short and dyed a bright aqua blue.

He'd been there ten years, longer than anyone else who wasn't the owner, Dolores, or her son Daniel. Maybe that was why he always felt like the Cool Kid around the place, or maybe it was because he was genuinely friendly with everyone. He was even housemates with Kiki, one of Lauren's closest friends at Cold World. Not that Lauren had ever gone to their place, which they shared with another couple of people she'd only heard about. It was important to have boundaries at work, she thought.

Of course, that was probably one reason why Lauren had never been one of the Cool Kids. Not back in school, not anywhere she'd worked, and definitely not here.

She resented that about Asa, just like she resented that little pinch he got at the corner of his mouth, like he was always thinking about some inside joke. He didn't take anything seriously, and that was something Lauren couldn't stand. She took *everything* seriously.

"Why are you here?" she asked now, the question coming out more churlish than she'd intended as she slammed the top of the Keurig over the K-cup.

"The meeting?" he said. His eyebrows shot up at her confused frown. "The first of December. Holiday season. The planning meeting. Did you forget?"

She *had* actually forgotten. Which was totally unlike her. Lauren lived her life with lists and systems and plans. Three months ago, she'd Googled "best skincare routine" and clicked through the results until she found one that was numbered and affordable and easy to follow, and now she did it every morning and night. She updated her Goodreads page religiously, not to leave reviews but just to ensure that she had some kind of record of every book she'd ever read. It annoyed her to get the biannual postcards from the dentist's office about her next cleaning, because she'd already put a reminder on her Outlook calendar at work to follow up.

"Shit," Asa said, squinting at her. "Is there a problem with your programming? I knew we'd see the effects of Y2K eventually."

"I didn't *forget*," Lauren muttered, even though by now it was obvious she had. She'd already hit the button to brew a cup of coffee, but it wasn't lighting up, so she hit it again. She could hear the churn of the machine as it started to heat the water, but still no coffee. If she was actually a robot like Asa loved to tease her about being, shouldn't she have more proficiency with the stupid thing?

"And you saw all the extra cars in the parking lot and thought, what?" he continued, ignoring her denial. "Maybe it's overflow from the Waffle House?"

She hadn't even noticed the extra cars. She'd been on autopilot, lost in her own thoughts. Scarily, she only had vague impressions of the twenty minutes it took her to get from her apartment to Cold World. She had a volunteer engagement after work, and even though she'd been preparing for it for months, *planning* for it, now that it was here it still tied her stomach in knots.

"I have—" *A lot on my mind*, she almost finished, but she didn't have that kind of relationship with anyone at work. And if she was going to start confiding in someone, it certainly wouldn't be Asa Williamson. She stabbed the Keurig button again with her finger, mentally urging the machine to start already so she could extricate herself from the awkwardness of this moment.

He set down his own mug on the counter, reaching over her to fiddle with the machine. Not for the first time, Lauren couldn't help but notice that he smelled good. Like, *really* good. It was one of life's true mysteries, because she felt like she'd know his scent anywhere, but she couldn't quite place what it *was*. Some mixture of cedar and citrus, not overpowering, never burning her nose like some colognes did. But always *present* whenever he was nearby, and sometimes she'd catch the tail end of it when she entered a room he'd just been in. She lived in fear that one day he'd catch her inhaling a big whiff whenever he was close, and she'd have to quit her job and move to North Dakota.

"There," he said as the Keurig whirred to life, dispensing a steady stream of coffee into her mug. As far as she could tell, all he'd done was lift the top and place it back down again. Of course he'd make it look easy.

"Thanks," she said grudgingly.

He settled back with his coffee. "No problem."

This might be the longest Lauren had ever spent one-on-one

with Asa. They hadn't exactly hit it off right away, despite his ability to charm his way into friendship with everyone else. Lauren wasn't even sure of his technical job title—he seemed to do a little bit of everything. She'd seen him working the gift shop with Kiki, serving hot chocolate wearing an apron the same color as his hair, even skating circuits around the rink, making sure everyone was traveling in the right direction and no newer skaters needed help.

And it was Florida, so they often needed help.

She'd started at Cold World only days before the staff holiday party two years ago, which was an awkward time to be the new person. She'd still been reeling from her job interview. It had been pretty standard until Dolores mentioned the need to get Cold World's books more organized. Somehow, that had set Lauren off into an impassioned speech that, embarrassingly, had brought actual tears to her eyes. When she'd finally come up for air, she thought she'd blown it. She must have seemed unhinged. Instead, to her surprise, Dolores had told her on the spot that the job was hers if she wanted it.

Since she hadn't been there long enough to *know* anyone at the holiday party, she'd spent most of it taking note of ways to cut costs at the next shindig. It was part of what Dolores had hired her to do, after all. Lauren thought they could dial back the sandwich platters since there were tons of leftovers, she figured a closed bar would be more money-saving and probably more responsible, and if there was already a Secret Santa she saw no reason for Dolores to separately give gift cards to each employee.

"Those come out of my own pocket, dear," Dolores had said when she brought it up, patting her hand kindly.

But one of Lauren's best—or worst, as in this case—qualities was her tenacity. For some reason, she had a hard time letting it go. She'd turned to the person next to her, who was piling his plate high with two each of the five different types of cookies. She hadn't learned his name, and normally someone with that many tattoos would've intimidated her, but there was something about his eyes that had seemed kind.

"It makes no sense," she said. "If you think about it, if everyone buys a twenty-dollar Secret Santa gift, and then they get a twenty-dollar gift card, doesn't it all come out a wash? If the gift cards are going to mean something, why not cancel Secret Santa?"

"Bold move," he said. "Running on a platform of *cancel Secret Santa*. How long have you worked here again?"

She'd felt her face heat. "Three days."

He'd pointed a cookie at her. "Love your initiative, though," he said. "Keep at it and by March we can get all the toilet paper down to one ply."

He held the cookie in his mouth and walked away, still facing her, one hand holding his plate and the other holding up crossed fingers as though he were actually hopeful. The most infuriating thing was that his tone hadn't even sounded sarcastic. It wasn't until a full minute after he'd walked away that it hit Lauren that there'd been a spark in his eyes as he'd left, and it hadn't been kindness. And a week later, she'd received her generous hundred-dollar gift card from Dolores along with everyone else, and a token coffee mug from Kiki as a belated Secret Santa present.

"This is a regift because my aunt gets me a new one every year," Kiki had said. "So don't feel bad that you didn't get anything for anyone."

"The holidays are kinda . . . intense around here, huh?"

Kiki shrugged. "Dolores thinks that we work so hard to make all our guests' holidays special, so we deserve something special, too. She's a little eccentric, but she's a sweet boss. You'll get used to it."

"Ah." Lauren ran one finger along the rim of the mug. It was white, printed with a rainbow and flowers and an aspirational quote that encouraged her to **BLOOM WHERE YOU ARE PLANTED!** "It's nice," she said hesitantly. "That she arranges the Secret Santa thing and goes out of her way to get everyone in on it."

"Oh, that's all Asa," Kiki had said. At Lauren's questioning expression, she gestured to her shoulders, as if telling a stylist where to cut her own bleached strands. "Long hair? Tall? Tattoos? When it comes to Christmas, he doesn't play. Secret Santa was totally his idea."

The guy she'd vented to at the party. Great.

Photo courtesy of the author

Alicia Thompson is a writer, reader, and lover of baseball. She has never caught a foul ball, but she was once two seats down from a Jumbotron proposal, and that has to count for something. She's currently taking in home games in sunny Central Florida with her husband, two children, and a cat named Luna, who has yet to hit for the cycle (aka has not escaped out of every door in a single day, although with the numbers she's been putting up . . .).

VISIT THE AUTHOR ONLINE

AliciaThompsonBooks.com
AliciaBooks

Ready to find
your next great read?

Let us help.

Visit prh.com/nextread